The Firm

The Firm

Sullivan & Connolly

MICHAEL J. WALSH

O'Malley & Finnigan
Washington D.C.

ISBN: 978-0-578-31964-3

O'Malley & Finnegan, Washington, DC

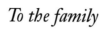

To the family

CHAPTER 1

Michael Sullivan wanted to get to the office early his first day to impress the partners they'd made the right decision hiring him over several others. After a mile ride from the small apartment he shared with his wife, Mary and their infant son, Jack, he got off a bus in the middle of third street and walked to the corner of third and Roosevelt. There he paused and looked up at the fifteen story National Bank building, the third largest in the city. He'd become an associate in the city's oldest law firm located on the top floor. Built in the thirties, it served as the bank's head office. Still formidable in 1982, a bit old fashioned, and not in the best part of the business district, which had moved up town to Seventh Street, it housed a dozen or so law firms, insurance companies and accounting firms. The Firm's windows on the fifteenth floor commanded an enviable view of the river and the city's east side.

He entered the lobby with its four elevators on the left, and two steps to the bank on his right, nodded at the gentle looking bald headed man behind the cigar store counter and headed for the farthest elevator with a flashing green light overhead. Others followed, the doors closed, the elevator rose to the top floor and he got off and headed down a long hallway with marble flooring, flanked by doors with frosted glass emblazoned with such names as "Federal Mortgage Company," "Weinstein Jewelers." He rounded the corner and confronted two double doors of frozen glass framed in dark brown moldings. The tenant listed:

Barron, Walker, Youngman & Hamilton
Attorneys at Law

A side panel contained the names of the lawyers in small black lettering:

Samuel K. Barron
Howard L. Walker
Johnathan B.Youngman
Matthew S. Hamilton
John T. Jensen

Of Counsel:
Barton Youngman
Frederick S. Willoby

He pushed open one of the doors and saw an empty reception desk fronting a blank wall with gold laminated wall paper. Comparison with the hall could not have been more stark; the reception area contained brown modern wood chairs with bright orange colored seats, two coffee tables and lamps with orange lamp shades, an obvious attempt by a well meaning decorator to bring modernity to an old office suite.

Having been interviewed by all members of the firm, he had a good idea of the office layout including his own office located to the right off the entrance. He proceeded past his office down a dark green carpeted hallway to the offices of John Jensen, Matthew Hamilton and Samuel Barron on his right. Howard Walker and Johnathan Youngman's offices were directly across the hall from Barron's. Next to Youngman's office, a law library held state and federal reports, supreme court cases dating back to the first issued and many textbooks dealing with various areas of law. He turned and walked back up the hall past the library, a small conference room containing tax volumes and a large room for three secretaries.

He saw nor heard anyone, so he quietly proceeded to his office. Eight a. m. and he realized he was the first lawyer in. He felt a tremendous thrill. His office, more than a young lawyer could hope for. Three huge old fashioned sash windows looked out on the majestic Concord River. Cars streamed across the Warrington Bridge from the eastbound freeway on to Culver Street into the business district. The sun reflected off the magnificent antique bookcases standing against the wall opposite his desk filled with priceless volumes from another era. A small antique desk, built during world war one, sat near the back wall with three matching antique caned chairs in front. Michael gazed out the window at the city just getting underway.

Not a fancy office or glamourous, as some offices in newer buildings, but it was everything he dreamed about. An old fashioned law office; ethics, and longevity the firm's hallmarks. That's what the firm had going for it; dignified lawyers doing their work quietly and efficiently. Now, he was a member of the city's oldest firm founded in 1895.

Michael Sullivan wanted to be a lawyer from his earliest remembrances. Not because he thought lawyering would be a lot of fun or an easy way to make a living; but only after reading biographies of the great trial lawyers, John J. Fallon, Clarence Darrow, Louis Nizer and scores of others that he decided to enroll in law school, and become a trial lawyer. He loved competition and decided the court room an arena he could compete in, much as bull fighter loves the bullring. That's where skill, excitement and reward could be found practicing law. To be in the arena where you tested yourself against an opponent and vied for the jury's verdict. To convince twelve people of the merits of the cause. If there was "glamour" in the law, he sensed it lay in the court room

Michael Sullivan didn't have the time to be a serious student in college for several reasons: he spent most of his waking hours working at an advertising agency and when he wasn't there he played tennis, a sport he took up at thirteen, and became so adept he obtained an athletic scholarship making it possible to go to college. Lost in reverie he heard someone come into the office; it turned out to be Mrs. Beatrice Grantano, the lead secretary, veteran of twenty years at the firm hired as a messenger when she was eighteen.. She came directly into his office and said:

"Mr. Sullivan, Mr. Youngman asked that you see him when convenient."

"Thank you Mrs. Grantano," He waited a few minutes until he heard Youngman head for his office and then got up from the desk and walked down the hallway to his office. He arrived in time to catch Mr. Youngman in a fit of coughing, which he thought unusual, for a man forty four years of age. Youngman had a cigarette in his hand, a number of papers on his desk and looked like he wanted to get right down to business.

"How are you this morning Michael?"

"Fine Mr. Youngman, how are you?"

"Well I've got this cough which I can't seem to shake, but other than that I'm just fine thank you. Awfully glad you're with us. I thought I'd give you an assignment and see how you handle it. We have a judgment against this chap Daniels for a thousand dollars but we haven't been able to collect a dime. I've written letters, had some calls made and all we are getting is a stall and 'the check is in the mail' routine. I think it's time we execute on the judgment. Ever done that?"

"No I haven't Mr. Youngman .....but I can," he said with an air of assurance.

"Good! Take this file, it contains the complaint and judgment. You take it from there."

"Yes sir."

"Let me know how it works out." With that he turned to the papers on his desk indicating the conversation had come to an end.

My God, he thought to himself, I assumed the first project would be researching cases or drafting a pleading but this is front line action. Back in his office he quickly pulled the statute governing execution of judgments, read through it quickly and turned to the annotated cases. There he found what had to be done. Draft a writ of execution and take it to the sheriff who would go out and execute on the debtor's property. After drafting the writ he set out for the courthouse writ in hand for delivery to the sheriff. What a feeling of excitement—his first test.

He went to the court house civil division counter, asked for the sheriff, and was directed to one of his deputies. He explained the circumstances and asked how long it would take to execute the writ.

"I see no problem Mr. Sullivan, I have time I'll go out there this afternoon and see what can be picked up"

"Can I go along to see how it's done?"

"Sure, be back here in an hour."

By two o'clock that afternoon Michael was back at the court house excited about the prospect of performing so quickly and efficiently the task he had been assigned by the partner. He checked in with the sheriff, civil division, and waited until deputy Johnson, who later in the afternoon he called "Sam," appeared in full battle gear including a pistol strapped to his side. "Sam," a big burly red faced man about thirty five came swinging around the counter and said: "let's go barrister and see what we got."

The ride to a middle class section on the east side of the city was made in silence, only interrupted by the squad car radio cackling as sheriff deputies throughout the city reported into central dispatch at the court house. They pulled up in front of a two story gray split level home. No one seemed about and there were no cars parked in front or in the driveway or any sign of life. The deputy jumped out of the car Michael close on his heels. He tried the front door and when that brought no one, he went around to side of the house and with a tool Michael had not seen before pried open the widow effortlessly and climbed in.

"You stay here counselor, I'm going to take a look around."

In five minutes he opened the front door and beckoned Michael to come in. "We've got all kinds of good things in here that can be attached like a refrigerator, stove, television sets, at least two thousand dollars worth. I'll have them picked up this afternoon and taken to our central warehouse. The sale will fetch at least enough to cover your judgment and attorney's fees plus our costs. I'd say the mission was a success, let's go."

When he got back to the office from his sojourn he found a note on his desk to contact J. Youngman as soon as he came in. "Something wrong" he thought to himself. Without dwelling on the reason for the note he wheeled out of his office and down the hall to Youngman's. He looked in and saw Youngman engaged in a phone conversation, his feet up on the desk, half facing the window which looked into another part of the bank building. He waved a hand for Michael to come in, motioning him to a seat, and continued to talk on the phone. Michael sat down, and while waiting for the conversation to end, he observed Youngman and the office generally. While Youngman talked animatedly to the person on the other end of the line Michael's eye took in the room, one of two corner offices. The other directly across the hall occupied by the firm's senior partner, Samuel Barron. In the center of Youngman's office sat a huge antique desk, very expensive, backed by a beautiful credenza which contained stacks of papers and pictures of his wife and children. The wife, a striking blonde, and aristocratic looking. Around the walls old fashioned glass and oak wood legal book cases stacked one upon another completely filled with law volumes and journals. Adorning the walls were prints of English judges in various poses, all characterizations by "Spy." Michael sat in one of three chairs facing the huge desk. He judged it a very warm and comfortable office.

Youngman continued: "I think we can settle this case and I think we should settle it. The exposure is heavy if it goes to a judge or jury. The plaintiff's lawyer is not too heavily into it yet....if we nail him early with the fast money we can cut off the exposure." He paused obviously listening to the argument he was getting from the other end of the line. Then: "well let me see what I can do, if we can buy it for five thousand dollars I'm going to recommend it to the company"

Michael had some background information on Johnathan Youngman which he gleaned from reading Martindale Hubble, the definitive work, consisting of a compilation of biographies of leading lawyers and law firms in the United States. He found his academic background impressive: Stanford University undergraduate, Harvard Law. For someone from the Midwest, that would be a super echelon education and it put him in the hierarchy of local lawyers socially and legally. He also read he was a Lieutenant Colonel in the Viet Nam war serving on the staff of the Joint chiefs at the Pentagon which he also found impressive. The senior attorney, forty four years old, had a mustache, which alone set him apart from most and a very leathery sun tanned face. He reminded Michael of pictures he'd seen of British officers in the newspapers during world II, such as Field Marshall Montgomery who had a pinched mustache. Youngman was sleight, thin with a bird like face, the nose being the most prominent feature. Here was a man to be reckoned with and his demeanor did nothing to put the associate at his ease.

He abruptly broke off the phone call and turned to face Michael head on. "I've had a phone call from Howard West, Daniels's attorney, who told me he's sending us a check for fifteen hundred dollars covering our judgment and attorney fees and requesting a release of items held by the sheriff. I've never seen such quick action. What did you do?" He smiled, a pleased look on his face. Relieved, Michael described what had happened following their talk and Youngman's direction to collect the judgment. When he got to the part about the sheriff going through the window, Thornton slapped his knee, looked at him with a look of admiration and said: "That's what I call action. Nice job Michael. If you can accomplish that in that short span of time, you're going to have a successful career around here. That guy West and Daniels have been stalling us using every dodge in the book to avoid paying that judgment. You surprised them. Total and complete surrender."

"Thank you Mr. Youngman." He left the office on a cloud that afternoon. His first win. He could hardly wait to get home to tell his young bride.

CHAPTER 2

Mary Griffin met and married Michael Sullivan in 1982 after an eight month courtship. He had finished law school at Georgetown University in Washington D.C. and passed the District of Columbia Bar exam when they met. At the time she was working as a legislative aide to a Senator. He found her beautiful, intelligent, interested in politics, government, public service, Catholic and religious like himself. A perfect match. They came from similar backgrounds, she from a family of three brothers, private girls high school, College at Trinity in Washington D.C and extensive travel throughout Europe. He: three sisters, an intense interest in politics, world affairs, military service in the air force, work for a congressman on Capitol Hill, and travel in Japan. After graduation from law school he returned home state to prepare for the state bar exam. Mary transferred to San Francisco and a romance that started in Washington continued but at a distance. It consisted of her flying to his home town and he flying to San Francisco. It reached the point where the courtship became such a strain they decided the only action that could ease the pain of uncertainty and separation would be to get married. It took place after he passed the state bar exam and got a coveted job as law clerk for a state Supreme Court Justice.

Their wedding was spectacular, the bride beautiful, vivacious, gracious, animated; what he found fascinating were the many businessmen, executives, lawyers, doctors, friends of Mary's family, who, as they came through the reception line at the racquet club, greeted the bride warmly with great fondness and embraces and then turned to him, looked him in the eye and, in a confidential tone, said: "you are mighty lucky young man, she is a brilliant girl, take good care of her." At the moment it made him proud, later he came to appreciate exactly what they meant. What they were saying was: "there aren't many like her, you are an extremely fortunate man."

He got off the bus and walked a half block to the "Oliver" apartments where he and Mary rented a one bedroom ground floor apartment in a thirty unit complex. After he got the job at Barron, Walker, Youngman & Hamilton they moved to the city from the state capitol where he had served the one year clerkship with Justice William Wiseman. He reasoned, that with graduation from a prestigious law school, a one year clerkship at the State Supreme Court and passing two bar exams he would have a relatively easy time getting employment with one of the city's five largest law firms. That proved not to be the case. Each of the major firms had its own personality. One hired strictly locals meaning state law school graduates. One hired lawyers with eastern law school credentials, and most of those hired were graduates of Ivy League schools with law journal in their background or order of the Coif, something Michael didn't have time for. He completed law school in twenty four straight months while working on Capitol hill for a Congressman. That left little time for pursuits such as work on the law journal. He hoped the clerkship would make up for the lack of law journal on his resume. After twenty five interviews, he kept track of every one, he landed a job with the oldest firm in the city: Barron, Walker, Youngman & Hamilton. Its reputation based on preeminence in the field of municipal bonds.

. . .

Howard Walker, one of two senior partners, was sixty years old, very tough, stocky of build on a six foot frame, given to wearing dark brown suits. While he had a cheery smile and red rosy cheeks that made him look like a cherub when he got talking enthusiastically on a legal subject, his eyes glinted with sharpness that prevented any one mistaking him for a lightweight or a fool. For many years he practiced as a solo practitioner specializing in trial work, primarily defending life insurance companies from false claims and also had a number of spectacular trials in a wide variety of cases. Michael felt pleased to be around him and hoped to learn the intricacies of trial work watching him work. He didn't have long to wait. He hadn't been in the firm three weeks when Walker called him into his office at nine o'clock one morning. Seated next to the senior partner's desk was a little fellow dressed in a pair of gray slacks, blue sport coat, an ill-fitting shirt, a narrow black tie and a round face sporting a crew haircut.

"Michael," Walker began, "this is Tommy Thompson a client and good friend of mine who has trial date this morning at ten o'clock. I can't try the case as intended because of a conflict. I'd like you to stand in for me. He's been sued by a creditor who says he wasn't paid by Tommy here. Tommy owned his own business, a corporation. The short of it is: he did pay the Jones Egg Company, the creditor, with a series of checks drawn on Tommy's corporation which is now defunct. Our defense is the checks are corporate checks, not Tommy's individual checks and the Egg Company must look to the corporation for payment, not Tommy individually. Tommy and his corporation were two separate entities and the creditor, the Egg Company should not be able to look to Tommy for payment"

The client turned to Howard Walker with a beleaguered look as if to say: "I don't understand it all but if you say it will work, ok." He turned to look at Michael and realized he was not going to get the senior partner to try his case, but a young rookie lawyer. Walker gave reassurance to the client: "Michael is just out of law school. Smart! Has been clerking for Supreme Court, Justice Wiseman, he'll get you out of this scrape. Besides this will be a trial to the judge, not a jury." Obviously, from the look on his face Tommy didn't get the distinction. He only knew he would feel much better with Walker trying the case.

Michael felt there was no use to protest to Walker publicly in front of the client or privately, that he didn't feel ready or he couldn't do it. Walker either felt he could handle it or Tommy was a pest whose case could not be settled and therefore there was no alternative to trial, and Walker just didn't have the time or inclination to tie up a half day or more trying a District court case

"Michael, you and Tommy spend a few minutes together and then I think you'd better head for the courthouse. Judge Burke sits promptly at ten o'clock and he won't abide a late appearance. What a crisis! Michael knew he had to do three things quickly. First, peruse the file which was small and determine its contents second, what to ask him on the stand and third make sure he got to Judge Burke's court room eight blocks away by ten a.m.

As they left the building and started walking the eight blocks to the courthouse, Michael became unconscious of the people passing on either side of him and those coming towards him, cars turning in front of him, honking, changing lights, he just trudged on block after block. For him there was he, the client and the case to be tried... his first. Before leaving the building he quickly skimmed the file and acquired the gist of the situation: Tommy had purchased from Jones Egg Company a truck load of eggs and paid for them on the spot by handing the driver of the truck a check which he signed as president of the Thompson Corporation. It turned out while funds were in the bank to cover the check when it was written, the owner of Jones Egg Company held the check two weeks without attempting to cash it and when he did the bank wouldn't honor it with the explanation the corporate account didn't have funds sufficient to cover the check. Thompson Corporation had become insolvent. While Tommy had some personal funds the corporation was totally bereft of same. From the basic set of facts Michael quickly constructed the defense—that while the plaintiff might take a judgment against the corporation for the amount of the debt as evidenced by the check, he could not take judgment beyond the corporation to reach Tommy individually since Tommy's liability was limited to his stock or equity in the corporation. Having set the defense in his mind, he began telling Tommy the questions he would be asking as they neared the court house.

"Yes, yes, that's true I paid all my bills with corporate checks, I never used a personal check." A light went on in his head and he said: "I get it. I get what you're saying."

Satisfied the client got the idea of questions he would be asked, he began to focus on the mechanics of getting to the court room and in place by ten o'clock since it was then nine fifty five and they were just entering the eight story court house on Fifth Street. As they came through the swinging front doors their gaze fastened on a milling crowd of people standing waiting for elevators on the left and right side of the main staircase. Some just standing smoking, others seemingly in a great rush. Strangely, he had been in the old building only one other time and that to file papers in the clerk's office on the first floor. He knew the District court, where the case was to be tried, was different from the Circuit court but he didn't know in what respects except it was a lesser or lower court. Built in 1922 the building, located on Fifth Street across from a park covered with emerald green grass and beautiful old oak trees, some fifty or sixty feet in height with leafy overhang, made a perfect setting for a court house. But the architecture was utilitarian and practical, and it's eight floors even more so. Twelve Circuit and six district court rooms were housed on seven of its eight floors with a jail on the top floor for prisoners held overnight or brought in from the prison farm for hearings, preliminary proceedings, or trials. Michael and Tommy squeezed into an elevator loaded with police, jurors, lawyers and witnesses and ascended to the third floor where they were the only ones offloading.

"Come on Tommy we're looking for district court room 3113 and we've got about one minute to get there." Sullivan swerved around the staircase set in the middle of each floor and barreled down the corridor three steps at a time with short legged Tommy in pursuit. After about fifty steps, his heart pounding, he spied district courtroom 3113. "Hon. Richard Burke" on the glass door encased in wood. Without looking to see if Tommy was still with him, he burst into the room and saw an elderly looking man sitting sideways at counsel's table inside a gated balustrade separating the Judge's bench, witness stand, and bailiff's desk from the twenty or so benches available for spectators. On the left of the bench a jury box which strangely enough had only six seats. Michael went straight for the counsel table to the left of the bench. A man, he judged to be the clerk or bailiff came toward him. "Are you here representing the defendant?"

"Yes sir."

"The Judge wants to see you and Mr. Beaudry in chambers. He's been waiting for you to arrive. Are you Mr. Walker?"

"No sir, I'm Michael Sullivan, I'll be trying the case in his place." For the first time Michael took note of the elderly gentleman sitting at counsel's table and concluded he represented the Jones Egg Company. He gestured to the elderly gentleman and Michael to follow him as he disappeared through a door behind and to the left of the Judge's bench. Michael experienced anxiety; and concern for Tommy who would not know what was going on. He knew he was scared enough just to be in court much less without his attorney present, secondly he felt completely at a loss as to what was going to happen or might happen in the Judge's chambers.

Beaudry entered ahead of him into a small office completely book lined with state reports, federal case books and assorted other books. The Judge sat behind a small unassuming desk and motioned the attorneys to be seated on a green leather couch which barely fit into the office.

"Gentlemen we'll get started in about five minutes. I've just been reading the file and it seems to me this is a case that should have been settled. "By the way", turning to Michael, he said: "I don't believe we've met young man, I'm Richard Burke as you've probably already guessed." Michael jumped to his feet and moved swiftly toward the desk with outstretched hand and said: "I'm Michael Sullivan, your honor with Barron, Walker, Youngman & Hamilton, and I'm representing Mr. Thompson and the corporate defendant.

"Well, that's fine, I see Howard Walker's name on the pleadings; I was looking forward to seeing him this morning—I guess he doesn't try these little cases anymore"

Michael quickly translated the statement which implied his senior partner was way too busy to be involved in a minor case before this lower court Judge.

"No sir, he fully intended to be here, but had a conflict. I was just called in this morning to try it." That seemed to assuage the Judge's feelings and he said: "Mr. Sullivan have you met Mr. Beaudry representing the plaintiff?" Michael turned to look Beaudry full in the face and quickly tried to size up the lawyer who would be the first of many adversaries he would face across a court room. Beaudry gave him a cursory look and a friendly handshake but obviously intent on putting the young lawyer on notice he was about to be "taken into camp." Michael noticed Beaudry had lines around the eyes that made him look tough but Michael sensed there was a goodness in the man. Nevertheless he knew this lawyer would give him no quarter. He was there to win quickly and get on with the next case.

"Pleased to meet you Mr. Sullivan." There was no patronizing by this senior lawyer. He was all formality and ready to do battle.

"Have you tried to settle the case?" the Judge asked, addressing neither in particular.

"Your honor, Howard Walker and I have talked a number of times and he made an offer but my client is not receptive and he wants his money. I'm afraid we must go forward unless Mr. Sullivan has something new to offer."

"I have no instructions to settle your honor and I would therefore join Mr. Beaudry in requesting that we proceed." The young lawyer had no idea whether he had any authority to talk settlement or not but when he heard Beaudry's statement and tone of voice, he took that to mean the matter had to go forward.

"All right gentlemen, take your seats at counsel table and I'll be out in a minute and we'll get underway."

Michael could see right away the Judge was not entirely pleased with the turn of events but not unaccustomed to it happening, resigned to sit on the bench and try the case. Leaving the Judge's chambers he bolted past Beaudry and made a bee line for Tommy sitting in the front row of benches looking apprehensive. Sullivan tried to speak calmly although he was nervous and trying not to show it to the client.

"The Judge will be out in a minute, you come up here with me at the counsel table. Mr. Beaudry, the other attorney, will start putting on his case first and he will call probably two witnesses. Afterwards, I'm putting you on and we'll be discussing how the order came about, when you were billed and how you paid. Have you got that?"

"I hope so," the client looked at him mournfully.

Judge Burke swept into the room from the door to the left of his bench and took two steps up to his chair and promptly seated himself and looked down at the parties.

CHAPTER 3

"This is the case of Jones Egg Company, plaintiff vs. Tommy Thompson and the Thompson Corporation, defendants: Number 59-1032. Mr. Beaudry you may proceed with an opening statement if you wish."

Beaudry came to his feet and said: "I know the court is familiar with the pleadings in this case and therefore I will waive my opening statement...." With that he sat down. Michael, found himself somewhat taken aback, since he had presumed you always make an opening statement in order to get your version of the facts in front of the court or jury. He was not sure whether this was some kind of a trick or not, and further, whether the client might be unsettled if he too waived his argument.

"Mr. Sullivan you may proceed with any statement you may have." He made a snap judgment—no opening statement. No need to telegraph his defense, inasmuch as opposing counsel was not going to show any cards.

"You may call your first witness, counsel," Judge Burke, all business, shot at Beaudry.

The lawyer called to the stand a well suited gentleman from the back of the court room to come forward and mount the witness stand. After he was sworn in by the bailiff he seated himself in the witness box to the Judge's left and stared out at both lawyers. Sullivan saw a well dressed business man who looked honest and would tell a creditable story. He appeared in the vicinity of fifty five or six and clearly contrasted with Tommy Thompson who had ill fitting attire on, and while not looking dishonest, could conceivably give that appearance to a Judge or jury because he looked nervous in the courtroom setting and uneasiness can be mistaken for dishonesty.

Beaudry, on direct examination, brought out the well dressed gentleman was Mr Damitor, owner and president of Jones Egg Company, which had been in business for twenty years and had hundreds of commercial customers in the metropolitan area. That they sold eggs to all kinds of businesses and restaurants and had sold eggs for years to Tommy Thompson's company and he knew Thompson though not well. "Yes," Thompson had been a "slow pay" but eventually he would pay the bill. That after a large shipment had not been paid for, he had had Thompson contacted by the accounting department and that department eventually got Thompson to issue a check to cover the amount of the purchase. In the normal course the check was dishonored and demand made on him for payment but he refused stating his business insolvent. He would not make good on the check so a legal action was commenced to collect.

It all seemed plausible and neat and Michael listened intently trying to figure out what to ask on cross examination, if anything, that would aid his case and damage Beaudry's. Before he knew it the direct examination was over and Beaudry intoned the fatal words: "your witness."

As he followed the direct testimony Michael began to formulate a line of questioning in his mind that he hoped would bring out some points for his side without aiding his opponent's case.

"Over what period of time did you do business with Tommy Thompson?"

"About five years." came the answer.

"Did you do business with Thompson or with the Thompson Company?"

"Well, really both. We looked on Tommy Thompson and Thompson Company as one in the same."

"Did you ever accept, or receive any checks in payment for goods from Tommy Thompson?"

"No"

"Every check you received was from Thomson Incorporated was it not?"

"Well, that's true, but……"

Michael cut him off and said: "Did Mr. Thompson ever offer to pay you himself or give you a personal check for payment for any goods your company sold to his corporation"

"No, he did not."

"Did you ask him to?"

"Not until his corporate check proved no good."

Realizing he was hitting at the heart of the matter, Sullivan struck: "Well then you always looked to the corporation for payment, did you not?"

"Well, yes," he stammered, "up to the time the company's check bounced."

"Thank you Mr. Damitor." No further questions.

Beaudry rehabilitated the witness with several questions concerning his client's knowledge or belief that Thompson and Thompson Inc. were one and the same but Sullivan had inflicted damage. The witness responded he essentially relied on the corporation for payment over the years. Beaudry desperately hoped the Judge would have caught the distinction—-that Thompson Inc. was Tommy personally, and his client had a right to rely on that fact. Michael knew instinctively he had drawn blood and it was an exhilarating feeling.

Two other witnesses testified for the Plaintiff telling of their investigation of Thompson Incorporated and Tommy business dealings. Michael decided not to cross examine. Now it came time to put on his case. He called Tommy to the stand. He knew it could be a disaster if his client failed to answer his questions correctly or if he asked the wrong questions. Without any chance to review the case and talk with the client in depth, he would have to rely on posing the right questions and Tommy's ability to establish the legal basis for the defense—the plaintiff relied on doing business with the corporation not Tommy individually. He looked directly at Thompson and with gentle questioning began to develop when and how he got into his business, the nature of the business, number of employees, method of payment for goods received. Finally he came to what he saw as the critical question and the key to his defense. Relying on the fact he established on cross examination, Mr. Damitor was always paid with a corporate check and not the personal check of Tommy Thompson, he asked the following questions:

"How have you paid for goods from suppliers?"

"By corporate check, that is, the Check of Thompson Inc."

"Have you ever used a personal check to pay for these goods?"

"Never," shouted Tommy, beginning to sense he might be getting control over the situation

"Have you ever been asked by suppliers or creditors to give a personal check in payment for goods or services?"

"No sir!"

Michael did not dare ask many more questions and felt lucky to get the answers Tommy had given. Beaudry mounted a ferocious cross examination: "Isn't it a fact you have signed personal notes for equipment purchased for your business?" Michael winced internally at this thrust and tried to show nothing keeping his eyes fastened intently on the witness.

"Yes sir I have but that is because the bank insisted that I co-sign for the equipment as a guarantor for the corporation paying for it. But no supplier of goods has ever asked me to sign as a guarantor for payment."

Michael, at that point, thought he had the most brilliant client-witness a lawyer could ever hope for and an honest one too. Thompson gave a perfectly plausible explanation to a trap question. Beaudry asked several more questions trying to badger the witness into saying he treated all the assets of the corporation as his own and creditors really looked to him personally for payment. But Thompson knew at this point if the other side had a personal check of his to any creditor, including the plaintiff they would have produced it. So he just kept repeating over and over in different answers "that all payments to creditors were made with corporate checks. All of a sudden it came to an end. The Judge allowed the lawyers to make closing statements and each took their seats.

In a sonorous tone Judge Burke delivered his opinion from the bench: "Gentlemen I've heard arguments of counsel, and listened to the evidence very carefully. As has been pointed out by Mr. Beaudry, the plaintiff's counsel, the issue is whether the defendant Thomas Thompson is one and the same entity as the Thompson Corporation. In other words should the corporate veil be pierced, as urged by Mr. Beaudry, or is Thompson's personal affairs and finances separable from his corporation in which he is the sole shareholder. I find the plaintiff should prevail against the Thompson Corporation for the evidence clearly shows a contract for purchase by the corporation which gave a check in payment, which turned out to be worthless although the check was issued when the money was there to honor it, but unfortunately the Plaintiff waited two weeks to cash it and by that time the account was in deficit. As to whether that liability should be extended to Mr. Thompson, I find the evidence is insufficient to show in fact he is indistinguishable from the corporation and therefore render judgment for the defendant Thompson. The evidence is quite clear he kept his personal affairs separate from those of his corporation and he paid, without exception, corporate debts with corporate checks. Finally he was never asked by this plaintiff to give a personal check at any time for goods purchased by the corporation or co-sign for any purchases from the plaintiff. It is my view the plaintiff was fully aware Thompson was doing business as a corporation and therefore accepted the risk of insolvency by the corporation. We will be in recess until two o'clock this afternoon.

Michael Sullivan wanted to shout, he'd just won his first trial. Instead, he came to his feet, as did opposing counsel when Judge Burke rose and exited from the courtroom. Beaudry crossed the isle separating counsel tables his hand extended and said:

"Congratulations Mr. Sullivan you did a good job. I don't like being beaten by a rookie but you did it fairly."

Michael melted like a wax candle. He felt a rush of warmth for this older lawyer, not pity only respect. "Thank you Mr. Beaudry it was a pleasure to try a case with you. I'm sure we will meet again." With that he broke off the conversation and turned to his client who sat stiff at the counsel table.

"Mr. Thompson, you won!"

"I don't understand; I thought I heard him say judgment for the plaintiff."

"He did, but that was against your corporation not you. You're the one we were trying to protect from the money judgment. A judgment against your corporation is near worthless." Thompson broke into a big smile: "I get it. The corporation has no assets.

"Mr. Sullivan, I don't think Paul could have done any better and I'm going to tell him so. I couldn't have paid that judgment; I probably would have had to take bankruptcy."

They parted on the court house steps. Michael felt a tremendous sense of worth, even cockiness as he headed back down the street to tell Howard Walker of his success. He went over the high points in his mind, the cross examination, the Judge's opinion from the bench. It was perfect, just the way he imagined it. In fact, he might have the makings of another John J. Fallon, the great "mouthpiece," made famous by the writings of Gene Fowler. Walker was pleased and not a little surprised. He thought to himself, the young man is not afraid. He might have been lucky but it's a good start. He praised the new associate and told him the next time he went to court, it would be to assist him in trial. Michael Sullivan felt very pleased with himself.

CHAPTER 4

That night, with a feeling of exultation, he told himself he had the making of a trial lawyer and as far as he was concerned there could no other role. Testing yourself in the arena against worthy advocates. Business lawyers, probate lawyers....no glamour. It took guts to go into the arena.

"Mary, I'm going to be a hell of a trial lawyer, he told her over a candle lit dinner. They had had a couple of drinks before and were in a happy mood. She listened to him and shared his joy and knew he had a tendency to get carried away with his own prowess. Nevertheless, she dutifully asked questions about the trial and he recounted with great relish every question and answer. And when he had fully exhausted the morning's effort she looked at him and he knew he had reached the limit of her endurance. They both laughed at the same time.

"I love you for listening, you wonderful girl, you're going to be proud of me yet."

"You idiot I am proud of you now, you don't have to prove anything to me. She believed he was going to do well and, in fact do great things, but she also knew with too much praise he could be insufferable. She kept to the middle ground, encouraging, praising and, if necessary, deflating. In short, even as a young wife and mother, she knew how to handle and encourage him to move forward.

They had a wonderful time that night talking about the future and how they would play an important part in the firm, about the sleeping child Jack in the next room and when they finally retired late that night they loved each other with great passion.

Initially, Michael met Matthew Hamilton the night he and about a hundred other would be lawyers were listening to a Hamilton talk about the state bar exam they were all about to take. Hamilton was an impressive fellow. He addressed the group, introducing himself as chairman of the Board of Bar Examiners and gave a stirring talk about the responsibilities of the Bar and what would be expected on the exam and how it would be graded. Afterward he interviewed a number of applicants, Michael among them. He asked a few per functionary questions and then seemed to get interested when Michael told him had gone to school in the east, had already passed a bar and served as an officer in the U. S. Air force.. As it turned out Hamilton had served in the air force. When he found out Michael had not been hired and still looking for a job he said his firm might be interested, although it looked like they were going to hire the son of the most senior partner in the largest law firm in the city. He had invited Michael to visit with him shortly after that meeting.

They met and he informed Michael they had decided to hire the partner's son. Disappointment followed, but only for a few days, when Michael learned he had been selected to serve for a year as law clerk to a state Supreme Court Justice. He quickly accepted as a great honor and something that would make his resume more attractive when he had to go job hunting again at the end of the year.

When his clerkship drew to a close, he remembered his conversation with Matthew Hamilton and decided to talk with him again as well as others since he had to get a job after his term at the court ended with a wife and baby son to support. He found it difficult to get interviews with firms even though his credentials were impeccable and he had achieved added luster as a Supreme Court clerk and passed two bar examinations. His hopes centered on a large law firm but it was not to be and after numerous rejections he wrote Matthew Hamilton requesting an opportunity to meet with him. He was grateful and encouraged when he received an immediate reply and an invitation to meet at the offices of Barron, Walker, Youngman & Hamilton. With dispatch he looked the firm up in the biographical section of Martindale Hubble, the compendium of leading firms in the city and the United States. He concluded this could be a sleeper firm, small with a great potential for growth. The oldest partner, Samuel Barron, sixty, Howard Walker, fifty five, Johnathan Youngman forty four, Matthew Hamilton forty and the youngest member, John T. Jensen, thirty four.

Before the appointment to meet with Matthew Hamilton he found everything he could about the firm. First and foremost it billed itself as the oldest law firm in the state, continuously in existence since 1897. The original partners were southerners and through the years it had prospered and by the time Michael Sullivan was scheduled to meet Matthew Hamilton the firm specialized in municipal bond work, corporate, transportation and insurance defense litigation.

The meeting with Hamilton took place on a Monday and Michael Sullivan, urged by his wife Mary, purchased a new suit for the occasion even though they didn't have the money for it. She convinced him he would get the job and be able to pay for the suit. He looked sharp and felt sharp when ushered into Matthew's office. He took an instant liking for the older man, who seemed to reciprocate immediately. From the first minutes they hit it off. Matthew explained that they had hired an associate the previous year but, unfortunately he had not passed the bar and as a result, he was contemplating joining the army in the Judge Advocate General's corps. Michael had already served two years active duty in the air force at the time of his discussion with Matthew and later achieved the rank of Captain in the Judge Advocate General Reserve.

Matthew told him if the young associate left, the firm would definitely be interested in talking to him. The meeting was cordial and Michael had the impression he would have been hired on the spot if the firm had an opening. They left it that Matthew would get back to him within a week if the associate joined the army. It turned out to be one of the most difficult weeks he had ever spent. Fraught with anxiety and concern because he had not yet landed a job and the hope he might get the call to compete for a job he decided to stay calm and pray. Of all the firms he had interviewed with, Barron, Walker, Youngman & Hamilton appeared to be ideal for him in size and he knew he would get immediate client contact and possibly the chance to try cases sooner than in a large firm.

On Friday the call came. "This is Matthew Hamilton. The fellow I told you about has decided to take an offer to join the military so I'd like you to come in Monday, if that's convenient to meet other members of the firm"

What a thrill to receive that call. He felt confident he could sell himself to members of the firm. On Monday at nine a.m. sharp he began the rounds, spending exactly one half hour with each of the five partners. They were friendly and courteous; he: positive and respectful and more importantly he liked each of the five men instinctively. Matthew Hamilton said he would call him in a couple of days and let him know whether the firm would hire him as a replacement for the departing associate. The call came the next day. Everyone liked him and the salary offered, twenty five thousand the first year. Michael said he was honored to join the firm and they agreed he would start the following Monday, August 1, 1983

He had not been with the firm three weeks, when Howard Walker called him in to his office and informed him he had to try a personal injury case in a few days and wanted Michael to assist him, in fact, he said he'd like him to try a portion of it, and he would be right alongside. He handed him the file and told him to study it and start contacting the witnesses requesting them to come in for interviews and pre trial preparation. A move to the big leagues he thought to himself. He already had one trial under his belt and this trial would be before a jury.

He set about studying the file and lining up witnesses since the trial was only four days away. The factual situation was simple enough. Walker's client had been hit in an intersection by a car that claimed the right of way. The dispute arose over whether the driver of the other car had forfeited his right of way by having the "last clear chance" to avoid the accident, and consequent injury to Billy Walters, the firm's client. As part of his preparation, Michael took stock of who would be representing the defendants, the Insurance Company and its insured. It turned out to be a young man, about Michael's age who had been practicing law for some time but more importantly trying cases for four years. A few weeks earlier Michael had been sitting in back of one of the courtrooms at the federal court house watching proceedings as a very young lawyer, impeccably dressed, and with great aplomb, addressed the Judge using a pointer and a large easel with an involved chart on it, illustrating the mystery of anti trust entanglements which he claimed his client not to be involved in. Other, older lawyers, seated at the counsel tables seemed completely absorbed in his argument, so to the Judge. Michael left before the bench ruling but had watched long enough to be very impressed with the young man's air of authority, confidence and overall demeanor. Being highly competitive, he liked to match himself against others and felt a grudging admiration for the young lawyer and the feeling he would like to have a go at him. Later he found out his name, Armand Jorgenson, an associate with one of the two largest firms in the city; the same lawyer he had watched in federal court would be opposing he and Howard Walker in the Walters's trial

The trial started off innocently enough. Michael sat beside Howard Walker and watched as jurors were called by random numbers and told to take their seat in the jury box to the left of the Judge's bench. The Judge, Dimitri Sammaneli, was a dapper fellow with black curly hair, slightly graying with a distinct twinkle in his eye. He wanted to be liked and as a Judge he did not strike fear into the hearts of litigants, jurors, witnesses or lawyers. Lawyers referred to as a settling judge. He would call attorneys into his chambers and point blank asked defense counsel his best offer. When given a figure (ridiculously low) he would turn to the plaintiff's counsel and say: "what do you need…" (meaning what do you need to make your client settle) The plaintiff's lawyer would give a figure (ridiculously high) and Judge Sammaneli would turn to defense counsel and say: "Well I think plaintiff's counsel has suggested a fair figure, could you come up with that?" The defense counsel knew, if he could state a figure that was low but higher than his first offer, the Judge would become an advocate for the defendant's figure and would lean on the plaintiff's counsel to talk seriously to his client about it because it was his opinion (the Judge's) a jury wouldn't do much better.

Plaintiff's counsel would come back with a higher figure and finally after haggling over a few hundred dollars the Judge and the counsel would agree to a settlement figure. Of course both the Judge and defense counsel knew the figure could not be too low because the plaintiff's counsel would be working on a one third or forty percent contingency fee to be paid by his client and any settlement would have to take that fact into consideration. Once the figure was agreed upon, it then became the task of the attorneys to sell their clients on the settlement.

In smaller cases the defense counsel would usually have the authority to settle up to a certain amount without checking with in insurance company. The job of the plaintiff's attorney was much more difficult. He had to go out to his client, who would be waiting at counsel table with perhaps a full courtroom of 40 or 50 jurors sitting in the back benches waiting to be called and with the witnesses waiting to testify in his behalf. A client who is psychologically ready to testify and has steeled himself for a great ordeal is not easily persuaded to settle his case unless he is equally paralyzed by fear.

The Firm

The plaintiff's attorney would exit the Judge's chambers, gesture dramatically to his client to follow him into the hallway outside the courtroom and then the attorney would use all his skills, psychological and legal, to point out to the client the merits of settling versus the pitfalls of not taking advantage of the offer, even though in the eyes of the client it is far from what he believes he deserves, and more importantly, what the jury would reward him based upon what to him is the obvious justice of his claim. After much haggling the client would finally agree to the figure. His attorney would signal the defense counsel a settlement had been reached, who would then notify the bailiff to notify the Judge the parties had settled and request a meeting be held in chambers. The lawyers would solemnly march into the chambers and the Judge proclaim, "well gentlemen have you reached a settlement?" Both counsel would dutifully reply that was indeed the case. Smiling, the Judge would call for the court reporter to come into his chambers and defense counsel would proceed to dictate into the record the terms of the agreement subject to corrections by plaintiff's counsel.

That completed, the lawyers would shake hands with each other, receive the congratulations of the Judge and thereafter return to their positions at counsel table. Judge Sammaneli then donned his black robe and re-appeared on the bench at which time he thanked all the prospective jurors for waiting so patiently to hear the case, explaining to them the fact the parties had settled their differences and this was preferable to a long and testy trial in which one party would lose. He went on to advise the jurors that, if they had not taken the time to come down to the courthouse to do their civic duty, and be ready to give it their best as disinterested jurors it might very well have turned out the case would not have been settled. He would then impart to them his philosophy that they played just as important a roll in the settlement of a case, as in trial with a verdict. With that he would thank them profusely and dismiss them to return to the jury room to await being called for the next trial.

"Case dismissed," he would state with emphasis and the lawyers and the Judge went on to the next case and the plaintiff to console himself that he had some measure of retribution.

Judge Sammaneli had not been able to persuade Howard Walker or Armand Jorgenson to discuss settlement in the Walters case with the result a jury had been picked and seated in the jury box listening to Judge Sammanelli tell them about the case before counsel gave opening statements.

"The plaintiff has brought this action claiming the defendant was negligent in driving his car at too high a rate of speed and in general not watching where he was going. The plaintiff claims that as a result of defendant's negligence his car was damaged in the amount of one thousand dollars and he was injured by being thrown about the car sustaining bodily injury to himself in the neck, shoulder and back and therefore was required to incur medical expense in the sum of two thousand dollars. In addition he claims lost wages in the sum of five thousand dollars and finally due to pain and suffering he has been damaged in the sum of one hundred thousand dollars.

Michael kept his eyes on the jury as the Judge spoke the words he himself had helped draft in the complaint. He could detect interest on their part, as exemplified by their fixed attention to the Judge's words and sleight leaning forward so as to not miss anything being said.

"The defendant, the Judge continued, of course, denies in his answer that he was negligent in any way and, in fact, alleges the accident took place because the plaintiff stopped his car suddenly without warning and therefore the plaintiff should recover nothing because he was contributorily negligent. The defendant goes on to plead that even if he should be found negligent by the jury, the claimant has not been damaged to the extent he claims. That ladies and gentlemen is a brief summary of the contentions of the parties. I will now ask the plaintiff's counsel to present his opening statement."

Howard Walker gracefully got up from the table, walked to the front of the jury box and placed himself squarely in front of the jury.

The Firm

Michael watched with great anticipation because he had heard from John Jensen, the youngest partner in the firm, that in his earlier days Walker had done a great deal of trial work and had been very successful. It gave Michael a feeling of comfort as he watched the elder man began to address the jury. As he listened he began to feel a sense of disappointment creep into his bones. He expected fire, passion and emotion. Instead Walker was low key, dispassionate and a couple of times lost his thought. A wave of frustration engulfed Michael because he knew he didn't have the experience to fully try the case and he looked forward to learning from Walker. Jorgenson's opening statement was short, smooth and in a subtle way cut through the plaintiff's case on damages by inferring ever so slightly, the case might be a sham.

Walker called the plaintiff as his first witness. He carefully took him through questions needed to establish his case and then turned him over to Jorgenson for cross examination. It took Jorgenson about a half hour but he carefully planted the seed in the minds of the jurors that the plaintiff might have some inflated ideas about the damages he had incurred, and whether, in fact, he was completely blameless for the accident.

It had been decided Michael would examine the next two witnesses, the plaintiff's wife and the only witness to the accident. The wife took the stand, the bailiff administered the oath and she primly seated herself in the witness chair. It was not completely lost on her that the cross examination of her husband, although gentle, may have quietly planted a thought in the jury's mind that perhaps she and her husband were over reaching.

The young attorney arose and walked slowly to the end of the jury box so that he looked down a straight line at her, with the jury—all twelve—on his immediate left. His intention being to keep the eyes of the jury on her as she answered his questions not to look at or pay any attention to him. He had seen the technique used in a criminal trial he had attended while preparing to defend an airman facing military discipline. While serving as a lieutenant in the Air Force he'd been appointed to act as defense counsel for military personnel accused of lesser offensives. He had not yet attended law school, so as a means of acquainting himself with courtroom tactics, he'd take an afternoon off from the air base to watch criminal proceedings in a nearby city. Michael had been impressed with the tactic, if the examining lawyer stood at the opposite end of the jury box, the witness could speak directly to him and the jury at the same time without having to turn his head back and forth from questioner to jury as if watching a tennis match.

He commenced his questioning dwelling on the event that took place after the accident, establishing the number of times the Dr. had been visited, the tests taken, the medicines used to control pain, how much time her husband had taken off from work, as well as her personal witness to the constant pain he suffered as a result of the accident. It went smoothly and she was obviously becoming more confident and at ease as she was getting the exact questions he said he would be asking her and she knew the answers to be given. She proved very effective on direct examination and he released her for cross examination.

Armand Jorgenson knew what he was doing and his experience, although not immediately apparent to the jury, was recognized by Michael about half way into his cross examination. He effectively brought out that her husband had been in a prior automobile accident; that he had received physical damage much like he was claiming to have received in the present case, and strangely enough on the same parts of his body where damage had previous been sustained. He also brought out that her husband had still been treating off and on from the prior accident with his current doctor, thus implanting in the jury's mind, that the physical damages claimed might be more or entirely from the prior accident rather than from the accident on which the claim was being tried. He sat down.

Thinking to himself that damage had been done and it would be useless to try to rehabilitate the wife through rebuttal examination, he excused her and called as a witness the only person who actually witnessed the accident. This gentleman, in his fifties, slightly graying at the temples, and neatly dressed, presented a picture of an honest disinterested by stander. Michael again took up his position by the jury box and directed his questions in a logical progression establishing that on the day in question he had been driving his car behind that of the plaintiff, and that suddenly from a side street the defendant's car had come without warning into the path of plaintiff's vehicle and the two had collided sending the plaintiff's car spinning out of control. In his own mind his direct examination had been masterful, the witness responded in an honest and straight forward manner and he was pleased with himself when he sat down. It worried him that Armand asked only a couple of perfunctory questions on cross examination and then released the witness for further questioning.

They agreed Howard Walker would handle the last and most important witness, Dr. Soberling. He relaxed as Howard Walker began to take the Dr. through his qualifications as an expert and then began to probe his diagnosis and findings concerning the plaintiff's injury and finally his prognosis for recovery. What Walker was looking for were those magical medical words uttered by the expert: "permanent injury"

"Dr. do you have an opinion based on your treatment, the history you took, your examinations and your entire familiarity with this patient, whether, within the realm of medical probability that the injuries he now suffers will be permanent?"

"Yes I do."

"And what is your opinion Doctor?" Walker asked, as he dramatically turned to face the jury awaiting the answer from his medical expert.

"My opinion is the injury is permanent."

Howard than took the doctor through the formality of explaining why he thought the injuries would be permanent and turned the witness over to Armand Jorgenson.

Armand wasted no time in tearing into the doctor, first pointing out he had only seen the patient on 5 or 6 occasions and on each of those occasions he had seen at least twenty other patients and therefore really hadn't spent that much time on the case. The witness fidgeted. He pointed out to the witness that X-rays showed no damage and therefore the "soft tissue" damage the doctor claimed the patient had could resolve within weeks of the accident which the doctor admitted was true. He also got the doctor to admit that there was no nerve damage, really no objective medical evidence, only the subjective complaints of the plaintiff. After about a half hour of this kind of treatment Armand let the doctor off the stand with a curt dismissal. "Thank you Doctor"

By this time it was clear to Michael they had clearly established the "liability" part of the case; that the defendant had caused the accident and therefore was liable, but they were taking a pounding on the issue of damages because of Armand's skillful cross examinations.

After Dr. Soberling testified, Howard Walker rested his case and the defense called one witness, Dr. Hiram Johnson. It was customary in a trial for personal injury that the defense lawyer could insist that the injured party allow himself to be examined by a doctor selected by lawyers for the defense. That being the case Billy Waters had been examined by Dr. Johnson for purposes of testifying at trial should the case go that far.

In his direct examination, Armand Jorgenson was very matter of fact as he led the witness through the various tests he had administered to determine, if and where the plaintiff had been injured. The doctor recited that the injured party claimed stiffness in the back and neck regions but medical history contained evidence of the prior vehicle accident that had resulted in injury to the same areas—so the probability was excellent he was still hurt from the prior accident. Also that the tests showed no "objective" findings. The distinct impression left by this testimony was, the man may not have been hurt at all, but if he was, the damage was sleight and the jury award should be minimal.

On cross examination Michael was astounded at Howard Walker's slashing attack. After a few preliminary probes about "soft tissue" injury becoming permanent and the doctor admitting that a probability existed but he didn't think that was the case with this plaintiff. Walker, red faced and in a highly pitched accusatory voice boomed at the doctor with a knowing look at the jury:

"Dr. were you paid to make the report from which you have just testified?"

"Yes. I was."

"How much"

"Two hundred and fifty dollars"

"And who paid you that sum?"

"I believe it was Mr. Jorgenson's firm," the doctor said looking rather confused and embarrassed.

"And finally, doctor do you do a lot of examinations for this firm and testify for them?"

"Yes"

"Objection," your honor. Armand Jorgenson was on his feet now shouting at the Judge that the line of questioning was irrelevant and a cheap way of attempting to prejudice the witness in the jury's eyes.

"Sustained" the judge fired back without hesitation.

"No further questions your Honor." Walker sat down, clearly exhausted. For his part Michael felt embarrassed by the attack on Doctor Johnson. It was unnecessary and even as an inexperienced lawyer he felt the attack might hurt rather than help the case because the jury would have sympathy for the Doctor rather than feel any bias on his part.

The Judge called a recess. Michael and Howard Walker sat together at the counsel table, Michael thinking the case had not gone well, especially in the handling of the two medical witnesses. And Paul, slumped down, showing a signs of exhaustion. Suddenly the bailiff appeared from the Judge's chambers and handed Michael a note. It read:

"Mr. Sullivan I know you are a new lawyer and probably assisting in the trial of your first case but I must admonish you never to leave the counsel table to question a witness as you did in my courtroom today. I believe this advice should be followed in every other court room you might find yourself in the future. The rule is no lawyer leaves the counsel table unless he has permission from the bench. I think you are going to make an excellent trial lawyer but suggest you heed this advice.

Best wishes, Dimitri Sammaneli,
Circuit Judge

Stunned and humiliated he felt like a fool. Howard leaned over and in a low voice said:

"Michael, I think we better try to settle this before it goes to the jury. I'm going to have a word with Armand.

I would take the chance of going to the jury, Michael thought to himself. There is clear liability and the man has medical damages and lost time from his job—surely a jury wouldn't be completely fooled by Armand Jorgenson and his very competent cross examination. Rather than voicing that argument to Howard, he kept quiet thinking this man has tried a hundred cases and knows more than I. I don't like it but his analysis would be more valid than mine.

"Ok, I'll advise the Judge of what we are doing"

Within five minutes Howard came back and confided he had a ten thousand dollar offer from Armand Jorgenson and he'd advised the plaintiff to accept it. Again, Michael felt a pang. They had sued for a hundred thousand dollars and he felt a jury might award twenty five thousand, but then maybe Howard was right, they might award five thousand. Juries were like that.

Afterwards Armand came over and talked with Walker for a minute and then turned to Michael and said "you did a good job with those witnesses." Michael smiled and murmured "thank you" but was still feeling sick to his stomach from the Judge's rebuke and the fact the case had settled. As competitive as Michael was he didn't treat the comment as patronizing from a young man his own age. He realized Armand had much more experience than he in far more important cases and meant it as a compliment and encouragement. From that day on he had a genuine admiration for Armand Jorgenson as a lawyer although they were never to meet again in court.

He didn't take too long feeling sorry for himself because the firm obviously expected him, even with little experience, to begin trying cases. Actually only three other attorneys in the firm were experienced enough to go into court: Howard Walker, who, as Michael had recently witnessed, was rusty and really not in good enough physical shape to take the beating of a three or four day trial, Matthew Hamilton, only rarely was called upon to try a case spending most of his time on corporate and municipal matters and John Jensen who had tried a number of cases but was primarily a "book" man and felt more at home trying cases to a Judge rather than the rough and tumble of a jury trial. Sullivan hadn't been with the firm more than four months when he realized he would be the one, as youthful and inexperienced as he was, to take over the brunt of the trials the firm might have to engage in. In that respect he was pleased because his idea of a real lawyer was not one who engaged in corporate, tax or probate law but one who spent his time in the court room—-where the ultimate test comes when a legal matter can't be settled in any other way. He realized it would be trial and error since the other men didn't have enough time to let him sit alongside for a year or two before ever being allowed to question a juror on voir dire. This put him at a disadvantage because he would be going up against older lawyers who had been trying cases for years or younger ones from the larger firms who would have had the opportunity of first spending two or three years just drafting pleadings and legal memorandums in support of motions, and the actual arguing of motions, before they were allowed to try a case on their own.

So be it. He would make up for his lack of experience by knowing more about any case he was going to try than any opponent he would face. In time he would catch up. Even though he was barely out of law school he felt an obligation, perhaps even a duty, to not only learn the law but to get clients. (He later learned the longer he practiced no one really expected a freshly minted lawyer to bring in clients) but, of course, he didn't know that at the start.

CHAPTER 5

He was sitting in his office pouring over a case when the phone rang and the caller introduced himself as Paul Samuels. "I got your name out of Martindale Hubble. I'm an attorney in San Jose, California and I have a client by the name of Winona Johnson. Her mother just died in your city leaving quite a large estate. Mrs. Johnson thinks her mother made a will under undue influence by her housekeeper and some other people. Would you be interested in taking the case?" To Michael, a client was a client and if proper terms could be worked out for representation and the firm had no objection, he would be glad to take the case.

"If you'll send me a letter telling me exactly what the facts are and I have a chance to digest them I'll get back to you."

"Fair enough. I'll dictate something today and you should have it by weeks end, and by the way, if it's necessary to try the case I will probably need to be admitted to your probate court. Any problem on that score."

"I don't think so but I'll let you know when we decide on whether we'll represent Mrs. Johnson or not."

It turned out the firm had no questions about getting involved since Mrs. Johnson offered to pay a retainer of five thousand dollars and pay on an hourly fee basis. Samuels's letter disclosed an abundance of facts that wove a tale of intrigue, untrustworthiness, treachery, betrayal and what Samuels concluded amounted to undue influence in the decision and drafting of the last will and testament of Mary Rogers Smith III.

Samuels memorandum detailed Mrs. Smith was the widow of Thomas Smith III who commenced his career as a real estate agent without a college education but with a charming personality, quick wit and an astute head for figures. He began selling houses making a modest income and before long he figured out investing in duplexes might make more money than commissions from real estate sales. He purchased his first duplex from meager savings putting a small amount down and placing a ninety five percent mortgage against the property. He quickly found two reliable renters and charged them a rent that more than covered the mortgage payment and other expenses. He knew from his real estate experience he could use depreciation to offset income from the property and avoid paying higher taxes. Within a year of his first purchase he bought a second duplex and duplicated his first experience quickly finding two more renters with the same results. After five years (he was conservative and patient) he parlayed the duplexes into purchase of apartment houses and within ten years he owned a string of apartments and on paper a wealthy young man at age thirty five. He married Mary Rogers, who like himself, had worked hard for a salary, had accumulated some minor savings, was very smart and had the same talent for figures he had. They made a perfect team.

She had vision and restraint while he had charm and energy. The heart break in their life turned out to be an inability to have children so in their forties they decided to adopt. Tom Smith had employed numerous lawyers in his real estate ventures and he knew one who could arrange for adoption of a child. The process involved a physician knowing his patient desired to adopt out her child as soon as it was born, arrange for the lawyer to draw up the necessary papers, go to the hospital, meet the mother and have her sign the documents. Subsequently, when the mother gave birth, the lawyer went to the hospital, picked up the child and delivered it to the adoptive parents. Later papers were presented to the court and a formal decree of adoption entered in the court records. This procedure occurred in Winona Johnson's case. Winona, as she was later called by her adoring parents, came to the Smiths as a five day old infant and became the light of their life. In every way she proved to be the perfect daughter. First in her class, high school valedictorian, on to a fine college for girls and at age twenty six marriage to a business man in California. Something happened shortly after their marriage. She became distant from her parents either because her husband didn't like them or she felt, as an only child, it would be better to keep her doting parents at a distance.

As time went on Tom Smith became wealthier and by age seventy five had amassed a considerable fortune based primarily in real estate and securities. During their lives the Smiths had made many acquaintances, but developed a special fondness for a young woman about the same age as their daughter, Winona. In some ways this woman, Debra Dulset, took the place of Winona after she married and grew estranged from the Smiths. She traveled with them, they spent holidays together and shared many experiences through the years. Debra did not marry and as she grew older spent more and more time in the company of the Smiths, particularly Mary. While this friendship flourished the relationship between the Smiths and their adopted daughter waned. When Winona finally had children, the Smiths, as proud grandparents, made every effort to see them and Winona was not adverse to this. Nevertheless daughter and adoptive parents remained apart.

Prior to his death Thomas made a will in which he left his entire estate to Mary. Before doing so he set up trusts for Winona's four children even though he had not had the opportunity to be with them or know them. Just before his death there had been a reconciliation of sorts between Winona, her family and the Smiths. They all had reached that point in life where family means more than sleights fancied or otherwise. Thomas was gone, however, Mary felt content; she had regained the love of Winona, and even more importantly, the grandchildren who were now grown and anxious to recognize her as their grandmother.

Not too long after Thomas's death Mary was in a severe automobile accident and after a long period she slowly started to recover when suddenly her condition grew worse and her physicians decided she required round the clock nursing care. At first two full time attendants were hired, by her friend Debra Dulset, in consultation with Winona. After about a month, and continued worsening of her condition, Debra decided to move in with Mary. Winona had no objection, although she had not been consulted before the move in. For two more months Mary lingered and then without warning she passed away. They notified Winona she was failing but she could not get to her before she suddenly died.

Samuels memorandum concluded with the revelation that after Mary and Thomas reconciled with Winona and her family, they both changed their wills to provide if either predeceased the other, the survivor would leave the bulk of their estate to Winona or her children if she died before them. These wills were drawn by Thomas's long time attorney and confidant, Willard Marshall, who was also a family friend and continued to counsel Mary on business and personal matters. During the last two months of her life she did not call Marshall for any legal advice even though his safe contained Mary's will. His first knowledge that something was wrong came as he sipped coffee at breakfast one morning two weeks after Mary's death when a headline and the story that followed caught his eye. It read:

"Wealthy Widow, Mary Rogers Smith III
Leaves Estate to a Friend"

The story noted, that although the deceased left surviving an adopted daughter and four grandchildren they had not been mentioned in a will executed shortly before she died.

Marshall abruptly paid for his coffee and literally ran three blocks to his office where he placed a call to Winona. He advised her he had a will in his safe previously executed by Mary before himself and two associates in which she was named the primary beneficiary.

"What does it all mean Willard?"

"It means, for some reason, your mother changed her will about a year after I wrote it for her and she did not consult me. You are the beneficiary of that will."

"I know nothing about it except Mary told me I would get everything upon her death. I was absolutely in shock when I learned Mary's will was being offered for probate and Debra was the executrix as well as the beneficiary. Mary must be worth two or three million dollars at least. What do you advise?"

"I would talk with your family lawyer if you have one."

"I do" she said with some relief in her voice.

"Tell him the story and see what he thinks. I believe there is the possibility of a case Winona and as a matter of fact you don't really have a choice you either contest the will or lose a fortune. You will probably have to get counsel here to represent you in the case of a trial. I can't do it because I represented your folks and drew their wills and would undoubtedly be called as a witness."

For Michael the case would be a tremendous challenge, certainly from a legal standpoint, but more importantly from a factual standpoint. The law in such a case is clear enough: if it can be shown the maker of the will was under undue influence, the will can be set aside and the will drafted by Willard Marshall substituted in its place. The difficulty, and in most cases the stumbling block, is factually proving the will submitted to probate invalid. It was understood between Michael and Paul Samuels, that if the case had to be tried, the division of labor would have Paul coming into the state to try the case and Michael would be tasked with marshalling the facts, getting the case ready for trial, talking to witnesses and preparing a pretrial brief.

Michael requested Winona come from California to meet with him and tell everything she knew about those involved with Mary at the time of her death. When she arrived Michael ushered her into the firm's conference room, got her a cup of coffee and asked how her flight from California had been. As she talked he watched her without seeming to and judged her to be in her mid-forties, roly poly with a very cheerful, honest face. To a trial lawyer, a plaintiff like Winona can be the difference between winning and losing. Her face glistened with honesty. Her demeanor, as they talked, was calm her statements forthright, not antagonistic over the very distinct possibility of being cheated out of a fortune in the five million dollar range. As to her appearance she had a tailored look which combined with her honest face made her very appealing. The question that flashed across his mind as he sized her up was how her opponent, Debra Dulset, would look.

As it turned out, Debra Dulset made quite an appealing witness as Michael later found out when he arranged to take her deposition. The estate of Mary Rogers Smith III had engaged the firm of Stark, Margolis, Watson & Levy to protect the validity of the will that had been submitted to the probate court. By this time Michael had become the firm's trial lawyer, and through diligence and hard work, had become quite adept at persuading juries and trial Judges of the merits of cases he undertook. The Smith case presented the toughest challenge he had faced, even though another attorney, Paul Samuels, would be trying the case. His part would, in many ways, be the most difficult part. Preparation is the most important part of any case that is to be tried. He had to marshal the facts, depose the witnesses and research the law they would cite in their trial brief.

The night before taking Debra Dulset's deposition he reviewed her complete file prepared by an investigator who worked from time to time with the lawyers in the firm. Everything was there, her habits, friendship with Tom and Mary Rogers and with Winona herself. The deposition afforded an opportunity to gather information and to judge what kind of a witness she would make on her own behalf. The next morning he arrived promptly at nine o'clock at the tenth floor offices of Stark, Margolis, Watson & Levy and the first person he met was the court reporter he had retained to record the proceedings and prepare a transcript. They were directed to a large conference room with a floor to ceiling window and a view of the city looking north. Within two minutes the door to the room opened and Debra Dulset swept through it, closely followed by Samuel Watson, her lawyer, who made introductions all around. Michael made a quick inventory of her demeanor. Dressed stylishly but not over dressed. She would be considered by most as attractive in a non-threatning way. Her figure full but not distracting. She appeared to be in her late forties. He expected her to be a hostile witness and would know soon enough whether her voice and body movements would be persuasive to a Judge or jury, not to mention the believability of her story.

By means of questioning, he saw the defense her attorney would present in court: she befriended Winona when they were in college together. She would come to Winona's home on holidays and spend as much as a week's time and eventually was accepted, not only as Winona's friend but a friend of Mary and Tom's. When Winona married and moved away, Debra remained friendly with the Smiths. Because she failed to marry she wound up spending more and more time with Mary and Tom, and after Tom died she became very close with Mary, sometimes even taking trips with her. During this time, Winona, her husband and her children grew away from her adoptive mother and father. Just a few years before Tom's death Winona and her parents were reunited. In her testimony Debra admitted she knew Mary had a will but not its contents, and further stated she presumed Winona and her family were probably named beneficiaries. She said, in answer to Michael's questions, that as Mary's health waned she essentially took over care of her to the point of being at her bedside night and day, along with nurses who were in attendance part time. Debra testified, about a week before her death, Mary advised Debra she wanted to change her will and make Debra the sole beneficiary. Debra contacted a lawyer had a new will drawn up and witnessed by the two nurses while Mary lay in her sick bed. The lawyer was present at the signing. Michael concluded the deposition asking Debra a few more perfunctory questions.

Her counsel appeared quite pleased and asked no questions. The deposition served to confirm that Debra, the sole beneficiary, would make a good witness in her own behalf; she appeared calm under tough questioning and had a plausible explanation why the deceased had chosen to leave five million dollars to her instead of her adopted daughter and grandchildren. She had been a life-long friend and present at the end while Winona and her family had spent little time with Tom and Mary. There was logic to this explanation.

It would be a difficult task to show Debra used her friendship with Mary to influence her to change her will. With the lawyer present when she signed and his testimony as to her soundness of mind when she executed the will the problem became doubly difficult. This fact concerned Michael but he saw it as Paul Samuels's problem knowing he had only to prepare the case not try it.

The court set the trial for December 15, 1992. Four days before trial Paul Samuels became seriously ill and informed the court of his inability to try the case and requested a postponement. Since all matters and court appearances pertaining to the case, from the time it had been filed, were attended by Michael, the Judge refused a continuance saying the case had been on the docket an inordinate amount of time and it had to be tried as scheduled. He left no choice. The Judge, knowing Michael to be a capable trial attorney, insisted his firm proceed to trial. No point in panicking; he knew these things happened in trials and often Judges, with heavy dockets, and so many cases to try, would say they could only postpone a case so many times. It made no difference whether $5,000 or $5,000,000 was at stake——-the defendant had a right to proceed without undue delay.

Michael knew the case forwards and backwards, the testimony the witnesses were expected to give and the burden of proof he would have to carry in attacking the validity of the new will. He also knew the capabilities of his adversary, Samuel Watson. He realized Watson knew he held the upper hand and knew, all too well, how to play it. He watched and learned as he skirmished with Samuel Watson in the discovery, deposition and motions phases of the case. Watson would be well prepared. The trial proceeded on the day appointed; Michael and Watson picked a jury, made opening statements and called the first witness to the stand. Winona told of her early years with her adoptive parents, her friendship with Debra during their university years and the fact she thought Debra was still her friend after her father died and her mother left alone. The fact Debra became close to her mother was a source of comfort, in fact, in the last moments before her mother died she kept in weekly contact with her concerning her mother's welfare.

On cross examination she admitted to Samuel Watson she had been estranged from her parents but the last year before her mother's death she had bonded again with her parents, who, for the first time since her marriage, were able to see and enjoy their grandchildren. "No" she could not say whether her parents had made a will that provided for she and the children but they had often mentioned they would do all they could for their grandchildren. "Yes" she assumed she would be remembered in any disposition of their property——-who else would they leave it to? "Did she ever consider that her friend and her mother's friend would, at the end, inherit her mother's wealth?" It never crossed her mind. "Yes" Debra had been attentive to her mother and perhaps she had not been as concerned as she might have been, but she had been busy raising three children and assisting her husband in his business. They lived in different cities a thousand miles apart and she knew her mother understood this and didn't resent the fact they saw each other infrequently.

Michael's other witnesses recalled how fond her mother was of the grandchildren and that she and Tom had been happier than ever with the chance to have Winona and her family back in the fold. One witness recalled how sick she was at the end and her opinion that Mary Rogers Smith III didn't have the capacity to make a will at the time the contested document was dated just a few days before her death. Other witnesses testified that when they tried to visit Mary or check on her condition Debra always blocked their efforts which they thought unusual because Mary was a woman who had always been extremely conscientious about visiting sick friends and expecting similar treatment in return. All this evidence was offered by Michael to create an inference in the jury's mind: that Debra had the opportunity and the motive to get the decedent to leave everything to her, coupled with the fact Debra knew of the long period of animosity between Mary and Winona's family and the lack of contact between the two in Mary's last months.

Samuel Watson moved for dismissal at the end of Michael's case on the basis the evidence introduced was insufficient to allow a jury to find "undue influence." The Judge, however, ruled enough evidence had been presented by the plaintiff to establish a prima facie case and instructed Watson to proceed with the defense. Several witnesses testified Mary Smith and Debra were not only friends but Debra had been like a daughter to the Smiths during the period of Winona's estrangement from them. That even when Winona became united with her parents they still looked upon Debra as a daughter and loved her as much as Winona. They saw nothing strange about everything being left to Debra. Howard Stern, a handwriting expert told the jury although the signature on the will was shaky that would not be unusual for a woman of her age and that he compared many documents containing her signature and found the signature on the will to be authentic.

Watson called Beatrice Tracy and Viola Taggert the two nurses who witnessed the will, each of whom said they saw Mary sign it. The last witness Samuel Watson called was the lawyer who drafted and witnessed the will's signing. Barton Jenkins took the stand. Michael had taken his deposition and knew what he would testify to and had determined he was a weak malleable individual who was anxious to do the bidding of anyone willing to pay his fee. Balding with a small mustache, diminutive of stature with furtive eyes he did not present the look of integrity that Watson would have hoped for, but he did have a fair legal reputation. On cross examination Michael hammered at the fact Jenkins had not seen the client before drafting the will and had done so upon the advice of Debra Dulset, who he had not previously known relying on her word that she was like a daughter to Mary who was bedridden and not well enough to come to his office. The will left everything to Debra. He admitted he did not know the value of the assets but was advised it was all real property and a few securities. He stated he was present at the signing of the will with the two nurses and he had asked Mary Smith a few perfunctory questions and based on her answers he judged her mentally capable of making the will. With that testimony Samuel Watson rested satisfied he had presented an air tight case. 5:30 Friday afternoon. In chambers the Judge told the lawyers he would allow Michael to present rebuttal witnesses, if any, the following Monday after which they could present their closing arguments.

Michael returned to the office dejected—he had put on the best case he could make from the facts. The question upper most in his mind was: would a jury believe that Mary was influenced by Debra and or others? On the surface it didn't make sense. If she was of sound mind she would not have spurned her grandchildren who she loved without qualification in favor of another. If Winona had been negligent in her attention to Mary in her sickness, Mary was not the type of woman who would abandon the future of her grandchildren out of pique. Winona accompanied him back to the office. He told her the truth as he saw it.

"We've put on the best case possible, Winona, the question is: will the jury buy what's reasonable and makes perfect sense versus the iron clad testimony of the nurse witnesses, the hand writing expert and the lawyer? Samuel Watson is no fool. He knows the burden we have to carry and he's fully aware a strong argument can be made the second will is perfectly valid. Before she could respond with her own thoughts on the situation the phone rang.

"Michael, Samuel Watson here. We've never talked settlement in this case. Do you think it's worth discussion?" He knew Watson had a lot of experience in trial and settlement, years in fact. Watson was 51 and through watching him work during the trial he knew that all times Watson knew exactly what he was doing and didn't shoot from hip or lip. If he was even broaching settlement talk he wasn't absolutely sure of winning but sure the odds were heavily in his favor.

"Absolutely," Michael said. "Give me your thinking." Watson went on to lay out what he thought were the strengths of his case and the weakness of Michael's.

"I admit you have a strong case, Sam, but I don't think our position is as weak as you think. I've got enough to get to a jury and once in their hands who knows. What's your offer?"

"One hundred thousand and all your client's costs and attorney's fees which I would calculate to be about one hundred and fifty thousand." Watson was pretty sharp—- laying out a lure. $50,000 for Michael and $100,000 for the client. Many attorneys would leap at being assured of a $50,000 fee giving incentive to talk the client into settling.

"I'll get back to you how long will you be in your office?"

"I will be here until eight o'clock working on my closing argument," he said laughing.

"OK, I'll be back to you before then."

He set down the receiver and reviewed the conversation verbatim. She sat there completely at a loss. Finally she said: "We certainly could use the money. Bill is doing well in his business yet we've got the children to educate and it would go a long way easing that burden. At the same time I feel a great loyalty to my mother and dad who worked hard for what they got and I know they took great pride in their grandchildren. I feel as though I'd be letting them down if I settled for the $100,000. I know you have a tremendous amount of time in this case and it will be difficult to pay your fee, so it does make sense to get what you can and pay our costs at the same time. What would you do?"

"I'd turn it down Winona; you've just made the best possible argument that could be made—you feel you'd be letting your parents down. Would you feel the same way if they offered $500,000?"

"That would be very tempting, but no, I think I would feel the same whether it's $100,000 or $500,000."

"All right I will call Watson and tell him no and If he has any other figure in mind to give me call before Monday. In the meantime I will be preparing to be in court Monday unless I hear differently from you."

After she left, Michael thought to himself Sam will come up from that figure and maybe as high as $500,000. He knows and his client knows we will appeal if we lose and they will appeal if we get a verdict. Appeals are lengthy and expensive. He picked up the phone and called Samuel Watson and with great courtesy turned down the offer, adding if there was any change to let him know. Watson was non-committal. Michael knew his neck was on the line with the firm because the case had taken a great deal of his time and no guarantee he would be fully paid even though the client had retained the firm on a time basis. He also was aware of the ethics of the situation—the client's wishes are the priority when it comes to settlement.

Early Saturday morning he sat at his desk working on a brief of the law and instructions he would ask the Judge to give to the jury before they retired to deliberate. The phone rang and he answered: "Michael Sullivan"

"Mr. Sullivan?"

"Yes, I'm Michael Sullivan," he said cautiously, not quite sure of the person on the other end of the line.

"My name is Johana West. I saw the article in the paper yesterday about the Mary Smith's will. I know something about that Mr. Sullivan; I spent a few days as a nurse for Mrs. Smith shortly before she died. I don't mean to be nosey but I know something about that will and it's not like what I read in the newspaper."

Michael kept listening still uncertain of what the woman wanted, but fully alert to get her story. As the story unfolded he began to take notes on a yellow pad beside the phone. She kept talking: "In the newspaper story it said Debra Dulset testified Mrs. Smith knew exactly what she wanted to do when she left everything to Ms. Dulset rather than her daughter. I don't think that is true. It's none of my business but I was hired by Beatrice Tracy a practical nurse taking care of Mrs. Smith. Viola Taggert, also a practical nurse, and Beatrice's associate couldn't come to work about 8 days before Mrs. Smith died so Beatrice called me to substitute. One day I overheard Debra talking to Beatrice about a will and some other matters." She proceeded to pour out to Michael what had transpired that day and when she concluded she said: "I wanted you to know because I think it's terribly unfair what they're saying in that trial according to the article I read. I think it's important you know but please don't involve me."

Michael could hardly subdue the excitement welling up in his chest. Early on, as she related her story, he knew he had a great rebuttal witness but she could not be subpoened because she lived in another state and couldn't be forced to testify. It would take every bit of his skill to convince her she must testify to see justice done.

"Mrs. West, may I call you Johana?"

"Yes sir, you may."

He could visualize her cringing with the phone in her hand. Such a witness will frequently become hostile when you ask them to testify. He continued in a soothing voice: "You obviously know enough about the case to know an injustice is about to happen and you care or you wouldn't have called me."

"Yes that's true, Mr. Sullivan but I don't want to be involved."

"I'll be honest with you Johana, I can't make you testify. What you've told me may be enough to save that injustice you are worrying about from happening. Do you have any grandchildren?"

"Yes sir I do. Two."

"I'm sure you love them." He heard her gasp at the other end of the line. He continued in a soft even tone; "I'm sure you would do anything for them. Mary Smith had grandchildren and she and her husband Tom loved them very much. She had a will that provided for her daughter and her grandchildren. That will will be superseded by the will Debra Pulset has filed with the court saying, in effect, Winona and the grandchildren get nothing and she gets it all. It's up to a jury to decide who should get what but to make that decision based on all the facts they are entitled to the evidence only you can furnish."

"Well Mr. Sullivan I hear you but I don't want to testify. I just wanted you to know so you could tell the court."

"I appreciate your thoughtfulness in calling me Johana but I can't tell the Judge—I can't tell anybody. Under court rules your testimony, given by you is the only way the Judge and jury can hear what you have to say. I've told you everything I know about the case and the fact, in my view, an injustice will be done if you don't come forth with what you've just told me. Will you please think it over?" Michael could tell from the tone in her voice she wanted to help yet she was paralyzed by fear, perhaps because of a reluctance to appear in a court room filled with press and inquisitive spectators. He continued in a firm but soothing voice: "I will have a plane ticket for you and you can be here by 4:00 pm tomorrow. We will have you put up at a hotel two blocks from the courthouse."

"Well, that's very nice Mr. Sullivan but I have responsibilities here and just can't take the time."

"Johana, I'll be in my office until 5:00 o'clock this afternoon. I believe you have a duty to the law, the Judge and the jury to testify. If you were in the same position as Winona would you want someone with your information to come forward—information that could determine the future lives of grandchildren like your own?"

"Like I say Mr. Sullivan I just can't testify but I will think about what you've said."

CHAPTER 6

When he hung up he realized he was dripping wet from the conversation. He had used every argument and approach he could think of. Had he raised enough to start her conscience working on her heart? He continued to work all afternoon on instructions and a legal memorandum for the court, glancing up at the clock every half hour. By four o'clock he'd lost track of the time becoming engrossed in the memorandum he'd written. In it he argued the plaintiff had presented sufficient evidence to allow the case to go to the jury. Once the jury got the case he had a fighting chance since the equities were in his favor if not the law. He felt confident the defense had not presented enough evidence for the court to grant a motion to dismiss.

He snapped out of his trance like concentration to look at the clock. It read 4:55 p.m. It's useless, he thought, I'll have to waive rebuttal and go to closing argument without putting on any further evidence. He finished his work at 5:30 p.m., bundled it into his brief case and left his office to enter the reception room. He opened the door and started toward the elevators. Just as the elevator doors opened he heard a faint sound. What was that? He hesitated and looked back at the office. Yes, he heard it now. A telephone rang for the third time. My God, could it be? He raced back and unlocked the door and grabbed the receiver on the receptionist's desk. It stopped ringing. It had rung five times by the time he reached it. He ran to his office and started going through the notes he had taken in the earlier conversation with Johana West. He found her number and calmly, as his hand would allow, dialed and said: "Johana?"

"I just called Mr. Sullivan, but no one answered. I've been thinking all afternoon, I went to see my grandkids —I thought about what you said. I don't know how much I can help but I will tell the truth about what I know." He felt as though he could hug her. Instead he said: "Johana, thank you. I'll meet you tomorrow when you land; and Johana it's going to be a real pleasure to meet you."

On Monday morning Michael and Winona were sitting at the counsel table, as he performed some last minute work on rebuttal testimony of his last witness. Sam Watson came into the court room followed by Debra Dulset. Once seated he leaned over and told Michael he would like to speak to him before the Judge came into the court room for the morning session. Michael got up and followed him to the back of the courtroom out of hearing of the clients.

"My client is willing to pay $200,000 plus cost and attorneys fees. That's the best I can do for you."

"Wait here Sam, I'll advise the client of the offer. He approached the table, leaned down and whispered in Winona's ear.

"No," she said just loud enough for Debra and Watson to hear it.

Michael turned towards Watson and motioned him to come forward. Shrugging his shoulders, he told Watson, "no dice, Sam we're going all the way."

Looking a bit taken back, Watson said: "Ok Michael. I thought that was a very generous offer. I think you've got a very stubborn client on your hands and you're forfeiting a handsome fee."

At that moment the Judge mounted the bench looked at Michael and said in a commanding voice: "Do you have any further rebuttal Mr. Sullivan?"

"Yes, your Honor, I have one witness. I call Johana West"

Once in the witness chair he began his direct examination: "Mrs. West, will you tell us your full name, where you live and what you do for a living?"

In answer to his questions Johana gave preliminary information about herself, her work and her family all of which was designed to give the jury a chance to weigh her veracity. Michael reached the crucial part of her testimony when he asked: "Were you acquainted with Mary Rogers Smith?"

"I was not an acquaintance but I did have an occasion to work for her for one day."

"How did that come about?"

Johana hesitated for a moment as though to gather her thoughts before answering: " On December 21, 1991 I received a call from Beatrice Tracy an acquaintance of mine who said she had been taking care of Mrs. Smith and the job required two people because of the patient's total helplessness. She said her assistant would not be available the next day and asked if I could substitute for her."

"And did you?"

"Yes, I went to the house that day and Beatrice met me and explained what was expected."

By this time, Michael, out of the corner of his eye, saw both rows of the jury box leaning forward sensing something dramatic might be about to be disclosed. Samuel Watson gazed at Michael with a slightly concerned look on his face wondering what could he possibly get from this witness. Even the Judge looked up from his notes and fastened his attention on the witness.

"Was Debra Dulset in the house that day?"

"Yes, she was."

"Objection, your honor all this is totally irrelevant."

"Mr. Sullivan is there some way you intend to tie up the presence of Mrs. West and Ms. Dulset in some form to this case?"

"Yes, your Honor, I intend to show that the presence of both of them in the house that day is very relevant to our proceedings today."

"Objection overruled subject to being tied into the case at later point. Proceed Mr. Sullivan."

"What, if anything was Debra Dulset doing to or saying to Mrs. Smith?"

"Well she was in and out of her room all day but she couldn't be talking to her too much"

"Why is that?" Michael asked with a look of intense interest on his face to match that of the jurors.

"Because, as far as I could see, she was mostly unconscious and when any sound came from her I couldn't make it out."

"Were you and Mrs. Smith in the room at the same time at any time during the day?"

"Yes. At least 4 or 5 times during the day and the night. It was obvious she, excuse me, didn't have all her buttons. Muffled laughter came from the jury box and the entire courtroom.

"Objection." Samuel Watson was on his feet with an angry look on his face and said: "I move the last be stricken from the record as being meaningless."

"It will be struck from the record."

"Can you explain a little more precisely her demeanor as you observed it?" Michael rephrased the question.

"I meant no disrespect sir," she explained in response to the courtroom's laughter. "I thought she was a very sick woman and really not able to communicate."

"Did Debra treat her as if she didn't have all her faculties about her?"

"No sir. Whenever I was in the room with Debra she talked to her like the old lady might be understanding everything she was saying. I thought that was a little ridiculous because it was obvious to me she couldn't understand anything"

"Finally, did you hear any conversation or conversations between Beatrice Tracy, Mrs Smith's nurse, and Debra Dulset?"

"Yes I did"

Samuel Watson was on his feet shouting: "Objection your honor. Anything she says would be hearsay and inadmissible as such."

Michael quickly gained his feet before the Judge even gave him permission to speak and turning to Samuel Watson, fully cognizant all eyes in the jury box were focused on him now that an objection had been raised to testimony they knew was important to the case said: "Debra Dulset is a party to this case your Honor and anything she said that was overheard by this witness would be admissible as an admission against Ms. Dulset's interest."

The Judge looked directly at Samuel Watson and said in a firm voice: "I agree, Mr. Sullivan. You may continue to question the witness."

"Can you tell us what you heard?"

"Ms. Dulset told Beatrice Tracy she had arranged to have Mrs. Smith sign her will the next day and a lawyer would be bringing it to the house. She wanted Beatrice and the lady I was substituting for to act as witnesses. She told Beatrice it was important that Mary look like she understood what was going on and if anyone should ever ask to tell them Mary was just fine. Beatrice protested telling Ms. Dulset it would be almost impossible to prop her up so she could follow anything being said or read and sign an intricate document like a will. Debra said: 'You just give her whatever stimulant needed so she appears all right for a half hour. That' all it will take. I'm prepared to give you and Viola a thousand dollars each for witnessing her will. There is only one condition and that is you must never mention the degree of her sickness to anyone. Once the will is accepted I guarantee each of you $5,000 dollars. I've already talked with Viola and she has no problem"

If Michael's examination of the witness was a play in a football game a replay would have shown Samuel Watson's face completely drawn of color and Debra Dulset gesturing and shouting: "she's a liar."

Michael imperceptibly glanced sideways at the jury box and thought, he saw some formerly placid faces turn hostile.

"What did Ms. Tracy say, if anything, in response?"

"She said it was ok by her as long as Viola was willing she was too."

"Where were you when you heard this conversation between Debra Dulset and Ms. Tracy?"

"I was outside the room dusting but the door was opened and I could hear everything said"

"Are you aware of whether Ms. Dulset or Ms. Tracy realized you were in the hall?"

"I don't know, but I doubt they would have been talking the way they were if they knew I was right outside the room."

"Did you ever tell anyone what you had heard?"
"No, not until I contacted you Friday evening."

"Your witness," Michael said so softly he could hardly be heard in the now hushed courtroom.

Samuel Watson seethed but tried to hide as much of his anger as humanly possible. What every lawyer dreads had just happened. He had been lied to by his client. He gamely mounted a ferocious cross-examination asking why she had not come forward. Had anyone paid her to testify? Had Michael or his firm paid her? Did she know Winona? Could she mistaken about what she heard? How far away from the room was she when she overheard Ms. Dulset's Conversation with Ms. Tracy? He kept her on the stand for three hours and he couldn't break her. She simply kept telling the story over and over again. Finally hoping he had cast doubt on her truthfulness and her motives he slumped down in his chair. The jury returned a verdict late in the day restoring the validity of Mary's original will by finding the second will had been obtained by fraud and undue influence.

That night he and Mary, and the two children broke out steaks they had been saving in the freezer, a bottle of wine Michael brought home and they sat around the dining room table as he recounted the day's events. Mary laughed and cried at his descriptions of the Judge, several jurors and Samuel Watson's cross examination of Johana

West. The children just cried because dinner was so late. The parents spoke of what it meant to Michael's career with the firm.

"Michael they will have to make you a partner now; you've been doing so well and the fee for this case will pay half the overhead for a year." She spoke passionately not for herself but for her husband who had worked so hard on the case.

"I agree but these are funny fellows. They're not used to going to court much less wining trials before juries. The firm has had municipal work so long it's become a monopoly in the state. The bulk of fees come from that work and they don't have to worry about adversaries. They may figure they don't need a partner just yet. I think if we are going to be successful as a firm we're going to have to develop a trial and business practice to go along with the municipal work." He had been with the firm four years and had been thrown into the trial practice almost exclusively when Paul Walker died at sixty four from a massive heart attack. From that day forward he was trying cases against lawyers with 10 and 15 years more experience and winning.

CHAPTER 7

Mary did a wonderful job as wife and mother and he depended heavily on her wisdom and judgment; only twenty-six, she in some ways was more sophisticated than he. Educated in the east and a world traveler before 21 she had the maturity of an older woman. She was pretty, intelligent and the same things excited them both: politics, government, foreign affairs, volunteerism and above all their faith. Her family, lived in California, her father an executive with a large furniture retailer well able to provide a comfortable life for his wife, herself and three younger brothers. His father, from a Irish family that lost their business in the depression, worked as manager of a retail store; while his mother, from a well to do southern family served as wife and mother to their four children.

"The partners have had it too easy with the municipal practice. It's like shooting fish in a barrel. Good money and easy work. Howard Walker tried most of the cases, before I came and now he isn't physically able to go to court.

Mary interrupted: "Michael we have two children and barely getting by. I think you should, go talk with Matthew Hamilton and point out what you've been doing for the firm for four years with your successful trial work. You've earned it. They owe you."

Mary had never complained before and seeing she was upset he put an arm around her and said: "You're right sweetheart. I've been so busy working and trying cases I haven't realized how hard it has been on you trying to manage on what the firm pays me. Tomorrow I will tell Matthew that we have to have more money. If I get any static, it will be time for me to start looking around. I'd hate to leave my eighty year old firm but man cannot live on prestige alone." At that she laughed. He could always make her laugh. It was an Irish trait he picked up from his father always quick with a quip with a dash of dry wit on the side. "On the other hand if I stay it can be built into something competitive with the big firms."

"Michael, remember when we first had dinner with the Hamiltons? I wasn't too certain Imelda Hamilton cared for either one of us. I got the impression she thought we were unstarts from eastern schools and should be knuckling under to her."

"You're probably right. You've always been nice to her but never to the point of kissing her backside. I think the woman has an inferiority complex." They talked until 1:00 am in the morning about the firm and his future there and finally fell asleep in each other's arms proud of Michael's win in Winona's case and determined to see where they stood with the firm.

True to his word, Michael got up early the next morning, showered, shaved and put on his best suit Mary had purchased for him at Brooks Brothers when he got the job at the firm. Fully suited he viewed himself in the mirror to make sure his tie was straight and looking back in the mirror he saw himself: a six foot one inch tall, fairly good looking thirty year old lawyer, with a slim face, close cropped hair and off kilter nose broken when he was ten years old. His eyes were brown with just the hint of a twinkle. The suit a gray pin stripe that gave off an air of professionalism. The shoes shined and wing tipped. Fairly impressive, he thought, as he left the apartment ready to get some answers from Matthew Hamilton.

At 10:00 o'clock, after Matthew had been in his office for an hour, Michael got up from his desk, walked down the hall and knocked on the door even though it was wide open. Matthew looked up and flashed his usual smile at the sight of Michael and said: "Michael, come in." He leaned back in his chair, welcome for a break from what he was doing. As usual his desk was piled with files and municipal bond transcripts.

"What's up?" he asked a smile still on his face. He was in shirt sleeves his suit coat hanging on a cloak rack in the corner. While most of the attorneys in the office worked with their suit coats off unless meeting with a client, Michael and the senior partner, Samuel Barron, kept theirs on; Barron because he was head of the firm and thought it proper to keep his coat on at all times and Michael because he thought a lawyer a professional and should dress accordingly.

Without hesitating he launched into his short prepared speech detailing why he thought he had earned the right to be a partner. Matthew kept his hands on his lap leaning back in his chair giving full attention to what Michael said. When he concluded, Matthew came forward in his chair and said: "Michael, you've have been doing great work and you're right. I think you have earned partnership. Since I think the others will agree with me let's talk about where the firm is going. Howard is 64 and definitely slowing down, not doing too much but still taking some pretty good money out of the pot. When he came into the firm he was our litigator but he has a bad heart and you've seen he's just about stopped trying cases and you've been carrying his and your load for four years. Sam is 70 and doing a fair amount of the municipal work and brings in more than he takes out. In three or four more years he will probably retire. Johnathan has pretty much the clientele he inherited from his father the senior partner before Sam. He takes out about what he brings in and hasn't seen the inside of a courtroom for years. John Jensen, we hired right out of law school to do business and trial work. As it turned out he's a smart lawyer but doesn't have the personality to be in court. That leaves you and me. What am I doing? I'm doing most of the municipal work which is the highest grossing work for the firm plus I'm bringing in most of the clients. After only four years we don't expect you to be a great producer of new business, but I've noticed you've developed a good following amongst your contemporaries this, and your proficiency in court, have been a great boon to the firm and I think you know that." Michael made no reply seeing Matthew wished to continue.

"I think we have a future. We have prestige amongst our contemporaries and longevity as the oldest, continuous firm in the state and the most important factor, a reputation for integrity. I need more help in the municipal work and you've got the personality and brains to get along very well with our municipal clients and the right hustle to get new ones. John doesn't have the right personality for the municipal clients and that's where I think you would fit right in." Matthew stopped and looked for Michael's reaction to his candid statements about the individuals in the firm, what they brought in and took out, their strengths and weaknesses, his representation Michael would be made partner, and that he considered he and Michael to be the future of the firm.

"Matthew, I appreciate your offer of partnership. If the partners go along I accept. I must say I love trial work and while I'm flattered you want me to work with you and Mr. Barron (Michael always referred to and addressed Samuel Barron, the senior partner, as Mr. Barron) I believe we have to build a trial practice if this firm is to go anywhere. I've thought about what the firm needs and you're right—you need someone you can groom and train to work side by side with you and Mr. Barron. I'm not that man."

Matthew had a look of deep disappointment. From what he had just told Michael it was apparent He and Sam Barron had talked about bringing Michael into the municipal work as a perfect fit for their practice and his participation would guarantee the firm would continue to hold a monopoly in the state's municipal field. He said nothing and focused instead on what the young associate said.

"I think we should go out and get an established lawyer to join the firm for a year as an associate; see how he works out in the municipal field; and if you and Mr. Barron are satisfied, make him a partner."

Matthew responded still hopeful of convincing Michael the municipal route would be the most advantageous avenue for him to pursue. "Yes, I can see what you are saying and it makes sense, developing a trial practice but I would prefer that you be the one to work with me and Sam. If you won't do that do you have anyone in mind who might fit our needs?"

"Yes, I know a couple of fellows in other firms who are still associates and doing mostly corporate and business law who would fit in nicely—-all educated at eastern law schools. I also think it would be a good idea, if the firm's municipal work would support it, bringing in an associate right out of law school. The municipal practice would then furnish a base to finance further expansion of trial, business and possibly tax areas."

Matthew got up out of his chair, walked over to the window and looked out at the river for a minute and said nothing. Without turning his head he said: "Michael you've got me excited! You're the first one in years who's said 'let's go, let's grow.' The seniors are about through; we have to grow to survive in this city. We can't just sit here and rely on the municipal law monopoly. I'll speak to them about partnership and I'm sure after your performance and the fee generated by the Winona Johnson case no one's going to quarrel with Michael Sullivan as a new partner earning his share of the profit."

Within a year Howard Walker died of a massive heart attack. Michael's trial practice increased immediately as he took on Walker's share of pending cases. Shortly after the death the firm name was changed to Barron, Youngman, Hamilton, Jensen & Sullivan. Taking Matthew at his word, after their talk of partnership, Michael began the search for a lawyer who could assist Matthew in the municipal practice, eventually becoming a partner. At the same time he began interviewing men who were about to graduate and take the bar. His first target was Bill Wilson, a lawyer he had become acquainted with shortly after taking the bar, who was on the verge of becoming a partner in a large prominent firm. He carefully explained what he had in mind, what the potential was and asked him to meet with Matthew Hamilton who could really explain what the practice would be in some detail and the prospects for partnership. Bill, only 31, tall, good looking and smart as a whip met with Matthew and they seemed to hit it off very well. Later he talked with Matthew about the meeting.

"He's good Michael; he's got the right temperament and he realizes there could be a real future for him here. At the same time he was frank with me and said he expected to be making partner with his firm in about a year, and had a lot of time invested in building a corporate practice."

"Did you tell him he could develop a business practice right along with the municipal work?"

"Yes I did. He seemed pleased with that and said he'd get back to me in few days. I think he's interested, but he's used to the big firm atmosphere. It may be too tough for him to give that up. A bird in the hand is worth two in the bush. And we're the two. We'll see."

Matthew had a good idea what Bill Wilson might do and that was confirmed a week later when he called and thanked Matthew for the offer. He explained he had talked it over with his wife and they decided the future for him lay with a partnership in their present firm with the opportunity of working with the firm's prestigious corporate clients. Michael and Matthew were greatly disappointed since they had placed high hopes in landing Bill Wilson who had a good track record as a lawyer and would have made a perfect fit for the municipal practice.

CHAPTER 8

In his teens Michael became interested in the game of tennis when a friend whose mother had been a local tennis champion asked him to hit a few balls at a public tennis court. Fascinated with the sport and its competitive aspects of one player against another and the mental toughness it required to play the game he immediately became aware of the styles successful players employed and worked to copy them. He'd played all sports including basketball, football, baseball and track but tennis was a game you won or lost on your own depending on no one else, except in the game of doubles. Within six months he became very good. Never took a lesson, but within the year had made his high school tennis team. By the time of graduation he had become state high school singles and doubles champion. This led to an athletic scholarship without which he would not have been able to go to college.

During his high school years playing tennis he met and played competitively against Blake Collins twice in state tournaments. After those encounters he lost track of him but within the past year learned he had attended law school at Harvard, after completing undergraduate studies at Princeton. He, like Bill Wilson, joined a larger firm in the city, smaller than Wilson's, firm but just as prestigious. Michael did some research on Collins and found out he too was on a partner track in his firm. He thought Collins could bring some strength to the firm and because he worked in corporations and business could probably be able to fill the slot he had tried to recruit Bill Wilson for. The educational background was perfect and he would appeal to a fellow like Johnathan Youngman, a Harvard graduate. Johnathan had been impressed with Michael's Georgetown law degree so Michael figured he would be overjoyed at Collins's Harvard J.D. He broached the idea with Matthew who said: "Sure see what you can do but I know his firm thinks highly of him and he'll make partner there within a year."

Within a week Michael decided to go after Collins "cold turkey." He called him and when he came on the line said: "Blake, this is Michael Sullivan. You may not remember me but we played tennis against each other in high school."

"Sure, I remember you, we had a few good matches. I remember you became a perfectionist but I didn't make the team at Princeton although I've kept up my game and would love to play you some time. Beyond a tennis game what can I do for you?"

Michael jumped right in: "I've been practicing law in town and I'm a partner with Barron, Youngman, Hamilton, Jensen & Sullivan. Me being the Sullivan. I wonder if we could get together for lunch at your convenience?"

"Well, sure," he said, a little haltingly, not really knowing what the call out of the blue was all about. After all, he hadn't been a close friend of Michael's or even an acquaintance and other than the fact they had played some tennis against each other there was really no connection. "Yes, I'll be glad to have lunch. Name the place."

"How about Billy Ryan's Monday at twelve o'clock?"

"Great I'll see you there." Blake Collins hung up and thought: this will be interesting. Whatever he has in mind He didn't want to discuss on the phone. Monday will come soon enough no use fretting about it. He turned back to the work on his desk and soon forgot about Michael's call. Michael put down the receiver and said to himself "This is tough work. I think Blake would be good for the firm but if they don't like him and don't offer the job after showing an interest in him it could make for an awkward situation. Better be sure it is workable before you say anything about coming with the firm and becoming a partner."

On the appointed day Blake Collins appeared at Billy Ryan's. Michael had already made a reservation and secured a table in the back, quasi public. Ryan's bore the reputation in town where lawyers, businessmen, stock brokers and rainmakers met for lunch and the waiters were all male and in uniform. A long bar with ten shelves high in front of a huge mirror carrying whiskey of every brand imaginable stood along one wall. Two bartenders were working feverishly to keep up with demand. Some patrons stood behind those seated at the bar waiting for one of forty tables with white table cloths and fluted napkins to open up. Dark wood dominated the room thorough out, so much so, that Ryan's could easily be mistaken for a London men's club. The habitués liked it that way. There were women, of course, but the place was too masculine to attract a large number of them at the lunch hour. Collins spied Michael the minute he made it past the maître d' and headed directly for his table. As he came across the room Michael, who had not seen him since high school days, saw a six foot slender man of twenty eight with wavy hair, handsome, and mature looking for his age. He had an athletic stride and a confident look on his face. His suit was light gray, tailored and Ivy League. Michael stood up as he approached the table and said in greeting: "Hi Blake good to see you, it's been awhile."

"Same, it's been a long time." Once seated they agreed on a round of beer and immediately launched into conversation about tennis, where they had been since their last meeting and their careers to date. Blake told how he had met his wife, when they were both undergraduates at Princeton, how he had pretty much forgotten about her when he went on to Harvard Law School, and then had run into her in Boston where she was working in an advertising agency after graduating from Princeton. One thing led to another and after he graduated and took the bar they came to the city and he got on with his present firm. Michael wishing to establish a rapport and actually having a good feeling about Blake told how he had met Mary in Washington D.C. after he had graduated from Georgetown University Law school and had taken the bar there. She was working on Capitol Hill for a U.S. Senator in a policy position. Within eight months they were married and they came back to the state where he grew up and after passing the state bar he was appointed law clerk to a Justice of the State Supreme Court. They talked in this vein for over an hour while eating lunch and a second round of beers, a friendship quickly developing. As interesting as the conversation was Michael decided he had to move forward with the purpose of the lunch. He had made up his mind Blake was definitely a fellow they could use if they could get him. He thought it time to make the pitch while the mood seemed right.

"Blake, let me be frank why I asked you to lunch." He proceeded to outline what they wanted in a new man joining the firm, the plan to expand and the prospect of a partnership for him after a year. Blake listened carefully not interrupting not asking questions. After ten minutes of explanation from Michael he asked: "What kind of a fellow is Matthew Hamilton? Why don't you want the municipal work yourself, it sounds pretty lucrative?"

Michael thought it an astute question, evidence the fellow quickly grasped the point: why should he be interested if Michael was not? "I'll be honest with you Blake I like the trial arena. The municipal work is too detailed and precise. It is extremely well paying and without a doubt it allows the firm a solid economic base from which to grow without huge financial risk. I believe in order to build a strong firm you have to have balance; municipal, corporate, estate planning and tax on one side and litigation on the other."

"Michael it sounds interesting and yes I would meet with both of you. If it's all right, why don't I come to your offices? How about the first of next week?"

"Blake that would be great and it's been really good to see you again after all these years. I hope we can work something out."

Without commenting on the last thing Michael said, Blake shook hands and promised to call the following week. Michael headed back to the office feeling good but not confident of the outcome of their talk. He went down to Matthew's office and repeated the conversation the two men had had, his estimate of Blake and his background. On Monday Blake Collins paid a visit to the offices of Barron, Youngman, Hamilton, Jensen & Sullivan. Not as impressive as the office Blake came from; still the firm was older and equally distinguished in the city. Michael met him in the reception area and they proceeded back to Matthew's office. They shook hands and a discussion ensued in which Matthew did most of the explaining, giving Michael a chance to observe Blake's demeanor and the chemistry between the two men. Blake appeared comfortable talking with the older lawyer and he thought at that point Blake would be perfect for the firm. He made a good impression, was well known amongst the younger lawyers in the city and clearly ambitious. Matthew took him on a tour of the office, which included a very impressive conference room surrounded on all sides by law books from floor to ceiling with a door leading into the secretary's pool. It was an impressive setting for what they were trying to accomplish in recruiting the young man. Blake asked questions which Matthew answered forthrightly revealing more about the firm that would normally be kept in house. Michael could tell Matthew liked what he saw. After Blake left Michael went back to the conference room with Matthew. He fixed two cups of coffee and handed one to Matthew and asked point blank:

"What did you think?"

"I think you did a great job of recruiting; he would fit in nicely with the bond work."

"Did he say when he would let us know?"

"In a couple of days."

Matthew paused thoughtfully for a minute before answering. "I think he's interested. He'd have a lot more leeway with a smaller firm then where he is now by the same token he could be like Bill Wilson, afraid to take a chance. We'll just have to wait and see."

Two days later Matthew came into Michael's office with a dark frown on his face. "You look like you just lost your best friend," Michael said. Are you the bearer of bad news?"

"Blake called me just now and turned us down. He was effusive about the firm but he didn't think it would be the best move for him at this time. I thanked him for visiting with us and we parted on cordial terms. Any other ideas?"

Michael responded: "I'm not ready to give up on this fellow. If he's who we want I'll get him but it may take a little time."

"Go to it Michael," Matthew urged, brightening up markedly at his partner's determination to go after Blake. "We've put a lot of time into this project and it would be a shame to have to start over."

With single mindedness Michael began to map out a strategy with tennis the common denominator. A week passed after the meeting with Blake before he called and suggested a game. Blake was delighted. "How about Saturday morning, I am a member at the Melbourne Club, I'll get us a court."

Michael showed up at the Melbourne Tennis and Racquet Club, the city's most exclusive, and met Blake in the men's locker room. He'd never been in the club and was curious to see the layout. Eight outdoor clay tennis courts and 2 indoors. 3 squash courts, 2 racquet ball courts plus a huge clubhouse containing all the amenities to be found in a first class club, men's bar, card room, paneled dining room all devoted to the racquet sports. He knew it cost money to belong to a club like the Melbourne and concluded Blake must have it or perhaps his firm paid the bill. All the courts were in use, except the one Blake had reserved, with both men and women playing singles and doubles attired in white from head to foot. He later learned week-ends were reserved for adults with junior players relegated to week days. They stepped on the court and began rallying the ball back and forth. He could tell after they had hit a few balls Blake was good and from the way he hit it back, aggressive. This had the makings of a real test. Apparently Blake played regularly from the practiced way he moved about the court. Michael, busy with trials, had tried to play as much as possible to keep his game sharp but he couldn't match Blake in playing time. After the first set, which Blake won six games to four, they sat down.

"You've been playing a lot Blake, I'm guessing. Too sharp for me in the first set."

"I try to play at least twice a week, it's the only exercise I really have time to get and besides it's good for business." Michael wanted to ask but didn't whether his firm paid for him to join. Instead he asked: "have you been playing here long?"

"Yeah, since I was about fourteen. My father belongs and I've been able to ride on his coattails."

For Michael that answered his question: he foots the bill himself—not the firm. Blake said, "let's do another if you're up to it."

"I'll manage it." They took up their positions on the court. Blake liked to win. Michael played enough players to know "winning" meant everything to some players and he included himself among that group. The second set would be for bragging rights. Blake got off to a four game to one lead, which seemed insurmountable yet Michael knew he couldn't keep it up, tennis being the game it is. He figured all he had to do was stay calm and keep playing his game. Slowly Blake began to make errors. The set went to 4-2, then 4-4. By the time the set reached 5-5 they were hitting the ball at each other like mortal enemies. Michael eventually came out on top in a tie breaker. They both collapsed exhausted on the bench courtside.

"A really great game Michael," Blake complimented him with a new found respect.

"We'll have to play the rubber match."

"Ok by me; sometime next week same time, same place."

"You're on," Blake said, pleased to have a chance to win the third set.

The Firm

When they parted Michael knew a lot more about Blake Collins then he could have learned in 20 conversations. Sport is a leveler— you can tell a lot about a person by the way they handle themselves in a sporting event. There isn't any room for posturing or faking; you're on the line and your best and worst traits can become immediately apparent without you even realizing it. Michael was impressed with what he had learned. Blake remained calm. He didn't swear when he missed a shot he just got ready for the next one. When Michael hit a winner Blake rarely commented unless the shot was truly spectacular. This was revealing in that it showed a limited sense of sportsmanship. He made no bad calls, that is, calling a good ball out. This too he found instructive; he wanted to win but not to the extent of cheating. All in all he passed every test Michael looked for and he took that as a good omen.

For the next four weekends they played a match at the Melbourne Club and each time talked in generalities afterward but nothing further about Blake's joining the firm. After they finished on the fourth Saturday Michael suggested they drop into the men's bar for a beer and sandwich. He had decided their friendship had developed to the point where he could restart the conversation with Blake suggesting he might reconsider his earlier refusal. They were seated in one of sixteen booths that surrounded the U shaped bar. Around the walls were framed pictures of tennis greats all of whom had played at the club at one time or another. John McEnroe, Pancho Gonzales, Jack Kramer, Rod Laver, Jimmy Connors, Frankie Parker and a host of others stared down at them as they ate their hamburgers and drank beer. They were starting on a second round when Michael broached the subject.

"Blake, Matthew and I were really disappointed when you decided to stay with your firm." He hesitated before going further not knowing whether the reaction would be adverse and even rupture a growing friendship or open up a new opportunity to make the case for joining the firm.

"I'll tell you Michael I felt bad myself. You all seemed like pretty nice fellows and I've thought a lot about it wondering if I made the right decision." Encouraged Michael seized the moment.

"Let's start all over again. Matthew really laid out everything when we talked in his office, even things we really didn't want to disclose to anyone outside the firm. You know everything there is to know about us. I think if you joined us we'd make a great team—you and I and Matthew. If you do the municipal work you're going to do as well as you are now and still have plenty of opportunity to do corporate work. As Matthew said you'd be partner in a year. I'd like you to go back and think about it, review it with your wife and get back to me. If we're going to make this firm a great law firm let's get with it!" He saw he had Blake thinking and he could do no more but wait for him to take a second look at his offer.

"I'll do it. This time I will really look at it, review every angle all over again. You know what? I hardly knew you before except by reputation and now that we've gotten to know each other I think it might be great fun to work together."

CHAPTER 9

They parted and Michael, elated, went home to take on the Saturday afternoon chores. He related the conversation to Mary and she listened without asking any questions. That was her secret weapon. She could listen to anyone and not be thinking of what she was going to say next. With this faculty she was able to analyze immediately what she was hearing from the speaker. When he completed his version of the conversation she said: "I think you and Matthew are going to an awfully lot of trouble; he turned down a very good offer why pamper him?"

He became a little miffed and responded to her question: "I think we need him or someone like him to do the municipal work. I don't want to do it and that is justification enough, I think"

"Well Michael, I hope you're right. I only know what you told me about him and he seems pretty ambitious from what you've described, I think we should just see what happens."

A week went by and they heard nothing. Michael was about ready to call and ask what the deal was but Mary cautioned: "Just stay calm, don't show your hand." He knew she was right and sure enough, that afternoon he received the call.

"Michael, this is Blake I wanted to call you first before Matthew. I have spent a great deal of time this last week talking your offer over with my wife and doing a lot of thinking on my own." Michael held his breath as he thought brother this has to be it, I've already put as much time into this search as I can afford. "I'm really honored and ready to come with you and the firm. I'll call Matthew. It will take at least two weeks to clear up the cases I'm working on here."

Relieved and exhausted Michael responded: "This is great. You take care of business, work the mechanics out with Matthew as to when you will be coming and we'll have a good talk when you're on board."

Blake Collins joined the firm and they were seven lawyers as the year 1987 dawned. The law was beginning to change from a profession to a business model. The days when a lawyer would join a firm, apprentice essentially for four or five years, depending on the size of the firm, become a partner, then a senior partner and finally retire were fading from the scene. Now billing by the hour, with maximum hours billed was the new model. Women were joining out of law schools taking their place side by side with the men, not only within the firms but in the court room. Whereas before a hand shake would suffice—no longer. Everything had to be in writing, for many lawyers would conveniently forget what they told their brother or sister lawyer orally. A new devise was coming into fashion known as "discovery." Discovery gave each side of the litigation a complete picture of what the other side had so that when a matter came to trial there would be no surprises. It was thought by those who advocated discovery it would expedite and refine the administration of justice. While it might refine trial practice, it did not expedite but served to delay justice long after it would have been accomplished in the '70's and the '80's. Discovery also served to make litigation costly with the advent of multi-depositions, interrogatories, cross interrogatories and endless hearings concerning what one side was refusing to divulge to the other. Discovery meant increased costs for clients, especially large corporations with deep pockets. Discovery meant not only one lawyer on the case, oftentimes 15 or 20 lawyers, each working on a separate phase of the case. It was a boon for the profession and costly for the clients. The legal profession was moving rapidly from "generalist" lawyers to "specialist." Sometimes very narrow specialties such as tax shelters, estate planning, energy and probate. The old fashion lawyer was like a football player who played defense and offense. He could try a case, write a will, handle a divorce, write a brief and argue it before an appellate court. In the year 1988 that sort of lawyer was in his mid fifties and fading. The "new" lawyer was a real hit at cocktail parties, if asked a question in his or her specialties. Outside of the specialty such a lawyer didn't have a clue as to what the law might be. Because of this trend Michael understood the firm had to adopt specialization in order to survive, which meant being able to offer clients a range of services with specialists available to handle each. That meant trial lawyers, tax and domestic relations lawyers, trust and probate lawyers and of course, the firm specialty, municipal work. Barron, Youngman, Hamilton, Jensen and Sullivan were of the old school. Bringing Blake Collins into the firm was the first building block in what he hoped would be a new and growing firm. Blake took to the municipal work like a duck to water and just in time because Sam Barron was doing very little and Matthew was trying to deal with an increasing amount of business as more and more municipalities were issuing securities to build schools, public works as well as state projects. The fees from these sources began to increase proportionately with a public building boom.

Matthew was delighted with the new associate and started integrating him into the municipal practice shortly after his arrival. As far as Michael was concerned it was working out perfectly and left him free to start building his own practice. When he first joined the firm Matthew had him doing a great deal of work with his clients and because of his personality and obvious knowledge of the law they began to call him as much as they called Matthew. If this caused friction between he and Matthew he was oblivious to it. His only motive was to work with the client he was assigned to and do the task that had to be accomplished. Besides Matthew was getting deeper and deeper into the municipal work and bringing in huge fees. Before long Michael and Blake with Matthews's knowledge were drawing up a list from which they would try to hire two attorneys from other firms. Although Blake was not yet a partner, the three of them decided to get lawyers with three to five years experience rather than taking three or four years required to train law school graduates. With this as a goal Michael and Blake began to view their choices in different settings, such as in the courtroom or at specially arranged lunches and even as tennis partners at the Melbourne club. Finally after a four month search and research period, including the wives of potential hires they settled on two who met their specifications, both graduates of eastern law schools. As luck would have it they had no where near the trouble encountered with the hiring of Blake Collins. Those approached to join the firm saw the picture painted by Michael and Blake and felt their future best served by joining a small growing firm rather than the 25 to 30 person firms they were leaving. It was decided that Thomas Hardy, Yale undergraduate, and Columbia Law School would go to the municipal side of the firm with Barron, Matthew and Blake. The other new hire, William Thompson, Stanford and Georgetown Law School, would join Michael, Johnathan Youngman and John Jensen on the trial and general practice side. Sam Barron would continue to work part-time in the municipal field. The other partners in the firm did not resist the recruitment of the two new lawyers leaving the hiring aspects to Matthew, without comment, as long as it didn't reduce their partnership too drastically.

As the year 1990 got underway Michael looked back at what had been accomplished. He and Mary were sitting in their living room Saturday evening having a cocktail before dinner. After he made partnership they were able to buy a house for themselves and four children: Jack, age 8, Sharon, age 6, Peter, age 4 and Kathryn, age 1, and a dog they called Shanahan after one of Michael's Law school friends. Nearby a neighborhood Tennis court and swimming pool made it a perfect place to live and raise children. The neighbors, in the main, were doctors, lawyers and other professionals working their way up the American social and economic ladder. The living room, where they were sitting, had windows, floor to ceiling that looked out on a green lawn anchored by a Japanese garden topped with a waterfall spilling out of a stone pagoda. Beyond the lawn a half acre of tall fir trees that backed onto Dominic Road. On the southern side of the house a large paneled entry way led into the living room with a large fire place at one end, a separate dining room with wall to ceiling glass looking out at the garden and taking in the same view as from the living room. Book cases flanked either side of the fireplace. Mary and Michael loved books and estate sales. They read biographies of great men and women in history, politics, campaigns for the presidency including all of Theodore White's series on the "Making of the Presidency." At night when the children were in bed they would sit up late reading in bed, chatting about what they were reading, even reading to each other.

"You know Mary," he began, "the firm is on the brink of busting out. I'm really excited. Blake is working out, we have three lawyers working on the municipal side plus Sam Barron and four doing general practice and litigation. From here we add a tax specialist and two more associates, one for business and one for trial. In no time we'll be eleven lawyers. From what I see we'll double that in two years. We've built the base."

She could see the excitement in his eyes and she was happy to hear the enthusiasm in his voice. They were building something solid and going to grow. Her time was taken up raising four children and Michael had little time to aid her in the work. He worked six days a week taking Sundays off if he didn't have a trial on Monday. No matter how busy they were mass at St. Benedict's took precedence. The six were in the front pew for 10:00 o'clock mass every Sunday. Michael made time to serve on the parish council as president even though he had just one child in St. Benedict's school. He felt as committed to the school as he did to his law practice. Mary through herself into volunteerism, not only at the school but in the

Junior League where she found an opportunity to bring her skills to work with the community brailling for the blind.

"Michael things are moving so fast we need to get away and spend some time together. We've never taken a vacation together without the children. I think we need a break."

A light came into his eyes and he took her hand: "Sweetheart I agree but I can't do it now. I've got trials booked for the next six months." She didn't argue but was sadden and struggled to keep a smile on her face. She knew how busy he was yet she also knew he couldn't keep going at his present pace so she vowed to let it go for a while and renew her plea in a few months. It turned out as Michael had predicted; within a month of their conversation the firm hired a tax lawyer, a recent graduate of the New York University school of Law and two additional associates. For the 36 year old partner the world revolved around his law practice although he was not totally unaware of the world around him.

Ronald Reagan had been elected in 1980 following four years of malaise under Jimmy Carter. Re-elected in 1984 he carried every state in the Union with the exception of his opponent's home state Minnesota. His second term saw the beginnings of a changing world which would ultimately affect him and all Americans profoundly. Soviet Russia, America's principal adversary and threat to democracy started to collapse at the seams. The Russian bear had stretched its tentacles across Eastern Europe occupying half of Germany in the process. It maintained surrogates around the globe. The United States had fought two wars to contain the red menace in check losing 81,110 dead and 245,437 wounded soldiers in the process. The collapse came in 1989 with the fall of the Berlin wall, separating East Germany from West Germany. Michael's generation had lived with the communist cloud from the time of their birth as their parents had before them. He served in the U.S. air force as so many others did when the call came, and was discharged as a first Lieutenant after two years of service. In 1988 George Bush serving as Reagan's Vice President for eight years, decided to run for President and was elected in his own right as the 41ˢᵗ President of the United States. The world remained at peace despite ongoing brush fires in Africa and the states that broke away from the Soviet Union after 1989. America stood alone as world leader.

Blake Collins became a partner as promised and he, Matthew and Michael held frequent conferences and meetings about the progress of the firm and the direction it was taking. One day in late December Matthew asked Michael to lunch. They agreed to meet at Taylor's Grill five blocks from their offices in the 15 story bank building. After they ordered Matthew brought up the purpose of his invitation to lunch.

"I wanted to get your thinking Michael on hiring another lawyer for the bonds. The municipal work is booming and Blake is really getting into it the swing of it and as a result he's doing nothing else and I've been thinking I might need another lawyer to assist us, Sam's not doing much of anything anymore." Michael listened, thinking to himself, what's this all about, Blake has been with us a five years and he and Matthew seem to be handling the municipal work without too much strain. Matthew continued: "I've had my eye on a young fella by the name of Doug Phelps who works in the city attorney's office. We've worked on a couple of municipal matters for the city and I was impressed with how he represented the city."

"How old is he?" Michael asked.

"I think he's about 34 I would guess and went to law school locally. He's not in the mold we've been hiring but seems knowledgeable in municipal work and he could be trained. We'd take him on as an associate." Michael made no comment thinking it might not be a bad idea to have a buffer between Blake and Matthew and it would give Blake competition for Matthew's favor and the bond business.

"That's one of two things on my mind. What's your reaction?"

"My immediate reaction is can we afford it and if you think we can and business is burgeoning, go for it."

"Well it might be a little tight," Matthew admitted; it would give us an even dozen lawyers and I'm sure he'll make his salary and then some for the first year, so I don't see a great risk financially."

"If that's the way you feel go ahead and pitch him. Have you consulted Blake or anyone else on this?"

"I wanted to consult you, I don't feel a need to consult anyone else." He said this in a tone of finality.

In the nine years Michael had been with the firm he had established enough trust with Matthew to the point where Matthew sought his advice more and more and tended to listen to what he had to say. Matthew headed the firm with Samuel Barron pretty much out of the picture; he took out most of the profit and, more importantly, brought in the highest fees yet he listened to Michael's ideas about the firm's future, the kind of law they should practice and his conviction they had to grow to compete.

"I think Blake should start branching into corporate as well as bond work, we need development there and he could eventually take over that end as well as work on the bonds." That's a good point," Matthew said, glomming on to the idea he could keep most of the municipal business —and not have any real competition from any single lawyer in the firm.

Michael had researched how the municipal business had come to the firm in the first place. It started with a single client in 1928 when Burtchell Wells, a partner, gave a legal opinion authorizing a county to issue bonds to finance a school building. Word got around the state you had to see Burtchell Wells if you wanted to build something and issue bonds to pay for it. The idea being, a municipality with a tax base could borrow money, issue bonds to pay for a project, and pay the bonds off with tax revenues. But it could do so only with a legal opinion acceptable to the bond buyers. And the New York underwriters would only accept Well's legal opinion. So Wells and the firm kept getting business; by 1940, even with the depression, his practice grew so fast he limited it to approving bond issues. His efforts generated half the firm's revenue. In 1936 a young associate, Samuel Barron, joined the firm and Burtchell Wells trained him to handle a few small bond issues. By 1975 Wells had long been deceased and Barron had created a monopoly in the bond field to the extent bonds issued by any entity in the state had to receive a favorable legal opinion from by Barron, Walker, Youngman & Hamilton to be saleable.

As the business grew Barron trained Matthew Hamilton to be a bond lawyer. When Michael joined the firm Barron, 70 had turned over most of the business to Hamilton. The firm continued to dominate the field because New York investment banks would only except the firm's legal opinion. In 1989 Hamilton went to New York at least once a month for closings at the big banks as business flourished. This increased his importance in his own eyes and that of other members of the firm. Michael felt Matthew had changed from the time they had met at the bar review and first discussed his hiring. While Michael had his ear and gave him ideas, Matthew tended to forget where the ideas originated and started to present them to the firm as his own. Michael thought of the bond business as a firm asset not belonging to any one lawyer. Matthew began to think otherwise. He gained confidence in his own abilities and didn't resent the fact Matthew took credit for his ideas, deliberately or unconsciously.

"The second thing I had on my mind," Matthew continued, is a move from our present offices to the Wilson Building. I ran into the leasing agent the other day and he said they had a whole floor available that could be built out to our specifications. I thought you and I and Blake could look at it and see what we think." The idea excited Michael as it reflected a new firm spirit and willingness to move up in the legal world.

"I think it's a great idea, we can't possibly add any more lawyers here and we do need space for expansion. Will the leasing agent get us a floor plan or do we have to have someone do it for us?" Matthew asked.

"No, we just sit down with the agent and his draftsman, give him an idea of what we want and they come back to us with a prospective law office."

CHAPTER 10

For the next six months excitement cursed through the office as they all began to review preliminary plans for the new set of offices in the remodeled Wilson building. Included in the sketches were twelve offices for the lawyers, another six for support staff, a conference room to accommodate sixteen chairs around the conference table and shelves on four sides of the room to house three thousand law books and treatises. They set aside additional space for another ten offices plus more secretarial space. Michael and Blake visited the offices at least once a week as they were being built out and were thrilled to see it take shape. Grass cloth wallpaper covered the walls in each office set against dark paneling with the same theme carried out in the reception area, hallways, and conference room-library. Rich forest green wall to wall carpeting covered the floors throughout the suite. They wanted the architects to create a "traditional look" and they were successful in doing so. Prints of English barristers and judges adorned the halls in addition to pictures of the early partners, dating back to the late 1890's. It was an office you would be proud to ask clients into; it had a quiet strength, the client felt comfortable and confident in such an atmosphere. One side of the dark paneled entrance held a gold plaque with the firm name: Barron, Youngman, Hamilton, Jensen & Sullivan etched in black letters with the names of all the lawyers listed vertically beneath. Everything fell into place and they moved into the new offices Sunday, October 1991.

Michael took Mary to the offices late Sunday night so she could see for herself the work they had wrought. She thought it magnificent and told him how proud they should all be. They wandered from office to office. Many were richly furnished and Matthew Hamilton's, the largest of all, had the most expensive look, with a large desk, framed pictures, plush furniture and book cases with early editions of state supreme court cases. When they came to Blake's office, Mary remarked about the "fanciness" of the office compared to Michael's which had a small desk, two facing chairs, his law school diploma and bar licenses hanging on the wall framed in black.

"My, look at the fancy furniture and the paintings. Looks like Blake is a Gaugin (Paul) fan. This is almost as plush as Matthew's office."

"Well," Michael explained, a trifle defensively, "Blake is big into the arts and I think he likes to give that impression to his clients. I'm just a trial lawyer, and I like my office spare—I don't need to impress anyone."

They sat in the library in the back of the suite with its long dark shiny conference table surrounded on all sides by shelves of law books. "This is a dream Mary. Remember how things were when I clerked at the Supreme Court: that little cubicle of an office, four hundred dollars per month and now we are here nine years later, I'm a name partner, we have a new house, three children and enough to live on, the firm has twelve lawyers and we had five when I started."

"God is good, Michael. We have our health, you're doing what you love, our family is growing—we'll have a fourth child in six months, we love each other what more could we want?"

"Nothing, still we're both interested in doing something for others as well as ourselves. I know you have your junior league work but maybe we should being doing more. I know some fellows from the University who have started a shelter for the homeless down on Beacon Street. One of the group asked if I would be interested in going down there of an evening and playing bingo with the drop-ins. I told him I would. Want to do that some time?"

"Can we take Jack and Sharon? They're old enough to learn from it."

"I'll find out. It would be fun for them to learn to play bingo and see how other people live."

So it happened that every Tuesday night they began showing up at the shelter with Jack and Sharon who sat among the homeless with their mother while Michael stood in front of the room calling out bingo numbers, joking and wise cracking with the players. Promptly at nine o'clock Michael announced refreshments would be served and he, Mary and the children moved to the other end of the room where a make shift kitchen sat behind a counter and they handed out sandwiches, cookies and hot coffee with other volunteers. It wasn't a full meal for the homeless who came through the line, yet for a short time they enjoyed shelter, food and a chance to forget their troubles and escape the weather. The patrons loved Jack and Sharon who were as friendly as puppies and made no distinction as to who they sat with or talked to. Even at their early ages they seemed to instinctively know the people they were playing bingo with were not like them or the adults they normally came in contact with but it didn't seem to make any difference. They treated the homeless men and women just the same. The players loved the two and cheered when one or the other called "bingo."

Not too long after they started attending the Tuesday sessions, they met another couple who started coming, John and Sally Kennedy, who, like the Sullivans, heard about the shelter and wanted to volunteer. John, four years older than Michael, tall, masculine, an Irish sense of humor, and a certain maturity that belied his age alternated with Michael calling the game and between the two keeping the room in stitches laughing for the full two hours. Sally Kennedy, like Mary, was calm with obvious inner strength and an equal partner with her husband. Mary liked them immediately and was even more impressed when she found out they had young children at home and had to hire a baby sitter to cover the time they volunteered to work at the shelter. As they became better acquainted, the couples exchanged information on backgrounds, Michael disclosing he practiced law and Mary cared for Jack, Sharon, Peter and the baby Kathryn and a lot of charitable work on the side. The Kennedys explained they were former New Yorkers who moved west to start their lives when John hired on with a local company building homes. John said home building was booming and the future looked bright so they decided to put down stakes. He said his parents and Sally's parents and all the brothers and sisters lived in Manhattan or Long Island and so they were the only pioneers in the family. They also had four children. The two couples continued to see each other every Tuesday night at the shelter and after the acquaintanceship reached the six month mark Michael received a call at his office from John Kennedy wanting to make an appointment to discuss a business matter.

"By all means John, just tell me when it would be convenient for you."

"Would this Friday at ten o'clock be ok?"

"Absolutely. I'll see you at ten and you know we are in the Wilson building?

"Yes I've been in the building recently, they've done a beautiful job of remodeling it. I'm looking forward to our meeting."

Michael hung up the phone pleased. It was always nice to get a new client, and he especially liked the idea of helping Kennedy a young man like himself just starting out. He gave it no more thought turning his attention to a brief to be submitted and argued on appeal on a case he'd lost at trial. Sharply at ten o'clock Friday the phone rang and the receptionist let Michael know John Kennedy had arrived for his appointment. Michael came out to greet him and then led him down a dark paneled hall way pass four offices to his. He invited Kennedy to take a seat in one of the chairs facing his desk and he took the chair next to him. He had a legal pad on his lap prepared to listen and record the client's problem. He employed this procedure with all clients finding that sitting beside them rather than behind a desk put the client more at ease, engaging in a conversation instead of a cross-examination. He found most clients nervous when they see a lawyer and usually upset about a serious problem they have no idea how to cope with. When the client is comfortable he or she feels free to unburden themselves and not withhold facts that could be crucial to solving their case.

"Can I get you some tea or coffee John?" he asked, before they settled in to discuss Kennedy's problem.

"Yes Michael I would, if you have tea."

"We do, and I'll join you." He picked up the phone and asked that a cup of coffee and a cup of tea be brought in. They chatted amicably for a few minutes before his secretary brought a small tray containing Darjeeling tea, lemons, sugar, black coffee and assorted cookies and placed it on a table placed between the two chairs. By this time the formality of the office had receded and it was obvious Kennedy felt completely at ease so much so Michael sensed he would listen and not ask questions of this man who seemed so in control.

"Michael I've never really told you what I do, because it wasn't relevant. Now it is. I've made quite a bit of money dealing in real property which I own here and in several other states. I build and own shopping malls, lots of them. I think about forty or more. They generate a tremendous amount of money. We recently finished building another mall. Sometimes we run into construction problems because of shabby work or faulty material. Seldom but it happens. Last week we, that is Kennedy Enterprises, Inc. were served with a complaint claiming we owe a builder ten million dollars. Mind you we've already paid over sixty million and the mall we're building is not yet finished. As a result we can't open, tenants are waiting and we're losing rents. Will you and your firm defend us?"

"That's what we do John. We try cases, we don't settle." Kennedy went on for an hour detailing enough facts for Michael to conclude Kennedy Enterprises had a valid defense and a counter-claim for damages. He informed the client they would answer the complaint and then engage in substantial discovery to find out why the Plaintiff, Boulder Construction Company thought they were owed ten million dollars.

"I don't think we owe them anything. They owe us. I doubt whether they will settle and as a matter of fact I won't settle. I want to teach these fellows a lesson and other companies we deal with not to fool around with Kennedy Enterprises and I think we can accomplish that going to trial and hopefully beating them."

"A trial will be expensive John, I'm sure your company has faced litigation before and it's not cheap."

"Yes we have, and it's never cheap and I've not found a firm I'm entirely comfortable with. When I met you I had the feeling you were a good lawyer and I had my people do a little checking and the answer came back, 'He's a top trial lawyer and as tough as they come representing a client. He's not cheap.' So here I am and money is no object."

After Kennedy left the office, Michael reflected on what it would mean to win the case and get Kennedy Enterprises as a full time client. His thinking went beyond remuneration the firm might receive from such a huge client; He liked John Kennedy and while they met through charitable work at the shelter they had not spent enough time together to become close friends. Now, having spent a couple of hours with him and learning what he had accomplished, Michael had tremendous respect for him and looked forward to developing the friendship.

With an unlimited budget for the defense and prosecution of a counter claim against the Boulder Construction company, Michael went all out taking depositions of past and current employees of the Company, lining up experts knowledgeable of material used in the construction of the mall and experts able to testify to the damages Kennedy's company suffered as a result of faulty construction and loss of revenue from tenants who would otherwise be occupants of the mall. Six months after their meeting the case was tried before a jury. The firm representing Boulder only had three attorneys and they were stretched to the limit in preparing for trial. They were short on witnesses and experts to counter Michael's lineup of witnesses. Each side presented their case, and in his closing argument to the jury Michael laid out the facts and argued Boulder had been more than just negligent, they had been guilty of fraud. As a warning to other construction companies he told the jury they must bring home a verdict in Kennedy's favor and against the plaintiff's claim to have its bill paid in full. The trial lasted two weeks, and every day Kennedy sat at the counsel table beside Michael watching him take over the court room, including the Judge, winning points on motions, using his experts to demolish the plaintiff's experts and showing his skill in cross-examination of plaintiff's witnesses. Two weeks absent from his position as the president and CEO of Kennedy Enterprises cost Kennedy money but his opportunity to watch Michael Sullivan in action more than made up for it. Whether they won or lost the case he decided all legal matters for him personally and for his corporation would be handled by Michael's firm. Not surprisingly, the jury came in with a verdict dismissing the plaintiffs claim and awarding Kennedy Enterprises five million dollars in damages. Coming away from his experience in the court room watching Michael at work Kennedy sensed the young lawyer had skills far beyond a court room but for the moment laid the thought aside content to have him serve as legal counsel.

. . .

Blake and Michael continued to have lunch on occasion to compare notes on the firm's progress, but more often Blake and Douglas Phelps, the lawyer hired to assist in the bond department, lunched together. They had become close as they learned the bond business and spent a great deal of their time with Matthew Hamilton working on municipal projects while Michael continued to try cases and build a trial section. Two years after Blake joined the firm, and later became a partner, He and Matthew agreed Michael should look for another lawyer to assist with the growing litigation the firm handled for Kennedy Enterprises. With the addition of Kennedy as a client, Blake and some of the general lawyers in Michael's section handled business matters for the company which were becoming increasingly complex as Kennedy continued to buy and sell companies. Michael had interviewed a number of young lawyers, and no one impressed until he interviewed Cormack O'Neill.

"Sir, my name is Cormack O'Neill, thank you for seeing me." As usual Michael came from behind his desk and offered the younger man a chair and sat next to him. As was his custom he thoroughly studied O'Neill's resume before the interview. His eyes ran over the three page paper and noted he'd gone to Boston College as an undergraduate, and law school at Fordham in New York, probably a Catholic he speculated. Between college and law school he spent two years in the Air Force as an officer, like Michael, coming out of the ROTC program at Boston College. He had a wife and young child. Looking now at O'Neill facing him Michael saw a full Irish face with large smiling eyes. His build was bulky and at five feet ten inches; he could be described as stout but agile. Michael liked his looks on sight. After a series of questions and answers Michael asked what sort of law he thought he would like to practice. He didn't hesitate: "I've studied the firm sir, you have a municipal law business practice and a trial section. I don't know if I would be good at it but I would like to be a trial lawyer. Let me add I'm looking for a job so I can do whatever the firm needs." They talked a while longer and Michael concluded the interview, saying:

"Mr. O'Neill I'll be letting you know within the week if that is satisfactory with you?"

"Yes sir," he came to his feet, shaking Michael's hand heartily and thanked him for the interview. As he left the office Michael smiled to himself and thought: "That big old Irishman could make a whale of a trial lawyer, he looks like a fighter with a sense of humor. He'd seen ten other men and women who sought the associate position, and of those he'd seen, he liked the Irishman the best. His trial section now had six, O'Neill would be the seventh and the fifteenth attorney in the firm. The firm hired O'Neill and it turned out he quickly became adept at trying cases to a jury. He had an Irish way about him that juries trusted. At first Michael assigned him smaller cases; as time wore on he assigned him more responsibility.

Michael and Mary became friendly with O'Neill and his vivacious wife, Nell who, while candid and outspoken, was always careful to respect the senior partner and his wife. (After the death of Samuel Barron, the withdrawal of Johnathan Youngman and the resignation of John Jensen to teach law, the firm changed its name to Hamilton, Sullivan, Collins & Phelps.) While the firm didn't have a caste system, there existed a line drawn between partners and associates and the partners wives and the associates wives, that is, except for Michael and Mary, who associated with both groups with equal ease. They worked at it realizing it important for firm morale to treat all members of the firm the same. Impersonality could be the death knell in a law firm. From the time Cormack O'Neil joined the firm as an associate, Michael sensed Blake Collins did not cotton to O'Neil and his wife, Nell. Possibly because Cormack could be brash and his wife Nell a little loud at firm gatherings. Seemingly Cormack had no idea of Blake's feeling toward he and his wife and never went out of his way to act other than himself when they were together. Whatever the reason, he grated on Blake. Michael became acutely aware of Blake's attitude towards the associate as time grew near for Cormack to be considered for partner. At partner meetings Blake measured what he said about Cormack but it became evident it would be difficult to convince Blake to vote for Cormack's partnership. His attitude also had an effect on Matthew Hamilton, although Cormack got along well with Matthew. Without notable fuss Michael took Cormack aside and warned him of Blake's feeling and how it might affect his chance to become a partner. Michael arranged to meet Cormack for lunch at Morrie's Place an Irish pub famed for a raucous atmosphere and a lot of Irishman talking loudly and laughing at each other's jokes.

Comfortably seated in a booth out of earshot, and after carefully studying the menu and giving their orders, Michael brought up the subject of partnership. "How do you and Blake get along?"

"Ok," he responded with a questioning look and modulated alarm. "Why do you ask?"

"You should be coming up for partnership this year and I've detected more than a trace of doubt toward you in meetings we've had. Have you and he had any discussions about your progress in the firm?"

"No, I've noticed he gives me a fairly wide birth but nothing overt. Do you think he'd try and block me?" Cormack asked in a clearly alarmed voice.

I'm not sure," Michael responded. Blake has been throwing more and more weight around since becoming a partner and he seems bent on staying close to Matthew...."

Cormack cut in: "He and Doug Phelps seem to be working on Matthew. The associates definitely have the opinion Matthew is becoming a legend in his own mind and those guys do nothing to discourage his image of himself. What's your impression?"

Michael was very careful before answering the query yet felt out of respect for Cormack he should be candid in his reply, knowing anything he said would surface eventually when the associates gossiped.

"I think you're right, Matthew is easily flattered and at times loses sight of what's best for him and best for the firm. It wasn't always like that; when I first came with the firm I looked upon him as a real mentor and felt pleased when he praised my work. We shared the same ideas about building the firm, but lately he seems to have grown away from the firm by the amount of money he and the municipal boys are bringing in. He seems more interested in cash flow than what's good for the firm. You've worked hard and I'm pleased with your work and I think I have the weight to convince the partners of the merit of your making partner."

Michael had a genuine fondness for Cormack, having hired him and watched him become an excellent trial lawyer. He held high hopes for him personally and his ultimate worth to the firm. He didn't know exactly what Blake's objections to Cormack becoming partner were but in his view it didn't warrant blocking him from partnership.

"What do you think I should do to appease Blake?"

"Do nothing different, keep your nose to the grindstone and if you can bring in significant business, I think it would make a good argument if push comes to shove on partnership. The main thing is to be aware of Blake's feelings and gauge your actions accordingly."

Taking Michael's suggestion to heart, Cormack made a determined effort in the next six months to bring in an insurance company insuring drivers against claims for property and personal injury damage. The firm had some auto defense work which brought in steady fees, and it hoped to get more. It turned out Cormack developed all kinds of different clients during his four years with the firm, some a little exotic, which may have caused Blake Collins apprehension about his becoming partner. One of his exotic clients, George Malloy was in charge of the claims department of Boniface Insurance Co. that happened to write twenty percent of the state's auto liability insurance. He and Cormack first met at a bar they both frequented, as well as a number of Malloy's adjusters. Malloy an outgoing, boisterous fellow had climbed quickly in the company, based mostly on his reputation as a tough claims adjuster who fought claims all the way to the state supreme court. Many of the larger firms in the city got Boniface's business but, either because they liked Cormack's jocular, Irish personality, or the fact his wife had become fast friends with Nell Cormack, Malloy began sending cases over for Cormack to defend. Cormac and other lawyers in the firm tried these cases as assigned by Michael Sullivan and in several instances Michael tried major cases himself all with favorable outcomes. Malloy took time to meet with Michael praising Cormack's work and complimenting him and all the attorneys that were now working on Boniface cases. He told Michael: "You guys are trying cases not trying to settle them for more than they are worth. Frankly the company likes your tenacity and your winning record. You've saved us thousands of dollars with your defense verdicts. We're thinking of taking some of our business from Sloan, Battery & Wilson, who we've been with the last ten years and moving it to Hamilton, Sullivan, Collins & Phelps. Can you handle it?"

Malloy and Michael were meeting for the first time and Michael sized him up as plenty tough and not necessarily impressed with lawyers. The man was aggressive and he expected his lawyers to be aggressive. That's how he moved up in the company. "Winning," he employed as a mantra. Michael answered the question confidently with certain preconditions in mind, knowing some of the casualty insurers forced their counsel to take low pay in return for getting their business and tried to dictate how a case should be tried.

"Mr. Malloy, we appreciate the business you've sent us and I attribute that to Cormack O'Neil who told me you are a personal friend of his. Yes we can handle whatever you send us; we might have to hire more attorneys to handle it, but I think you should know, we control the cases we take and we're always ready for close consultation and cooperation. We get results because we prepare cases assuming they will be tried not settled. You're the client and we tell you when we think a case should be settled and when it should go to trial and we abide by your decision. We work hard and we charge for that and you've been paying our bills so I assume you're satisfied with our billing," he concluded with a smile.

"I've got no quarrel with anything you've said; you people have done a great job for us and we'll pay for that. That's why we're moving some more of our business your way and we'll move more as long as we're getting the results you've been producing."

They continued the conversation fifteen minutes more discussing minor details. When they finished both were clear the firm would use its talents to the fullest and the company would abide by the firm's principles. Four months after Michael conferred with Malloy, Cormack was proposed for partnership by Michael in their seventeen member firm and accepted unanimously but not without a couple of comments by Blake Collins to the affect he hoped Cormack would not be so loud and disassociate himself from some of the characters he befriended. Michael thought, money counts with Blake. Cormack's bringing in Boniface Insurance prevailed over any dislike of Cormack's personality.

CHAPTER 11

One evening, not long after Cormack O'Neil made partner, Michael and Mary were enjoying a before dinner cocktail when the subject of Matthew Hamilton came up. She asked him where he saw his role vis a vis the other partners. He sipped his drink and watched as Mary carefully put her drink down.

"You seem preoccupied of late, is everything all right at the firm, I have the feeling something is bothering you."

"Oh things are all right," he said softly.

"No I don't think they are Michael, I've had the feeling for some time you're bothered. Let's have it."

He thought how perceptive she is. It's funny in a marriage how your mate reaches a point where she can sense how you feel—good or bad. In Mary's case she never pried, never nagged, kept herself in check at all times and knew instinctively when to reach out. She's smart, you can't fool her and there's no point in trying. He took a gulp from his drink, gave a sigh and eased into a response. "I have the sense the municipal boys are working on Matthew for more money and he's flattered enough by the attention to listen to their thinking. He's changed since I've known him. He seemed a simple straight forward trustworthy fellow when I first met him and some-one I really looked up to as a mentor. Now with big money coming in from the bonds he has hardened, even mean at times. He's been tough on the associates giving them the lackey treatment. I think Matthew believes the municipal section is carrying all the weight and should be compensated accordingly."

"How has he been toward you?" she responded quietly.

"Cool I would say, we don't have the rapport we once had. I think Blake has worked on him, and the only reason I can think of is, I make more money than he does and I guess he thinks because of the tremendous fees he can charge for municipal work he's bringing more into the firm than I can doing trial work and thinks he should be entitled to a greater share of the firm's profits. The other problem is I don't cater to Matthew, like the bond boys and he may see me as the enemy."

"Do you think you're being a little paranoiac?" she asked in a non accusing manner.

"No. I know what you mean but I don't think so. There's a definite chill in the air, it may be partially my fault because I have a tendency to give it back if shoved. The trouble I think is the bond fellows think the trial and general practitioner lawyers are second class citizens and should play second fiddle when it comes to sharing the wealth. What they don't seem to see or don't choose to see is that if you want a law firm and growth you can't be a specialty boutique. When you represent clients you have to be ready to go into the court room, if necessary, to defend their rights. Matthew has lost sight of that fact."

A look of alarm crept into Mary's eyes as she discerned the problem Michael described. She knew how hard he had worked to build the firm and a successful trial section; for him it was not the money, instead prestige of the firm, competition with other firms and reputation mattered most. He believed in treating people fairly, asking for a good days work for a good days pay. That system seemed to be in jeopardy at Hamilton, Sullivan, Collins & Phelps and she could see it grieved him.

"Well Michael, what do you want to do about it? You know I'm with you all the way," she said firmly and with conviction. Mary was tough, independent and had the same attitude as her husband: when someone shoves you shove back.

"We've put fourteen years into this operation Mary, I don't see doing anything precipitous right now. I'd prefer to keep working with these fellows to see if I can't make them understand what I've been talking about. The annual meeting is in October; I'm going to work on a plan to show them by actual numbers how the firm would work better, be stronger and in the long run more profitable if there is a greater sharing of the wealth and the worth of each individual in the firm recognized, even though some are bringing in more money than others. A law firm is like an athletic team, it's as strong as its players; it won't win with just a couple of stars."

"Now that you mention it I've notice Blake and Courtney have been a little distant around me. I've found that curious because he and I have always got along. But Michael I've got to confess I've had misgivings from the time you brought him into the firm. "You didn't see it; Blake wants money and power that's his goal. I've never completely trusted him—a little too slick."

"How about Courtney?"

"She's ambitious, I like her and we get along ok but she's dominated by Blake. She's buttered Matthew's wife up; I never have. Imelda is loud, brash and pushes Matthew all over the lot. I don't think she likes me and never has which has been no help to you. I think she's the one driving him on the money. He can't make it fast enough for her; she spends it like a drunken sailor."

He laughed at her bluntness and said: "My God you've got the woman pegged to a T. She demands respect from the associates. It's criminal to see how she lords it over their wives. I notice the wives of the municipal associates know which side their bread is buttered on and go out of their way to flatter her. On the other hand at firm parties I see you getting around to all the wives, of partners and associates alike finding out how they are doing and I do the same with the men. It's the only thing holding the firm together and I know they look up to us."

"I'm glad it's out on the table Michael. Let's keep trying to buck people up and make them feel it will be all right. You're number two and we owe it to the younger ones since you recruited most of them." He reached over and kissed her and said: "Sweetheart it's so great to have you behind me; you don't know what a relief it is to talk about it. We've worked so hard you just hate to see it come apart because of greed. That night they slept soundly and the next day he went into work with a renewed resolve to make things work.

. . .

The phone rang in his office and the receptionist informed Mrs. Talbot Morris wanted an appointment. "Put her through Maggie. Hello Sheila, how are you? It's been a long time."

"Michael can Talbot and I see you this week?"

He noted a bit of worry in the tone of her voice, even anxiousness. Michael made it a practice to never ask the client to explain much on the phone, preferring to get them in as soon as possible while the story or worry is still fresh in their minds. From experience he knew that once they were able to tell their story, a burden lifted from their shoulders to his. That was the roll of the lawyer. First settle the client down, analyze the facts and give them some idea, even if preliminary, where they stood legally. The successful lawyer will say, in effect, "give me your trouble, I'll take care of it, don't worry."

"Come in this afternoon Sheila, if you wish, or tomorrow morning if that works better."

"Oh thanks Michael we'll be in first thing in the morning."

On the dot at 9:00 the next morning the Morrises were escorted to his office, offered coffee and after everyone was seated they related their story.

"It's been a few years since we've seen you," Talbot began tentatively and things have gone well for us. We've had two more children and I'm no longer a carpenter; I build houses, lots of them and Sheila takes care of the four kids. You did wills for us a couple of years ago. I don't if you remember, but Sheila and her two sisters are beneficiaries of trusts set up by her father...."

"And that's what we want to talk to you about," Sheila broke in.

Michael nodded, encouraging Talbot to go on and he proceeded to lay out the problem. "Sheila's father, Barney Rushing, owned Rushing Storage with buildings all over the United States. He set up three separate trusts for Sheila and her two sisters, now worth about thirty million each. He named his right hand man in the business, Howard McNaughton, as trustee of each trust. We think he's been taking from the trusts by expensing items that don't seem kosher; he refuses to answer questions we've had about taxes and general trust matters. He doesn't seem to answer to anyone. We want to do something about it....we really need to know what's going on. Sheila is the oldest, so we feel responsible to do something about it. For example: what are the trusts holdings; is he buying and selling stocks for the short term? We simply want to know are the beneficiaries being protected?"

"The short answer is yes. Something can be done about it. The remedy is a cause of action defined as breach of fiduciary capacity. When a trustee breaches what we call a fiduciary duty, and there is evidence he's using the trust for his own benefit, that is, not looking out for your best interests, you can go to court and charge him with breach of his duties as trustee. That means filing a law suit, seeking discovery of what's been going on with his handling of trust assets, asking he be replaced and if he's breached his duty, damages."

As Talbot spelled out their frustration with the trustee, Michael began to think through an approach that would began to get at the root of the problem, and if necessary a litigation approach that might have to be taken to obtain a favorable outcome. When Talbot concluded his narrative of their complaints, Michael sat up and began to explain what he had been mulling in his head.

"Did you by any chance bring a copy of the trusts with you?"

Talbot reached into a brief case sitting beside his chair, pulled out documents and handed them to Michael saying: "On the chance you might need these I brought copies along, each is similar except for the names." Michael took one and began reading. Silence prevailed while he slowly read each page. When he finished and flipped the last page into place, he turned and said:

"The first thing that caught my eye is a provision stating in the event a controversy or dispute arises concerning administration of the trusts, the situs of litigation would be the state of Colorado which is to say if we wish to challenge the actions of the trustee the jurisdiction or place of trial has to be Colorado. And the law of that state would govern the case."

"But the trustee is in Marina del Rey, California, where Rushing Storage is located and he runs the company," Sheila inserted.

"True, Sheila, but the suit would be filed in Denver and he would have to defend it there," Michael replied. He went on: "My thought is to go to the corporate headquarters in Marina del Rey, talk with Mr. McNaughton and find out what I can. It may be possible to get what we want without filing suit which will be very expensive."

"Michael we don't care about the legal expenses," Sheila quickly responded, "It will be well worth it if this can be resolved without legal action....the sooner the better. If not than we are prepared to pay whatever it costs." Talbot nodded assent.

"All right, here's the plan. I have a trial next week that will take ten days to complete if all goes well and it goes to the jury. In any event, as soon as it's over, I will call McNaughton asking for an appointment advising I represent you. If your sisters are interested, we will represent them too which could help on the costs. It would also show McNaughton you're all on the same page."

Talbot answered emphatically: "If they want in, ok, but we're prepared to foot the legal costs ourselves. What happens if you can't budge him?"

"If that turns out to be the case I would fly to Denver and find a law firm to represent you there. We would, of course, remain in the case as co-counsel and I would try it, so that we will have complete control and the Denver firm will be in an advisory capacity."

For the first time since they entered the office Talbot and Sheila broke into a smile and it was apparent they felt something had been accomplished. They had confidence in Michael and it showed on their faces.

"Ok it's set. I'll call you before I go to California and report my findings when I return."

. . .

The following week Michael tried the case he had spoken about to the Morrises and was greatly disappointed when the jury rendered a verdict against his client for two hundred thousand dollars for breach of contract. He had not lost a case in some time and he took it very hard. He believed, however, the Judge had erred in his instructions to the jury and the appellate court would reverse the verdict and send it back for a new trial, nevertheless it would result in more legal expenses for his client and trying the case a second time, unless it could be settled for a much lesser sum. Mary consoled him saying a loss is bound to happen once and a while, and he couldn't win every case he tried. She knew most attorneys considered themselves superior trial attorneys if they won fifty percent of the cases they took to trial. Michael had a much higher percentage. He complained to her it was an important case and a valued client. Once back in the office he snapped out of his momentary depression and called Talbot Morris as he had promised and told him an appointment had been made to meet with Howard McNaughton in California mid-week to probe him on the workings of the Rushing trusts.

As he strapped himself into his seat on the Boeing 757 destined for Los Angeles his spirits lifted as his recent defeat receded from consciousness and he mentally prepared for his meeting with McNaughton. On landing he took a cab for the six mile ride to Marina del Rey and booked into the Ritz Carlton Marina del Rey hotel arriving at four in the afternoon. His first act was to empty his brief case of his notes and legal memorandums regarding breach of fiduciary duty, under Colorado law and all the information he had been able to garner about the trustee. For five hours he poured over the documentation and prepared what he called a potential cross examination of the witness. He intended to size up what kind of witness McNaughton would be on the stand and whether the man appeared honest or dishonest. He'd cross examined enough witnesses to know when a witness was lying or even shading the truth. Occasionally he'd been proved wrong but in most instances his instinct proved correct. He didn't attribute it to a sixth sense; it came from experience watching the way people shifted in their seat, or looked away or dropped their eyes, all telltale signs of lying. When he finished his preparation he went down to the hotel restaurant, ordered a New York strip steak, a bottle of California wine and drank half. By the end of the meal he began to feel sleepy and at ten fell sound asleep.

In the morning he caught a cab outside the hotel and took the short ride to the headquarters of Rushing Storage. The eight story building, housing the corporation, did not particularly impress, but the setting made up for it. One block from the shimmering Pacific Ocean, surrounded by small sail boats, a few yachts, in a marina set against a slate blue sky, and the sun coming up like a ball of fire in the east the building took on a majestic look. Michael felt good and confident, as he always did, just before trial. Once fully prepared, a calm came over him and he felt focused on the task at hand.

He checked the tenant information board in the lobby and noted the corporate headquarters occupied the top floor. Promptly at nine o'clock he presented himself to a receptionist in her 40's who gave the impression she brooked no opposition no matter how important the visitor appeared. After he announced his name the receptionist had an immediate change of attitude and confided that Mr. McNaughton expected him and would be right out to take him back to his office. Five minutes later a man in his mid-fifties appeared from a corridor to the left of the receptionist and introduced himself as Howard McNaughton. Michael rose from his chair to meet his grasp and quickly took stock of the figure confronting him. Short at 5' 8" and muscular McNaughton carried himself upright in a superbly tailored dark blue suit with a barely perceptible white pin stripe. Piercing eyes behind rimless glasses, gave him a humorless look.

"Glad to make your acquaintance," he said as he gestured Michael to follow him down a long corridor leading to a large impressive office at the end with floor to ceiling windows allowing a magnificent view of the Pacific Ocean and the marina. Not feeling in any way intimidated Michael complimented McNaughton on the view he had from his office. McNaughton proceeded to sit behind his desk even though a circular conference table was available, and a couch with plush chairs located nearby. Michael assumed this arrangement was calculated to give some sort of advantage to the man behind the desk. Actually it gave Michael a clue as to the man's personality—not entirely sure of himself and apprehensive about the lawyer's visit. Taking it as a sign the man was going to be defensive, Michael initiated the conversation.

"As I advised in our phone conversation, I represent Talbot Morris and his wife Shelia and her two sisters and I wanted to meet you and ask a few questions about their trusts. As he said this he noticed a slight tightening of McNaughton's jaw muscles yet the man remained silent.

"They seem to know very little about the workings of the trusts. What the investments are and how often the assets are sold assuming the assets are mostly in equities."

McNaughton leaned back in his chair and looked a little more relaxed since this appeared to him a nonthreatening question. He gave a general answer the trusts had approximately thirty million in each invested in stock and bonds without specifying the type or number of securities.

"That's a significant responsibility for you, especially with your duties as president of Rushing Storage."

"Well....yes, most of my energies are taken up running the company but I have several investment firms that assist and advise me on the trusts investments."

"What firms are they?" Michael shot back. McNaughton stiffened and said: "It's really irrelevant what firms they are and I can assure you they are trustworthy and well established."

"I assume they are yet I think my clients are entitled to know what firms you're using and an accounting of any and all investments those firms have made on behalf of the trusts." He said this without threat but as a matter of fact. Shifting in his chair, looking threateningly at Michael, McNaughton exclaimed: "There is no requirement in the trust document that requires this information to be disclosed. I give an overall report annually to the beneficiaries setting out the amount of income generated, tax returns and on several occasions I have doled out sums to each of them as I deemed appropriate and of course they have received principle on their birthdays of 25, 30, 35, all as required by the terms of the trusts. I think I've been fairly open handed with Sheila and her sisters."

Again, in a calm voice Michael said: "I don't think they are accusing you of any wrong doing, they just want to know more about the trusts and how they're being invested. I think they have a right to know that."

Red faced McNaughton came back at him standing up with a hurt look on his face and told Michael he had been the right hand of Barney Rushing, Sheila's father. He began to pace around the office, explaining how right out of college he joined the company and before long he caught the eye of Rushing. He grew to be his closest assistant and the old man trusted him implicitly and it was

his wish that he manage the trusts for the children and in his opinion he had done so with great fidelity. Again, Michael assured him
he had no reason to think otherwise, but that it would be very
helpful and would allay any fears on the children's part if he would
first, make quarterly reports and second, furnish the companies and
funds the trusts were invested in. "This should satisfy the beneficiaries." McNaughton remained standing and said he would think
about it and let the beneficiaries know his decision. Michael stood
up and graciously put out his hand and said with a disarming smile:
"That will be fine, but since I'm representing the beneficiaries I
suggest you advise me of your decision. I will expect to hear from
you within the next ten days." With that exchange the conversation
ended and Michael said he could find his way out and left the building. McNaughton looked after him as he left and thought to himself: "this guy is going to be trouble but I can stall him by making a
few adjustments." What Howard McNaughton didn't realize is that
he completely misjudged his young opponent. Michael always came
on softly, so as not to alert the adversary; if that didn't achieve the
goal he followed with litigation.

Once outside the building, he glanced at his watch and saw it
was only eleven o'clock. The sun lit the marina and he decided to
spend a few minutes wandering around the dock, looking at the
boats gently rocking in the clear blue water. What a place, he
mused, everywhere he looked he saw suntanned people painting
their boats, tinkering around the masts of the sailing ships getting
ready to set sail through the channel out to sea. The whole scene
resembled a painting and gave him a thrill and a sense of how beautiful life and people can be.

McNaughton turned out as he suspected after his talk with the
Morrises. He'd been unchecked since Barney Rushing's death and
he clearly saw himself as smarter than most people and that held
true for Michael Sullivan. Only thirty eight, Michael had gained
enough experience with men like McNaughton to know the biggest

mistake they make is to take other people for fools. They never know what hit them when the blow comes. They're never prepared for it. Michael Sullivan made his living on opponents like Howard McNaughton. The bigger they think they are the harder and faster they fall.

CHAPTER 12

On the plane ride home his thoughts turned to his situation in the office something he found himself doing with more and more frequency. Blake Collins had consolidated his position in the firm recruiting a number of the associates into his orbit, all this accomplished by entertaining in his home and in several clubs he had memberships in. He and Phelps would often drink with them after work, they were clearly flattered by the attention and thought Blake carried real clout with Matthew. Michael on the other hand, grew more and more estranged from Blake and Matthew. His relationship with the associates and the partners remained strictly professional. They knew him as brilliant lawyer and admired his integrity and independence yet they understood Blake had Matthew's ear and thus the path to partnership. Matthew did nothing to defuse this impression and in fact went out of his way at times to let the firm know Blake was his man. Those associates who were smart thought Blake obsequious but did nothing to alienate him because fees from the municipal section were pouring in and becoming partner would greatly enhance their financial position.

Two weeks after his return from California Michael received a packet from Howard McNaughton. He opened it not expecting to find too much and his hunch proved right. The trustee sent a four page document setting out the history of the trusts, income generated per year, taxes paid, distributions and expenses. Conspicuously missing, the number of shares held in each company, the number of buys and sales of each stock, brokerage fees and itemized expenses. The two firms handling the trust accounts were disclosed. Not much of an accounting but sufficient to allow the trustee to believe it would satisfy Michael and the beneficiaries.

Talbot and Sheila Morris reviewed the contents and based on Michael's suggestion decided he should contact law firms in Denver and then fly there, interview the firms he had picked and recommend the one he thought should serve as co-counsel. He knew the trustee was represented in Denver by the fifty member Brownstein firm so he decided to retain a firm of similar size and reputation. Matthew knew of Michael's representation of the Morisses and the problems they were having with the trustee and when told he would be flying to Denver asked for what purpose.

"I'll be looking for co-counsel to file suit in Denver based on a breach of fiduciary duty."

"How much of your time will it take out of the office? And will we be paid?" he asked with barely hidden sarcasm, the way he'd been addressing Michael for over a year.

Without a hint of rancor in his voice Michael replied matter-of-factly: "I'll be gone about four days and you should know the Morrises pay their bills within days after they've received them unlike a lot of our clients."

"Alright, check in when you get back I'd like a say in who we go with in Denver." Michael made no reply and left the office determined Matthew would have no say in Denver counsel, that he would reserve the choice to himself based on lawyers he interviewed. The following Monday he took the two hour flight to Denver's Stapleton International Airport arriving at eleven thirty in the morning. Before leaving he arranged to meet with attorneys at Bodkins & Murray a forty five person firm and Adkins, Baumstein & Murray with sixty lawyers. And three firms the following day. At each firm they scheduled him to speak with a preselected lawyer, a specialist in trust litigation. In advance Michael had prepared a slim downed version of the facts designed to interest the litigators at each firm. It turned out to be the right approach. Two of the firms provided junior partners for the interview. Probate specialists at a third firm spent an hour going over the case, but gave the impression they would be inclined to settle rather than try the case. They also seemed hesitant to mix it up with defense attorneys at the Brownstein firm. By the time he visited the fourth firm Wednesday afternoon no decision had been made and he felt a little discouraged because he had not run into anyone with the tenacity needed to go up against the trust attorneys. Before leaving for Denver he consulted Martindale Hubble, a publication that carried biographies on most of the prominent attorneys in the United States. He knew he could engage lawyers at any of the firms he visited and they would be happy to have the business. Yet he wasn't satisfied with the crop he had interviewed. At five thirty he visited the last firm on his list, Ritter, Bellini & Swartz.

"Good to meet you Mr. Sullivan, we've been waiting to visit with you about the Morris case." This from a good looking young lawyer with a crew cut, square jaw, about his age and a firm handshake. I'm Austin Beene and this is my boss Peter Murray. Michael turned his gaze to Murray who greeted him with a warm smile. Murray, like Beene, was tall six feet two or more, dressed informally in sport coat, gray slacks and a nondescript tie.

"Sit down Mr. Sullivan and tell us about the case, it sounded promising on the phone when you talked with Austin. Michael proceeded to review the facts and he noticed both lawyers gave unfeigned attention to every detail. When he concluded Murray said: "I'd like you to meet Bill Ritter, we call him Tex. He's the senior guy here and I've spoken to him about you and a little about the case. Murray placed a call and sixty seconds later Tex Ritter came into the room. Dressed in a perfect fitting gray pin stripe suit, straight from Saville Row wearing black cowboy boots, tanned with a rugged face and a beautiful smile.

"Mr. Sullivan, pleased to meet you sir," he said in an Oklahoma twang. Everybody sit down," he gently commanded. They all moved to a small conference table in Murray's office. It impressed Michael they brought in their top man in the seventy five man firm; it indicated to him they wanted the business and had taken the trouble to talk about the case. Nonetheless, he wanted to hear what they had to say about the case. Ritter appeared to Michael to be in his early sixties and opened the conversation.

"Peter here has been giving me a run down on your case and let me tell you what we'll do for ya. First, we don't know enough to state positively we'd win but we can judge that pretty quickly after discovery. Second, we aren't cheap four hundred and fifty for me or Peter less for associates and paralegals. Three, we don't settle cases, we try them unless, of course, the client directs us to settle. Fourth, the Brownstein firm would be the opposition and they're tough and we like nothing better than to beat 'em which we've done plenty of times before. It really gets under old Sam Brownstein's skin when we do. Fifth, we'd like to get the case and co-counsel with you. That about raps it up. You can let us know, I presume you'll be going home tonight. Michael remained silent during his soliloquy while he listened and studied Tex Ritter. He liked what he saw. A tough no nonsense trial lawyer who enjoyed beating the brains out of the opposition. At the last moment he'd found his co-counsel.

"I don't need to wait," he said, "we'll go with your firm with the caveat the clients approve. I'll call you Monday."

Just like that, it was over. Bill "Tex" Ritter broke into a broad smile, and said : "You won't regret it Michael. Your clients will get their monies worth and we'll get unparalleled joy beating ol' Sam Brownstein."

On the plane ride home he felt a great sense of relief and jubilation at landing Ritter's firm, and felt no anxiety informing Matthew of his choice. The next morning Matthew, like clockwork, came into his office and asked some general questions about his trip and Michael briefly described his experience with each firm and the full interview with the Ritter firm. Hamilton's face hardened somewhat at Michael's emphasis on the fact the firm litigated rather than settled.

In the early years Matthew tried some cases but as he became more and more involved with the municipal bond practice under Samuel Barron's tutelage he became soft and his instincts were to settle everything possible when it came to trying cases.

"Why not go with a probate or trust firm, they're specialists and it seems to me they would have a better handle on the Morris case?" Michael understood this to be an attempt to question his judgement and possibly to try an override it, and he responded:

"That was my first impression, but the more I learned about the trustee, the more I think we need the toughest lawyers we can find. Be sure I'll lay out the whole result of my search to the Morrises and let them make the choice. This approach seem to mollify Hamilton and he left Michael's office with a parting shot:

"I hope you know what you're doing." Silently Michael mocked his remark saying to himself, "Thanks for the encouragement." Talbot and Sheila were overjoyed with his handling of the matter and quickly signed on to engagement of the Ritter, Bellini & Swartz as co-counsel and authorized the filing of a law suit and request for discovery.

. . .

When Michael started practicing law at Barron, Walker, Youngman & Hamilton his outside activities and interests included his religion, family, law, politics, history and tennis in that order. His interest in history and politics began at an early age. He recalled his parents being excited about someone they referred to as "Jack," or "Kennedy," and they seemed so enthusiastic about his wife Jacqueline and she seemed so attractive when he saw them on television and he remembered how his father would say: "He's a great president." As a boy of eight he was dazzled by the aura and excitement that surrounded "Kennedy," and he thought the President clever.

Then on November 22, 1963 he watched television with his parents who were stricken when CBS news anchor, Walter Cronkite took off his glasses and mournfully announced to a shocked worldwide audience "President Kennedy died at one pm Central Standard Time, two o'clock Eastern Standard Time, some thirty eight minutes ago." The result of an assassin's bullet. On Sunday morning two days later he and his father were watching television news while his mother fixed breakfast. The picture showed Oswald, the shooting suspect, being escorted by police out of a holding cell, when suddenly a man in dark suit and gray hat stepped out of a crowd in front of Oswald and a sharp crack was heard, Oswald slumped forward and everyone jumped on the man in the dark suit and wrestled him to the ground. Michael's father shouted to his mother: "Get in here, someone just shot Oswald." His parents were sad, everyone they knew was sad. He and his family watched the Kennedy funeral on television as the casket wheeled up Pennsylvania Avenue on a horse-drawn caisson. Behind the caisson a singular black horse with a saddle and boots in the stirrups turned backwards followed. Michael felt sad for the President's little son who saluted his father's casket as he lay in state in the Capitol's rotunda. World leaders marched from the White House to St. Matthew's Cathedral with Bobby Kennedy, Edward Kennedy, and the widow in the lead. The nation watched in mourning and grief. He watched the television as the funeral cortege came across the Memorial Bridge to the President's final resting place in Arlington National cemetery. He watched as the eternal flame flickered above the simple grave on a hill below the Custis-Lee mansion, the home of Robert E. Lee, head of the Confederate army during the civil war. With his parents and the world he watched Bobby Kennedy, the Attorney General and Edward Kennedy, the Senator from Massachusetts lead the widow away as the cameras panned the disbursing mourners. His parents were in shock and he felt like a "king" had died. He'd watched the Vice President being sworn in as President of the

United States on a plane carrying the President's dead body. The First Lady, blood still on her suit, witnessing the swearing in. In his eight year old eyes he thought it unfair that "young" Jack Kennedy should be dead and this funny fellow with the broad brim cowboy hat should be the new President.

In school he began to read about the men who had been President and what their backgrounds had been like. He read about the life of Al Smith, who in 1928, ran as the Democratic nominee for President and lost to Herbert Hoover. Historically they said he lost because he was a Catholic, like himself, but in 1960 "Kennedy," an Irish Catholic was elected breaking a barrier that had existed since 1928. Michael, like millions of others, young and old, watched what the new President would do with great apprehension. As a youngster he was vaguely aware America's enemy was communist Russia. All school children were taught the evils of communism and their goal of world domination. In the Pacific the Chinese were another enemy headed by the old communist, Mao Zedong. This common theme ran throughout television and newspapers. As he grew older he followed the rise and defeat of Goldwater in the 1964 election. Television brought Cronkite, Huntley, Brinkley, John Chancellor to the screen at the Republican National convention at the cow palace south of San Francisco. He watched Eisenhower condemn the press to a wildly cheering crowd; Nelson Rockefeller, Governor of New York, booed by Goldwater's conservative delegates. In his teens he decided the Republican Party closest to his way of thinking. Many of their nominees were self made men, and he identified with their principles, limited government, fair taxation, fiscal responsibility, pro-life, representative of small business and a strong military.

Under Lyndon Johnson the country went from military advisors under Kennedy to a full scale war in Viet Nam, a faraway place nobody had ever heard of. For ten years (1964-1974) the war raged on in the countryside. It frayed the fabric of the country. By splitting public opinion for and against the war Lyndon Johnson forfeited his re-election and the voters elected Richard Nixon.

Elected to Congress in 1946, Nixon joined John Kennedy a young veteran from Massachusetts, in the House of Representatives. Both served in World War II. They rose quickly, Nixon to the Senate in 1950 and Vice President in 1952 and Kennedy to the Senate that same year. In 1956 Kennedy lost in a bid for Vice President but succeeded winning the Presidency in1960 defeating his old nemesis Richard Nixon. After losing the 1962 race for Governor of California, Nixon turned to the law joining the New York firm of Nixon, Mudge, Rose, Guthrie & Alexander. He gathered a coterie of young lawyers and aides at the law firm and laid the ground work for a comeback win for the Presidency in 1968 against a weakened former Democrat Vice President Hubert Humphrey. All these events registered with Michael Sullivan and he developed a desire to someday be apart of the ebb and flow of the country's fortunes.

. . .

While Michael interviewed law firms in Denver, Blake Collins invited Matthew to lunch at the University Club an exclusive male bastion. A member for some years, Matthew put Blake up for membership. No other member of the firm, including Michael, received a similar invitation. It gave Blake a superior feeling knowing he and Matthew were the only members of the firm afforded an opportunity to meet wealthy clients. In addition Blake belonged to a number of private clubs where he was socially active. Michael on the other hand preferred to devote his non legal efforts to volunteer work with civic clubs, the bar association his church and a political club he joined shortly after joining the firm.

On arrival, Matthew and Blake went directly to the men's dining room on the second floor and there they were greeted by the tuxedoed host. "Welcome Mr. Hamilton and Mr. Collins, I have a table prepared for you." Perhaps fifty men were seated at tables covered with white table cloths, silverware and glistening crystal. Waiters dressed in black pants, white shirts, black bow ties and black vests, stood along the walls ready to come to a table at a guest's beckoning finger. The room, half full at twelve thirty, found the two partners following the host, talking and waving to friends, as they moved toward their table. When they were comfortably seated Matthew took a breadstick from a silver dish in front of him and as he munched on it. "What do you think of Michael's trip to Denver?"

"Oh I think it's ok but really a waste of time; we'd be better served if he was back here trying cases."

"I've found him becoming more and more independent and I don't care for his attitude. You, Doug Phelps and I are working ourselves to the bone bringing in all the money and he wants a good share of that. The general practice side is just not bringing in what they're taking out." Matthew said this in the nature of a probe to test Blake's reaction.

Carefully, Blake replied: "I agree he's been a little distant and I'm not so sure he's pleased with your leadership." Knowing this would whet Matthew's interest, he continued: "He's been preaching to the associates the importance of general practice and trial work to the firm, and it's a given he's become one of the most successful trial attorneys in the city and probably the state. There's nothing wrong with talking to the associates except it leaves the impression municipal work is just icing on the cake. He thinks you place too much emphasis on its importance over other work the firm produces."

Matthew took the bait and red-faced hissed: "If it weren't for you and I, there would be no firm. I'm getting a little sick of his attitude." The food came the discussion ended and they proceeded to eat their roast beef sandwiches with relish. By the time a waiter brought dessert Matthew had settled down and began discussing a problem he had with one of his municipal clients, when Blake brought the conversation back to Michael and the firm.

"You know Matthew the annual firm meeting will be on us before you know it and I think there's going to be a play for more points from the trial-general practice boys." Knowing he had opened up a delicate subject, Blake continued: "any change in points would have to come from you. Speaking for myself I'm content with what I'm making."

"Well that's nice of you to say that Blake and I don't mind giving up a few points; I think you should have more than any partner except myself. You've been responsible for bringing in huge fees this year on the municipal side."

"That's nice of you, but I don't think Michael would be too excited about me taking out more than him. Have you thought of that?"

"No I haven't. I think he can be talked into it, he has nowhere to go." They finished their lunch and returned to the office and the subject of profits did not come up again since the annual meeting was six months off.

Every year the partners met in October, when the fiscal year came to a close; they reviewed progress made during the year, discussed potential partners, reviewed expenses and allotted partner shares for the following year. From the time Michael joined the firm as an associate and later as partner Matthew Hamilton held the largest number of points and biggest share of the profits. Michael's share had risen each year but after Blake became a partner his share rose rapidly until it almost equaled Michael's. Although the meeting would not take place for months Michael began to develop a plan he would present to the partners that would create an equitable distribution of profits and prepare the firm for future growth.

CHAPTER 13

After he returned from Denver Michael plunged into the case load piling up on his desk, many awaiting trial. In October an intriguing case came to him through a referral. A young woman had gone to a reputable doctor at the Medical Institute to have an intrauterine device inserted into her for birth control. After using the devise for some time it began to cause pain and she asked the Doctor to remove it; he told her it was no longer there. In her first interview with Michael she told him she continued to have pain and nausea so she went to a second doctor who examined her and found no sign of any problem. For another three years she continued to have pain, nausea, and lack of energy. She came to suspect the device had not been properly removed. She told Michael her ordeal lasted four years until a naturopath found the intrauterine device. He listened to her story and had great sympathy for her suffering.

In a firm meeting to review cases the firm would accept he brought the matter to the attention of the partners and asked for permission to proceed with a law suit to recover damages for her horrific experience. The fee for the firm's services to come from a settlement or success in trial. If neither were achieved, no fee. Matthew voiced no opposition and seemed ambivalent about taking on a contingent fee case. Blake Collins, however, voiced disapproval arguing it would take too much of the trial section's time and be difficult to persuade a jury that two of the city's most prominent doctors were guilty of malpractice. The other Partners sided with Michael when he said he would take the case on his own, using no firm resources, extra time expended to be over and above the time he normally put in and expenses paid out of his own pocket including expert witness fees. Blake Collins withdrew his objection based on Michael's willingness to absorb expenses and the partners unanimously agreed to undertake representation of Shelley Brownstone and her husband Bart.

Michael judged Shelley to be a very appealing witness in her own behalf. At five feet two inches she looked small, very trim and had a freckled farm fresh face he knew the jury would be sure to trust. Her Husband, Bart, had spent four years watching her suffer, taking time off from work when she couldn't get out of bed, doing most of the household chores. Shelley lost her job as a result of her illness, her employer stating she took too much time from her job and he had to hire someone else. Michael filed two lawsuits, one for Malpractice against the doctors, and a separate suit on Bart's behalf for loss of consortium. (loss suffered by the spouse caused by the actions of the defendant doctors) Then he made an appointment to see Dr. Peter Schmidt who found and removed the offending intrauterine device. On the appointed day he arrived early at Dr. Schmidt's office. One patient remained to be seen by the doctor. Michael had deliberately scheduled the appointment as late in the day as possible so the doctor would be free of seeing patients and more inclined to relax and spend the necessary time to go over all aspects of his medical diagnosis and removal.

Keeping with his usual practice, Michael prepared extensively for the visit. He read medical journals and articles involving the device implanted in Shelley Brownstone and read cases dealing with the subject and in so doing became an expert fully equipped to question the doctor. He worked out a direct examination that he'd use when the doctor took the stand. (the doctor had no idea he would be called as a witness.) When he and Dr. Schmidt sat down in his office after the last patient had been seen and the office assistant departed for the day the doctor sat casually behind his desk, obviously starting to simmer down after a busy day of seeing patients.

He viewed Michael quizzically. He was in his late fifties, steel gray hair and clear blue eyes. Before they talked he shorn himself of his white coat and put on a checked sport coat that gave him a younger look, but no less impressive. He folded his hands in front of him on the desk and asked Michael what he could do for him. The man appeared twenty years older than Michael and an expert in his field but the young attorney had cross-examined enough doctors not to be intimidated by them, young or old. Through experience he was well aware of their limitations and knew doctors testify medicine is not an exact science and for every doctor who testifies one way another can be found to testify the opposite way. Michael had a legal pad on his lap and asked the doctor if he minded if he took notes and the physician had no objection.

"As you know I represent Shelley and Bart Brownstone," he began. "I know her story from her viewpoint; I wanted to find out what she told you and how you diagnosed her problem."

"Well," he started out unhesitatingly, "she came to us as a new patient and I believe she said she'd been referred by another doctor, it's in my notes, but I can't remember who. She explained she had an IUD inserted in her approximately four years ago and over that period had suffered pain constantly, to the point she had to lay down part of the day. After two years she asked to have it removed, by the doctor who inserted it; he told her it wasn't there but she continued to have pain. When her condition got worse she went to a second doctor complaining she thought she might still have all or part of the device still in her. He examined her and told her he found no evidence of the IUD and hinted her pain could be psychosomatic."

Michael interrupted: "Did she name either doctor?"

"No, I didn't ask her, perhaps I should have. My sole interest was to diagnose her problem and try to help a young woman in obvious pain and terrified about what was happening to her mentally and physically."

"What did you do for her?" Michael probed.

She told me she went to a naturopath who told her she still had the IUD in her and that was the source of her pain. "I examined her, took x-rays and blood tests. She passed all the tests but the pain and suffering continued. My last thought, although it seemed duplicative since she had been assured the device had been removed by two doctors was to go into the uterus to make absolutely sure the IUD had in fact been removed. At that point I decided a hidden IUD had to be the cause of the problem. I agreed with the Naturopath's diagnosis. Michael couldn't believe the candor with which Dr. Schmidt went to the heart of the problem.

"What did you do next?" he asked casually not wanting to disrupt the doctor's narrative.

"I scheduled a probe and you know what I found: the device wedged up within her uterus, infection had set in. I immediately removed it and within a week she reported her pain had ceased and she felt like she felt before the IUD had been inserted. That told me we had found the cause of her four year ordeal."

"Would it be a normal occurrence for it to be left in the uterus even though the doctor thought he had removed it?"

"Well, yes it can happen, but it seems to me that when she continued to complain of pain after he said he removed it, logically he should have gone back in to make sure it had in fact been removed."

"Was that done?"

"To my knowledge it was not done," he said without more.

Michael knew his next question and the answer he received were crucial to the case and assumed the doctor would be aware of it as well.

"Doctor when she went to the second doctor with the same complaints that she came to you with what should have been done?"

"I assume the doctor, if the same specialty as mine, Obstetrics, would put her through the same tests I did and based on her history rechecked the device to make sure the original doctor removed it."

"Did he do that?" Michael asked softly

"Apparently he did not."

"Assuming these two doctors were the same specialty as you, should they have done a re-check based on her complaints."

"I believe they should have."

At that juncture Michael knew he had a case and thought: this gentleman may or may not wish to become a witness but he's honest and won't back off the truth. With that in mind he posed the ultimate question looking square into the doctor's eyes. "Was it negligent they did not recheck of the uterus?"

Dr. Schmidt lowered his eyes, his head dropped and he said in a voice not much more than a whisper: "Yes, in my opinion it would be."

Those words were the confirming seven words every lawyer wants to extract from a doctor in a malpractice case. Dr. Schmidt would be the perfect witness if he testified. They talked in generalities for five minutes more about the patient-client and Michael shied from suggesting he would like the doctor to be a witness. The doctor, well knowing he had made an important admission, was careful to give no further opinions or question who the other two doctors were. As soon as he left the doctor's office he went immediately cross town to his office and dictated a three page memo to the file recalling exactly the words spoken by the doctor. He looked at his watch when he finished: 10:00 p.m. He locked up the office and left for home. Mary was not happy at his late arrival.

Ever loyal, Mary was happy to see him when he came through the door. "You must be exhausted," she said with genuine concern. He looked burned out, his face flushed as he dropped on to a couch. "I kept your dinner warm, I think we can have a drink before you eat, get some color back in your cheeks and we can talk about why you worked so late tonight.

"Are the kids in bed?"

"Yes, all except Jack, he's still studying." She fixed him a double scotch and water and a single for herself and brought them back from the kitchen and handed him his.

"You are a saint, sweetheart," he said taking the offered drink. He took a healthy swallow and let out a sigh. "Oh that tastes good." He felt the warm sensation in his throat and began to relax. "Remember I told you about the lady who came in to see me about six months ago feeling she might have a medical malpractice suit?"

"Yes, I do recall. It made me sick when you told me what happened. In fact I felt infuriated at the thought it happened."

"This afternoon, late I visited with the doctor who finally removed it, and he, in effect said it amounted to negligence not to have discovered it once she asked to have it removed. That's tantamount to winning the case before we try it."

"You must feel great."

"I do. I'm going to ask for a million in damages. It may seem a bit high but after what she's been through, unnecessarily, she deserves it."

"Will the firm get the whole fee if you win?"

"Yes they will, it goes into the firm's coffers which will be split in December."

"I hate to see you work so hard while Matthew and Blake shoot fish in a barrel and charge exorbitant rates for it," she lamented.

"I know, that's the luck of the draw," he philosophized. At the same time he realized if he could persuade a jury of the righteousness of his cause the payday might reach as high as two hundred and fifty thousand dollars for the firm equal to a good slice of municipal work and three times as hard to come by.

She looked so beautiful standing there in her nightgown he wanted to reach out and squeeze and hug her. She caught the look she knew so well and said; "Not now, you've got to eat and get some sleep. There will be times for games later." What a gal, he thought, she really loves me. Dutifully he finished his drink, ate the warmed over dinner and fifteen minutes later lay beside Mary in bed sleeping like a baby. She smiled at his ambitiousness and rolled over content he was home and safe.

. . .

Hamilton, Sullivan, Collins & Phelps continued to prosper in 1995, following a trend occurring in law firms across the country; as business picked up they added more lawyers to fill the need. After making partner Michael moved his family to a new neighborhood, purchased a five bedroom home with access to tennis courts and swimming pool and settled in for a long stay. Most of the families in the community had children in grade and high school with a smattering in college. Their neighbors were professionals: lawyers, doctors, accountants, architects and businessmen. Most of the wives, with children still in school, were stay at home moms, the exception being those women who had attended law or medical school and chose to practice and be mothers part time. All the women were involved in charity work with the Junior league, Assistance league or other nonprofit corporations. They served on boards, cared for the poor, manned lunch counters at the local grade and high school, ran thrift shops and brought meals to shut-ins.

Mary spent twelve years raising the children and doing charity work with the Junior League and wanted to go back to work. She found a woman who agreed to take care of the children when they got home from school freeing her to take a part time job with the Winthrop Foundation. The Winthrop brothers inherited their wealth from the paper making industry. "Billy," the oldest set up a foundation at an early age to distribute grants to all sorts of charities. George Winthrop devoted his time to making money and spending it as quickly as he accumulated it. Married with three young children, a socialite wife who gadded about town, and a mistress George saw himself as a Bon Vivant, a man of wealth and a power in local politics. He found that by giving money to politicians, he could get his phone calls answered. His specialty was to pick an up and coming politician and bet on him like you would on a horse, that way if the politician turned out to be successful and you were an early backer the rewards in power could be significant. George loved to hob nob with and entertain the Governor and the state's two Senators who he backed early in their careers.

William "Billy" Winthrop never married, and at fifty led a simple life. Unlike his brother, he turned down dozens of invitations and kept pretty much to himself and a few card playing cronies. When George asked him to contribute to a political campaign, he obliged simply because he thought it good business to stay in with the "ins" as well as the "outs."

Mary found the work exciting; managing investments, reviewing applications for grants and recommending grant recipients to "Billy" and his board of directors. Between the two Sullivans they were well on their way to moderate wealth despite expenses of private school education for their four children, mortgage payments and general costs of living. The nature of his practice took almost all his time and though he'd been invited to join numerous social and golf clubs he always declined with the excuse he didn't have the time. He changed his mind when asked to join a new tennis club with five outdoor courts and a single covered court, swimming pool, sports shop and a snack bar. He decided to work on his tennis game as much as his trial schedule allowed. A natural athlete, and winner of two state high school tennis championships, he earned an athletic scholarship at Georgetown University and played four years on its championship teams. After college he entered the Air Force for two years and continued to play, participating in two Air Force World Wide Tennis Championships, the last at the Army-Navy country club, outside Washington D.C. When he wasn't playing in the tournaments he toured the capital on his own and fell in love with the city.

In the first years after Blake Collins joined the firm he and Michael played regularly once a month. That ended when Blake joined the Dorsett Club where he could play with the city's elite. They played a few times more and then the invitation to play stopped. Mary and Courtney Blake got along together and worked on several Junior League committees, but socially went their separate ways, Mary working with her church and the Winthrop Foundation, Courtney playing tennis at the Dorsett and lunching with young women her own age and status.

In July 1995 Blake and Doug Phelps decided to throw a party at the City Museum which housed the most famous art work in a five state region. The cost of the party to be absorbed by the firm, the justification they gave: to attract a hundred or so of the city's most successful young businessmen and their wives in the hopes of boosting the firm name and prestige and attracting clients. They gave the party a theme: "Wall Street," encouraging guests to dress like, bankers, brokers, traders in the "roaring twenties." When Michael and Mary arrived at ten p.m. Saturday night the party appeared in full swing. A ten piece band sat on a platform at the end of the room; two bars flanked the band on either side. In the center a giant table laden with ham, roast beef, pasta, salads, and an assortment of fish, fruits and desserts. All set out lavishly for the two hundred guests who twisted and gyrated as the band blared out jazz tunes. By twelve thirty a.m. people were stumbling around if they weren't dancing to the frenzied music. Most of the city's elite were present, half of whom looked unsteady on their feet and that included a startling number of women.

The Sullivans watched this spectacle develop and as it got wilder and wilder they lost zest for the party. When a lawyer Michael knew stumbled into their table, noticeably drunk, slipped and spilled his drink, gained his balance and stumbled off in another direction Michael turned to Mary and said: "That's it Mary!" he had a disgusted look on his face. "This thing is an embarrassment to the firm. It smells of hedonism. These people are making a spectacle of themselves. Let's go, we won't be missed."

"I'm with you sweetheart. I suspect this party will break up when the police arrive." He led her out into the dark night and they felt the fresh air on their faces and a sense of relief to be out of the museum.

"That was a depressing scene Michael."

"It's a symptom of the times," he seethed. The restraints are off and even the people we know are back there carousing with the rest. Blake and Doug let the thing get out of hand. I know it's a private party but it reflects unfavorably on the firm; all the partners and the associates were in the thick of it."

They reached their car in the lot and he helped her in and after they were seated and the ignition turned on he reached over and kissed her and said: "Thank God I'm married to you, some of those wives in there looked like they could go home with someone other than their husband. Let's get out of here." They drove home holding hands.

From the beginning the two were close, their interests common: the law, foreign affairs, politics, religion, the Catholic Church and their children: Jack 12, Sharon 10, Peter 8, and Kathryn 6 enrolled in St Bartholomew's grade school. Mary found Millie, a nanny, who loved the children and when her husband died of a heart attack, Michael invited Millie to come live with the family, and because her children were grown and lived in other cities, she accepted.

Early in September Michael's attention turned to the upcoming annual partnership retreat. As far as he could see, the firm had reached a fork in the road: they had to decide whether they were going to be a specialty firm, or a general practice firm with the bonds a specialty. Matthew Hamilton and Blake wanted total control which simply meant the three municipal partners would take out the highest percentage of profits, their rational being they produced the most revenue and therefore were entitled to the highest return. This only made sense in Michael's mind if the firm did nothing but Municipal work. Since it did not, the other fourteen lawyers had to bill at normal rates and perform work in other facets of a law firm such as litigation, tax, probate, corporate, family and labor and employer law. In short, the bond lawyers billed at very high rates while the general lawyers billed at lower rates resulting in four bond lawyers bringing in half the fees, and fourteen general lawyers bringing in the other half. He felt the firm's profits should be split evenly amongst the partners with a reasonable bonus to any partner that produced an outstanding amount. He also believed the bonds were a firm asset not belonging to any one partner. A chasm between Matthew, Blake and himself had widened in the last year, probably because they realized he intended to make a pitch at the annual meeting as he'd done the year before when he argued the firm had to be governed by equitable principles and fairness in compensation, which meant sharing a greater percent of the profits with the associates, something he had been advocating for a long time.

Matthew's position had always been, an associate should work at least six years before making partner, and even then, they should be considered junior partners for compensation purposes. In contrast, Michael thought that kind of thinking would eventually tear the firm apart; a terrible waste for a firm that had practiced law for a hundred years. An announcement was placed in the state bar bulletin that year, and sent to all members of the bar proclaiming: "the firm of Hamilton, Sullivan, Collins & Phelps "celebrates its one hundred years in the practice of law" The name of the original partnership formed in 1895 was listed first and all the others that followed ending with the Hamilton firm in 1995. Michael intended to make clear at the meeting what lay ahead for the firm if the current direction didn't change. He realized his best might not be enough and he might lose the argument to greed over reason yet he knew he had to try. He owed it to the firm and the many lawyers who served it faithfully for a century.

CHAPTER 14

In preparation for the meeting he began to write a narrative from notes he'd made over the years based on twenty or thirty conversations with Samuel Barron, the senior partner who died in 1992 at the age of 77. Barron joined the firm in 1940, then a young man of twenty five, and a recent graduate of Vanderbilt University Law School. In their discussions Barron regaled him with stories about some of the characters who had played roles in the firm over the years. Like "Wee Willie Watson," a fabled trial lawyer who liked to tipple and the greater the trial the more he tippled. Barron said the man was brilliant when trying a case to a jury. In summation he would be intoxicated, not unnoticed by the jury, but his logic and grasp of the facts were so clear the jury sat spellbound as he painted a picture of the case on a fresh white canvas. They couldn't wait to see how the finished picture looked. When he sat down that picture stayed with them until they came back into the courtroom from deliberations with a verdict in favor of "Wee Willie" who stood about five feet six inches. Then there was Miles Sloan, a giant in the twenties, who specialized in railroad law. His fame reached such proportions, he frequently appeared before Congress to testify on the intricacies of railroad regulations. In the thirties the firm was led by Alfred Lawton, a distinguished gregarious gentleman, who besides being a great lawyer enjoyed being a leading light in the Democratic Party and a friend and consultant to Franklin Roosevelt in the thirties and early war years. Lawton raised prodigious amounts of money for the party and knew many of the nation's corporate titans. Barron made it a practice to question older members of the firm what it was like to practice in the first part of the century and their stories he passed on to Michael. The firm had its share of scoundrels and wastrels. Barron liked to tell the story of Roger Farley, a young man very talented in the law, who spent most his time drinking, playing tennis and dallying with other men's wives, so the story went. With great relish Barron related to young Sullivan a typical day at the office for Roger during his truncated time with the firm.

"'Old Roger' (thirty five years old at the time) would come traipsing into the office about ten o'clock in the morning, two hours late, and go right to his desk where he looked for his 'tennis book' and called a tennis playing partner for the day. He'd arrange a match for two in the afternoon, preceded by lunch at his club of two dry martinis, soup and a sandwich. The routine never varied. With the game wrapped up by four o'clock he showered, returned to the office, made a few business calls, then calls to a string of lovelies to see who would be available for the evening's entertainment. Barron claimed Roger got away with his indolent routine, first because his father was very wealthy and gave all his business to his son and secondly the father sent other clients Roger got credit for while others did the work. "Old Roger," Barron would say, and laugh as he did so, looked quite the specimen at six feet three inches, blonde hair, blue eyed virile male. He loved the ladies and the ladies loved Roger. Ultimately he brought honor to the firm, not for his legal exploits, but by answering the call to arms in World War II. They made him an officer in the infantry; in an act of great bravery he saved the lives of twenty men in his platoon when he charged a machinegun nest manned by the Germans, lobbing a hand grenade that silenced the gun but cost him his life. The newspapers made much of the fact he'd been a pillar at the firm. The senior partner declared

Roger gave up a promising practice and a great future to join the army for his country. Barron concluded the tale telling Michael he'd actually signed up when it was discovered he'd fathered a child and determined the service afforded the best opportunity to leave town quickly.

By creating a narrative Michael hoped to impress on the partners the significance of the firm's century of law practice, the men responsible for its continuity and pride in Hamilton, Sullivan, Collins & Phelps continuing its place in the legal annals of the city and state. He reviewed the financial history of the firm, studying revenue and expenses over the last ten years. What partners had brought in and taken out in profit. He calculated the number of clients and the revenue generated by the firm's general practice contrasted with the fewer number of client's and larger revenue brought in by municipal lawyers, noting the discrepancies between the two. Finally he charted what would happen to the firm's competitive reputation if it continued in its present course. It took three weeks to complete the narrative, working at night. Satisfied with the result he reviewed it with Mary two days before the meeting at a resort fifty miles from the city. "I think it's all you can do Michael, whatever happens is for the best. Try to keep it on a non-emotional basis, sometimes you get a little worked up and lose your audience."

On the eve of the meeting, Michael met with Blake, Phelps, Dudley Peterson and Cormack O'Neil reviewing in a general way his thinking and asking for their support. Peterson and O'Neil listened carefully; they were in the general law section, had been recruited by him and held him high regard. Both listened but were noncommittal probably because they feared Blake Collins and Matthew Hamilton more than they admired Michael. At the end of Michael's presentation Cormac indicated he would give his backing to any proposal he offered.

Michael J. Walsh

The next day all six partners arrived at the resort within an hour of each other and checked into separate rooms. The meetings were to be held in Hamilton's room and began promptly at one p.m. The afternoon session, led by Matthew, covered the state of the firm, now eighteen strong, followed by ad hoc recitations by each partner regarding cases they were working on, their caseloads, prospects for new business and whether to hire one or two associates for the coming year. At four o'clock, Dudley Peterson, took drink orders. Several had beer, including Michael; Matthew and Blake had scotch and soda. Dudley sat out a spread of ham, turkey, crackers and cheese and the conversation began to flow at a more relaxed pace, as the drinks took hold. Several partners, after the first round, started to refer to Dudley as "garcon." Much laughter would ensue after these calls for "garcon." Outwardly the meeting proceeded smoothly, nevertheless, Michael sensed anxiety in the room, as in prior years, "points" moved up on the agenda. At five thirty Matthew ordered his third scotch and announced "points" next on the agenda. Suddenly outward frivolity eased off and everyone struggled to compose themselves after two rounds of drink. Having been around his partners for years, he knew their drinking habits. After four drinks Matthew's eyes became glassy and if you had a point to make it had to be made no later than the fourth drink. On the other hand, Cormack could down seven whiskeys and look perfectly sober. Michael sipped two beers aware he had to hit his fellow partners at just the right point or the game, as he saw it, would be over. Cormack and Dudley Peterson knew they would come out on the low end of points awarded so they drank freely, although curious to watch what they knew to be a showdown on point distribution. Blake and Doug Phelps stopped drinking scotch at two as they carefully eyed Michael downing his two beers. They had no intention of being caught unprepared or surprised. Matthew shrugged off the effects of three drinks and offered his suggestion for distribution of points.

136

Hamilton	29
Sullivan	16
Collins	19
Phelps	17
Peterson	10
O'Neil	9

A stunned silence followed. No one spoke, each quickly calculating mentally the impact on his own share. A clear picture emerged; Michael lost points and the bond lawyers gained giving them sixty five percent of the profits leaving thirty five percent to the trial lawyers. Whether this had been worked out in advance with Collins and Phelps, Michael had no way of knowing but he considered it a very clever ploy for Hamilton to be giving up points he held the previous year in favor of Collins and Phelps.

Blake Collins broke the silence: "You shouldn't be giving up all the points, Matthew, if anything, Doug and I should be giving up points." Michael believed Blake's outburst feigned and made to look generous in the eyes of Matthew and the other partners. In response to Collin's protest Matthew offered to give up another point if Blake, Michael and Phelps would do the same with the points going to the two junior partners. He thought this should resolve the matter and announced the new offer not bothering to consult the others.

Hamilton	28
Sullivan	15
Collins	18
Phelps	16
Peterson	12
O'Neil	11

O'Neil, apprehensive and anxious to seal the deal, since he gained extra points, attempted to play the role of peacemaker speaking with the intent of injecting humor into a tense situation said: "I'll drink to that." An audible sound of relief could be heard. They all raised their glasses, except Michael. Everyone looked at him out of the corner of their eyes, watching for the reaction they hoped would not come, knowing full well it had to. The one exception, Matthew Hamilton, who reached for the bottle of scotch and poured himself another drink thinking the trouble had been avoided with the loss of only a few points. He completely misread his position. He had either deluded himself into thinking he owned the firm and could do as he pleased surrounded by sycophants who feared to take him on, or he realized Michael to be his only threat and could be handled easily. He didn't appreciate the fact his co-senior partner had become a very astute, tough trial lawyer, who, through dint of hard work, had been slowly and painstakingly building a very profitable law practice, a highly respected member of the bar and the glue holding the firm together. Blake could not understand Michael's willingness to absorb humiliation and loss of points for the purpose of building and holding the firm together. Matthew didn't understand loyalty; the others did but they understood who held the cards and because they were young and couldn't or wouldn't see the future they were going with Matthew unless Michael turned him around. He knew he must make the try even if it resulted in failure, for in his mind, the firm was more important than any one partner or associate. Somewhere along the line Matthew lost sight of that.

He started slowly, deliberately: "Last year at our annual meeting I raised the point I thought we needed a policy for distribution of income. I provided you copies of an article in the 'Practical Lawyer,' the best I've seen on the subject. We don't have a policy." All eyes fastened on him as he spoke; they knew he was putting his finger on a crucial issue effecting each of them individually as well as the firm. Could he affect change? He faced a jury of five, two of whom were with him he believed. He needed five. He determined to be unemotional, only reason could persuade lawyers. "It is essential for each partner to know exactly what to expect, not the money he will earn but how his share is determined. We have six partners five of whom are very close in age. He handed each a sheet of paper with the following written on it:

Name	Age	year-Partner	years-Practice
Hamilton	54	19	24
Sullivan	41	9	14
Collins	39	5	12
Phelps	38	3	12
Peterson	36	2	12
O'Neil	34	1	7

"Within two and a half years we will have at least two more partners, a total of eight. In 1992 we were eight lawyers now we are eighteen. What has been our method of dividing income? Receipts! There is no other explanation. Why is there such a disparity in points between the bond lawyers and the trial lawyers? They all work hard for the firm. I have worked longer, been a partner longer, have as much or more experience than Blake yet I have three points less. Dudley has practiced as long as Doug Phelps, has as much experience yet has four points less. Why? The obvious answer is receipts. Are receipts a valid measure he asked rhetorically looking directly at Matthew Hamilton. I think not. However, I would accept that method as sole criteria if the partners competed on equal footing. That situation does not exist in the firm presently. It will not work where a firm relies on a major client or a specialty such as estate planning or a monopoly like municipal bond opinions. The reason is simple. Non municipal lawyers bill a hundred dollars an hour for their time, municipal lawyers bill at five hundred dollar per hour. The issue is:

Should the municipal lawyers make more than non municipal lawyers based on higher receipts?" No one moved, or interrupted waiting for Michael's conclusion. He knew he had their full attention, because each had a stake in their future and that of the firm.

"I believe we all want a successful law firm. If the bond lawyers want more money they should form a boutique bond firm. If they don't want such a firm I believe the profits have to be distributed more equitably. Four partners, myself, Blake, Doug and Dudley have to bring in more business if the firm is to grow and prosper. We've brought in some but because of our ages it is nowhere near enough to sustain us in the future. With age we will be able to bring in new business. We are fortunate to have the bonds to sustain us while we grow. Bonds, by themselves, are not sufficient to allow growth. I pointed out at last year's meeting, the municipal work is unique because it is a monopoly. It comes to us. The bond business has been in the firm since 1926. Blake came to the firm in 1986 to help Matthew in bond work. Doug came into the firm for the same reason in 1989. All partners should share in the proceeds of the bond business not just the partners who do bonds. Any of the men in the firm can do bond work, illustrated by the fact, Tom Hardy, an associate has done very well since he's joined the bond lawyers. Twelve other lawyers have chosen general practice including three partners. If we all work the same hours, but in different areas, the fact one area of law brings in more doesn't justify more profits go to those in that area. If the bonds were a profitable corporate client such as Kennedy Enterprises, which I brought in, a bonus would be justified. That's not the case with the bond business. The bonds have been nurtured over the years by many lawyers. They are the firm's asset, not any one partner's." Here he struck at gravamen of the issue, equity.

"All should participate in dividends from the firm's specialty not just those who inherited it or assigned to work on it." He paused and looked at each partner, knowing he'd made a reasoned argument, logical, persuasive, and irrefutable.

All had stopped drinking attuned to every word he spoke, realizing this had been well thought out, and not some emotional appeal on his own behalf. He talked sanity to them and they realized it whether they liked it or not. There could be no doubt about his sincerity, not for his benefit, but for their future and the future of the firm. He continued: "Statistics for the last four years show our general law practice brings in about half of what the municipal practice brings in. If we want a law firm that is competitive with the top five firms in the city we are going to have to work hard and bring in new business." Michael had laid the groundwork for his conclusion; he'd identified the problem, the effect on the firm's future and now he would offer a solution.

"In the past year I have given a lot of thought to a policy for distributing profits. I have discussed it with major players in other firms without disclosing our current method. I find that, uniformly, they distribute profits evenly amongst partners, no matter what function the partner performs. They realize the profits come the work of each partner. In other words one partner may be working in a less lucrative field but he earns the same as a partner working in a more lucrative, but necessary practice. Why do they run their partnership that way? Because they realize to have a full service law firm, one that can serve all needs of a client, they have to offer all sorts of legal specialties: tax, probate, litigation, corporate, appellate. I think under such a system, people feel equal, they trust each other to work for the good of all and high morale is generated. People are treated equally for their talent. I think Blake and I are equal, the same for Doug and Dudley. Our percentages should be equal; if one of us has an outstanding year that person would be entitled to a commensurate bonus. Under Matthew's proposal, bond lawyers have sixty two percent of the points, non-bond lawyers thirty eight. I propose a shift of six points making the percentages fifty eight to forty two." He handed them a sheet containing new figures.

Hamilton	25
Sullivan	17
Collins	17
Phelps	16
Peterson	15
O'Neil	10

He had come to the heart of the matter. Each in his own mind, still clouded by alcohol, could calculate where they came out in the new submission. Hamilton gave up four points, Michael gained two points, Blake lost one point, Dudley gained 3 and O'Neil lost one. After they had time to adjust to the numbers, Michael concluded: "I believe the policy should be in writing setting forth the criteria for distribution of income and take into consideration, age, maturity, length of service, reputation in the community, productivity, quality of work and business getting ability."

No one said anything for about twenty seconds, the other five partners looking at Matthew for a response. He looked at Michael as though he was seeing him for the first time. The look he had on his face was one of admiration for what he deemed a brilliant pre-sentation. He seemed stunned by it. "Well that was quite a speech, you've obviously done some homework, we can all appreciate that. I think what you've said makes sense." All eyes were on Matthew but Michael looked at Blake and saw anger in his face but held his tongue.

"Any comments?" asked Matthew, as he look around the room knowing, the issue was out in the open and had to be dealt with. He realized it put Blake in the spotlight since it affected him adversely. O'Neil spoke first and said he thought the proposal very fair and sensible. Dudley echoed O'Neil. Doug Phelps, with a finger to the wind, remained neutral not wanting to antagonize either bond or general partner, yet inwardly he approved. Michael felt at that point Matthew Hamilton might go along with it. It kept him as the chief earner, it made the non-bond lawyers feel recognized as an important firm asset. He also knew the lawyers in the firm felt great respect for Michael and his sense of fair play, but those factors mattered little to Matthew. It put the bond lawyers in their place and made him look good to the others since he relinquished the most points.

"What do you think Blake?" Matthew asked, interested to see his response, suspecting it would be negative.

"I think it was really a good presentation, he said non menacingly. But I couldn't agree less. I'm as interested in growth of the firm as Michael. In fact, he, I and Matthew have had many conversations about it. Michael recruited me specifically to help Matthew in the bond practice. We built it up. Doug Phelps was brought as it continued to grow. Now we've brought an associate to help us. We're all earning more money than we could have possibly dreamed of, not because of the law side, but from the bond revenue. I agree we all want a law firm with all the specialties we can develop but the bond income is what sustains us and as long as that area is carrying us and has every possibility of growing, I think we should encourage it and those who are performing it. And I think we do that by giving greater initiative to the bond lawyers. What we do makes it possible for the firm to make profits and that should be rewarded. I think, unlike Michael, our present system does that, It rewards those who bring in the most, and at the same time creates more profit for those who are not doing municipal bond work. Something they wouldn't be getting but for our work."

"I couldn't agree more," Doug Phelps chimed in. "The fact we make a little more only helps the general lawyers to make more and I think Matthew and Blake and myself deserve recognition for the work we do by way of a bigger bonus, a few more points or higher share of the profits whatever you want to call it."

Matthew saw he had to step in and bring the meeting back to a social level before all sense of camaraderie dissipated. "Ok, I think we've heard two views; I suggest we digest what we've heard and take it up in the morning. It's seven o'clock, time for cocktails followed by a steak dinner I've ordered for us at the lodge. Remember we will meet again here at eight a.m. sharp. Tomorrow the ladies will join us for the wind up, cocktails and dinner at the lodge." With that said everybody got up and helped themselves at the bar hoping to bring some conviviality back into the meeting. But after the hard three hour session, the drinks didn't diminish the sick feeling they had that trouble lay ahead for the firm.

At dinner the wine flowed; Blake and Doug Phelps, fairly inebriated, let it be known they had won their point even though a decision would not be announced until morning. By ten o'clock everyone was far enough gone, after steaks and five bottles of wine, to slowly leave the lodge and head back to their rooms drained from the day's meeting. With a heavy heart Michael retired knowing the outcome and he pined as much for himself as he did for the future of the firm. He fell into a dead sleep for two hours and awoke when he heard voices in the room next door. His mind alerted he propped himself up on his elbows and looked at his watch. The luminous dial read one thirty. He rolled over and put his head back on the pillow. He started to doze off but through his drowsiness he heard his name: "Michael." Alerted, he sat up in bed now fully awake. He remembered Blake and Phelps had elected to room next door. He could hear them carrying on a spirited conversation, still inebriated, and talking loudly not aware of who might hear them. Phelps kept repeating the phrase: "Keep it down," but his roommate paid no heed. Michael listened.

"Blake, Michael might be right. What he said this afternoon made sense."

In an angry voice Blake shot back at him: "It makes sense for him, he gets two points and I lose one and the junior partners get more than they deserve yet we're supposed to keep bringing in the big fees and share it with everybody. You heard what he said, now let's quit the argument and get some sleep," he said dismissively. He heard Doug roll over and say: "I hope you're right."

Sick at heart, Michael, lay back down in his bed thinking about the firm and the course it would take. He knew it was over when Blake attacked his proposal and the others sat mute afraid to express their opinions. He thought it interesting, that Doug, who clearly understood the stakes, and could have swayed the others, sat silent. His admission to Blake that [Michael] "…might be right," meant he recognized the truth of Michael's argument but decided to opt for short term gain.

The following morning they were all up, showered and shaved sitting around Matthew's apartment eating breakfast of fruit, pastries, orange juice and jugs of hot coffee. Matthew finally came out from his bedroom and all eyes turned toward him, awaiting the decision central to the firm's future. He greeted everyone with cheerful: "Good morning gentlemen," and slowly poured himself a cup of coffee. They continued eating saying nothing.

"I don't want to take up to much of our time today on business. We have golf lined up at ten o'clock and the ladies will be joining us around three o'clock. Again the schedule calls for cocktails at six and dinner at seven at the lodge. He paused for effect, and then looked up and said: "I've had a chance to think over our discussion yesterday. I put forth a plan where I gave up points, the junior partners received one each, Blake got three and everyone else stayed the same. Michael put forth a plan and argued persuasively for it. Blake and Doug argued against it. I believe we get more stability and equity by me giving up points. Does anyone disagree?

Matthew had Michael in a corner; if he argued against it he would look greedy, if he said nothing he would lose face. Michael realized his argument had fallen on deaf ears confirmed by the conversation overheard between Collins and Phelps. That being the case he decided to lay out concisely what he viewed as a wrong turn for the firm. Looking directly at Matthew, he spoke very softly every eye on him for his reaction to the challenge.

"I think it very generous of you to give up points to the junior partners, a gesture I believe is misplaced, not because my points remain the same but rather it leaves the municipal partners with a major share of the profits and relegates the litigation partners to junior partner status. I think that formula ultimately damages the firm and that's my concern."

"All right Michael I take that as a dissenting vote. Any other dissenting votes?" Michael looked at the junior partners and saw a look in their eyes that said: "Thanks Michael for trying but we don't have the cards." Jumping at the opportunity to close the match out Matthew said triumphantly, "hearing nothing further I adjourn the meeting. We'll see you all at the lodge for cocktails and the associates and their wives will be joining us." Matthew, Blake and Phelps quickly left the room, the others tarried for a moment giving Michael a handshake. Peterson left, only Cormack remained.

"Look at it this way Michael, the firm's going to grow, the municipal work is a monopoly, it will grow and we're all going to make more money. You argued for principle and lost; don't worry it will all work out, everything you said makes perfect sense and those guys are going to eventually see it that way."

"I wasn't concerned about money Cormack, the firm and its ability to compete and grow and you people were my concern. I'm afraid I lost an important battle for lack of support."

"We were with you Michael we just didn't think you had the cards to trump Blake And Matthew." With that exchange they parted and Michael walked slowly back to hisroom. The first thing he did, once in the room, was to call Mary alerting her to the situation. He dialed home and she answered. "Are you all right?" she entreated.

"Yes, but we lost. He filled her in with the details of the meeting the day before including the conversation between Blake Collins and Phelps and the handling of his proposal by Matthew that morning. He told her he loved her and would tell her the whole story when she arrived that afternoon. Feeling tired and a little let down he fell asleep barely waking in time to meet Mary at the lodge.

CHAPTER 15

They saw several lawyers and their wives in the lobby of the lodge, and talked cordially with each. Mary suggested they walk along the golf course and talk about where things stood. The sun beamed down from a cloudless sky and the mighty furs along the fairways furnished cooling shade. Fall kissed the leaves orange and gold as they began to drift on to the course.

"I'm appalled at those spineless jellyfish Cormack and Peterson forfeiting principle for a few dollars. Nothing surprises me about Blake and Doug Phelps. Greed is their motive," Mary lamented. "It's disappointing after the way you've worked for the firm, putting your heart and soul in it from the very first day. Those turncoats don't deserve you."

"Well Mary we had a good run, let's get through tonight and when we go home we'll sit down, sort it all out and figure out our next move. Jack, Sharon, Peter and Kathryn still need to be educated and we've got to figure out where we are financially."

By the time they walked four holes on a path running along the fairway a calmness descended upon them. They spoke of their faith, trust in God and the fact He had always done what was best for them. When they reached their room darkness had fallen and they decided to take a short nap before walking over to the lodge to join the firm's cocktail party and dinner. Blake and Courtney Collins were the first ones they ran into as they entered the lobby. Courtney was charming and Blake acted as though nothing had occurred in the last two days to change the relationship between the two couples. Mary and Michael were themselves, as always, making small talk and laughing at the jokes. They moved from couple to couple and Mary saw how much the associate lawyers respected Michael. She saw it in the eyes of the wives who had been told by their husbands of Michael's prowess as a trial lawyer. The wives gave her great respect because she had always gone out of her way to welcome them into the firm, unlike Imelda Hamilton, Matthew's wife. Mary understood their fears and hopes for themselves and their husbands. Imelda Hamilton treated them as inferiors, while Mary did everything in her power to counteract the senior partner's wife's condescension. They looked to Mary as their patron, not Imelda.

Someone announced dinner being served in the dining room and they all filed into a room especially set aside for the eighteen lawyers and their wives. The tables were set in a U shape, the head table set for six and two extended tables seating fifteen and sixteen guests each. The meal proceeded cordially, salad served first followed by filet mignon steak, and vegetables capped off with apple pie a la mode. The wine flowed freely and voices grew louder and louder during the meal as the group loosen up and laughter erupted as the wine worked its will. When the company finished dessert Matthew, at the head table, flanked by his wife, Blake and Doug and their wives, took a spoon and rapped a glass for attention. Michael and Mary had been seated by place card at the end of one of the two tables, a clear sleight, and breach of protocol when they should have been seated at the head table, Michael being a senior partner. It did not go unnoticed by the gathering. Mary speculated it had been done by Imelda, who despised she and Michael because they'd never bent the knee though they were always courteous in their dealings with her. That apparently didn't satisfy her need for complete domination and subservience. Matthew told of the firm's history, personalities, longevity, and the growth in the number of lawyers. Then, in a more serious tone of voice, he said he wanted to address the firm's present status and its future. Mrs. Hamilton, sitting at his side, beamed as she looked out on her court. Blake

Collins, next to her, looked smug.

"As you all know we've just completed our retreat, and what a meeting it was, celebrating our most successful year. I have all of you to thank for that, and I want to especially thank Blake Collins and Doug Phelps who have contributed mightily to our success with their hard work and loyalty. We would never have been to accomplish what we did without their efforts. I am looking forward to working with them and all of you to make 1997 even a greater success and for the firm to prosper in the years ahead. He sat down midst applause. Blake leaped to his feet and said:

"Matthew, we couldn't have done it without your leadership, we thank you for the inspiration you've given to all of us."

Michael and Mary kept staring at the head table, knowing full well they had just been dismissed before the entire firm. All present understood the slight. No one, except the partners and their wives knew exactly why Matthew ignored Michael and his contributions to the firm, but they knew enough to realize Michael was out and Blake was in with Matthew. Michael felt like he'd been sucker punched in the stomach without warning, made to look like a fool before his peers. The tragedy of it all—the necessity to pile on after his defeat in the partnership meeting. For himself, he could take it, for Mary she didn't deserve the humiliation. They sat with smiles on their faces to stunned to do anything else. He'd given his all for the firm and this was his reward. After Blake sat down, Matthew invited everyone back to his suite for drinks.

"Let's skip it," Mary said, "we don't owe that hypocrite anything."

"No, my thinking has always been when they hit you never let them have the satisfaction of knowing they've hurt you. Oh, they know you'll hit back but they are never sure when and pretty soon they relax. That's when they are ripe for picking."

"All right I'll go; I'm not sure how I will act."

At the party, it soon became evident many in the firm sensed the change and only a handful could be seen talking with Michael or Mary who gave no sign of the wound they had suffered. After a respectable time they left and the drinking crowd stayed until early in the morning. Blake and Doug Phelps were still basking in their new found celebrity as number two and three in the firm.

On their way back to their room they held hands and Michael said: "Listen, sweetheart, we'll take our licks, but we can't be defeated; we're way too tough for that. When we get back to town we'll sit down and talk this whole thing through and decide what's next for us."

"I know you're right," Mary said softly. It really hurts to have been betrayed by those you did so much for."

When they got to their room they fell into each others arms, forgetting for a while the public humiliation they had just endured.

. . .

The annual year end meeting, scheduled for December 5, would not take place for another two months. So on their return to the city Michael and Mary talked through the whole episode at the retreat and searched the past to see where the relationship with Blake and Matthew started to deteriorate. Putting together all the events and episodes going back three years they surmised the problem arose when Michael began asserting himself as a senior partner and laying out his vision for the growing firm. At first it met with Matthew's approval and enthusiasm; as time went on and Blake began to work closely with Matthew and the municipal work flourished with the state's booming economy, Blake began to drive a wedge between Michael and Matthew, apparently vying for "position" from which he could dictate firm policy, and with it, distribution of profits. His view conflicted with Michael's in that profits came first the firm second. In such a contest the winner is inevitably greed. The problem facing him: what to do in the face of overwhelming opposition to his views. In their initial conversation, after the retreat meeting,

Michael J. Walsh

Michael and Mary reviewed their situation. They had four children, Jack thirteen, Sharon 11, Peter 9 and Kathryn 7, a good size mortgage and their first child ready for high school. The early years with the firm had been difficult financially, but Mary had managed to make a dollar walk around the block; later years proved far more profitable and they began to build a substantial financial base. In 1993 the firm had its best year and Michael decided to invest in the stock market. Through a good friend at a local brokerage he placed six thousand dollars in a broker's possession to invest as he thought best. The broker, Jeremy Bonds, bought six thousand dollars worth of stock in an initial offering of a Cable Company. The stock split eight times within a short time and produced thousands of dollars in gain. By 1995 Michael had an investment account worth over a million dollars. If they had to leave the firm they knew they had enough resources to carry them forward until he could re-establish himself.

"We've got two months until the December fifth annual meeting and I'm inclined to wait until that meeting to see what the environment is. If Matthew and Blake are intent on a force out, they'll make it clear, and I'll know what I have to do. Matthew's been talking about space in the new Armstrong building which means a large expenditure for furniture, equipment and a higher fee for square footage then we pay now. He's also asked to draft a new partnership agreement. I'm definitely opposed to taking on more office space for the sake of show and if the agreement makes the litigation side of the firm second cousins, I would have no choice but to leave. But I see no point alerting those fellows to our thinking now. If we go we'll have to think about business I could take with me and how to go about it."

"Michael, I think it wise we presume you will have to leave and you'll be on your own. You're a great lawyer, you've proved that and you will make it no matter what happens. If you make the decision on December fifth, we still have to the end of the month to plan for

152

the New Year and I will certainly keep working to help us out. As far as the children are concerned, they love you and whatever we do they will be with us one hundred percent."

"I think the other consideration is: bonuses will be decided at that meeting and I don't want to prematurely jeopardize my chance of getting one. So we'll ride out the next two months and be ready to leave if there is no other option."

Michael went ahead with his cases and trials showing no resentment after the events at the October retreat. As far as Matthew, Blake and Phelps were concerned Michael had been whipped, had fallen into line and would make no more fuss over direction of the firm. They based their thinking on the fact the firm was making so much money Michael would never for a minute consider leaving such a profitable situation. They were courteous but condescending. The rest of the firm, particularly the associates and administrative personnel, treated him with the respect he had always enjoyed.

Just before thanksgiving Matthew called Michael and asked him to come to his office immediately. Thinking something important had come up, he got up from his desk and walked down the hall to Matthew's elaborately furnished office. Once in the room, Matthew began shouting at him: "I think you've been conspiring against me for a long time and I'm sick and tired of it."

Taken aback, Michael shot back: "I don't know what you're talking about, can you be specific?"

"I don't have to be specific you've been fighting me for a long time," he shouted, his face flushed.

Michael, had no idea what he was talking about and denied any conspiracy, professing ignorance as to the accusation. The tirade continued and Michael headed for the door saying in a loud voice: "This guy is absolutely crazy!" He returned to his office shaken and sat as his desk pondering Matthew's unexplained outburst. He half expected him to come down the hallway to apologize but that didn't materialize. "This cannot go on," he said to himself, Blake has this fellow's ear, or he's starting lose it in the gray matter. Either way this is intolerable." That night he told Mary of the Matthew's irrational confrontation, and she felt, while Blake's influence may have caused Matthew's unsolicited rant for no apparent reason, the man exhibited psychotic behavior and as far as she was concerned it amounted to the last nail in the coffin. But she said nothing to her husband knowing full well he was terribly upset by the outburst, which attacked his integrity and loyalty to the firm, something he had given unstintingly.

On December fourth, the night before the partnership meeting, Michael and Mary called the children into the living room and briefed them on what the stakes were for the next day. They all took it calmly but from the looks on their faces it was apparent they knew their lives could change if Michael left the firm. They loved and trusted their parents, so from the oldest to the youngest they asked no questions and merely said: "Dad we're with you whatever you do."

After the meeting with the children Michael laid out his plan for the meeting the next morning. If, by some miracle, they decided not to sign a new lease for office space and the partnership agreement proved not too onerous to sign, he would remain with the firm long enough to work out his next move. If not, he'd inform his partners of his intention to dissolve the partnership. Mary said she understood, and without betraying the anxiety she felt, said she would be standing by the phone awaiting the outcome.

The meeting, scheduled for eight thirty December fifth, took place at Matthew's club, which he'd recently been invited to join. Seventy five years old, the club enjoyed the reputation as the most prestigious in the city. Michael had been invited to the club as a guest many times but never had any interest in joining. Shortly after Matthew became a member he moved, within a respectable time, to have Blake inducted as a new member with the firm paying initiation fees and dues.

Just as he invariably did for trial, Michael arrived early to survey the field. The manager directed him to a private room set up for the breakfast meeting with waiters standing by awaiting the guests arrival. They exchanged pleasantries and Michael sat down at a round table covered with a white table cloth, glistening crystal glasses and silverware.

"Coffee sir?"

"Yes, Please."

A waiter poured a steaming cup of black coffee; Michael swallowed and enjoyed the first taste of the brew. He looked around the room noting heavily framed pictures of English gentry and rural scenes of the country. A glass chandelier added to the formality of the room with its dark mahogany walls. Coming into such a room could have been intimidating to some but Michael had been in many such rooms in clubs all over the country where he stayed while trying cases. He felt very comfortable and calm considering the fact he was on the verge of severing a connection he loved and had taken pride in from the time be began practicing law. He smiled. He felt just like he always did when the potential jury came into the courtroom, took their seats and prepared for the voir dire; (questioning of the jurors) highly alert, aware of everything and everyone around him, ready for combat, having fully prepared, not only his own case, but that of his opponents.

Cormack O'Neil, the first to arrive, looked dapper and obviously pleased with his status as a new partner with an increased share of the profits. He and Michael chatted amiably as if the meeting to take place was just another meeting. Cormack seemed in high spirits. Within minutes the other partners arrived and took seats around the table, Matthew directly across from Michael and Blake on his left. The waiters received a signal from Matthew and immediately eggs, bacon, Danish, sausage, potatoes, on warm plates and orange juice and coffee arrived from the kitchen. He ate slowly and listened to the chatter around him; the partners were in a good mood and as far as they were concerned trouble had been avoided to everyone's relief and the firm would go forward with the future looking brighter than ever. Michael had had his say, and having lost seemed prepared to "go along to get along."

By nine fifteen plates were cleared away and Matthew called the meeting to order. When he had everyone's attention he reached into his briefcase, sitting beside his chair, and brought out a stack of documents. He passed two documents to each partner and said: "I'm handing you a copy of the new lease for our move to the Armstrong building and a new partnership agreement which contains profit percentages and all the items we agreed to at our October retreat. I'd like us to take a few minutes to read each document and then let's discuss them. Fifteen minutes went by as each man slowly read the documents, some making notes in the margins. Matthew, who had drafted the agreement, and was familiar with the text ordered more coffee and sat back to watch the partners reaction.

For Michael's part, he had no intention of signing the lease so he turned his attention to the partnership agreement. Half way through he knew he would not be signing it. He expected the agreement to set out the shares discussed at the October meeting. He was not prepared for clause thirteen—voting rights. That clause gave voting rights on partnership decisions to the number of points held by the respective partners which meant the municipal partners would have a voting plurality of fifty eight to forty two which in turn meant the municipal partners would favor their specialty to the neglect of the rest of the firm. Michael realized if the firm's biggest client, the municipal business, faced competition from one or more firms the firm would be in danger of collapse. He saw that danger and had articulated it as clearly as possible at the October meeting. After each partner signaled he'd read the documents Matthew asked for comments. Blake spoke first stating he thought the two documents pretty much set out his understanding and he, for one, could sign them. On cue Doug Phelps chimed in saying, "ditto."

Each man followed Blake's lead and volunteered they would be prepared to sign as Blake indicated.

Michael said nothing and Matthew thinking he had unanimity pronounced: "Well gentlemen that does it, if we all agree we might as well put our signatures on the agreement and I'll notify the leasing agent we're prepared to sign the lease."

"This partnership is dissolved gentlemen!" Michael heard himself say. Matthew, with a stunned look on his face said: "What did you say?"

In a strong calm voice Michael repeated: "This partnership is dissolved, I will not be signing the agreement. I see no point reiterating what I've argued in the past."

For a moment, perhaps fifteen seconds, no one said a word. Shocked at what they heard. The first to speak, Cormack O'Neil, sounded like he had a bone stuck in his throat. "Oh no, Michael don't say that, we need you more than ever!" The other litigation partners found their voices and said his leaving would hurt the firm and himself. "Everybody loses," they said. Michael heard Blake gasp when he made his announcement, yet he said nothing. Doug Phelps, realizing Michael's arguments in October had been right and harm could come to the firm in the months or years ahead tried to play the role of peacemaker urging Michael to take twenty four hours and think about it. Matthew quickly took advantage of Michael's announcement, and in a hostile voice said he would begin drafting the necessary papers claiming it amounted to a "withdrawal" and asked when he intended to leave. Michael told him, "December thirty first."

The meeting immediately broke up and by the time they reached the front door of the club, it was evident the partnership had received a blow. Some were sad and alarmed; they felt Michael had been loyal to the firm and kind to each of them. Of all the partners, Matthew and Blake had adjusted to the reality and by the time they left the club they had hardened their hearts and accepted the dissolution as beneficial. He walked out with the partners but half way back to the office excused himself saying he had to go to the court-house a few blocks from the club. He made a beeline for the nearest public telephone. He thought he should be sad and depressed, he told himself, but to the contrary, he felt euphoric freed from the tremendous burden he had been carrying consciously and subconsciously. All he wanted to do now was call Mary and give her the word he would be leaving the firm and when. He felt so excited he had to calm himself down to dial the number. He heard it ring three times and then Mary's voice came on: "Michael," she exclaimed.

"It's me sweetheart—the deed is done. I think they were in total shock. They didn't have the slightest inkling it was coming. They obviously assumed we'd roll over and play dead."

"I don't care about them; how are you? Are you all right?"

"Believe me I feel great! I don't know how tough the future is going to be but we start a new challenge today. I've got twenty five days to find new office space, files I can take with me, law books to buy, office equipment and a secretary. I have the feeling these fellows are not going to be easy to deal with now that the applecart is upset. When it dawns on them they're liable to blame me as a renegade spoil sport and not themselves for their own folly. I can't wait to see you and I'll give you all the details."

"All right," relief sounded in her voice, once she digested the import of his message. I'll be waiting for you with open arms, come home early if you can."

He returned to the office, and as expected, not one of the partners came to his office to discuss the meeting. He realized by noon everyone in the office would have the basics of the meeting. He left the office from time to time during the day and noted the secretaries were extremely courteous, even solicitous. The four or five associates he ran into in the hallways were more than courteous; he thought he saw a look of admiration in their eyes and body language that said: "You've got guts Mr. Sullivan, we admire you." He knew he would be missed by most of the associates and office personnel because he treated everyone equally, encouraged the associates, unfailingly courteous to staff and had a dry sense of humor that made people laugh. He would miss the people yet he realized, for him, the last chapter in the firm Hamilton, Sullivan, Collins & Phelps had come to an end. To that he said: "When the Lord closes one door He opens another."

When he walked through the door that evening Mary and the children were waiting gathered about the fireplace in the living room, with a roaring fire sending out warmth. Mary brought him a scotch and he settled into an easy chair next to the fire. Rain began to beat against the floor to ceiling windows that looked out on a Japanese garden surrounded by green grass, and beyond tall fir trees forming a miniature forest. A warm setting for the story he told recalling the events of the breakfast meeting at Matthew's club. He recounted every detail he could remember from the time he entered the club until the partners left. The children listened, wide eyed. They loved their father; to them he was a great hero still they were old enough to know he had been hurt badly and at their young ages they found it difficult to understand why anyone would treat their father in such a fashion.

From the time Jack and Sharon were four and two they went to the office on Saturdays. They looked forward to it at the end of each week. Michael prepared cups of hot chocolate and sometimes he let them speak into his Dictaphone and play back their voices to their screeching delight at hearing their own voices. Often they wandered into other offices of partners or associates working on the weekend and asked them questions much to their amusement. Matthew gave them mail and asked them to deliver it to the various offices. When Jack and Sharon got older he'd take them down to the library, give them yellow legal pads to draw on while he worked on briefs. At three or four in the afternoon they all came home and the children told Mary of all they'd done and who they talked to. As the firm grew in numbers they understood their father was a senior partner, a trial lawyer and they were proud of him and all he and their mother had accomplished. As he told the story of the meeting they knew their lives were about to change and their father had lost his job.

Mary felt both relief and concern for she knew his life had been miserable the last two years as he watched the change and those men he brought into the firm go in a different direction—a direction he believed set a course for disaster. But now it had come to an end. They would start again and she knew success lay ahead because her faith remained unbounded, both in herself and Michael. In her own way she was the rock on which the family relied. Michael expressed doubts from time to time. She never gave failure a chance to gnaw at her. The future remained bright, and her fearlessness carried Michael and the children through many crises and they loved her for her quiet strength.

After the children were in bed they sat before the fire holding hands talking softly. Already he brimmed with ideas; he admitted fear but knew movement the key to avoid freezing up. One of his first moves would be to fly to Los Angeles to secure Boniface insurance company's business brought to the firm by Cormac O'Neil and which Michael controlled as head of the firm's trial section. If he could keep this client it would provide a base upon which a new firm might be constructed. John Kennedy placed a great deal of business with the firm as well as a considerable amount of litigation. If Kennedy went with him rather than Matthew, he would have to hire at least four new lawyers just to service Kennedy Enterprises. He realized Matthew would not sit still and let those clients go with him without a fight to the death. Therefore he felt it imperative to contact his clients as soon as possible to alert them to the break and the choice they would have to make. Go with him or stay with the firm? Mary encouraged him to go to Los Angeles and fight for the insurance account. Michael carried the firm's insurance litigation, without him, Matthew would be at a disadvantage trying to hold that business. The same held true for Kennedy. At the end of the conversation their spirits lifted, knowing they had the wherewithal to found a new firm. They went to bed and had the first peaceful sleep they'd had in months.

CHAPTER 16

The following day Michael booked a flight to Los Angeles to meet with Robert Northcutt, head of Boniface Auto Insurance Company. Friday that same week he sat in the company's reception room waiting for a ten a.m. meeting with Northcutt who he knew and had worked with on numerous big cases in which he'd won spectacular defense verdicts saving the company millions of dollars in claims.

"Matthew has already been on the phone to us Michael," he announced, as they shook hands and Northcutt led him back to his office on the seventeenth floor overlooking Wilshire Boulevard. The executive was short and squat, sporting red suspenders and a short crew haircut. His outfit belied the man's confidence in himself. He had risen rapidly in the ranks of the company through sheer bravado, nerve and calculated daring. He took risks but not outlandish ones. He'd saved the company millions by knowing when to hold them (go to trial) and when to fold them. (settle the case) Part of his success he owed to Michael Sullivan's skill as a trial lawyer. "Matthew says the firm is best suited to handle our account." He said you're just a solo attorney now."

They sat on a sofa in Northcutt's office facing each other and he continued to speak: "I can't make a decision now Michael but if you give me a good argument, I'll bring it to the board of directors. We are talking business here, not friendship."

Very calmly, in a resolute manner, Michael stated why he should keep the account and could do the job the firm could not. He explained, while the firm had trial lawyers, they had nowhere near his experience. Moreover, he had his eye on a young lawyer his own age, Paul Connolly he intended to have as a partner who happened to be one of the best trial lawyers in the city. If awarded the business they would hire additional lawyers to service the account. He would personally give the account his full attention as his firm's second biggest account, Kennedy Enterprises being the first.

"Do you have the Kennedy account now?" Northcutt interrupted. He knew the reputation of Kennedy Enterprises and if Michael had that account, his new firm would have a solid footing.

"I don't have it yet, however I will be talking with John this afternoon and I will have an answer to your question before I leave Los Angeles tonight. Michael summed up his argument saying he had worked with Northcutt for ten years, "I think I've proved myself."

"Get back to me with the Kennedy decision. It will carry significant weight with the board. In the meantime for my money, you have the account and you continue to work with me. But it's not that simple. Not too many of the people I work with here are big risk takers. In many ways I can make the argument we should go with you, or if not you, some other firm. I don't have that much confidence in Matthew Hamilton without you in the firm. There's no point in wasting time, if you're to keep the business you should know right away. I'll put together a conference of decision makers Monday morning and I should have an answer for you Monday afternoon."

With that the meeting came to an end with a friendly close. "No matter how this turns out Michael, I wish you the best of luck if you don't make it with us."

He got in his rental car and headed out Sepulveda Boulevard to Los Angeles International Airport. He didn't know if he'd secured the insurance account with his presentation; he realized if he had not come it would go to some other law firm based on Robert Northcutt's comment about Matthew and the firm's chances of keeping the account. If he didn't get it Matthew wouldn't either.

In his mind that justified the trip. He turned in the rental car and went to United Airlines to await his flight. He called John Kennedy at a special number Kennedy had furnished him with where could be reached day or night. He called. Kennedy answered. Michael proceeded to advise him of the break up, why it occurred and that he intended to leave the firm and set up his own firm. That he (Kennedy) would be asked if he wished to continue to use the firm as his lawyers or go with Michael in the new venture. When he finished explaining everything Kennedy said: "Michael My business and my personal affairs stay in your hands. If you have to hire more lawyers to handle Kennedy enterprises I'll make sure you have the wherewithal to do that. Furthermore I will not wait to hear from Matthew Hamilton; I will call him when I hang up with you and advise him my business and files should be sent to you. Is that all right with you?"

Taken aback Michael could only say: "John, thanks for your trust. I appreciate you're taking a risk putting all your business with me when I'm just forming a new firm. You won't be sorry."

"I don't consider it a risk Michael, I've got the best lawyer in the state and thankful for it. I'm with you all the way. Also I'll call Northcutt at the insurance company in Los Angeles and tell him I'm your client and he would be wise to have you as his attorney. I'm in Madrid and about to catch a plane for London but as soon as we hang I'll make those calls. Good luck."

True to his word Kennedy called Northcutt with his recommendation and before Michael boarded the plane for home Northcutt called Michael and said: "Boy you work fast. I just heard from the famous John Kennedy singing your praises. Believe me that is going to play well with my Board. We won't be meeting on Monday, it couldn't be arranged but I'll call you as soon as I have a decision. Merry Christmas."

"Thanks for the call Robert and a Merry Christmas to you and yours."

The Firm

That week end Michael and Mary felt apprehensive; Kennedy Enterprises gave the firm a solid start, yet to insure continued growth, they needed an affirmative answer from Robert Northcutt of Boniface Insurance on Monday. If he gave a negative answer it meant a rough start. They knew Michael would retain most of his individual clients, but that business could be sporadic. Without two major clients, like Kennedy Enterprises and Boniface Insurance it might take years to build a new practice.

Michael had known and tried two cases against Paul Connolly, a talented trial lawyer in the firm of Kelley & Dunstin. Forty years of age, quick on his feet, knowledgeable of the rules of evidence and quick to see the essential issue in a case Connolly would make a perfect match with Michael's skills. He too had gone to Georgetown University law school graduating a year after Michael. If he secured the insurance company he intended to approach Connolly suggesting they form a partnership. This carried risk, Connolly might not turn out as expected, leaving Michael vulnerable, still he dismissed this as an extremely remote possibility. He'd seen enough of Connolly to make a judgment; he'd recruited and hired most of the associates at Hamilton, Sullivan so he felt confident in his judgment of lawyers.

Over cocktails they discussed the situation. Always upbeat, Mary offered encouragement telling Michael; "I think you're going to get the account, getting Paul Connolly to come with you may prove more difficult. I know his wife Teresa from the Junior League, we've never been on any committees together, but I do know she's a tremendous worker. She's a "go getter," and from everything I've heard a responsible wife and Mother. They have two children in grade school."

"I got Blake Collins to come to the firm and that took a lot of cultivating, to our detriment, but it's ten years later and I've built enough of a reputation in the legal community and the trial bar that a man like Paul might jump at the chance. He's one of thirty five lawyers in his firm and strikes me as the kind of a fellow who would like to strike out on his own. If it's good news on Monday, I'll have him on the phone Tuesday."

They admitted to each other they were scared about the future. Fifteen years building a law firm and suddenly finding yourself cut loose was frightening. Their faith made the difference. Their faith was the essence of simplicity: based on an unshakable belief in God and the role they must play in the scheme of things. Their parochial school upbringing taught them their role was to know, love and serve God above all. They were of the world and must contend with it every day—this they realized—and they knew they would not be alone. That always, God walked with them and they did His will as it was revealed to them. Pope John Paul II said at the outset of his papacy, "Do not be afraid." They took that philosophy literally to mean: "Do not be afraid I will be with you until the end of your days." This faith gave them an underlying confidence to keep moving forward each day, a new day a new opportunity. Work hard and things will turn out for the best. Mary had a saying she attributed to Father Junipero Serra, founder of the missions in California: "Always look forward, never look back."

Robert Northcutt called Monday and advised Michael the board had postponed the meeting; he would have an answer in about a week.

. . .

Christmas Eve, December 24, 1996, sitting in his office at Hamilton, Sullivan, Collins & Phelps, with just a few lawyers still around, and the partners gone Michael dictated into a machine as he thumbed through files letting clients know the status of their cases and his plans to leave the firm. A light snow fell outside and he could see it accumulating on the streets. He made a mental note to get down to the parking garage in the next hour or face spending the night in town, or worse, in his office. The phone rang. "Michael?"

"Yes, speaking."

"Merry Christmas Kid, I've got a present for you."

"Robert?"

"Yeah! The boys gave you the go ahead but you've only got six months. If you prove you can do the job we'll renew the option."

"Does Matthew know?"

"No. But he will. I'm saving it until after Christmas. No use ruining it for him now. I'll send a confirming letter; there'll be nothing about the option, just that we are going to retain your services."

"Quite a Christmas present Robert. I thank you and I'll work harder than I am now, if that's possible. I know you went on the line for me and it could be your neck if I don't make it. I'm not going to let that happen. In six to twelve months they'll promote you and give you a raise for giving them such good advice."

"Michael, I'll take it to the bank, I think you'll do it just like you've been doing it. You will have to hire some "savvy" lawyers because I'm going to dump a lot of tough cases on you."

"All right, I'm moving the operation to the Lincoln Building and I've leased plenty of space with options on more. Stay in touch and have a great Christmas. My best to the family." He hung up and walked to the window and gazed absently at the falling snow. "Thank you Lord," he said softly, thoughts already racing through his brain, the first to contact Mary, and the second to call Paul and invite him to lunch. He returned to his desk, trying to contain his excitement, and calmly dialed home. "Mary?"

"Michael, have you seen it outside? You've got to get out of there before you're snowed in and the children are all waiting for you to come home. It's Christmas Eve, you know?"

"Mary?"

"Yes."

"Robert Northcutt just called and said we have the Boniface account for at least six months and permanently if we do a good job. We're going to have a great Christmas." He heard her crying silently at the other end of the line. "Don't cry my sweetheart, it's all going to work out...I know it is."

She controlled herself and told him she was crying for joy not fear. She called it tears of relief. The pressure had been mounting since the firm meeting in October and she had done her utmost to contain her worries, trying not to show him or the children her concern for the family. Within a few minutes of the call he wrapped it up and turned his attention to driving home through, what had now become, a driving snow storm. He whistled, and sang carols in unison with the radio. The driving was haphazard, he didn't care; all he could think about was getting home and celebrating Christmas with his family. "The future is now," he thought.

They met at a little restaurant near Paul Connolly's office. Connolly, an inch taller than Michael's six feet one inch, strode into the restaurant, spied Michael already seated, moved to the table and they shook hands. Handsome in a rugged sort of way, deep set eyes, black hair, parted on the left, high cheek bones, a dimple in his chin (like Cary Grant) and thin, not skinny. Dressed in a dark gray pinned striped suit, he looked every inch a trial lawyer. They knew each other and on two occasions jousted in court. Michael winning one and settling one. In both instances Michael had been impressed with Paul's manner and his quickness on his feet. He knew the law. In Michael's view, a good trial lawyer had to be quick of mind and Paul, in his view, passed muster on that score. Once seated Michael got right to the point explaining briefly what had occurred at the firm, his plans, and the important point, he would be taking clients with him, including the Boniface Insurance Company which required more lawyer power than he could furnish on his own. He painted a picture of risk and opportunity knowing Connolly to be a junior partner in a prestigious law firm. Michael proposed a partnership.

Luncheon dishes were carried away and they engaged in a deep discussion. The last patrons left the restaurant unnoticed by the two lawyers as they continued talking. At three thirty the owner approached the table and announced the dining room closed until dinner. They adjourned to the bar still deep in conversation. At five thirty they stood and shook hands.

"Michael, I'm with you "if," and I don't know how big the "if" is, Teresa will go with me. I'm excited we can make it work."

"Let's do this Paul; you and Teresa have dinner with Mary and I tomorrow night and we'll just talk the whole thing through again with the ladies. If this ship is going to sail we want the principals on board."

"Great idea. Until tomorrow night then." They agreed, parted and went their separate ways.

The following night they met at Murphy's Irish pub both had frequented before. The men ordered tankards of Guinness Stout, the ladies, scotch and soda. Teresa O'Hara Connolly proved to be a beautiful woman, a perfect match for Paul Connolly. She had dark hair like Mary which she wore pulled back, a joyous demeanor and wore a St. John's knit that clung to her frame. She and Mary hit it off immediately, when they discovered they had come from similar backgrounds. Catholic girls high schools, Catholic Colleges, and lawyer husbands, from Georgetown. Teresa and Paul had two children, Peter and Samuel ages five and six. Like Mary she had been in the Junior League and did the same kind of charitable work Mary had been engaged in with the League. The two couples talked until midnight and like the conference between the men, the bartender had to tell the four of them the pub was closing. They sealed the deal at midnight. Sullivan & Connolly, a new "firm" came into existence. They all saw eye to eye. Fees to be used first to pay expenses. Michael, because he had practiced longer and had a major share of the business, would be senior partner, profits shared on an equal basis, with a bonus for bringing in a major client. He to practice what he preached to his former partners.

· · ·

On New Year's Eve numerous associates came to wish Michael well and to say they would miss him, even at risk of irritating the partners. At noon the office became quiet as staff and lawyers left early to get ready to welcome in the New Year. He left his office and started to walk around the almost empty offices of Hamilton, Sullivan, Collins & Phelps and a certain nostalgia came over him. There were people he would miss, many of them his own hires. He looked out the window for the last time knowing a part of his life had come to an end. Time to move on. As he continued to take in the view he sensed a presence in the room. He turned to see Matthew standing in the door way with a strange look on his face. Before Michael could speak Matthew snarled: "It looks like you stole the Boniface Insurance Company from me."

Taken aback by the surprise and suddenness of the attack, Michael paused for just a moment before responding: "I asked to be considered just like you; they obviously thought I could do the job."

"I think they made a mistake and they will regret it." But that's not what I came for. I wanted to make sure we have a complete understanding; we will keep all the files you've worked on except those clients who want us to turn their files over to you and the same goes for wills and trusts. We, of course will be paying you your equity in the firm. Outside of that I don't think there's much to say except we disagreed and it's a shame. We will go on to build a bigger firm without you. It could have been different."

"I understand perfectly and I agree it is a shame, as far as the firm goes I wish you all the luck in the world, as far as I'm concerned things happen for the best."

Matthew Hamilton turned and left Michael's without another word.

CHAPTER 17

January 1997 began with swirling snow and cold temperatures but Michael gave no thought to the weather when he opened the door to his new office suite on the sixteenth floor of the Lincoln building. Seven o'clock in the morning; he wanted to be the first to arrive and savor the beginning of Sullivan & Connolly. Stepping back into the hall, he admired the lettering in gold above the door: "Sullivan & Connolly" and the engraved plaque on one of doors, listing two attorneys, Michael Sullivan and Paul Connolly. They were the firm but before long other attorneys would be listed on the plaque below their names. He went back into the silent reception area and looked to his right at the conference room. Small but adequate for now he thought. Bookshelves filled with legal treatises and case reports lined two walls. Prints of Paris by Michel Delacroix adorned the other walls. In the center a long table with eight captains chairs served as a conference table. A deep blue wall to wall carpet complimented the room. Proceeding down the hall to his own office he passed Paul Connolly's office and three empty offices reserved for associates still to be hired. His office, not as fancy as the offices of his former partners Matthew Hamilton and Blake Collins, looked out over the city. At seven thirty Paul Connolly came in and sauntered down to Michael's office.

"Early on the first day eh..."

"Good morning Paul," he said with a welcoming grin, "you're pretty early yourself. I made a pot of coffee get yourself a cup and sit down. Connolly accepted the invitation and cup in hand seated himself, stretched out his long legs and relaxed in his chair.

"What's the first order of business?"

"The first thing I have to do is get Maggie Thompson and the new girl she hired typing dictation I brought with me. I set up an informal docket until Maggie can get it organized and I have to be in court at nine for the Casey case set for trial next week. Do you have any cases on call?"

"Yes, two as a matter of fact, can you handle those for me before the presiding Judge?"

"Yes, I'll be glad to. I think it's a good idea if we spent a couple of minutes going over the day's events."

"Good idea, keep abreast of what each of us is doing." From that day forward the partners met each morning to coordinate events. Michael realized the key to a successful law practice involved communication between lawyers. Everyone should know, within reason, what case, client and business they were handling, if for no other reason, to avoid conflicts. They continued to follow the practice from the day they opened for business.

Just as he anticipated, cases started coming in from Boniface Auto and within four weeks, Sullivan & Connolly had enough business to secure their financial picture for the next six months. That, with ongoing Kennedy business matters, required the hiring of more lawyers. Between the two partners they were able to hire three associates, two for trial and one for business matters. All three were very experienced and about to make partner in their respective firms but chose to go with Michael's new firm for the reasons that motivated Paul Connolly. With the addition of a book keeper and two new secretaries they expanded into the extra space Michael had planned for. After the first week he completely forgot the painful breakup of Hamilton, Sullivan, Collins & Phelps. That was history, Sullivan & Connolly would make history.

Michael worked as hard as he had ever worked, the difference being he now worked for his own firm. It was solely up to he and Paul whether the practice soared or failed. The fact so many of his individual clients, he acquired over the years, moved their files to his new firm, he found gratifying although he wouldn't learn until later, Matthew and Blake were shocked at the amount of business they lost when Michael left the firm.

One of the first pieces of business Michael turned his attention to after leaving Hamilton, Sullivan was the trust litigation between the sisters and the trustee of the Barney Rushing trusts. Attorneys for both sides were gearing up for the battle of titans, between Ritter, Bellini & Swartz, the Denver firm hired by Michael as co-counsel and the Brownstein firm representing the trustee. Michael scheduled a deposition of Howard McNaughton, the trustee, for late march 1997 in Los Angeles and decided to handle it along with an associate from Ritter, Bellini & Swartz. In preparation he had several conferences with the Morrises and Sheila's other two sisters. Through discovery, Austin Biene, the attorney with Ritter firm in Denver, obtained e-mails, correspondence, notes, stock and bond orders that had passed between trustee and his financial advisors. These were turned over to Michael and he poured over them every night in his office looking for clues that would lead to a breach by Howard McNaughton of his fiduciary duty as trustee. In his search he discovered a letter the trustee had written to a hedge fund, Bancock Inc. directing the sale of a certain security. He knew an investment of any of the trust's assets in such a fund would be a breach of duty. Austin Biene hired a private investigator to find out everything possible about the fund, its principal assets, track record, and what duties the fund performed for the trustee. Within a week a report came back to Biene. He noted the fund was located in Las Vegas and the principals had dubious, though not criminal backgrounds. The fund itself held investments in bundled second mortgages, junk bonds and legitimate securities of which the mortgages and bonds were "high risk" investments. Biene passed all this information on to Michael just before he flew to Los Angeles with an associate from Ritter, Bellini & Swartz.

Although the deposition would not be taken until Monday morning, Michael and the associate, Alfred Tonkin, arrived in Los Angeles Saturday morning to set up a one room law office in their hotel suite. Michael in one room working on questions for the deposition and the associate in another room he converted into a law library. They worked all Saturday, framing questions, revising, discussing and then revising again. By late that night the various phases of approach were worked out and Michael knew he was ready, leaving all day Sunday to study and set up the format for his questions. To Michael the taking of depositions took on the importance of the trial itself; he used it as a means to size up a witness and get the witness on the record where he had to testify the same way he testified in the deposition. If at trial he tried to change his testimony, Michael stripped him bare on cross examination. Alfred Tonkin had never been to Los Angeles so after they had breakfast Sunday morning Michael told him to take the day off and enjoy himself. Michael went to mass at the Church of the Good Shepard in Beverly Hills and once there he forgot all about the deposition instead concentrating on the mass.

As a grade schooler he served as an altar boy, and since he did so after Vatican II, he didn't have to memorize Latin responses like his father did in the thirties. From his days in grade school he had grown to love the mass which Catholics recognized as a re-enactment of the Last Supper when Christ created communion. When he grew older and traveled throughout the United States and later Europe he marveled the mass remained the same; it might be said in French at Notre Dame, Spanish in Madrid or Italian in Rome but always the same and celebrated twenty four hours a day in some part of the world. For an hour he listened to the sermon, knelt, stood sat and received communion. For Michael the mass became an important part of his life—it gave meaning to life.

When he arrived back at his hotel he decided to call Mary and fill her in on his situation and find out how she and the children were doing.

"The children are just fair, Jack and Sharon have come down with the flu and Peter and Kathryn are trying to comfort them and miffed at me for trying to keep them away from the two older ones. How is the case shaping up?"

"Really great. I've come across some documents that could cause a breakthrough and I'll know better after I take Howard McNaughton's deposition tomorrow. Al Tonkin is with me; he's been working his tail off on a legal brief so I gave him the day off and only God knows when I'll see him again short of nine a.m. tomorrow." They talked for another half hour and when he hung up he sat back on the bed and mused to himself, what a great wife he had and four wonderful kids. Knowing she and the children were all right had a calming effect on him, so much so that by nine o'clock he had put on his pajamas and fallen sound asleep, no longer concerned about tomorrow's challenge.

When he and Al Tonkin arrived at opposing counsel' office in downtown Los Angeles, they were greeted by the court reporter he had hired to transcribe the deposition and the three sat chatting for a few minutes before a secretary appeared and asked them to follow her to a huge conference room that looked out on the sunny skyline of Los Angeles. The sun rose like a ball of fire in the east backed by a pure blue sky. Howard McNaughton sat at the table with a number of lawyers sitting on either side of him. As each introduced themselves, Michael took their measure. All were from the Denver firm representing the trustee with Melvin Osgood the lead defense attorney. Michael's quick take on Osgood, who he had not met before, could be summed up as one of wariness. The man looked his age, crafty, experienced and a competent trial lawyer. He dressed impeccably with thinning hair and looked in the range of fifty five to sixty. To have him present meant the opposition considered this to be one of the most, if not the most, important depositions to be taken in the case. Perhaps even crucial.

Sitting directly across the table from the witness, Michael addressed him in a non-threatening manner, noting they had met previously at his office in Marina del Rey, followed by a series of questions concerning origination of the three trusts, how he became trustee of all the trusts, if and who he had chosen to use as financial advisors, and how the assets had been invested during the term of the trusts. McNaughton grew more and more confident as the deposition proceeded. At the two and a half hour mark Michael asked offhandedly if any of the trust advisors had suggested any but conservative investments.

"No they did not," he blurted out without thinking.

Michael struck: "Did you ever make any investments on your own in behalf of the trusts?"

McNaughton looked to Osgood on his right briefly as if to ask his counsel, "Do I have to answer this." Then said: "Yes I have."

Michael pressed: "What kind of investments?"

"Mostly bonds, municipal bonds, triple rated, that's pretty much it."

Now came the point in the deposition where you can win or lose the case. It became clear to Michael McNaughton had become apprehensive on the line of questions being asked and he could see Osgood had a look in his eye that could foretell a guided missile on the way yet he had no grounds to object until he heard the question and certainly no time to warn his client because he had no knowledge that Michael wasn't just fishing. (looking for an incriminating answer) Michael never asked a question he didn't know the answer to. He didn't fish or hope the witness would be unlucky and disclose damaging information. He never counted on the witness, he counted on his own preparation and knowledge of the witness.

"Did you ever invest trust assets in a hedge fund?"

Stammering, clearly shaken by the question, and trying to buy time for his attorney to intervene, McNaughton finally answered: "What's a hedge fund?" he asked, as though hearing the term for the first time. Melvin Osgood sat still, his face frozen, hoping against hope his client had the sense to tell opposing counsel he didn't invest in any "hedge fund," but if he did, he did so without knowledge it was a "hedge fund" and besides the trusts had profited hugely from the investment.

"A hedge fund is one that can be very profitable but carries a high risk. Most hedge funds require at least a one hundred thousand dollar investment because they only take high rollers. Do you know what a high roller is Mr. McNaughton?"

"Well, yes. It refers to somebody who places large bets."

"Like a gambler?" Michael said in a barely audible voice but loud enough for the court reporter to hear it and put in squarely in the record.

"Well, yes," he mumbled, white faced. The answer was faithfully recorded by the reporter

Michael could see McNaughton hadn't figured out he knew about his investments in the hedge fund. "Ever hear of Bancock Inc, a hedge fund?"

Osgood jumped in, sensing trouble. "I object on the grounds of relevancy. This line of questioning isn't going anywhere."

"For the record, I will be making it relevant with further questioning. You may answer Mr. McNaughton, your counsel has made his objection."

"I don't recall the name, I'm not sure I've heard of it."

Michael continued in an unperturbed voice: "It's located in Las Vegas, Nevada."

Again Osgood objected forcefully: "He says he can't recall counsel. Any questions you ask about it are immaterial"

Michael looked directly at the now flustered witness and hit him with the next question: "Bancock Inc. is a hedge fund with a billion dollars; it manages for selected clients. Does that refresh your recollection?"

"Now that you mention it, I think I've heard of it." Osgood sat silent, realizing what was coming, his only hope now: his client would not lie.

Michael pounced: "Have you invested your own funds in this hedge fund?"

"Well, yes, I might have."

"You would surely remember if you invested one hundred thousand dollars would you not?"

"Yes I believe I did." Osgood breathed a silent sigh of relief believing the hurdle had been cleared.

"Did you make a good profit from your investment?" Michael posed innocently.

Thinking he had passed the test McNaughton said confidently: "Now that you've reminded me I believe I made a phenomenal return, twenty or twenty five percent."

"Based on that success did you decide to invest trust funds in that fund?"

"Well I might have."

"Did you in fact send a letter to the Bancock fund directing them to invest five hundred thousand of trust monies into their fund?"

"I don't recall such an order."

Michael deftly slid a sheet of paper to the witness and to Osgood, after having it marked as plaintiffs exhibit 1 for deposition. "Does that refresh your recollection Mr. McNaughton?"

The witness stared at it unbelievingly. Osgood had looked at it and stared impassively straight ahead. Before he could answer, Michael added authoritatively: "That letter has been authenticated by Bancock and they retain a copy of it."

Defiantly McNaughton answered, his jaw muscles twitching: "Well, yes I did invest in that fund and it produced a handsome return for the trust."

Michael cut him off: "That fund is high risk, is it not, regardless of the result?"

"Well, yes it is but it was well worth it and again the trusts benefited from it."

Quickly, Michael moved on to other points, pointless as far as he was concerned and done merely to surround the hedge fund answers with nonrelative information. The goal had been accomplished, the damage done with the defendant admitting to investing trust funds in a risky hedge fund. That amounted to a prima facie case of breach of fiduciary duty. With the deposition concluded Michael and Alfred got up, thanked the grim faced attorneys on the other side of the table and took their leave.

"Let's take a cab to LAX Al, we got what we came for."

"Brilliant, Brilliant, Mr. Sullivan, I couldn't have done it better myself."

Michael eyed him with mock displeasure. "Just kidding, just kidding," the associate added.

Four hours later Michael sat in his office content with the knowledge the burden of proof in Morris v. McNaughton, had shifted to the defendant. On Monday Michael called the Morrises to fill them in on the deposition and his belief it went well.

"I don't know if you're invested in hedge funds or junk bonds; if you are, that's ok. For the trustee to invest Sheila's money it's not ok and that's what he's done. The fund in Las Vegas pools investor's money but does not register with the Securities and Exchange Commission. There is no protection for the investor from the state or federal government. I think Mr. McNaughton is vulnerable on the issue we're trying to sink him on. What I really want to discuss is the trial set for three weeks from now. The Denver attorneys will be coming to my office for strategy and final preparation and I think Sheila and her sisters should be on hand for any client decisions that have to be made."

The Morrises listened carefully and Talbot said: "It sounds like you struck gold on the deposition, does that put us in the driver's seat?"

"Yes and no." Michael replied carefully: "It gives us a real wedge but they have plenty to defend him with. But yes, I think it puts the monkey on their back to show the fellow faithfully administered the trust on behalf of the beneficiaries. We'll review the whole case next week when everyone is here."

"All right," Sheila said, "I'll make sure my sisters are here for the conference next week in your office. I assume you will notify them they should come and give a time and place. Same for us." Michael assured them he would send a letter that day.

. . .

Friday, the follow week, Michael and Paul, with their clients, Sheila and her sisters, Abigail and Gretchen and Arthur Biene, from the Ritter firm in Denver met in Sullivan & Connolly's conference room at ten a.m. Michael announced the agenda. First he reviewed the results of Howard McNaughton's deposition. Arthur Biene outlined the impact of statements made by the deposed and the law that applied to such statements. He pointed out McNaughton sounded shifty, evasive and in some cases an outright liar. Thus his veracity could be attacked. Second he made a grievous admission he invested beneficiary funds in a hedge fund. Michael discussed the evidence and exhibits to be presented at trial and Paul concluded with the legal brief that would be submitted to the court at trial. Instead of taking a break for lunch, Michael had lunch brought in and they reviewed with the witnesses what they would be asked on direct examination and what to expect on cross examination or if called as a hostile witness. (Putting an opposing lawyer's witness on the stand so he can be cross-examined before having a chance to give direct testimony to his own attorney.) Arthur Biene expressed cautious optimism. He added the Judge hearing the case in Denver might not view McNaughton's admissions as dispositive as he did, which can always happen when a case is tried.

As the time approached four in the afternoon, Michael summarized the case as he saw it and said he wanted to suggest a new tact. Having spent the whole day preparing them for trial, he had decided to come at the problem from a different angle. He started slowly so they could adjust to a different approach. "I think Melvin Osgood of the Bernstein firm is smart enough to realize Howard McNaughton's deposition has created a serious problem for their client. Still, he is one of the best litigators the Brownstein firm has, and that firm likes to win. I have a hunch He knows he could lose because of his client's behavior and might like to get out of the case without losing face. The way out for him is to settle the case. It will take some enticement—an amount of money that would give him and the firm some bragging rights."

Arthur Biene, interrupted: "Excuse me Michael but I think we can win this thing there's no need to give them anything."

"Let him finish, Arthur," Talbot Morris interjected impatiently. "Hear him out, then we can discuss it."

"I did jump the gun Michael, I'm sorry, Please continue," He nodded at Talbot acknowledging his admonition.

Michael continued: "My thought is to offer a million dollars and go up to two million, if necessary, to settle the case."

An audible gasp went up from the assemblage but before they could voice objections, he calmly proceeded to outline his thinking. "If we should win, they would appeal. That's costly. If we lose we will undoubtedly appeal and I think ultimately be upheld on the law, however an appeal is time consuming and expensive. I'm sure McNaughton's attorney, Melvin Osgood will advise against settling; by the same token, after that deposition, McNaughton's not going to be looking forward to going through the same thing on the witness stand. I'm thinking he will reject his attorney's advice not to settle."

"I wasn't too enthusiastic when I heard the word "settle," said Arthur Biene, "yet you may have a point. If we make an offer will they take it as a sign of weakness?" he addressed the question to the group in general. "On the other hand the Bernstein firm may see it as a way to get out of difficult case, collect some hefty attorneys fees and satisfy the client. Plus the client may be tired of litigation and harassment by the trust beneficiaries."

Michael resumed: "The settlement would include not a replacement trustee but a distribution of the trust to you, the beneficiaries, which would require the acquiescence of each of you, the trustee and more importantly the Judge's willingness to go along with the settlement and dissolution of the trusts."

They all started talking at once; Michael listened without saying a word, but the upshot turned out to be if the trusts could be dissolved and distributions made to each beneficiary in the amount of ninety million dollars, thirty million each, they would go for the settlement. The plan encompassed two elements: first, acceptance of the offer by the defendant and the Bernstein firm; second, dissolution of trust assets and sign off by the trustee, court and beneficiaries. The meeting broke up with the understanding a week before trial Michael and Arthur Biene should make an offer of a million dollars with the ultimate amount no more than two million and a condition the court agreed to a distribution of trust proceeds. They extended the offer one week before trial as Michael suggested based on the theory McNaughton would be very anxious as the trial date grew near and his clients stood to receive a ninety million on a one or possibly two million outlay.

Days before trial no response had been received from the Bernstein firm. Michael knew there had to be a response because the defendant's attorney had a duty to pass any offers on the client. He surmised McNaughton was being cagey not wanting to displease his counsel by looking too weak, but savoring the opportunity to get out of a humiliating experience as a witness, get a good deal of money in the bargain, and get rid of the harassing beneficiaries. Showing his attorneys he had no intention of giving in easily he proposed that any settlement should include payment of his attorneys fees by the trusts. McNaughton believed the beneficiaries, for their part, were not so interested in winning as they were breaking the trust, and obtaining their inheritance.

On Friday, the eve of trial, Melvin Osgood called Michael, now considered lead counsel for all the beneficiaries, and said: "We will settle for two million dollars and McNaughton's attorney fees and costs paid from the trust." He conveyed this in a patronizing manner as if to say: "We don't really want to settle this case because we think we can beat you, but to satisfy our client we are making this offer which we consider extremely generous."

"You're asking twice what we offered," Michael said in what he hoped sounded like a very surprised and disappointed voice.

"Well that's the offer, our man won't take less."

Michael knew better and asked: "What are your costs and fees in this case?"

"We've got a million in costs and fees," Osgood responded triumphantly, daring Michael to take that offer back to his clients, hoping they would balk at it. The thinking of the partners at Bernstein turned on the fact if they went to trial and won or lost, an appeal would surely follow and their fees could reach three million dollars.

Michael understood their thinking and bet on McNaughton buckling if a counter offer was made, not what they were asking, but too attractive for the reluctant Mr. McNaughton to turn down. He counted on the trustee standing up to his counsel and taking the bait.

"Ok, he answered after a purposeful pause, signifying he would take it to his clients but with feint hopes of acceptance. "It's now five o'clock here; I'll try to get a response to you by nine your time. Where will you be?"

"I'll be in my office until ten p.m. tonight. If I don't hear from you, call me tomorrow at the office at ten a.m. at the latest, and remember we've advised the court this thing is on for Monday morning. If we're going to do anything it has to be done tomorrow at the latest, because we'll be here preparing for trial Monday morning."

"So will we, but I intend to be back to you by nine." He hung up and asked his secretary to arrange a conference call with Arthur Biene and the Rushing sisters.

"It took some time Mr. Sullivan," she said apprehensively because it had taken an hour and the clock read six p.m., five p.m. in Osgood's Denver office.

Michael began: "Everyone on?" All answered in the affirmative. "Here's their offer, they want two million, we had topped out at, and they want the trusts to pay another million in costs and attorneys fees." A collective groan sounded from the listeners.

"No way," Sheila said and her sisters agreed. Talbot Morris spoke up and said: "What do you think Michael?"

"Our offer at this point is one million dollars. They've countered with two million plus fees and costs. I think they're bluffing. I'm reluctant to give them much in fees. However, we've come this far so I'd go back at them with one million five plus five hundred on fees, a total of two million versus their offer of three million. More groans.

Again, Talbot Morris asked a question. "I understand Michael's thinking Arthur what do you think?"

"I think Michael's right. Remember at our earlier conference we said offer a million but settle for two. That's essentially what Michael is suggesting. Remember two million to get ninety million is a bargain. Fortunately I think we're dealing with Howard McNaughton not his attorneys. They wouldn't settle for less than three million but unfortunately for them they have a nervous client."

"Sheila, I think we should go with our attorneys. If you have to go to trial and possible appeal, we're talking in the range of four million dollars. What do you say ladies?" he asked the sisters.

"I'd like a moment to talk it over with Abigail and Gretchen,"

The Firm

Sheila said. "Their husbands aren't here and I'm sure they would like to know what their husbands think."

"That's an excellent idea Sheila; it's now eight thirty and I told Osgood I would be back to him tonight by nine his time. Let's adjourn for a half hour and you can all talk it over and then call me back.

The clients called back after a half hour talk with their husbands. Acting as spokesperson, Sheila announced: "We're with you Michael and let's hope Howard is as weak as you judge him." They laughed at her portrayal of the trustee.

"I suggest you all stand by; Osgood will have to pass on our new offer, and assuming he can reach his client, get back to me with an answer. If they don't accept our offer, I'm telling him we will see him in court Monday morning.

The phone rang at eight fifty in Melvin Osgood's office. His papers laying on the desk in front of him ready to make any argument necessary. Personally, he felt fairly confident his offer of three million would prove too steep for Michael's clients. He barked into the phone: "Michael give me your best shot."

"They turned down your three million offer, and here's their best shot: one million five, and five for fees and costs. That's one million over our first offer! I might add your fees were a very tough sell. It would be my suggestion you take it because it's final. If it's not acceptable we'll see you in court Monday."

"Two million—that's it?"

"That's it," Michael said emphatically. And that offer is open until midnight tonight, tell your client that. I'll be sitting in my office awaiting your call."

"What if I can't locate him?"

"I repeat, the offer is on the table until twelve tonight. I'll be here."

"You're a hard man McGee, Osgood laughed. I'll track ol' McNaughton down and get back to you."

At five minutes to twelve Michael watched the clock as he had become more and more concerned the last half hour. He'd fully expected Osgood's call before the deadline.

The phone rang as the clock hand showed two minutes to twelve. "Michael, you tyrant, my guy "caved," you've got a settlement. A million five for McNaughton and five for the firm. Congratulations."

"Listen, Melvin, I did you a favor, you could have been looking for your client to pay you out of his own pocket which might prove hard to collect, and remember it all depends on the court going along with it."

"I don't think that will be a problem. He's spent hours on this case with all the motions, briefs and oral arguments, besides there are political considerations and he won't be too enthusiastic about trying the case and having to hold for one side or the other. This way everyone wins. I hope you are well paid for your work, that deposition you took of McNaughton scared the hell out of him. I think he feared the Judge might impose sanctions for fooling around with that hedge fund. We'll work with the Ritter firm on the settlement document and presentation to the court. I can't say I like the result but it's been nice dealing with you."

"The same goes for me. I'm sorry about your losing five hundred thousand in fees; maybe you can collect it from your client."

"Fat chance, Michael; the least we can say is it's over, we will have to wait for another time to try a case against each other."

CHAPTER 18

Just before the year came to an end Michael took a deposition one afternoon in the law offices of Chester, Wilson & Judge, one of the larger firms in the city. Jim Bronson represented the person deposed and after the deposition ended he asked Michael to drop by his office. Michael followed him from the conference room down to his office and once ensconced in an office chair with a cup of coffee in his hands Michael asked: "Do you want to settle the case?"

"No, not all, he said with a straight face, I'm going to kill you at trial."

Michael Laughed and said: "Jim, you didn't call me in here to tell me that."

"You're right," he admitted with a sly grin, although I will say we will probably settle this thing before it's over sparing you a beating at trial. No, I asked you to come back to the office to find out if you were aware your old firm has broken apart?"

Stunned, Michael tried to keep a poker face and said with as much calm as he could muster:

"Where did you hear that?"

"I just found out before the deposition, one of my partners got a phone call and passed it on; apparently it's all over town on the tom toms."

"No, I didn't know, what are they saying?"

"That Blake Collins and Doug Phelps pulled up stakes and took some associates with them.

Cormack O'Neil and Dudley Peterson are staying with Matthew Hamilton, and they're now known as Hamilton, O'Neil and Peterson. What's that going to do to the monopoly?"

"It's going to kill the goose that laid the golden egg," Michael replied sardonically. He got up from his chair, thanked Bronson for his hospitality, assured him they would have one last meeting before trial and another meeting to discuss settlement before trial. Just as he reached the door to leave, Bronson called out: "It's none of my business Michael, but why did you leave?"

He deemed the question impertinent, nevertheless he decided to answer: "I disagreed with the way the firm was being run and since I didn't have the votes I decided to leave and start my own firm. Best move I ever made."

"I'm sure it was, Bronson sympathized, realizing he had interesting information others did not and knew speculation would be rife why the old established firm suddenly came apart after seventy five plus years. Sullivan, one of two senior partners, just doesn't up and leave unless there is a serious problem he thought. Michael's explanation gave him the answer.

Michael could hardly wait to get out on the street and digest what he learned. His initial reaction—satisfaction in making the decision to leave the firm. "If you'd only listened to me the firm would still be in business. What a waste." Excitement turned into sadness, for the old firm had withstood the pressures of seventy five years and survived when so many others had failed. Another sensation took hold of him. Elation that he had his own firm and things happen for the best; this would be his attitude and answer if anyone asked what he thought. He had to call Mary and give her the news. It meant the end of the old and beginning of the new for themselves and Sullivan & Connolly. He reminisced, first there was the firm: Hamilton, Sullivan, Collins & Phelps now there were three, Sullivan & Connolly; Collins, Phelps and Brock; and Hamilton, O'Neil & Peterson. The king is dead he thought, "Long live the king."

On the way home he bought a couple bottles of wine and a dozen red roses. He figured they should celebrate. Celebrate what? The misfortune of others? No. They would celebrate having the guts to see a bad deal for what it was and the sense to get out before it crashed. They would celebrate their good fortune avoiding a wreck and the start, they hoped, of a new firm to take its place among the city's best law firms. Mary fixed dinner for the children so they could eat alone. The roses pleased her and she understood the significance, it was his way of saying: "we won kid, we're out of there without bitterness and our leaving is going to look pretty good; I'm sorry to say those two firms, Hamilton and Collins are going to fight each other to the death over the municipal business. They touched glasses and drank to the new firm.

. . .

In her initial interview with Michael, Shelly Brownstone told him she had gone to a naturopath in desperation to see if he could diagnose her problem. She described the office and the practitioner and said she was extremely apprehensive, even a little scared, to go but she had lost faith in the doctors she had gone to. He listened to her tale and told her he thought the device remained in her uterus and the source of her pain and suffering. He examined her said "This is your problem," with more confidence and professionality than either of the two physicians she had previously consulted. "There are remnants of the devise still embedded in you uterus. I can't take it out but I recommend you see Dr. Peter Schmidt an OBGYN I frequently refer patients to. In a few days I'm quite sure you will feel well again."

His prophecy proved correct. Dr. Schmidt confirmed the naturopath's diagnosis and removed remaining parts of the device. A few weeks later she couldn't believe the difference in her health. She told Michael she conceived her third child and chose doctor Peter Schmidt as her physician.

In reviewing the case Michael felt the Naturopath had to be a witness to describe his diagnosis of the device. Moreover, while the doctor was not a physician, his testimony would be devastating to the competence of the two doctors who had examined her and advised she had no residue from the device in her uterus. Three weeks before trial he decided to visit the Naturopath to make sure of his willingness to testify and gauge his potential as a witness. In preparation for the visit he boned up on the practice of Naturopathy. The doctor turned out to be in his early fifties. Michael had called ahead to make an appointment and on entering the doctor's office he found it unimpressive. The furniture in the waiting room looked worn and chipped and a few outdated magazines lay on a table next to four chairs. No receptionist greeted him and a bell rang when he entered. The doctor came out dressed in a shirt and tie and a pair of worn slacks. He stuck out his hand warily in greeting.

"Thank you for seeing me doctor," Michael said politely, "I won't take too much of your time," although it was apparent he had plenty of time, there being an absence of any patients waiting for his services. On first impression Michael liked the doctor, Kelley Smith. No pomposity and very courteous. He had a small nondescript office with one chair which he invited Michael to sit on. A quick perusal of the room revealed bare walls painted a light shade of green, a window looking out at a building across the street, the desk with a couple of files on it, a bookcase to the right of the desk with what look to be medical books and manuals, and a framed certificate on one wall presumably from Naturopathy school.

Michael explained the reason for his visit. In acknowledgement the doctor pulled a file from a stand up four drawer file to his left against the wall. Delving into it he explained how Shelley Brownstone had come to him, and after hearing her out he decided without hesitancy her pain came from a IUD device still in her. "She was a sick young lady and I could see she had reached a point of desperation. She told me of her experiences with doctor Richard

Phillips and doctor George Marshall and that they had made her feel stupid for complaining about a devise they assured her was no longer within her."

"What were you able to do for her?" Michael asked

"Not too much. I examined her and told her she still had parts of the IUD in her uterus causing her pain and once removed her recovery would quickly follow. I referred her to Dr. Peter Schmidt for removal of the parts remaining in her. I received a note sometime later telling me she was pregnant and thanking me for all I had done, which wasn't too much. I really felt sorry for her; those doctors fouled up, no excuse for it."

When he concluded Michael asked him if he would testify in court in her behalf and tell the story he just related. Surprisingly he had no objection. Most witnesses in his position refused to testify, especially in this case where his testimony would cast doubt on the competence of two noted doctors. The Naturopath, in Michael's opinion, could not be shaken on cross examination. He looked honest, and his voice had a calm manner, always appealing to a jury. After talking with the naturopath he decided to visit with Dr. Peter Schmidt hoping to find out more about Shelley's giving birth to the new baby and what he knew about the prior history. Schmidt was forthright and gave Michael information he knew he could use at trial. Perhaps in rebuttal. As Dr. Schmidt gave his narrative, Michael took notes on a yellow legal pad.

The night before trial Michael worked in his office preparing jury instructions to be presented to the court in the morning. The phone rang.

"Michael, Paul Castilani." Michael had tried several cases against Castilani and considered him a worthy adversary. He, and Bobby Henderson had defended doctors in at least twenty cases not losing a verdict between them. "We've talked it over with our insurance clients; we think the case is worth a hundred thousand. This is a one time offer."

Without an edge or any show of animosity in his tone Michael pointed out the complaint sought one million dollars in damages for pain and suffering, loss of consortium for the husband, Bert Brownstone, plus two million in punitive damages for what he deemed egregious conduct on the part of Castilani's client and his fellow doctor.

"That's absurd Michael. We represent two of the most noted gynecologists in the city and our expert will testify their actions in this case were perfectly reasonable and the accepted standard of care in treating Shelley Brownstone."

"I will, of course, pass your offer on to Mr. and Mrs. Brownstone and will let you know before we go to trial tomorrow. If I were you I'd prepare for trial." The minute he hung up he called the Brownstones and relayed the whole Castilani conversation to them. The defense lawyers knew sometimes a case goes on so long the plaintiff becomes exhausted so that when an offer of money comes and the chance to forego trial with all its complexities is offered, it can look extremely tempting. Shelley Brownstone was not buying. She told Michael she had been through too much pain and suffering, and the doctors should be exposed so other patients would not have to go through what she gone through for years until she screwed up her courage and went to a Naturopathic doctor.

"No Michael, let's go to trial, I would rather lose than settle for what they're offering."

The next morning Judge Randell Arthur requested the lawyers join him in his chambers before he called the jury panel. Arthur had the reputation of avoiding trial by getting the lawyers to settle. "That way no one loses," he argued, often persuasively. Castilani, spoke for the other defense lawyer reiterating his offer and the Judge urged him to make it two hundred thousand, reasoning he could save the court's time and humiliation of the two doctors charged with malpractice. To Michael he urged acceptance of the two hundred thousand settlement in view of the fact the track record for malpractices verdicts in the county were few and far between. Michael rejected the Judge's suggestion and Castilani and the other defense attorney told the Judge they doubted their clients would go above the one hundred thousand dollar offer still on the table. Shelley refused to settle.

"All right gentlemen somebody is going to lose this case. I'd make your clients well aware of that fact. I'll advise the clerk to empanel a jury. Be ready for voir dire in fifteen minutes."

They left the chambers and took up positions at their respective counsel tables facing the bench where the Judge presided. The jury box set to the right and down from the bench. Michael had arrived very early to take the table nearest the jury box so they would be able to study his clients during the course of the trial, and at the same time have a view of the defendant doctors sitting at counsel table across the room.

Each side during voir dire questioned some fifty perspective jurors. Some were dismissed for cause because the questions they answered demonstrated they could not be fair and impartial, and six were challenged peremptorily. (without cause) By the end of the day the jury had been picked and the Judge announced adjournment for the day with opening statements scheduled for the next day.

"Opening statements gentlemen," the Judge intoned. Michael had asked Shelley to dress very simply, not too showy, dignified, the mother of three, who suffered irreparably and unnecessarily. She looked very innocent and honest sitting there beside him. As her advocate he gave an impression of authority; from his questions on voir dire the jury could tell this lawyer was going to give them a competent presentation of his client's case. To an observer it would have been clear he was not intimidated by the Judge, the prominent doctors sitting across from him, their capable lawyers or the jurors themselves. At the Judge's instructions he rose slowly from his seat, requested the court's permission to address the jury and planted himself squarely facing the twelve.

Opening statements tell the jury how the story a party is about present will play out. From the outset, it is important the jury trusts the lawyer because in the statement he makes he tells them what he is going to prove and makes a covenant with them, that if at the end of the trial he's proved what he said, they must vote for his client in their verdict. It's vital they keep their commitment in mind as the trial proceeds. Some members will dare the lawyer to prove it, some will not like the lawyer but if he's proved his case most will feel his client deserved to win. Michael knew he had a sympathetic client who had undergone a tremendous ordeal as a result of trusting two doctors. By the same token he was not unaware that most people, and jurors are no exception, believe doctors above reproach, learned and not prone to mistakes like the allegation made in Shelley's case.

In a brief twenty minute speech he stressed the reliance and faith she had placed in the defendants. She believed when they told her there was nothing wrong with her they implied it all might just be in her head. He focused on the fact she felt confused and that perhaps the doctors were right. That in a desperate attempt to find the source of her ills, she went to a Naturopath, who, without fanfare or difficulty and without a tenth of the medical training the defendants had, quickly recognized the problem and solved it. He acknowledged the defendants had solid reputations for competence in the local medical community, but that doctors make mistakes, usually when they don't listen carefully to their patients. He told the jury that occurred in the present case through negligence and as a consequence his client endured four years of pain and the fear she could never have another child. Her husband had suffered as well and he too was entitled to recover damages for loss of consortium.

Paul Castalini, immaculately dressed in a gray pin striped suit, a conservative tie and black wing tipped shoes approached the jury box, stopped and pointed to the doctors at the defense table, dressed in dark blue and gray suits and said, as the jury directed their gaze at the distinguished looking physicians all in their late fifties. "These medically accomplished gentlemen are on trial today for something they are not guilty of. Their professional reputations are at stake in this trial; they have been charged with negligence in their treatment of this patient. In short they have been charged with malpractice ladies and gentlemen, the worst accusation that can be made against a physician. They have chosen to fight this charge and in the course of this trial we are going to show you they did everything they could to help Mrs. Brownstone and to the contrary their treatment was within the standard of care required of physicians in their specialty." The other defense lawyer made similar statements arguing their clients were not to blame, and in any event the plaintiff had visited their clients once and never returned. If she had returned, the chances were certain, they would have found the problem readily. Therefore she herself was negligent.

As the trial unfolded Michael called Shelley who clearly and forcefully conveyed to the jury the horror she and her husband endured during the four year old ordeal. He called neighbors and acquaintances of the couple telling of their observations of her distress and their knowledge of her visits to the physicians and her frustration they could find nothing causing her agony. Michael called the Naturopath who discovered the device as his final witness. The doctor first testified as to his credentials, education and the type of medicine he practiced. Paul Castalini came to his feet as did his fellow defense counsel objecting to further testimony from the Naturopath, arguing he was not a physician of the status of their clients and therefore did not qualify as an expert and his testimony would have no bearing on competence or non competence of their clients.

"Mr. Sullivan, your response," the Judge looked down at the plaintiff's counsel with a look of inquiry that said: "They've brought up an interesting point, and you better have an answer for it."

"My response, your honor, is the case law does not require that we produce an expert witness although I believe we have a res ipsa loquitur situation here. (The thing speaks for itself) Dr Smith, although not an MD, has sufficient medical background to describe what happened with his patient and how he diagnosed the problem. He is entitled to tell that story and it is for the jury to decide whether his testimony is creditable. I therefore respectfully request permission to continue my examination." Castalini was on his feet starting to mount further argument when the Judge cut him off. "I agree with Mr. Sullivan, he's not an expert witness, nonetheless, he's entitled to tell what he did and what he concluded, you may proceed Mr. Sullivan."

Michael proceeded to take Dr. Smith through everything that happened during , his treatment of Shelley Brownstone, and before Castalini could object, to say she had been treated shabbily. Castalini objected vehemently to his opinion being offered and asked it be stricken from the record. The Judge refused and gave defense counsel an exception if they later wished to appeal the ruling. Castalini and the other defense counsel mounted a full day and a half cross-examination of Dr. Smith, Shelley Brownstone and her husband. They could not shake them in their testimony. Castalini went one question too many at the end of his exam of Dr. Smith when he asked: "Isn't a fact doctor you have no more knowledge than I do as to whether these defendants were negligent?"

"Based on my own experience and medical knowledge, I would say they were grossly negligent in not listening to her complaints and not finding the device in her uterus."

Castalini immediately moved to strike the answer but the Judge, with just the barest hint of a smile said: "You asked the question Mr. Castalini, I'm going to let the answer stand."

Without batting an eye and maintaining a stone face Michael knew they had just scored at least a field goal with the jury which could get the case beyond a motion for dismissal.

On the third day of trial the plaintiff rested and the defense counsel were on their feet the minute the jury returned to their room. They asked the Judge to dismiss the case based on the argument Michael had failed to prove negligence and that was particularly true since he called no medical expert to testify on the issue of negligence, much less gross negligence. The Judge patiently listened for an hour to the arguments of the lawyers and then from the bench ruled he believed the evidence was sufficient to present the case to the jury and dismissed defense counsels motion.

During the recess Michael explained to Shelley and Bert Brownstone his greatest fear had been overcome by the Judge's refusal to dismiss the case. Had that occurred they would have to immediately appeal the decision. Now since Judge ruled against defendants, the case could proceed with the jury making the decision, not the Judge.

On the fourth and fifth day of trial Castalini and the other defense counsel put their doctors on the stand and each explained what they had done, how solicitous they were of the plaintiff, the fact they'd never been sued before and in Mrs. Brownstone's case felt it unfortunate but they had exercised the standard of care expected in the community. In cross examination Michael explored generally what each had done, why it had been done and as a final question why it turned out the third person to see her, a naturopath, accomplished what they could not. They were prepared for the question and each responded differently, and in Michael's opinion not enough to satisfy the jury. When the defense rested Judge Hayes asked Michael if he had any rebuttal witnesses.

Just one, your honor."

"Call your witness counsel."

"I call Dr. Peter Schmidt."

While Dr. Schmidt took the stand and was sworn in by the bailiff, Michael took out a yellow sheet of paper with writing on it and placed in front of him so it could be seen by the witness and especially the jury. To this point in the trial he believed he had made enough of a showing to make the jury look at the case carefully, in other words there existed a chance the jury would find negligence. With Dr. Schmidt the case could be nailed down or lost irretrievably. Unlike all the witnesses he had called, Schmidt had not reviewed the case with Michael before appearing as a witness. After Shelley had her baby Michael visited with Dr. Schmidt briefly and had not seen him since until he now sat in court ready to testify under subpoena. Michael had in mind the element of surprise and the doctor's honesty. If he hedged or equivocated defendants would most assuredly prevail.

Carefully Michael probed with preliminary questions. On the stand Doctor Schmitt looked impressive with his gray hair, alert eyes and obvious knowledge and honesty in his answers. The jury gave him their undivided attention. The initial questions dealt with his medical education, medical specialty, length of practice. Having established a foundation for the ensuing questions he asked:

"Dr. are you familiar with the defendants in this case?"

"Yes I am."

"How well do you know them?"

"Dr. Marshall I am slightly acquainted with. Dr. Phillips and I attended medical school together and have maintained a friendship over the years."

"Are you aware generally aware of their reputations in the medical community?"

"Yes I am."

"What is it?"

"I would say they have outstanding reputations in the medical community." (Michael winced inwardly at the answer but his face showed he expected such an answer.)

"Did you have occasion to treat Mrs. Brownstone in the last year?"

"Yes I did."

"Can you tell us the circumstances?"

"Dr. Kelley Smith referred her to me with a diagnosis she had the remnants of an IUD in her uterus. I examined her, confirmed his diagnosis and removed the offending parts. She felt better immediately and later she came to me pregnant with her third child.

"When she first came to you did you take a history?"

"Yes I did."

"Can you tell us that history?" (Michael watched closely how the witness reacted to his questions and felt confidant of his truthfulness.)

The doctor opened a file folder that he brought with him, consulted it and then gave his answer: "Well, as I said she came to me with a history of pain over a period of years, said she had finally gone to a naturopath, Dr. Kelley, that he diagnosed her problem as a part of an IUD still in her.

"Doctor, as a part of that history did she tell you that Dr. Richard Phillips, one of the defendants, had suggested she employ a contraceptive device and that he placed an IUD in her with her permission."

"Yes, she did."

"Did she also tell you she had decided to have it taken out and when he went to do it he told her it had come out of its own accord?"

"Yes, she explained that to me."

"Did she tell you she began to have abominable pain and headaches and she believed the device was still in her so she went to Dr. Marshall because she no longer trusted Dr. Phillips?"

"Yes."

"And did she tell you he told her, after examination, she had no IUD in her."

"That is true."

"And finally did she tell you how the device was actually discovered?"

"She told me she went to a Naturopath in desperation and he found a small string attached to the device. He referred her to me and I removed it."

"Did she then conceive the child you delivered twelve months after removal of the IUD.?"

"Yes, that is true."

During this part of his examination Michael never looked at the yellow sheet before him. Now he looked away from the witness and turned his attention to the sheet. As he did so the jury simultaneously turned their eyes on him and they too looked at the yellow sheet sensing something dramatic was about to take place. The witness sat comfortably unaware of the jury's interest in Michael and the yellow legal sheet. Michael renewed the examination. He started the questioning and the jury could see he was referring to notes on the yellow sheet.

"Dr. Schmidt, you are here under subpoena, are you not?"

"Yes. I was served yesterday afternoon late."

"Now, Doctor," Michael leaned forward, fixing his gaze directly on the witness: "You and I met in your office on September fourth this year when you agreed to see me and discuss Mrs. Brownstone's case. Is that not true?"

"Yes we met in my office late in the afternoon." By now, the doctor sensed Michael Sullivan had something more in mind then the time of day. He knew not what but anticipated the worst.

"And at that time I reviewed with you all the facts as I knew them and you told me exactly what you testified to this afternoon. I also took notes during our conversation, did I not?"

"Yes I observed you were taking notes as we spoke."

"And you had no objection to that?"

"No. I understood you had your job to do and I had mine. I did not object."

Michael paused. Fifteen seconds elapsed before he looked down at the yellow sheet in front of him. "Did you not tell me, and here I am quoting: 'that was the worst case of medical negligence I've ever seen in my practice.' "

Pandemonium broke loose amongst the defense attorneys, both on their feet at one time shouting: "objection. Objection the witness has not been called as an expert." Twelve heads swiveled to look at the Judge.

"Mr. Sullivan you may be heard on this objection."

"Your honor, defense counsel is correct, this witness is not called as an expert, but he is called as a treating physician and he has testified, I believe, truthfully, about a conversation he had at the time of my visit with him. I submit his testimony is relevant to the issue in this case." He is also a rebuttal witness to expert medical opinion brought out during the defense case." He sat down.

"I'm going to overrule the objection, you may answer Doctor and you gentlemen have preserved your exception."

"I'm sorry Mr. Sullivan can you ask the question again?"

"Will the court reporter read the question back to the witness?" Michael prompted in a very deliberate voice looking now squarely at the Judge. The reporter took notes in hand and read the question back to the witness and all eyes focused on Dr. Schmidt.

"Yes, Mr. Sullivan I did say that."

"Was that your impression of what occurred in this case?"

"Yes sir it was."

The court room became deathly still; out of the corner of his eye Michael saw the jurors looking at the defendants table.

"One last question Dr., Have you and I talked or seen each other between the day we met in your office and this afternoon as you testified?"

"No we have not."

"Thank you Doctor; your witness," he offered barely above a whisper. Michael slumped down in his chair, exhausted yet knowing the witness would never be shaken on cross examination. Defense counsel whispered together among themselves and then Paul Castalini stood up and said: "No further questions." Paul Castalini and the other lawyers concluded any further cross examination would result in the witness repeating the forbidden word: "negligence."

"We rest your honor, Michael said wearily.

"All right Gentlemen we will have closing arguments tomorrow morning and I want to have this matter to the jury by tomorrow afternoon. Adjourned for the day." Black robe flying, the Judge retired to his chambers.

CHAPTER 19

The following morning Michael addressed the jury, stressing the pain, turmoil and fear Shelley Brownstone had endured for four long years. That she had entrusted her body to two physicians, who held themselves out to be experts in their field, but it took a Naturopath, with not even a quarter of the training, to diagnose her problem. Why and how could it happen? Because they were negligent, in fact, they were grossly negligent which can be remedied by awarding punitive damages as a warning to those in the profession to pay attention to what their women patients tell them instead of suggesting, in subtle ways, their problems might be in their heads. "That's what happened in this case," he emphasized slamming his fist into the open palm of his hand.

Castalini and his cohort argued persuasively that their clients used their best judgment at all times, and inasmuch as they found no evidence of the device on their respective exams, that what happened was a freak accident, none of the defendants had ever been charged with malpractice and only a defense verdict would restore their reputations. The Judge instructed the jury on the law, told them to apply the law to the facts and sent them off with the bailiff to deliberate.

By late afternoon the jury remained in deliberations and at six o'clock they were dismissed for the day. The next day Michael and his clients arrived in the courtroom at nine o'clock to await the verdict; the defense attorneys had arranged to be called at their offices when the jury signaled it had reached a verdict. Under these circumstances the jury remains confined until all counsel are in the courtroom and the Judge is ready to call the jury in. Michael chose to wait in the courtroom with his clients while the jury remained out, knowing what a lonely and frightening feeling a client can have during deliberations. The defendants were not required to be present when the verdict was read, it being sufficient if their lawyers were present.

The time passed slowly, ten, eleven..... At noon Michael and the Brownstones went to lunch at a little diner with twelve stools within walking distance of the courthouse. They ate in silence until Shelley couldn't stand it anymore. "What's happening in there Michael?" She blurted out uncontrollably.

"I honestly don't know," he said, turning to her, knowing anything could be happening, but he personally thought some jurors were either holding out for the doctors or they had moved toward the plaintiffs and were arguing over damages. He favored the latter theory and decided to tell her. I'm guessing they are going to bring in a verdict for you and I'm not saying this to make you feel good. It's just my gut feeling. I've been in this situation well over a hundred times waiting for a jury and I've been surprised many times, both good and bad. The problem is the wait is excruciating for the lawyer and the client."

The afternoon moved on and by four o'clock the sun began to fade from the courtroom and by five darkness cast a black mask on the windows. The three sat alone in the courtroom except for the bailiff who sat at his desk reading a book and getting a little fidgety knowing the Judge would keep the jury working until at least six thirty before dismissing them for the evening which meant he wouldn't get home until eight o'clock after an hour commute.

Suddenly they were startled by a sharp knock coming from the jury room, followed by two more knocks. Johnson, the bailiff, literally shot out of his seat and bolted down to the room. "This is the bailiff!" he said in a calm manner, "what do you need?"

"We've reached a verdict, will you tell the Judge?"

The bailiff went to his desk, phoned Judge Randall Arthur and reported the jury signified they had reached a verdict. The Judge advised the Bailiff to notify all counsel and parties and report back when everyone was seated awaiting the verdict. They had deliberated fourteen hours, and now the waiting was over, the die cast. The Judge entered from chambers, ascended the bench and noticed the room had filled with spectators, probably lawyers and others working late in the courthouse, and heard the jury was about to render a verdict in a high profile medical malpractice case. He looked to his right where the jury sat and asked: "Have you reached a verdict?" The foreman, a distinguished looking man in his fifties, stood and addressed the court: "We have your honor."

"Please hand your verdict form to the bailiff. The foreman did so and the bailiff handed it to Judge....... He read it aloud:

"1. We the jury, duly empaneled, find in favor of the plaintiffs.
 2. We find the Plaintiffs suffered special damages in the amount of 10,000 dollars from the Defendants.
 3. We find the Plaintiffs suffered general damages in the amount 1,000,000 dollars from the Defendants.
 4. We find the Defendants should be assessed punitive damages in the sum of 2,000,000 dollars."

The Judge looked startled but quickly regained his composure. In a solemn voice he asked: "Is this the verdict of each of you?"

Rising to his feet the foreman responded in a clear grave voice that resounded around a deathly still court room: "It is your honor."

Michael Sullivan kept looking straight ahead waiting for the Judge to dismiss the jury and retire to his chambers. Paul Castalini, pro forma, requested the jury be polled. The Judge did so asking each individual juror if their vote was as shown on the verdict sheet. Each answered in the affirmative. The Judge thanked the jury for their service, dismissed them and retired to his chambers.

The door closed behind Judge Arthur and Michael turned to Shelley who had tears streaming down her cheeks. A hum then a buzz and then outright shouting ensued. Shelly's husband hugged her and Michael at the same time. Several lawyers approached and tried to grab his hand, some spectators shouted: "Good for you." "Nice going."

Out of the corner of his eye, while all of the well wishers were still congratulating him, he caught a glimpse of Paul Castalini and his co-counsel still seated at the defense table looking stunned like they were in a stupor and couldn't talk. Thoughts coursed through his mind as he stood in the middle of the tumult. This is unbelievable, they gave us exactly what we asked for. This is major and sure to upset the medical community. So be it. She deserved it after suffering four years of unrelenting pain and with punitive damages the jury has really sent a message to the profession: damages for negligence and punitive damages for gross negligence.

By the time he reached his office, four blocks away word had reached Sullivan & Connolly: "We won." Paul Connolly greeted him at the door and behind him the associates, paralegals, secretaries stood, all shouting, laughing and slapping him on the back. All he could do was to smile his broadest and protect himself from the pounding. "Champagne all around," someone shouted over the din. "To the boss," he toasted with an imaginary glass raised in salute. "To the boss," they repeated. Later Michael compared it to being in the winner's locker room at the Super bowl after the game. Fifteen minutes passed before he was able to break away, as the party grew louder and louder, and more lawyers from other firms in the building crowded in to join the celebration. Cell phones were cracking in law offices across the city: "There's a new top gun in town." With the verdict he joined the small number of elite trial lawyers in the city.

"Michael, what's all that noise I hear in the background?"

"We're having a little party right now Mary. Get this—the jury gave Shelley Brownstone, a million dollars in pain and suffering general damages and surprises of all surprises two million in punitive damages. What would you like for your birthday Mrs. Sullivan?"

"I can't believe it, you must be out of your mind."

"Something like that. As soon as I can extract myself from this crowd, we are going to have our own party. See you in a half hour. Boy do I love you."

Within the week Paul Castalini and the other defense lawyers filed motions for judgement notwithstanding the verdict and in the alternative a new trial. Both motions, pro forma, were denied by Judge on the basis he had made no error in his rulings or instructions given to the jury. Michael expected an appeal but it never came. Later he found out why; the insurance companies and the medical society didn't want the vast publicity an appeal and affirmance of the judgment would generate. Thus Sullivan & Connolly got their first large contingent fee immediately, enough to cover office expenses for a year.

. . .

From his earliest years Michael Sullivan had been fascinated by history, politics and political leaders. He remembered sitting with his father watching television. The president had been assassinated November twenty second and Lee Harvey Oswald jailed as a suspect. They saw Oswald being transferred from his Dallas jail when suddenly a man broke from the watching crowd of supporters shooting Oswald at point blank. Michael remembered the pandemonium on the television and in his own household. Confusion and speculation reigned supreme. His sisters and brothers were too young to comprehend what was taking place, yet at eight years he understood and realized his parents were extremely distraught. No one knew what was happening. Everyone feared a conspiracy to bring down the government. He remembered his father saying: "This would be a good time for the Russians to start trouble for us.

They stayed glued to the television for days. On the day of the funeral they watched the widow and the President's brothers, Bobby and Ted and many of the world's leaders attend mass at St. Matthew's Cathedral in the nation's capital. And then the burial at Arlington National Cemetry. They watched mesmerized as the widow lit a perpetual flame on the flat grave. The world watched shattered by what they were seeing. Only eight years of age, Michael realized the world changed over three days. It wasn't until years later he and all Americans realized the change had not necessarily been for the better. A series of shots from the upper reaches of the Texas Depository building in Dallas, Texas changed the world, As time passed Michael began to go back before the Kennedy years and sort out what prefaced the fatal event. With his father he watched the presidential campaigns in 1964 and 1968 driven by the civil rights movement and the war in Vietnam. As he came of college age in 1973 the war had become unpopular, but still dragged on. Michael was fully in tune with the policy formulated by John Foster Dulles, Secretary of State under Dwight Eisenhower—containment of the communist cancer by surrounding the Soviet Union with anti-communist states and confronting the communists wherever they stuck their heads up.

Richard Nixon had won a close election over Vice President Hubert Humphrey in 1968 and promised to wind the war down by slowly withdrawing troops from Viet Nam. In 1973 U.S. troop levels in Viet Nam sat at 68,000 reduced from a high of 549,000. Nixon had hoped the South Vietnamese could defend themselves; it turned out they could not and negotiations took place to end the war.

In his first year of college, Michael joined the Air Force ROTC program. (educating future officers for the United States Air Force) At the end of his college career he went on active duty for two years. His experience in the air force crystalized his thinking about the need for a strong military. The war ended but America remained on a war footing. The strong men in the Kremlin were determined, as ever, to spread their secular philosophy and totalitarianism to the outer reaches of the earth and they had a wiley ally in Mao Tse-tung, the face of communism in China.

He felt the years ahead would be dangerous for America, especially since it lost a war for the first time in the country's history. A hostile press, military ineptitude on the part of U.S. generals and not wanting to lose an election on the part of a devious Lyndon Johnson, caused the debacle, and tragically the loss of fifty thousand American soldiers and countless Vietnamese. He felt it should' not and could not ever happen again. The war polarized young people—some said war never again. They came to be known as the "doves." Others, more realistic in their appraisal, wished for peace but realized with the communist snake still at large, there could be no peace until it was severed at the head, and beyond that there was no assurance another monster might not rise up to confront America's freedom. They came to be known as "hawks."

While in the air force Michael saw duty in Japan, Germany, England and Italy and many other bases around the globe. He looked and he listened and concluded the world would be preserved for the "doves" by the "hawks" applying realism to the dangers found in every part of the world. He classed himself as a "hawk" with the hope of a peaceful world based on a strong America, ready to back up its leadership with military might. During his years in the Air Force he had plenty of time to read and think. The books he found most interesting were four written by Theodore White. Each covered, in order, the presidential campaigns of 1960, 1964, 1968 and 1972 from a reporter's point of view. Imitators have since tried to emulate Teddy White's insights and prose but no one has succeeded yet. Michael studied the campaign of 1928 between Herbert Hoover, a successful business man and engineer and Al Smith the four term Catholic governor of New York. He read of the prejudice and bigotry Smith faced as the first Catholic to run for President. In White's *Making of the Presidency*

1960 he faithfully recorded how John F. Kennedy became the second Catholic to run for President and had succeeded despite wide spread bigotry.

He followed with great interest the 1976 election campaign, as Nixon's successor, Vice President Gerald Ford struggled against an unknown peanut farmer, a one time Governor of Georgia and Naval Academy graduate, Jimmy Carter. Carter won. Ford lost narrowly, defeated, due as much as anything to the disgrace of Nixon resigning the presidency in the summer of 1974 and thereafter receiving a pardon from Ford. All these elections he found fascinating and felt strongly about the outcomes for the country. As early as high school, his sympathies lay with the Republican Party, whose nominees and platform were more in keeping with his own ideas. The old Democratic coalition made up of unions, Catholics in the north and liberal easterners began to come loose at the seams; instead being replaced by interest groups pulling the party to the left.

In 1980 Ronald Reagan, one time screen idol and two time governor of California, stunned the liberals by sweeping past the incumbent, Jimmy Carter, entering the White House after four years of the Carter presidency. The country had high hopes for the peanut farmer from Georgia, but he never lived up to his billing. The economy went soaring off the tracks and Carter blamed the people claiming there was a "malaise" in America. Reagan brought optimism and conservatism. He inherited an abysmal economy yet by 1984 he had the country on its feet and by 1989 his administration had successfully, through its defense buildup, brought the Soviet Union to its knees. He demanded the Berlin Wall be torn down, which was only a segment of the iron curtain sealing off all Eastern Europe from the west. With destruction of the wall came the end of the cold war and Russian withdrawal from Eastern Europe and breakup of the Soviet Republics—all because of Reagan's leadership. The United States won the forty nine year old cold war. (1945-1989)

During the Reagan years Michael and Mary saw the births of their four children, Jack in 1983, Sharon 1985, Peter 1987 and Kathryn 1989. In the early years of practice he dabbled in politics, serving as legal counsel to the county Republican Party. As a result he soon became known to state party leaders and the congressional delegation. His involvement turned out to be beneficial to the firm, in that, many of the people he met in politics became clients. By the time he formed Sullivan & Connolly he'd been active in politics for fourteen years. City leaders noticed an urged him to run for office realizing he he'd make a perfect candidate. He always declined, saying he had a law firm to build and a wife and four children to support. They accepted his reasons, and understood his dedication to the law, but in the back of their minds they felt the day coming when they might change his mind.

CHAPTER 20

As the second year of Sullivan & Connolly drew to a close Michael and Paul were having a drink with Tom Donovan, the first associate they made partner. While they had planned to wait four years before adding a partner, Donovan had proved so exceptional, not only in bringing in business but in his acumen as a litigator, that they felt compelled to make him an equity partner after only two years with the firm. His personality and work ethic meshed with theirs. The meeting took place at the University Club where Michael and Paul gained membership after forming their firm and brought other attorneys in when they joined the firm. It was Saturday afternoon, a few days before Christmas, and the three sat in a corner of the huge library apart from other members in the room reading newspapers, a book or chatting quietly over drinks. Two stories high with wooden beams across the ceiling and crown molding throughout. Two walls covered with books with a balcony around the upper portion of the room allowing members to ascend a spiral staircase leading to the balcony which in effect created a library on two floors. Entering the room from the lobby one could easily assume they were in one of the country's great university libraries. The room, turned out to be the pride of the club as a place for reading, research and a place where much the city's business took place every day. The power elite met at the club charting the future of the city and state. Half the members were lawyers, the rest, doctors, businessmen, politicians, accountants, bankers and a smattering of educators. Michael and Paul knew most of them, including Matthew Hamilton and Blake Collins from the old firm. Michael hadn't seen either since the breakup, except for one occasion when he ran into Blake unexpectedly in the library and they spent a few minutes talking about what happened to Matthew and the firm after they left.

Blake told him, within eight months of his departure with Doug Phelps, Matthew's firm had been completely torn asunder. Blake had left with five others and later merged with a firm of twelve lawyers. Matthew Hamilton lost every lawyer who had been with Hamilton, Sullivan, Collins & Phelps and now found himself with a firm of seven lawyers, three women and four men. Collins told Michael his firm had wrested most of the municipal work from Matthew, and as a result of the breakup, other firms were moving into the bond business.

The three partners ordered scotch and Michael proposed a toast to: "The continuing success of Sullivan & Connolly." They lifted their glasses and drank to the firm. It had been a gratifying two years for the infant firm, the high point being Michael's verdict in the Brownstone case. From that day forward business began to come in a steady flow. Paul had fully taken over the Boniface account and worked with four lawyers defending cases brought against the insurers. Michael and Paul tried the big cases building up a consistent series of wins, enhancing the firm's reputation as the top trial firm in the state. Other large firms began to send cases to Sullivan & Connolly when conflicts arose with their clients.

"To recapitulate," Paul said: "we have three partners and seventeen associates. I see the need to hire at least four or five more this year. What do you think of converting two or three of our present crew into business lawyers?"

"How long would it take?" Michael asked with some hesitation.

For some time Michael had intended to keep the firm exclusively in the field of litigation, but from his experience at Hamilton, Sullivan he realized to grow you had to diversify and be able to furnish the client with a full line of services. That meant developing a business side of the practice at some point. Paul told him it could take up to a year.

"How should we go about it?"

"We can hire laterally or right out of law school."

"I've been thinking about it; if we want to be the best firm in the city we're going to have to add specialties sooner or later so this is the year to begin. Let's do it Paul. Kennedy's business has been mostly litigation but he's told me if we had some business lawyers he'd move everything over to us. You make the hires, get the best people you can find even if you have to pay more. I think to start we'll have to hire laterally, it takes too much time to bring a new hire along. I don't think it wise to try and convert some of our trial lawyers into business lawyers. After the initial hires we'll build the business practice with the best lawyers we can get out of law school."

"To do it Michael we'll have to plow back a good portion of our profit," Paul warned.

"Can you go with that Tom?"

"I can Michael, spend money to make money."

"All right then. That's set. Now I think we should hand out some generous bonuses to our associates and staff and cut back on our split. How about that?"

"Agreed," Paul and Tom said in unison.

"To bonuses," Paul laughed raised his glass. "When you asked me to partner with you Michael you said it would take money to make money and paying associates top dollar would pay off in production but more importantly, loyalty. I believe that has happened."

Tom opened another line of inquiry: "What are your thoughts about making a partner or partners this coming year?"

"I favor it, and I think we should be looking at Billy Johnson."

"I have no qualms Michael and I assume we'll wait to the end of the year and keep an eye on him and if he still looks like the one we want, bring him in. Also I should point out if we hire laterally to build the business practice we will probably have to make the hires partner."

Billy Johnson had come right out of law school and in six months had astonished the partners by winning two rather large personal injury cases and settling two more for large sums, bringing substantial fees into the firm. Such a performance was extraordinary. Michael had hired him and was not surprised; he sensed his intelligence, and as a trial lawyer himself, thought he could judge who would or wouldn't make a good litigator. Billy Johnson was the best prospect he'd seen in all his time practicing law and he had not been disappointed. His preparation for trial was meticulous and though he had little experience he gave adversaries fits by dint of hard work and quickness of intellect. Within a few years Michael projected Billy would be working with him on major cases and after that taking on the big ones himself.

The partners finished their drinks, agreed on their share of the profits and bonuses on a paper napkin and adjourned to the dining room for a steak dinner. 1998 came to an end and their two year old firm had made its mark on the city's legal establishment.

. . .

On his way home from his meeting with the partners Michael's thoughts turned to Mary and the children. What a great wife she had been, giving valued advice, taking care of the family, from daily upbringing of the children, to running the household, being a pal and a backer of everything he did. He'd turned forty four and she forty and they made it a goal to travel all over the United States with the children, on what they called educational tours.

Without the children, they travelled throughout Europe, she for the second time. Before she met Michael Sullivan, she took her first trip while still in her teens. With a group of classmates she took an ocean liner from New York and they went on a grand tour through sixteen countries. Now on their first trip together she acted as guide introducing him to the great treasures she had discovered before they were married. After the fall of the Soviet Union their travels took them to Eastern Europe through Czechoslovakia, Poland, Hungry, Bulgaria, Russia, Romania and then to Western Europe and Germany, France England, Ireland Italy and Spain. When traveling they made it a practice to get up at seven in the morning, breakfast by eight and on the street by nine, jumping on and off sightseeing buses, walking, riding trains and subways, driving miles in rental cars. They kept a madcap pace all over Europe. Of all the places they traveled, Mary favored Rome, the city of light, while Michael fell in love with Paris the first time he saw it. They took the excursion boat around the Seine, listened to the bells of Notre Dame as they passed under it, jumped off at the Louvre and walked through the Tuileries Gardens. He hummed a tune from the movie *High Society*, *"Samantha I love you...."*

By the time he arrived home he was brimming with high spirits. He parked the car in the driveway and headed for the front door. Before he could open it, Mary appeared framed in the doorway calling out his name: "Michael, Michael," her voice shattering the night air, Jack has been in a serious accident; the hospital just called, we've got to get over to St. Agatha's."

His mind clamped tight, he became quiet, focused just as he had taught himself to do at the opening of a trial. The first step—get to the hospital as quickly as possible but not recklessly. He assimilated the facts as she recounted them on their way. He bracketed the main facts swiftly. Jack had been riding in a car with a friend and the friend's mother when another car came crashing through a red light, hitting them broadside, spinning the car around and around until it came to a stop a hundred feet from the point of impact. Mary could only tell him all three were taken by ambulance to the hospital and their condition serious.

Arriving at St. Agatha's, Michael let her out at the entrance and drove to the parking lot. As he ran toward the hospital he had a chance to think through what was happening. He'd been so happy and now only God knew what lay ahead. His thoughts raced back to Jack as a young boy and the great times they had together. The boy was a competitor, loved sports and showed promise of being a leader. He loved his dad and followed Michael around when they were cutting the lawn. They played catch together and now he competed as a tennis player. He tried to chase the question from his mind, will he be able to do these things? Then a destructive thought raced across his brain: is he in danger of death? "Try to stay calm." He knew life was about to change, how he didn't know, but it would not be the same.

"Michael, over here. This is Doctor Patofsky. He's just come from surgery." He wheeled around and saw Mary and a tall man in a blue surgical gown with a net on his head standing next to her. They were still thirty feet away and it was all he could do not to break into a run. He acknowledged the doctor, said nothing and waited, searching the Doctor's face for a clue as to Jack's condition.

"Mrs. Sullivan, I've just come from surgery: your son has been hurt very badly, two broken legs, a broken arm, some internal bleeding. He's gone from the operating table to intensive care. We're hopeful he's going to make it, as to the future of his legs, we can't tell yet. I'll be on his case until he's out of danger."

"How dangerous is his condition?" Michael barely got out.

"His head injuries are minimal, it's his body that's taken a beating, legs, arm, abdomen. We believe the spine is intact. He'll make it but it's going to be a long pull.

"Thank you Doctor," he said and turned to Mary: "Let's go to the chapel and pray." He took her hand and they walked to the little chapel on the hospital's ground floor. They found it empty so they knelt in the front pew praying silently for their son's recovery.

Michael lost both his parents, as did Mary, all within two years of each other. It had been devastating. Mary was pregnant with Jack and couldn't even attend her father's funeral. They were still suffering from their losses and now this accident to their oldest hit them hard. Intellectually they both knew that when disaster strikes some people turn bitter, others turn to their beliefs in a higher being to sustain them. Grounded in their religion they accepted what had happened to Jack. They, like anyone in their situation, couldn't find a rational for what had just occurred, but they believed their God willed it for the best. Bitterness was not an option, prayer their strength. After five hours they left the hospital exhausted with Jack still in intensive care.

Michael told his wife he would go back to the hospital in the morning and stay with his son until he left intensive care. Mary would stay home and take care of the other children. In the morning he awakened at eight and arrived at the hospital at nine. He called Paul Connolly and told him he would be out of commission "as long as it takes. Please assign my cases to others; I don't know how long I will be gone."

In the next month he spent most of each day at the hospital for the first week and a half. He sat outside the intensive care unit praying for his son, sometimes with Mary; then they moved him to a private room and the boy was overjoyed to see his father and mother there to greet him. They had not seen each other since the day of the accident. They had Jack in a body brace and his arms in slings, still he had a light in his eye and a smile on his lips.

"Dad will I be ok?"

"Yes, son," he said with all the courage he could muster, "you're going to be ok, the doctors say it's going to take some time but let's not worry about that now. Your mother, Sharon, Peter and Kathryn are so happy that you've come this far, we know it will all work out and you'll be home with us soon."

His son looked pale and obviously exhausted from days of trauma, his head lay back on the pillow and Michael assured him he would be right there in the room if he needed anything. After the boy fell asleep Michael got up from his chair near the bedside, went into the hall and called Mary. "They've got him set up in a private room sweetheart, he's going to be ok, tell the children. I'll stay with him here tonight, and if you can, come around at noon tomorrow and spend some time with him. I'm going to stay with him until he feels comfortable on his own."

"Michael, you have to come home to get some sleep, they've got nurses and doctors watching him round the clock."

"I know, but I'm staying here. I told Paul to take over until we get through this crisis. I didn't tell Jack, but this is going to be a long process of rehabilitation."

For the next three months he spent half his time at the hospital, half at his law practice and the rest in bed. Every day Jack made progress and he began to see he was going to make it and his father was right there to reinforce that confidence. Mary and the children came at least once a day bolstering his spirits; their dedication served to speed his recovery. During the recuperation period Michael and his son grew close and the boy looked upon the father as a hero as well as his dad. They had long discussions in the afternoon and Michael told him about some of his cases, even described some of his trials. They talked of the news, the family or something one or the other had seen on television. Soon they had him walking. The father took him to rehabilitation, waited while he worked with the specialist, drove him home and then to his office where sometimes he worked until eleven or twelve at night, for his practice had fallen behind with the four month absence to take care of his son. The firm suffered from his not being there full time and Paul made everyone work harder to pick up the slack. Every day they talked, and Michael made many decisions but left running the firm to Paul Connolly.

Never for a moment did he regret taking time off to be with his son; he told his partners he would make it up to them, and knowing him as they did, they never doubted nor resented his being gone. Just the opposite, it turned out to be a lesson not lost on the firm, that family and loyalty are what is important in life. They all knew they had witnessed an example of great love of the father for his son and his family. His example they would all emulated.

On his first morning back at the firm full time he asked the entire office to assemble in the conference room. Sixty people packed into the small space with a few standing in the hall, all eyes on the senior partner, flanked by three other partners and a brace of associates. Everyone in the room loved the "boss," as they referred to him out of earshot. Oh, they griped once and a while about an assigned case, a bonus not adequate, too much pressure on the eve of trial, still they trusted him, the future of the firm, his ethics and his basic fairness which they had all had experienced since joining the firm. To a man or woman, the lawyers believed they were on the ground floor of what would be the premier firm in the city and even the region; they toiled for Sullivan & Connolly and they were proud of it ready to do what it takes to support one man's dream—a truly professional law firm and not a business as so many law firms had become in an age when partners left their firms to go to the highest bidder amongst other law firms and took associates with them. Loyalty, out of favor. Greed the prevailing ethic.

Lawyers were not the only ones on the bandwagon of pragmatism. On Wall Street, the era of Ivan Boesky and Michael Milken prevailed. The "junk bond kings." They sold bonds that were junk enabling corporate raiders to buy up major companies, load the company with junk bond debt, sell the company's assets, cut employees and expenses to pay off the debt, all under the heading of "making companies more productive, improving profits and enriching the shareholders." The result: companies going out of business, layoffs, and the country headed for recession, attributable to greed on the part of Wall Street's "masters of the universe" as described by Thomas Wolfe in his novel of Wall Street avarice, *Bonfire of the Vanities.*

"I want to thank you all collectively as I have already thanked some of you individually for the effort you've put forth for the firm in my absence. You have proved no one is indispensable and it gives me more confidence than ever to know this operation continues no matter what. My son, Jack, is doing fine and his near death experience taught me more about compassion and understanding others than I've ever known. I will try and bring that knowledge to the table as we strive to build the future for ourselves at this firm. Again, thank you all for your good work." Before he could finish his words they broke into spontaneous applause. He waved and could say no more as tears came into his eyes and he choked back a sob. They understood and slowly began melting away from the scene. Paul Connolly put his arm around Michael and led him from the room.

CHAPTER 21

2001, a new year dawned. The firm had grown to sixty five lawyers, and a new president had been elected after a tumultuous battle between the two major parties. George W. Bush the declared winner on the date of the election after all the votes were counted, but the sitting Vice President, and challenger, Democrat Alfred Gore refused to concede unlike Richard Nixon, who graciously declined to contest the presidential outcome when Kennedy won in 1960 based on fraudulent votes in Illinois and Texas. Instead Gore hired lawyers and relied on the Democratic Florida Supreme Court to change the result in his favor. The Republicans, led by former Secretary of State James Baker, in the administration of Bush's father, George H. W. Bush, quickly countered the Democrat tactic by going to federal court and ultimately the Supreme Court to challenge Gore's claim—that a partial recount in Florida would prove he won the election in Florida and thus the presidency.

To rule in Gore's favor, the court would have had to allow the voters in Florida a full manual recount. The court held to do so would be a violation of the equal protection clause of the constitution and by a vote of 7-2 dismissed Gore's claim. With that dispute resolved, Bush became the forty third President of the United States. In doing so he became the second man in United States history to sit in the oval office after his father had served as President, the first being John Quincy Adams who followed in the footsteps of his father John Adams who served as the second President of the United States.

The Firm

Satisfied Jack would fully recover with the passage of time, Michael plunged back into work. He wanted to expand the firm's practice into other areas which meant hiring tax lawyers and three more business lawyers. Paul recruited the business side and Michael assumed the task of recruiting the tax lawyers. In doing so he decided to fly to New York and interview graduates of New York University Law School, reputed to be the best school in the country emphasizing the training of tax specialists. It occurred to him the Internal Revenue Code would not be shrinking any time soon, despite political calls and promises for simplification; in fact Congress would continue to pass more and more laws, as well as exceptions, requiring expert advice for those in the business community and the firm's growing list of individual clients.

He arrived at LaGuardia Airport on a Monday morning and drove a rental car into the city and into the lower level parking entrance of the Waldorf Astoria Hotel on Park Avenue and checked in.

Michael loved the Waldorf. He, Mary and the children stayed there for the first time in 1995 and they all loved it. The children went down to the balcony overlooking the ballroom and like children sitting on the stairs while their parents were having a party with grownups watched the tuxedoed gentlemen and ball-gowned ladies waltzing around the floor below and then came back to their parent's room and reported on eye opening scenes they had just witnessed. For his part he liked to go out on the street and walk north on Park Avenue and over to Central Park. He and Mary arranged for a sitter to take care of the children one afternoon and they took a cab up to the Metropolitan Museum of Art at sixty sixth street to view the wonders contained behind the walls of that magnificent structure; afterward they sat on the front steps and watched the people coming and going under a slate blue sky. At either end of the steps vendors staked out their territory selling hot dogs, cold drinks and ice crème.

Michael J. Walsh

On their last day in New York, Michael took the four children on the Circle Line Tour which boarded its passengers on the West Side Pier and proceeded around Manhattan Island with a magnificent view of the World Trade Center, Manhattan skyline, Brooklyn waterfront, Yankee stadium, Gracie Mansion the George Washington Bridge, around the northern boundary and Baker's field, home of the Columbia University Lions football team and back to the starting point on the Hudson River. One and a half hours of pure joy. They couldn't wait to tell Mary all the things they had seen. Jack said: "mom you wouldn't believe the World Trade Center, one hundred stories." After they had flown home and for weeks after they talked about all the things they saw in New York. Mass at St. Patrick's, a visit to the observation tower in Rockefeller Center, the excellent lunch at Windows on the World restaurant at the World Trade Center, lunch at "21" and through Michael's concerted effort a private tour of the United Nations and the security council. The children had seen and learned more in a week then they could have in six months at school. He and Mary believed it important that the children at a young age get out and see something of the world other than the parochial experiences they had at home.

He had breakfast by himself at Oscar's in the Waldorf and afterward walked down to Washington Square, the site of New York University Law School. Arrangements had been made to interview eight students hoping to connect with two and persuade the two to come west to the city. Of the first four he found one young man who seemed like he might fit in. Michael reviewed his resume and liked what he saw: Columbia Law School and in the process of finishing his masters at NYU. William Newton presented himself in a dark suit, white shirt and conservative tie. Seated in the student lounge, Michael asked some periphery questions and then got down to brass tacks, telling the young man he needed someone who wanted to work hard for a fair salary and grow with a firm that intended to be the best in the

224

city. If he was married that would be even better based on his experience married younger lawyers had greater responsibilities and apply themselves accordingly. Newton looked over six feet, jet black hair, heavy eyebrows and a mouth that hinted at mirth. It was his eyes that attracted Michael, they fastened on him as he described the firm; the man proved a good listener, the mark of a good lawyer. He decided to offer him a job. Newton didn't hesitate, he accepted.

"What about your wife? Shouldn't you consult with her?"

"No sir. We talked about it before we met; she said if you like Mr. Sullivan, and you trust what he says, take the job if offered. My wife is pretty sharp. When do I start?"

Inwardly Michael felt elated while his face reflected nothing but warmth for the new recruit.

"You'll start as soon as you and your wife can gather you're belongings and make the move. My wife, Mary will start looking for some housing for you and you might start doing that for yourselves."

"Thank you sir, I appreciate the opportunity, you won't be sorry." The young man left and Michael thought to himself: this young man has a maturity beyond his years, he'll be instilling confidence in clients the minute he starts practice.

Three other applicants came to the lounge, all very intelligent, with excellent grades, two in suits and one in a sweater and jeans. "Sweater and jeans" got ten minutes and a courteous "thank you" from the founding partner of Sullivan & Connolly and Michael guessed he was the smartest of the eight interviews. To his thinking, a savvy applicant would not show up in casual attire. The next two young men were interesting and carried high grade averages in the field of tax. But neither fit the bill he looked for—a lawyer with high acumen and personality, often a rarity. The two gentlemen had acumen but it would be in the back room of the firm. He needed lawyers who would mix with the clients, and who inspired clients to trust their advice. Again, he gave a courteous "thank you, for taking the time to meet with me."

The last and only woman interviewed had a degree in mathematics, spent a year at Cambridge University in England after graduating from Georgetown. She sat down and addressed him as "Mr. Sullivan." Without meaning to, Michael could sometimes be intimidating, in his look, his dress, his relaxed demeanor although he gave off a non-threatening appearance to most.

"I'm Susan Struthers and I'm interested in your firm."

He didn't resent the bluntness, although he viewed the situation as one in which the question was not whether she was interested in the firm, rather whether the firm had an interest in her. She wore glasses, steel rimmed, her hair pulled back tied in discreet red ribbon. Her Suit, an impeccable charcoal gray, the only jewelry, small gold earrings and a single gold band on her wrist. Although dressed simply, the fact she was a very attractive young women could not be disguised. Struthers at five feet ten inches in low heels had a look of confidence.

"Why are you interested in tax Ms. Struthers?"

"I've always been fascinated with mathematics, numbers and in many ways tax is akin to it. In my studies at NYU I've found innovation is part and parcel of the tax practice. You find a way to save a client taxes and soon other clients follow. I think it a challenging field."

"I see you went to Georgetown, how did you get there?"

"My father went to Georgetown and the law school and I have a brother there now and another about to go. My Mother went to Trinity in the District, so it seemed only natural to wind up there. Besides it pleased my father."

"If you moved how would your parents feel?"

"Well," she laughed, "I'm single and I like new places and I'm sure they'd prefer I stay at home but they are broadminded enough to wish me well whatever I do." Her smile was infectious;

it lit up the room. He liked her and thought she'd have the same effect on the clients, in addition, her grades left no question about her intelligence.

The interview ended, he stood and grasped her hand and told her he'd call her in week. She smiled again and he knew he had a winner and only the fourth woman to join the firm.

He left the law school and caught a cab back to the Waldorf. It started to rain and the drops pelted against the cab's window and he could see people rushing along the avenue, black umbrellas bent against the wind. He loved this scene: the cab ride, yellow cabs dodging in and out jockeying for position between traffic lights. Daylight still prevailed and he watched the thirty, forty, sixty storied buildings lining Park Avenue fly by. What bustle, everything moving at once, sidewalks teeming with people. New York stirred the blood and the sense of competitiveness in him. What a city. The cab pulled to the curb in front of the hotel, he paid the driver and headed for the lobby.

"Hey Michael," not expecting to meet anyone he knew in New York, he turned sharply and spied Blake Collins coming across the lobby.

"Blake, what are you doing here?" Michael said with genuine surprise and even a tinge of nostalgia remembering the good times they had had playing tennis in the early years, before the break up destroyed the old firm; better to look forward than back. They had gone their separate ways, the friendship never to be the same. Still there remained a sense of competition, both had gone on to build new law firms from the ashes of Hamilton, Sullivan, Collins & Phelps and Michael knew he was far ahead in the race.

"I'm back here on municipal business trying to make a living."

Michael looked directly at him now as he approached and saw he had aged. Gray hair had replaced the black and actually made him quite good looking. Dark eyebrows accentuated his gray hair. In contrast Michael at forty five didn't have a gray hair in his head and looked ten years younger than his age. They sized each other up and simultaneously shook hands.

"Have a drink at the Bull and Bear?" Blake suggested.

"By all means, lead on."

The bar, one of the most famous in the world, was jammed with men in pinstriped suits and quiet ties, beautiful women, wives and girlfriends all crowded the bar and surrounding tables. Dark wood the predominate décor and soft lights casting a romantic glow made the bar a magnet for the banking and Wall Street investment crowd with a sprinkling of lawyers and advertising executives for added flavor.

Snatches of conversation saturated the air: "Dow Jones;" "puts and calls;" "The charity ball at the Pierre, are you going?" "The old gray lady ain't what she used to be." (New York Times) The bar didn't pretend to be the local bar, but the topics were the same: who's in, who's out, what's selling, what stock to dump. Not a scene you would see back home. Only in New York.

Blake ordered a double martini, which Michael noted with interest to be a powerful starter and he remembered Blake always going easy on the first drink and certainly not a martini. He ordered a scotch and water and they took their drinks to an isolated corner at one end of the room. From there they could view the action and talk at the same time. After a few preliminaries and deep draughts from his drink, Blake became expansive. Michael asked with genuine curiosity what he knew of members of the old firm. Blake ordered another double, and fully relaxed, began to recount what happened since they last saw each other. The room faded into the distance, the sound muted as the two revisited the past for a few brief moments.

"You left in January, eight months later Doug and I and others left the firm. Matthew came to New York, immediately and made the rounds of all the banks and investment houses that underwrite bonds. He ran us down, telling lies about what happened and about

Doug and I personally. His story line: we were trying to steal the business. How do I know this?" he asked rhetorically, "because Doug and I came back here and made the rounds of all the banks and financial institutions we'd dealt with before the breakup and they told us what Matthew said about us."

"Did they believe him?" Michael asked, interested in learning the whole story.

"I don't think so, because as time went on, we began to get half the bond business and at the end of the year we got a huge break when the state put out a large issue and we won the right to render the legal opinion even though Matthew undercut us on his fee. From that point on we started to snake more and more business from him and the coup de grace came when Peter Bolling left him and came over to us."

"Did you recruit him?"

"No, he came to us and said he couldn't put up with the tantrums Matthew Hamilton was in the habit of throwing. He said Bert Thurman and Matthew were fighting like cats and dogs, in fact, it got so bad they had offices at either end of their suite and didn't talk to each other."

"What's the situation now?" Michael probed.

"Matthew's down to Bert Thurman and five associates. No one from our old firm is there, they've all gone their separate ways. Five are with me and the rest went to separate firms. It's so sad."

By now two double martinis and two scotches had been absorbed and a certain melancholy settled on the conversation. Michael spoke after a proper silence and suggested they have a final drink and then he had to pack and get ready for the flight home.

Blake perked up, signaled for the waitress and ordered a third round. When the drinks arrived Michael volunteered: "I think the breakup was the best thing that could have happened; I didn't think so at first, but it forced us to go out on our own and I've never looked back."

"Well, yes," Blake hesitated, it's been hard for me, we've merged twice with other firms, have twenty five lawyers and I'm going to slow up a bit. I've already told my partners."

"Why would you do that at age forty three," Michael interrupted, genuinely startled? You fellows have worked hard, been successful, why let up now?"

"It's not as it appeared. With the mergers came friction, three or four wanted to be big fish and insisted business getting is the chief component of the firm with rewards paid out accordingly." It crossed Michael's mind when he heard this that Blake had taken the same position at the time of the breakup only then he didn't have to be a business getter, the business came to him. Apparently things were different now in his own firm where they stressed getting business brought the rewards and he had never been a "business getter."

"I've got interests besides the law; I've spent a great deal of time promoting the arts in the city and some of my partners don't quite see the value in that field since it doesn't bring in any business. I've decided to take a reduced role in the firm and go 'of Counsel.' Another reason is Doug Phelps is leaving our firm and taking most of the municipal work with him. When the old firm broke up the monopoly came to an end and three or four firms are now competing for the business including some out of state firms. It's dog eat dog, no longer shooting fish in a barrel as Samuel Barron used to say."

"Will you continue to practice?"

"Oh yes, I still have a corporate practice and that will keep me busy and still leave time for outside activities I enjoy. I understand Sullivan & Connolly is doing all right, in fact, you fellows are getting the reputation as the toughest litigators in town. I remember that case we tried together when I first came to the firm. It happened to be my client and you offered to try the case to a jury. We won and I got a big kick out of it but decided then I didn't want to be a trial lawyer. I didn't like the arguments, questioning the witnesses. No give me the quiet of the corporate boardroom."

After three double Martinis Blake was riding high and Michael felt a little mellow so Blake ordered another double. "No more for me Blake, I've got to excuse myself and get ready to go; it's been good to see you and get updates on our old associates." With that he got up, shook hands and left, leaving Blake with his fourth martini eyeing the "swells" at the bar.

High in the sky, thirty thousand feet above New York he settled in for the ride back home and reflected on what Blake had said. Life really comes full circle he thought. I left firm and now the firm is no more. Everyone scattered to the winds—the golden goose killed. Blake told him that before he and Doug Phelps left to form their new firm, Matthew had avoided them stating he wanted nothing to do with them personally and would associate with them on a professional basis only. Blake said they rejected that proposition out of hand and left. Matthew tried to salvage the firm, keeping two partners who left him within a year. He then joined forces with a brilliant lawyer, Bert Thurman who had a temperamental streak and they clashed from the outset causing fear and frustration amongst their associates. Blake told him Matthew began to drink more and more and this affected his performance. And now to put a finis to the old firm Blake had decided to quit the race to certain degree. The strange thing about it was Michael didn't feel any elation at besting his old adversaries. He had tried to save the firm because they had built something together and the future looked bright but greed came between success and failure and so it had all come to an end, but for him it was the beginning—Sullivan & Connolly, sixty five lawyers, and according to Blake, the best reputation for litigation in the city. It's funny, he mused, if you just keep going when it looks the darkest, the Lord will provide, certainly that is true for Mary and myself.

How Ironic, Blake was abandoning the competition and Matthew, according to Blake, slowly disintegrating, while he, Michael, moved forward at full speed building his own firm in his own image powered by his own ideas of how to practice law and maintain integrity and loyalty among his lawyers, and at the same time, giving clients their monies worth. Indeed by the end of 2001 Sullivan & Connolly had become the "go to" firm, despite being half the size of the city's three other major firms.

CHAPTER 22

In the early years of their marriage the Sullivans lived next door to the Pearsons. Dick Pearson just starting out as a grain broker while Michael began practicing law at Barron, Walker, Youngman & Hamilton. The couples often fraternized and each couple had two small children who played together. Dick became a trader at Barnes & Company, an old line firm trading in wheat and grains that traced its beginning back four generations. The current head of the Company, Cyrus Barnes tried to keep up the firm's reputation but lost interest in running it marking most of his time participating in the social life of the city.

After four years the Pearsons moved away from the neighborhood to a bigger house as Dick Pearson grew more prosperous as the grain business grew more prosperous. Dick turned out to be the golden boy at Barnes & Co., indispensable to Cyrus "Cy" Barnes. The couples drifted apart though Mary continued to see Sue Pearson at social functions. Midway through the year 2000 Michael received a call from Dick, asking if he could see him as soon as possible.

An hour later he sat across from Michael in his office pouring out a tale of betrayal. In ten years he had aged from the young man Michael had known; his hair had turned gray and at forty five he looked fifty five. He dressed as a successful grain broker, pin striped suit, wing tips, rep tie and the look of a veteran. After a warm greeting he broached the problem. Since they had lost track of each other Dick had indeed become successful and wealthy. The company star, its chief revenue producer and a favorite of Cy Barnes. As the relationship grew Barnes looked upon Dick Pearson as a son and gave him more and more responsibility running the company. Recently he'd been given a new assignment rehabilitating five old grain elevators Barnes had been able to pick up for next to nothing. They sat at portside in the city, empty, run down and producing no revenue. Dick moved first to borrow money from several banks to refurbish the elevators to make them into serviceable facilities. This meant taking on millions in debt with the five elevators as collateral plus a guarantee signed by Cy Barnes, guaranteeing repayment of the loans. The deal meant risk, but Barnes had faith in Dick's abilities having watched him make a lot of money for the firm in his sixteen years as trader and eventually chief operating officer.

At the same time he managed the company he took to the road three weeks out of every month for a year. His target customer: the Japanese with its boom economy. Meeting with Japanese bankers every week he put together a consortium that would purchase or lease tankers, sail them to the U.S. and come down river to Barnes & Company's five grain elevators, load their holds with grain and return back to Japan. Orders were placed with Barnes, whose traders under Dick's direction, lined up grain producers who shipped their product by rail to the five grain elevators, each of which had tracks running alongside. Barnes & company handled the entire transaction for a fee. They bought the grain from the producer, shipped it to the elevators, loaded it onto the Japanese ships and guaranteed delivery. For this service they were paid handsomely.

At the same time he negotiated with the Japanese, and later the Koreans and Taiwanese to insure purchase of wheat, he and his traders roamed the country putting together a network of grain sellers to keep the elevators full. Within twelve months a contingent of buyers and sellers had been assembled and Barnes & company reduced debt and enhanced its equity position in the five elevators labeled the "golden geese." They hailed Dick Pearson as a hero and the company's success was recorded in the Wall Street Journal, with

Cy Barnes taking all the credit, leaving Dick's singular achievement out of the article, except for one sentence mentioning his name. Cy Barnes chief activity was promoting himself. His father, grandfather and great grandfather had built the business while he gradually succeeded in diminishing it through inattention, that is, until Dick Pearson joined the company and took the company to new heights and profitability. Barnes bragged at his clubs about his prowess but the men who knew him considered him a blowhard, but gave him credit for rejuvenation of the Company, especially after the Wall Street Journal article.

Based on his latest "success" Barnes recruited five prominent business men in the city to serve on his board of directors, chief among them Bernard Samuelson, head of one of two major banks, and like Barnes he had inherited his position as a result of his father and grandfather's successful acquisition of a majority of the bank's stock. Barnes and Samuelson often spent afternoons at the University Club drinking and playing cards, and while always done discreetly, they showed a liking for the ladies, not entirely unknown by their wives who spent an inordinate amount of time outdoing each other socially and didn't seem to mind their husband's piccadilloes as long as it didn't interfere with their pleasure or lifestyle.

Samuelson was sharper than Barnes and didn't have an ego. He told Barnes he would come on the board, if he could be chairman and his bank the company's top lender. The obvious conflict didn't seem to bother either of them. Samuelson's real motive: get to know Japanese bankers thru Dick Pearson's connections. He liked Barnes and his social connections but held him in low esteem as a businessman.

With operations running smoothly and cash flow streaming from various projects, Dick turned his attention to investments and diversification of assets. Ships carrying cargo from China and Pacific Rim countries continued to come into port and he urged Barnes to invest in warehouses to hold merchandise until it could be shipped around the country. The idea being the warehouses could be depreciated over a short period under favorable tax rules allowing the company to reduce its taxes while increasing equity. Barnes's equity increased since he held a majority of the stock. Over the years Barnes had given Dick a few shares of stock as a bonus at Christmas amounting to one percent of the outstanding shares; other than that he held eighty percent the other nineteen percent being held by his friends and members of the board.

As Dick continued to build the business Barnes became fonder and fonder of wine, women and song. This disturbed many of the employees; but not Dick since he received a handsome salary and didn't have Barnes looking over his shoulder. He understood his work built the business for Cy Barnes yet he didn't resent it because he enjoyed the work and knew his reputation was growing throughout the industry. One day in early March Barnes came rushing into his office unannounced, flush of face and seated himself down in a black leather couch which sat across the room from Dick's desk. The office was simple, a few pictures on the wall of men fly fishing, Dick favorite sport, a conference table with four chairs, a book case full of leather binders containing records of sales and purchases of wheat and grain and little else. If one walked in off the street they would be struck by the utter unpretentiousness of the office. It seemed a perfect fit for Dick Pearson's business needs with no frills to impress visitors.

"Dick, I've got problems," he began

"Well it can't be that bad, we've been able to solve our problems in the past and come back stronger than ever."

"It's not the business Dick, I've got personal problems, my wife is a spendthrift, that I can handle, I belong to five clubs to keep up appearances and that's manageable. No I've got myself in some real trouble at the gambling tables in Las Vegas."

"How much do you owe?" Dick said, not bothering to hide his shock; he suddenly realized he'd not kept track of Barnes, thinking he'd been blessed to be left alone to run the company.

Barnes hung his head and didn't look at him but uttered what sounded like "two million dollars."

"Did you say two million dollars? Did I hear that right?"

"You did."

"When? How?" he asked incredulously.

"Well, not all at once, gradually." He sat slumped down on the couch, half ashamed and half fearful, rationalizing it was 'his money,' he had lost.

"Where did you get that kind of money? It certainly hasn't been coming out of the company's coffers. I know you've paid yourself some hefty dividends, but not that much."

"Well, he stammered, I'm pretty well known down there as a high roller and when I show up they give me chips and in the beginning I had some respectable winnings, then I started to plow it all back and the casinos let me put it on the tab. I was there this past week end and Meyer Butsky, one of the owners, took me aside and said there would be no more tab until I paid the two million, worse he said I have two months to pay up or else his backers would demand satisfaction, he didn't threaten, but I couldn't mistake the way he said it. I have to sell the grain elevators."

"That would kill us," Dick erupted, "we worked hard to get those elevators; they are the backbone of our business. They produce a steady stream of cash flow."

"Can we survive if they are sold?" he asked pleadingly.

"Probably, but the business wouldn't be worth much by the time you pay your gambling debt; we'd be down to selling product and the warehouses which are not paid for yet."

"I have no choice! I need your help to sell the elevators."

"Why should I sell myself out of a job?"

"I'll give you half the proceeds of sale if you can sell them. That will give me at least a million and a half which will pay three quarters of the debt and still leave me the owner of Barnes & Company and some prestige intact."

"Who knows about this debt?" Dick asked, thinking quickly about Barnes's offer to split the proceeds of sale.

"No one, not even my wife. When I go to Las Vegas I tell everyone I'm going south on business. The casinos, I'm pretty sure, haven't broadcast my presence as far as I know and no one at the clubs I frequent has ever raised the subject. So no, I'm confident no one here knows."

"Are there any potential buyers?"

"I met a couple of New Yorkers in Las Vegas and they got interested when I told them about the grain elevators, I was doing a little bragging and I detected a small gleam in their eyes. One of the fellows, Oscar Boorstein asked if I ever considered selling. I said: 'not a chance,' and of course that happened when I was only down a hundred thousand and saw no problem covering that amount."

"What business were these men in?" Dick said

"They told me they owned a number of businesses without any specifics but I surmised they were involved with a holding company with a number of subsidiaries. The man gave me his card. Barnes took his wallet from his breast pocket, laid it on the table and fished out a number of business cards. After a moment searching he handed one to Dick who read it aloud.

"Oscar Boorstein, President, JBL Limited, One Chase Manhattan, New York, New York. Fancy looking," he added.

"What do you say? Fifty percent of the proceeds if you can make the sale."

"I'll think about it and let you know tomorrow."

That night he talked it over with Sue, his wife, and they decided he could do worse. If successful on a five million dollar sale he would have enough to go into business for himself or a new buyer might want him to stay on and manage the business for a while at least at his present salary and maybe more. The next morning he received a call at his desk from Barnes asking, almost pleading for an answer.

"I've decided to do it, however I want your word that I will receive half the proceeds and I presume we're talking about a cash sale not cash and stock or stock alone from this JBL Limited."

"It has to be cash I have one month to pay my marker or God only knows what those Vegas villains will come up with. You have my word." Dick thought, you fool, they're in the business of gambling don't blame them for your bad judgment.

Once assured of Barnes's promise, he set about determining the value of the elevators, aware any buyer would do that independently and he wanted his own appraisal to back up his offer of sale. At the same time he made a quick analysis of the cost of bringing the elevators up to a state of the art condition and figured one million would do it. Within days contractors were at work making the necessary upgrades. Fifteen days had elapsed since his discussion with Barnes and Dick was satisfied with the company's equipment and its balance sheet. He called Boorstein in New York, identified himself and said he understood from Cy Barnes, his "boss" that JB L Limited might be interested in Barnes & Company's grain elevators. Boorstein sounded very cool to the suggestion.

"When I saw your boss in Las Vegas I asked him if he had any interest in selling his business and he said 'no,' what changed his mind?"

Realizing an inquiry might be made, Dick decided to give a straight answer. "He has a few debts he wants to pay off and is looking to sell assets to do it."

Men like Oscar Boorstein are very careful; they want to see if they are dealing with a fire sale situation or not. Moreover they have ways of doing a top to bottom investigation of any potential investment and Boorstein sounded like a fellow who guessed the debt Dick spoke of was connected to the tables at Las Vegas.

"I'll tell you what Mr. Pearson, you come to New York, say in a week and tell us what you've got to sell and we'll see if there is something in it for Barnes and ourselves."

Armed with photographs, balance sheets, production figures and a roster of Japanese bankers, Dick arrived in New York the next week as promised. Before he left he advised Barnes of his conversation with Boorstein, including his answer of why he wanted to sell. Barnes gave off a cry and started to object but Dick silenced him saying: "Cy you can't fool with these guys, they're sharp. The first thing they'll do is investigate your record in Las Vegas, and don't think they can't get it. If they want the elevators and the Japanese contracts they won't care what you owe or how desperate you are to pay off gambling debts. They'll pay a fair price because we won't sell unless we get one."

"What do we do if they try to low ball us?"

"We turn it down and figure some other way to get you out of this mess. Don't worry, we have a first class product and a money maker and besides I have half of this deal and we're not selling for cheap."

. . .

"So you've got incentive!" Boorstein concluded.

"You bet I do and that's why you can be sure I'll be honest and give you everything you need to know to make a decision."

"Do you have authority to negotiate?"

"Yes, I believe I do, subject to Barnes's final approval; if the price is right he'll go along."

"What happens if he won't?"

"In that event, if I think the price fair, I would convince him of that and he'll listen to me."

"Ok, that's fair and square, I believe you're up front Dick, so let's leave it at this: within the week Jim Larson and I will come out to your place and look over the physical plant and the elevators and you give your books to our accounting firm here in New York and I'll alert our lawyers to start a preliminary draft of a contract for a cash sale. We put up no earnest money. We make a deal in two weeks or we don't."

"Do you have to run it by a board," Dick asked.

"Yes, of course, but that can be accomplished with a phone conference, and if we say it's ok, it will be ok. The board is not a worry. Ok?"

"All right, I'll see you and Jim Larson in about five days, right?"

"You got it."

Dick Pearson flew home and thought about his conversation with Boorstein. He'd done the right thing by being on the up and up. He felt sure he had established a basis for trust which would make the sale much easier. In his dealings at Barnes & Company, from the very beginning, he treated all his customers with complete honesty and never lost one through lack of trust, suspicion, or undercutting resulting in loss of business. Some might argue with this philosophy but in the long run those using deceit often ended up in bankruptcy, jail or both. Big and fast profits with Jail for the finale.

Five days later Oscar Boorstein and Jim Larson flew into town, booked into the Wharton Hotel, curtesy of Cy Barnes, and went to work. Following Dick from elevator to elevator, they inspected every foot as they went through, talking to the managers, asking questions of Dick. At the end of their first day on the ground they said they had seen enough. "We're interested," they told Dick, "we don't think a lot of Barnes but we trust you." That night Barnes hosted the two men at his home, inviting the board of directors and their wives in a lavish display of food and wines, hoping to impress the visitors with his wealth and station in the community. Dick and Susan had deliberately begged off allowing Barnes to be the star of his own show.

The two New Yorkers were cordial, even charming but underwhelmed by the display. They had plenty of experience dealing with stuff shirts with inflated egos and usually bought their businesses at bargain rates because they saw through their façade—wealth and no brains. The New Yorkers were second generation and they hadn't gotten where they were buttering up phonies. They respected Dick because they deemed him honest and sharp where his boss appeared borderline ethically and stupid. Their deal would be with Dick Pearson. In parting they advised Dick to bring Barnes: "You come to New York next week, we're interested and we'll talk more and see where it goes."

After they departed Dick and Barnes speculated where the "deal" was headed.

"I think we've made the sale old boy, Barnes gushed. You should have seen those guys at my house charming the ladies, telling jokes to the board; we got along famously. They realized I'm well off and don't need to sell if we don't get our price."

"I don't know Cy, I think you're underestimating those fellows. They're tough and smart, they make a price and that will be they're bottom line."

That took some wind out of Barnes's sail and he responded: "Dick we've got to sell, I've got one week and I've already had a call from Meyer Butsky."

"What did he say?"

"I told him we were on the verge of a sale of assets and I'd be able to pay seventy-five percent of the debt within a week."

"Was he satisfied with that?" "Barely, he wanted to know when he'd get the rest."

CHAPTER 23

Dick Pearson and Barnes flew to New York, Barnes dozing most of the way while Dick reviewed the approach he intended to take with Oscar Boorstein. The appraisal he received of the firm's assets came to four million seven hundred and fifty dollars, which included the improvements ordered for the grain elevators. He guessed the JLP Limited appraisal would come in at least four million and they'd make an offer to buy at three million five hundred thousand. He didn't discuss this with Barnes but decided to listen to the offer and see Cy's reaction. He hoped for the best price, but if Barnes went for the first offer he received, he'd have enough to get himself out of hock for a month or two and Dick stood to make a million plus.

The night before the meeting they booked into the Waldorf Astoria and Barnes wanted to party the minute they settled in their rooms. Dick begged off saying he'd meet him down stairs for dinner and fend for himself after that. The turn down didn't deter Cy who knew the night spots and some female acquaintances he decided to look up. At breakfast the following morning he complained of a headache and told Dick he'd been on the town and had a wonderful time although he'd had too much to drink. Even with a hangover Barnes maintained a commanding figure at six feet two, steel gray hair combed straight back with the part on the left side, steel rimmed glasses and dressed in a suit tailored on Saville Row, London. Well aware of the look he so studiously cultivated, coupled with his aloofness, he intimidated a lot of people and women seemed to think him handsome. Dick never succumbed to his charm having watched him for years and knew the façade which housed a limited capacity. In Dick's eyes Barnes lacked substance, but he fooled a lot of people. The New Yorkers looked upon him as a good natured dunce, and decided to deal with Dick exclusively.

At 10:00 a.m. they arrived in the lobby of One Chase Manhattan in lower Manhattan after taking a cab from the Waldorf. Once in the building they were directed to the fifty fifth floor and when they got off the elevator they were confronted by an armed guard sitting at a desk directly in front of them. When they introduced themselves and advised who they were there to see he made a call without even looking at them. He received the answer he expected and gave them each a visitor's pass and directed them to the right down a long hallway lined with offices each having two secretaries sitting outside. They finally reached Boorstein's office, and Barnes found it imposing. Beautiful art on the walls, windows on two sides overlooking Wall Street, rich oriental rugs, antique furniture expertly placed strategically around the room. Dick, having been in the office two weeks previously, felt comfortable but knew, from the look on Cy Barnes face, he believed he was in his element; that he had been born to be in offices on Wall Street in lower Manhattan. A very important man, the President of a very successful business, Barnes & Company, coming to do business with equals in New York.

Boorstein rose from his desk to meet them and gestured toward Jim Larson already seated on a leather couch in a sitting area in one corner of the office. "Welcome Cy, you remember my associate, Jim Larson, let's all sit down and get re-acquainted. Boorstein acted humbly, ushering them over to chairs ranged around the couch, and then ordered coffee, Danish and orange juice. As they ate Boorstein inquired about their trip and whether they had any trouble getting to One Chase.

Barnes responded to his questions, doing all the talking, and assumed he and Boorstein were the principles in the conversation and that Dick and Jim Larson were just subordinates. Boorstein did or said nothing to abuse him of his assumption. He'd dealt with many men, like Barnes, and felt no need to alert them to the fact they really weren't very important, better to let them think they had command of the situation until they found out, on their own, they didn't. They were usually out of Boorstein's sight before they realized they had been had.

"I assume you gentlemen will be flying home tonight so I suggest we get down to business. We are interested in buying all the assets," he said, without emphasis or fanfare in a cool modulated voice. "We have examined all aspects of a purchase, from our viewpoint, of course. We do not wish to dicker over price. After careful consideration our offer is three million dollars."

"That's preposterous," Barnes exclaimed. We have an appraisal that shows net worth of four plus million dollars, and we've just spent a million bringing our grain elevators up to state of the art. No I won't hear of it," he blurted out. The New Yorkers didn't blink, their faces set in stone. Silence.

Dick Pearson spoke up and said, "Gentlemen do you have an office where Mr. Barnes and I can consult?"

"We do. Jim, will you show the gentlemen to Ray Meyer's office. I'm going to give you a number if you change your mind. Jim and I will remain in this office and be available for any further consultation you wish to pursue."

Barnes mumbled, he didn't see any need for further discussion but would listen to anything Dick had to say. The two left and followed Jim Larson down the hall to the Meyer office. He told them they could get food or anything else they wanted by picking up the phone and ordering it.

"Just like room service," he said.

"Thanks Jim," Dick said and closed the door.

"I'm sorry I blew up Dick," Barnes said, now penitent. "I've probably blown the deal but I don't care. Those fellows are trying to get the elevators for cheap. I won't let them do it!"

"You can't blame them Cy, they're business men and I think they know they don't have to deal at arms length with us. They know you have to sell."

"That may be so and the Las Vegas boys are a week away but if I have to sell Barnes & Co., the whole kit and caboodle, I'd hate to do it. I need enough to pay off my debt and still have a some to live on. They're not offering enough."

"That may be true but look at the flip side. If you make a deal to sell only the elevators, you still have a going concern that's been around for seventy years and all the prestige attached to it. The company made money before the elevators and it will make money if they're gone."

"You've got a point there Dick, but I won't sell at three million when it's valued at four million dollars."

"That's true about the market value, but are there any buyers around interested? I don't think so."

"Ok let's sit tight for a few minutes. I'm starving and I think you'll think clearer on a full stomach." He picked up the phone and before he could say anything a voice at the other end said: "Yes sir, what can I get for you?" Dick placed an order and within ten minutes a knock came at the door and a table wheeled in covered with a white table cloth, linen napkins, sterling silverware, sandwiches and two pots of hot coffee. They ate in silence, momentarily forgetting their circumstances, giving into hunger generated by the tense atmosphere in Oscar Boorstein's office. Food was a welcome diversion.

When they finished Cy Barnes pushed back from the table and said: "What do you think we should do?"

"You were pretty steamed up when they told us what they intended to pay and that established you had pride and don't want to be taken for a sucker. That's in our favor. The question is can we save your pride and still come away with a sale?"

"How?" Barnes asked forlornly.

"Let's do this. We go back and offer three million, seven hundred and fifty thousand dollars, that's a million less than our appraisal, but still under theirs, I'm guessing."

"What happens if they don't budge?"

"We walk," Dick answered "and you sell Barnes & Company, pay off your debt, and we split whatever is left."

"Do you think, if we leave, we'll ever hear from then again?"

"It's a gamble. If it works, you will have your pride, a sale and most of your debt paid off. If it doesn't you'll still have the business, the elevators and maybe you can work out a deal with your Las Vegas friends. The question is do you have the guts to walk out if they nix our offer."

Barnes tightened his jaw and tried to look firm, inwardly he felt sick at the thought of having to face the Nevada gang without the money when they come calling at the end of the week. "Ok I'll do it," he said with little conviction.

"Good. Let me do the talking, and when I say it's time to leave, thank the gentlemen for their courtesy and follow me out the door. These guys are tough and if they turn us down, they won't bat an eye when we leave, but I'm betting they'll come around." He picked up the phone, dialed the number Boorstein had given him and heard Boorstein's voice. "Yes."

"If you fellas have had your lunch and are still willing to talk we'll come down to your office."

"Come right down, we've been expecting your call."

This time Boorstein invited them to sit around a round conference table in a corner of the room next to a window, the late afternoon sun streaming through creating a warm setting though the men sitting at the table were deadly serious and not feeling particularly warm towards each other.

Dick opened with a discussion of his appraisal, pointing out it was a million, seven hundred and fifty thousand more than JBL offered. He said he agreed with Barnes the offer on the table was not acceptable. He explained that over lunch they had carefully reviewed what they could accept, and the figure they reached amounted to far less than they had hoped to receive.

"And what is that figure?" Boorstein interrupted, his eyes not moving from Pearson's, realizing the deal would be cut with Dick, not Barnes. He wondered how tough the younger man would be and whether he could convince the old man to go through with the sale.

"Three million, seven hundred and fifty thousand!" Dick said firmly looking Boostein and Larson directly in the eye.

They looked at each other and Boorstein spoke, not menacingly, but with a firmness that matched Dick's. "No, we think our offer made sense. I invite you to change your mind."

Barnes looked at Dick and he could feel his insides shrink, his mouth went dry and a red flush slowly mounted in his face. He said nothing.

"No Mr. Boorstein our offer stands." Dick replied calmly. "I think it's a fair price for you and something we can live with." Silence followed.

Boorstein broke it up and said: "Well gentlemen I'm sorry we couldn't cut a deal, but that's the way things go sometimes."

Dick and Barnes got up from the table, shook hands with their two adversaries and without a word made for the door. The minute they were out of the office Dick said: "Don't look back, just keep going. They were silent as they headed down the long hall toward the front office, Barnes dejected. In a strange way Dick felt elated; they had the guts to turn down a bad deal and along with it Dick's million and a half dollar share. They took the elevator down fifty five floors and stepped into the lobby. Only a few steps had been taken when Dick heard his name called. A uniformed guard came abreast of them and asked if either of them were Richard Pearson. "I am sir."

"There's a phone call for you sir, can you take it over at the information desk?" He followed the guard while Barnes waited at the glass doors opening on to the street. He picked up the receiver and said: "Hello?"

"All right you young whipper snapper, you got it, three million, seven hundred and fifty thousand, sold American. Call me when you get back and I'll put our lawyers on it."

Dick smiled and said: "Mr. Boostein I presume?"

"You got that right Mr. Pearson."

"Nice doing business with you Mr. Boorstein." And they both laughed.

"Any time kid, you have guts, and your boss seems to have some too."

He calmly handed the phone back to the woman at the information desk and slowly made his way back to Barnes waiting impatiently at the door. "We've made the sale," Dick said flashing a triumphant smile.

"What?" Barnes grabbed the lapels on Dick's suit coat. "We what?"

"That was Boorstein on the phone, he didn't want to let us get away without sewing up the deal."

"My God," Barnes shouted and heads in the lobby turned to see if a madman was loose. Quickly he recovered a semblance of calm and complained to Dick as they reached the street: "Hell we were crazy, he probably would have paid five million for those elevators."

"I don't think so Cy, you've got your three million seven plus and you've kept the rest of the business and the prestige that goes with it."

"This changes things a bit for me Dick, I'm going to spend a couple days in New York and arrange to work out a pay schedule with my Las Vegas "bankers." I'll see you back at the shop in a couple of days. And by the way thanks for your help."

Back at the Hotel Dick called Susan and told her: "We capped the deal and we have a half of three million seven hundred and fifty dollars coming to us from the sale. I can stay or leave Barnes & Company but there will be time enough to figure that out when I get home."

CHAPTER 24

Michael took copious notes while Dick Pearson, in a two hour narrative, explained what happened in the sale of the Barnes & Company grain elevators. From experience, he considered it vital to get as much from the client as possible in the initial interview because, with the passage of time, they tend to remember less and less of the facts.

"Do you want to take a break," he queried, hoping Dick would not stop, yet realizing he seemed about played out.

"No, I think it best I continue while everything is fresh. To continue, when I got home from New York, I went back to running the company and working out the sale with Boorstein transmitting title to the elevators. Barnes stayed in New York for the week playing around at some of his familiar haunts. Two weeks passed and I hadn't seen or heard from him so I called him at home on Friday and he made excuses why he hadn't come into work and said he'd be in Monday. He came in Monday alright and the only thing I wanted to do was to ask about my share of the money. Boorstein told me he had sent a three million three hundred and seventy five thousand dollar cashier's check to a bank account Barnes set up in New York after we finalized the sale.

Around ten o'clock he came into my office and gave me a big hello and sat down. I said: 'Where is my share of the sale proceeds?' He kind of slouched down and told me he had paid two million to his Las Vegas creditors because they wouldn't take a down payment of a million and a half as he had planned. That left a million seven hundred and fifty thousand which he decided to keep; a million to capital to make up for the loss of income from the grain elevators. Then he gave me a proposition: 'We'll split the seven hundred and fifty thousand and I'm going to give you a raise.'

'What about our agreement?' I asked him.

'Well.' He said, and he had a mean look on his face, almost like a kid who'd been caught stealing 'I just decided it would be better to put the money into the business after paying off the debt and, well, I thought you would understand and besides I was under a lot of pressure when we talked about selling and I wasn't thinking very clearly.'

I told him we had a deal and if he didn't keep his word I would do whatever it took to collect my money."

Michael asked, "What did he say?" knowing the probable answer.

"He said he wished I wouldn't take it that way, that he had been my mentor and benefactor for sixteen years and that I should be satisfied with three hundred and seventy five thousand dollars for a few hours work in New York. He said both of us had been under pressure and we'd both be out of a job with Barnes & Company if he hadn't been able to pay off the debt. I told him I was through with him and his company and I would pursue a legal remedy to collect the debt. I told him to get out of my office and it would be vacated by the end of the day. He looked stricken. I don't think the old fool had the slightest idea I would tell him to take a hike. That's the story Michael." Three hours had elapsed and he'd written forty pages of notes, the makings of another interesting law suit.

"What can be done?" Dick asked, exhausted from his narrative.

"You've made an oral contract with this fellow without reducing it to writing. That would have been preferable. I believe we can get around that.

"That's right, I trusted his word; it never occurred to me to have some sort of paper written up. I worked for the man for sixteen years, and knew he had a loud mouth, and was a phony to boot, but I'd never seen him break his word. So much for trust."

"Normally an oral promise is unenforceable because it violates, what we call, the parole evidence rule—it can't be performed within a year. If we get around that problem, and I think we can, we'll have this stuff shirt before a jury within a year. Let's do this, I'll put a few of our people on the case and we'll develop a legal theory that will get us into court. From that point on we'll build a case against Mr. Barnes that will lay him open before the people who he thinks think so highly of him. From what you've told me, we can make it so hot for this fellow he might be afraid to go before a jury and risk his carefully built up standing in the community."

You could see the anxiety drain from Dick Pearson's face. Michael Sullivan inspired that kind of confidence in his clients. He was tough and they sensed it. He relished going after people like Barnes, the cheaters, the liars, the bad actors and better yet he got paid for it. Their battles were his battles, he and his firm's top litigators gave no quarter. When they took a case the client hired the toughest lawyers in the city. Michael had become, "the man to see."

A few weeks later they met in Michael's office and he outlined for Dick the tactics they would follow. First a demand letter to Barnes demanding the face amount of his share of the sale proceeds, and if that didn't bring a response a lawsuit filed under a theory Michael's research team came up with to avoid the parole evidence rule. They decided to allege a breach of contract theory known as promissory estopple. Michael explained the complaint sets out the facts exactly as Dick related and the enforceability of the contract relies on Barnes's offer to share the sale proceeds and Dick's acceptance of the offer by taking steps to affect a sale. Under the theory of estopple Barnes is estopped from claiming lack of written contract because Dick acted based on Barnes's verbal promise. Dick's testimony would be used to establish the facts of the case and Boorstein and Jim Larson's testimony to verify Dick's version.

As the time for trial grew near Michael made plans to fly to New York to take the depositions of Boorstein and Larson;

not knowing what to expect. He had to know where they stood; would they tell the truth or cover for Barnes hoping for some favor in return? Two weeks before trial he flew to New York and met with Boorstein, Larson and their attorneys in the law offices of Levine, Swartz, Bamberger & Weitzman on Madison Ave. Barnes had his own attorney present having decided not to come at the last minute.

Michael questioned Boorstein, first taking him through preliminaries dealing with JBL limited and then his history running the company. Proceeding with his questions Michael noted Boorstein made a very good witness, admitted to having his deposition taken many times and had been called as a witness in several trials involving the company. Michael found the witness couldn't be tricked or be led where he didn't want to go. His answers were calculated but appeared to be honest. Carefully he took him over his initial meeting with Dick Pearson and asked what he knew about Barnes's motivation for sale of the elevators.

"Mr. Pearson said, very candidly, that his Boss (Barnes) had incurred a gambling debt and had to sell to cover his losses."

"Did that make you think you could buy the elevators at a relatively cheap price?"

"No it did not. I sized Mr. Pearson up as a very sharp young man and the fact he disclosed this information told me he wanted a fair price or he wouldn't deal. To the contrary, I wanted to buy as cheap as possible but I realized that would not be feasible with Mr. Pearson. I did not know Mr. Barnes at this point."

"Did you inquire of Mr. Pearson what his role in such a sale would be and whether he had authority to make the sale?"

"Yes, we both did, Mr. Larson and myself. We didn't want to waste time dealing with Pearson only to find out he had no authority to deal."

"What did he tell you?"

Barnes's lawyer almost jumped out of his chair with an objection: "I object. Such a conversation would be pure hearsay and inadmissible at trial."

Michael calmly answered: "Mr. Pearson is a party and therefore if his conversation is combined with the testimony of Messers, Boorstein and Larson, the total conversation will be admissible counsel. I'm instructing the deponent to answer the question."

Turning to Boorstein he urged: "You may answer the question sir, and counsel your objection is saved for the court to rule on at trial."

Barnes's counsel knew what was coming next and he only hoped Boorstein would disclaim any knowledge of a deal made by Barnes to give Dick Pearson half the proceeds of sale.

Continuing his testimony, Boorstein said: "He told us he'd been given the authority and said he wanted to be perfectly honest with us; that he had an interest in the sale and that if he was successful Barnes had promised him half the proceeds."

"Why do you think he told you that?"

"I asked him myself and he wanted me to know that he stood to gain money from the sale but it must be for a fair price or he wouldn't make it, in other words he wouldn't dump it just to get his half."

"Did that affect your wanting to buy?"

"No. After he left we commented he could be trusted and wanted to warn us of his interest, yet that wouldn't affect his effort to get the best possible deal for the elevators. We felt he was straight up with us and that made the deal more enticing."

Michael knew then he had struck at the heart of the case and if he could coax the two gentlemen to testify in court, Barnes faced a tough time trying to convince a jury Pearson concocted a fairy tale. He also knew Barnes's attorney would have to tell him of Michael's lethal deposition of the two New York executives. After another hour of cross examination and rehabilitation the depositions ended.

Barnes's counsel could not shake the witnesses testimony of Dick's meeting in New York, their evaluation of the elevators in person and the second visit in New York with he and Barnes to consummate the sale. The Senior partner of Sullivan & Connolly flew home secure in the knowledge he was ready for trial in the case of Pearson vs. Barnes and Barnes & Company.

. . .

He awoke at eight the next morning after the flight home and Mary begged him to stay and get some rest but he demurred insisting they needed him back to work. The minute he hit the door and walked into his office, the intercom sounded and he heard Paul's voice asking if he could come down to his office.

"Sure Paul, can you bring a cup of black coffee with you when you come?"

"Ok, I'll be right there."

Once seated in Michael's office he handed him a cup of steaming black coffee and took a sip from one he brought for himself. "How did the deposition go?"

"Great. The JBL boys were stellar; they didn't bat an eye and gave me the same story Dick had given me. For once everyone is telling the truth except Barnes. It'll be interesting to see what he has to say in the wake of Boorstein's and Larson's deposition. How have things been going here?"

"Very well except for a problem that's developed involving Ben Armstead."

"What's Ben's problem?"

"He's leaving the firm and taking three associates with him and..." he held up his hand to stop the inevitable question, "and he's taking the Boniface insurance account with him."

The euphoria from the day before drained from Michael like water dripping off a man stepping out of the shower. "What in the world is going on?" he groaned, visibly shaken. Desertion always concerned him as he and Paul built the firm. In six years no one had left and they numbered seventy five lawyers. To their credit they had done everything to share their good fortune with their fellow partners and particularly the associates believing this method best to build and enlarge the firm. For six years the formula succeeded. Every lawyer hired, with a few exceptions, had been hired right out of law school and been the brightest and hardest working lawyers they could find. They expanded the firm, from exclusively trial lawyers, to corporate, securities, estate, probate, labor adding to their basic insurance defense practice salvaged from Michael's prior firm.

"Have you talked to him to see if he can be persuaded to stay?"

"Yes, to no avail, maybe he'll listen to you."

Michael reached for the phone and called Armstead. "Ben can you come down and see me, I'm here with Paul Connolly and he's just informed me of your plans?"

"Sure Michael, I'll be right down."

Within sixty seconds Ben Armstead came trooping into Michael's office. As he took a seat Michael studied his features and realized he had aged dramatically the last five years. Sometimes you get so busy you don't get to sit down a talk with fellow lawyers and this happened to Paul Connolly and Michael Sullivan as the firm grew rapidly. Ben had been hired as the sixth lawyer in the new firm and Michael kept him alongside at the counsel's table during trials. He taught him the art of cross examination, how to size up witnesses and close with a jury. Many in the firm thought Ben the fair haired boy who might someday succeed Michael. When he was ready Michael had turned him loose and he proved he had the makings of a great trial lawyer. Of all the people in the firm Michael was sure he'd rise to senior partner. To have him leave and take lawyers with him and an important client would be a real setback for the firm not to mention a grave disappointment to the founders.

"Is there anything we've done to make you or your wife unhappy Ben?"

"No," came the answer in a voice Michael judged to be apologetic.

"What's the problem then?"

"The firm is getting too big for me. I can see the day when you'll have over a hundred lawyers, maybe more in the next five years. I loved it when we were sixteen, I used to know everyone and they knew me. I loved trying cases with you and being able to pop into your office at any time, but I haven't been able to do that the last year or so Michael, you've been too busy and I've been too busy. Don't get me wrong, it's no one's fault, it just happens when you get bigger."

Softening his features Michael said: "I can understand wanting to be part of a smaller firm, I've been part of one twice, including this one. But you can't stand still, Ben, you've got to keep competing, the practice of law is changing rapidly, clients want full service they can't rely on small boutiques with a couple of specialties. That's why we've grown and will continue to grow, it doesn't mean the challenge of law is gone, in many ways it's more exciting; cases are bigger, the stakes and the risks higher—I don't shrink from that. By the way I'll be competing with you for the Boniface Insurance account. I don't know what arrangements you've made with them but I'll soon be finding out."

Alarmed, Ben blurted out: "They'll stick with me, I made sure of that before I decided to leave."

Realizing he couldn't change Armstead's mind he told him: "I would not have thought that of you Ben, they were our first big client and I let you work on that account without ever worrying about that account leaving much less being raided. You disappoint me."

"I wouldn't be too disappointed," Armstead retorted sulkily, "That's how you got the account in the first place."

"Wrong!" Michael shot back at him. I announced to my partners at Hamilton, Sullivan, Collins, Phelps & Peterson, I was leaving the partnership, it was only after I had done that that I competed for the Boniface company. The difference is you raided the account, by your own admission, and then informed Paul you were leaving and taking three associates with you. I question the ethics of that. Let's not quibble Ben, you let us know when you're leaving and we'll try to make it as smooth as possible. I'm truly sorry you're leaving because, as far as I am concerned, and I think I speak for Paul, we were looking forward to having you as our senior partner. That's not possible now so I wish you good luck and be assured we will try to keep the Boniface account."

Ben Armstead arose from his chair, prepared to leave, knowing from Michael's tone the meeting was over. He exited the office, turned in the doorway, looked back at Michael and Paul and waved.

The partners sat in silence for about thirty seconds before Paul Connolly said: "Where did we go wrong?"

"I don't thing we went wrong when we picked him. He appeared eager as anyone in the firm yet at some point he changed. Maybe his wife, or a growing family caused the change. There are some who are not meant for this Paul; we gave him everything we had, taught him every trick and now he'll be competing with us. Betrayal is difficult still you're seeing it more and more in the practice. For some, the motive is greed, for Ben he didn't want to keep up the pace. I'll call Bob Northcutt and see if Ben is bluffing on getting the Boniface account."

He asked Maggie, his secretary, to get Northcutt on the phone and when he came on she said:

"Mr. Northcutt, Michael Sullivan calling, may I pass you through to him?"

"Hi Michael, I think I know what you're calling about."

"Good, I have Paul Connolly here with me, I'm going to put you on speaker phone, do you mind?"

"No, go ahead."

"Bob, we've just had a chat with Ben Armstead who informed us he is leaving the firm and taking with him a new client, Boniface

Insurance. What's going on? We could have used some warning, we go back a long way.

"Michael, I apologize to you but my hands were tied. I have been told to stay out of it or lose my job. They warned me not to alert you."

"By whom?"

"Tom Beecham, the President,"

"Why?"

"As far as I can figure out Beecham and Armstead have become fast friends, social friends. He's been coming out here once a month for the last year and every time he comes he brings his wife and she's become close to Tom's wife. The two men play golf. Tom told me about the deal with Ben; I argued with him and said Ben couldn't handle it and he told me to stay out of it."

"What about the board, were they made aware of the decision?"

"They do what Tom says, remember his old man is the major stock holder in the company."

"Would it do any good to talk with Tom directly," Michael said.

"I don't think so Michael, It's a fiat accompli. I've seen the letter of termination you'll be receiving from Tom"

The partners looked at each other, the only discernable emotion detectable—anger.

"Gentlemen I'm sick at heart but I've got thirty years in the company and I'd like five more before I retire."

"Ok Bob, we'll await the letter." Michael hung up the phone.

"Nothing like loyalty versus survival, still I don't blame the poor guy," Paul said.

Michael reflected for a moment and then said, "Paul, let's have the firm meet at ten a.m. tomorrow morning, coffee and doughnuts. I want Ben and the men he's taking with him excluded. I want to tell everyone what's happened and where we go from here."

"Good idea, I'll get out the word."

On the way back to his office Paul O'Connell mused about he and Michael, especially how Michael had placed such high hopes in Ben Armstead. Within another six years he would surely have been number three in the firm. How strange life is and how easily certainty becomes confusion and frustration. He knew his partner had taken a real blow and admired how Michael had kept himself under complete control in their just ended phone conference with Bob Northcutt. I've had a couple of days to absorb the shock he thought, I'm sure Michael is still in shock. As requested he arranged to have the staff alerted to the next day's meeting. When they were all assembled, Paul called Michael in his office and advised: "The folks are ready, come on down."

Michael opened the door to the room where they were all gathered and immediately all conversation stopped, eyes turned toward him expectantly.

"At ease," he said smiling as he made his way to the front of the room. With that said they all relaxed. The saying was a carryover from his days in the Air Force and they all knew what it meant.

"I'm sure you've all heard Ben Armstead is leaving us, along with Tom Fredricks, Toby Johnson, and Johnathan Harding all associates," he began. "What you may not know is they have managed to take the Boniface insurance account with them." An audible gasp could be heard throughout the room.

Michael continued: "I know that many of you have worked on the account and are presently handling cases. I have ascertained from the company the transition will take about two months but I want to assure each of you no one will lose their job because the account is lost. You will be assigned to other matters. Further I fully intend to fill the void left by the loss of Boniface. With our reputation as trial lawyers we will gain more insurance business than we can handle. With respect to the gentlemen leaving, it will be a loss, but we wish them well. As far as the future of the firm, I anticipate it will continue to grow and hope all of you will grow with it. The law is changing, getting more competitive and this firm will compete because if you don't you regress and fall into a rut. Our policy has always been to treat everyone here, lawyer and non lawyer equally. We are not and will not become a firm where the profits are kept at the top and not shared with the workers. I think you all know that. Since the founding of this firm we have never lost a lawyer. Now we have and could in the future. If we do I hope you will come to us and tell us your intent so the parting is amicable. That's pretty much of wanted to say. I found out yesterday these men were leaving so we wanted to let you know as soon as possible that this firm will not suffer from this loss and your jobs are secure. Thank you." They stood and applauded loudly as he and Paul exited the room. He didn't see Armstead again until years later.

CHAPTER 25

Before a month had gone by the court set April 21 for the trial of *Pearson vs. Barnes.* On the eve of trial Dick Pearson and Michael met in his office to prepare direct and cross examination. Nearby, Boorstein and Jim Larson were safely ensconced in the executive suite of the Empire hotel ready to testify on the second or third day of trial. Though they volunteered to testify, Michael placed them under subpoena to be sure they didn't change their minds at the last minute. After Michael filed the complaint, Brad Smith, Barnes's attorney, offered to settle for one hundred and fifty thousand dollars. Dick Pearson turned it down considering it a scornful gesture. The case proceeded with discovery no further talk of settlement.

Michael had a concern going forward. Dick, although a relative young man, had had a heart attack in early January, and while fully recovered, he remained worried about his heart and the stress created by the law suit. He hadn't raised the issue and Michael had not asked about it, by mutual consent.

After a light supper of sandwiches and coffee at seven o'clock, they adjourned to the conference room where Michael began to review the questions he intended to ask on direct examination. Over the years he had developed a technique he found helpful in preparing witnesses for trial. He first ran through the questions and listened to the witness's answer. Then they discussed the question until the witness understood what Michael expected when he asked the question. Critics called this coaching the witness but he considered it important as a way to strip out irrelevant testimony witnesses tend to give trying to boost their bono fides. For

Michael it was vital that the witness understand the import of his answer to the question, which had been carefully tailored to the facts of the case. When satisfied the witness was properly prepared on direct examination he repeated the exercise for cross examination. In order to give the witness confidence when cross examined, Michael gave him the answer to every question he assumed opposing counsel would hit him with. When cross examined at trial the witness quickly became aware the questions being asked were the ones Michael said he could expect. The answers flowed to the consternation of the cross examiner.

Over the years he came to understand that once prepared and programed with the answers the witness subconsciously burned the answers into his brain and when a question was asked, he automatically gave the answer desired with great confidence. He compared it to cramming for a final exam. During the examine you retain all the answers, afterward everything drains from the brain and it returns to normal. He seldom became concerned about his witnesses on cross examination because they knew what was coming and were thoroughly prepared.

At nine p.m. they had just finished direct examination and Michael asked Dick if he wanted a break. He did and asked if he could make a phone call. When he returned from making the call he sat down and looked at Michael who sensed something had happened during the call. Dick was perspiring and his hands shook. Gently, Michael asked: "Are you all right?"

"Michael, I can't go through with the trial tomorrow. I just talked with Susan, she's frightened I will have another heart attack. Ever since I've been here preparing I have felt a fast beating of my pulse."

Atrial Fibrillation flashed across Michael's mind, he knew all about it from a client who had for years. You have to lay down to get the pulse back in rhythm. It races up and down and it's frightening. "Do you have A-Fib Dick?"

"I think so, right now I feel nauseous."

Instantaneously Michael shifted gears. He got Pearson to lay on the floor and found a pillow to put under his head and said: "Ok Dick I'll get hold of Brad Smith right now; I'm sure he and the court would agree to a set over....."

"No No," Dick whispered in a pained voice. "Michael, see if you can settle this thing tonight. I just can't go to trial. I don't think my heart will stand it."

The situation had suddenly become attenuated. He couldn't go against his client's wishes and to go forward amounted to fighting with one hand tied behind his back. He saw no option and quickly decided to follow the client's request. In a calm and somber voice he said: "All right Dick, I understand your concern, I'll do everything I can and I'll start right now."

When he first accepted the case he told Pearson it might well be settled before trial thinking Barnes would be hesitant to have the story of his betrayal played out in open court and from there to daily newspaper headlines that were sure to appear as the trial dragged on. So far it hadn't happened. He had taken the depositions of Barnes, Oscar Boorstein, Jim Larson, the chairman of the Board of Barnes & Company and each of the deponents, except Barnes, told of the deal to pay Dick half the sale price, and in the case of the board chairman, Barnes bragged to him after a few drinks he planned to pay Dick five hundred thousand dollars, not the one million, seven hundred and fifty thousand promised.

He dialed Brad Smith's number at home; his wife answered and told him Brad was still at the office. He thanked her and dialed Smith's direct line.

"Hello, Brad Smith," came the answer.

"Brad, Michael Sullivan. "Getting ready for tomorrow?"

"Just like you," came the friendly reply.

With a small knot in his stomach, growing by the minute, Michael ventured: "Shall we talk a bit about tomorrow?"

"I'm game," Brad answered. Michael didn't know Smith had Cy Barnes sitting directly across from him in the large conference room at Burns, Jordan & Smith. "In fact I was about to call you with a little probe on settlement."

Michael felt the knot in his stomach start to dissolve. This might work out after all, he cautiously thought. Dick continued to perspire, his face ashen. Michael gestured for him to stay down on the floor. "Your first probe, I recall, came to a hundred thousand dollars and my client turned that down as a ridiculous gesture.

"How does seven hundred and fifty thousand sound?"

"I can't do that Brad, however, I'll pass it on although I'm sure the answer will be no."

"Well, that's it. I'm going back to work here and if you have anything for me, holler."

Michael hung up and looked at Dick now supine on the floor. He went and got a pitcher of ice water, pulled up a chair next to his client and handed him a glass and said: "How are you doing fella?"

"A little better, what did he say?"

"He offered seven hundred and fifty thousand."

"I want to settle, but I just can't do it for that. What shall we do?"

"Fortunately, I think he wants to settle too because he admitted he intended to call me, so at least we have the ball up in the air."

"He expects me to contact you with his offer and get back to him with a counter offer. Initially I'm going to tell him seven hundred and fifty is not enough and we will have to go to trial.

"What if he turns down a counter offer?"

"If that be the case we are in big trouble. We will have to go to the court house and try to settle it in the morning. He'll guess I'm on the run and can't or don't want to try the case and we'd be lucky to get two hundred thousand dollars."

"What will you do?" Dick asked, putting his head back down on the floor.

"I'd do just what I said and gamble Barnes is just as reluctant as you are to go to trial."

"Oh Michael I'm sorry I've let you down," Dick moaned, clearly in pain.

"Look Dick," he said soothingly, "I know you're sick, I can see that and I don't blame you or Susan a bit. Let's go for broke and hope for the best."

Again he dialed Smith's office. The time: 10.00 p.m. Knowing it would be Michael, Brad Smith answered and said: "What's the word?"

"The word is 'no dice,' you've got to do better. I've been working with Dick all night and my witnesses are staying at the Empire. You've got to do better!"

At this moment Brad felt a shifting of the burden. He had no counter offer, instead the threat of trial and a client who wanted to settle but settle cheap. He hung up and told Barnes what Michael had said.

"Do you have any liquor on the premises?" Barnes asked. Without a word, Brad got up from the table, walked down to the end of the conference room, pressed a button partially hidden from view and slowly a bar swung out from the paneled wall and behind it seventy bottles of liquor sat on four glass shelves. He reached in, took two glasses, poured half a glass of scotch in each, walked back to where Barnes was seated and placed one in front of him. Barnes emptied half of it and placed the glass on the table. He wiped his mouth with the sleeve of his impeccably tailored suit coat.

Brad in shirt sleeves and suspenders raised his glass and said: "Cheers, we can bluff these guys and say we're ready to go or we can go back to them with some figure above seven hundred and fifty thousand dollars."

"Bastards," Barnes groaned, "what do you think?"

"I'd go back at a million and see what they do."

"He doesn't deserve it," Barnes grumped again. "Call Sullivan, that bastard and tell him a million and no more." He slammed his fist down on the table, drank the rest of the Scotch and held his glass out to the attorney asking for a refill.

"Michael, Brad here. My client says one million and no more and he means it. I'll admit he's not too enthused about going to trial (this in a lowered voice) but he's so tight fisted, my guess is he'd be willing to roll the dice."

"I don't think that will cut it Brad, I appreciate your efforts but my guy has been stung by a real bad boy and he thinks he has earned his commission. I think a jury will agree."

"We'll just have to see on that Michael. It's now 10:30, I'm leaving the office at 11:00. If I don't hear from you we can talk or go to trial in the morning."

Michael hesitated for a moment for affect and then said: "I'll be back to you by 11:00 with an answer. When he hung up he had the feeling Brad Smith was in the same position as he—his client didn't want to go to trial either.

Before renewing conversation with Dick he got him to sit in a chair, take more water and finally to walk around the room to get his bearings. "Thanks Michael, I'm feeling better; I think my pulse is back in rhythm.

"How can you tell?" he asked, curious to hear the answer.

"the pulse slows to a constant beat, you can actually feel it happening. Honestly I'm much better now. What did Smith say?"

"He said one million dollars."

"That's better than seven hundred and fifty thousand. What do you think?"

"I think we've got these fellows on the run, still we must be careful. There comes a point where their back goes up and there's no more talking they just want to go to trial, win or lose. I don't want to push Barnes that far, he's not the most stable person in the world. I think we should go back at them for one million five hundred thousand. This will be the first time we've countered. If they balk, you can probably get the million or go to trial."

"Go for it!" Some color had come back into his face and with it a fighting spirit.

At exactly 10:55 Michael dialed Brad's number. "Ok Michael I've got my hat and coat on, you caught me just as I was leaving."

"Well take off your hat, leave the coat on and see if we can get down to business. One million five is our offer. You save your guy three hundred and fifty thousand."

"You assign me an impossible task, but, of course, I will pass it on."

Michael detected a slight note of relief in Brad's voice. He had a capped offer, and whether Barnes cared more for his reputation than his pocket book he was about to find out. While they waited for Michael's call, Barnes fixed himself another double scotch and began to feel somewhat mellow as Brad carried on his conversation with Michael.

"What did our arch enemy say?" Barnes said trying to show his attorney he had complete control of himself, despite downing the equivalent of six scotches.

"One million five hundred thousand and no one hundredth dollars."

Barnes slammed his empty glass on the table, got up and fixed himself another drink. He came back to the table, said nothing and stared at the full glass of scotch. Brad Smith remained silent, knowing the crucial moment had arrived. Did this fellow have the guts to go to trial or would he give in to save his precious reputation?

Barnes picked up the glass and drained it, set it down on the table and said: "Ok, on one condition, that I get two years to pay it. I can't pay it all at one time."

Looking very serious Brad said to his half intoxicated client: I don't know if I can sell the two year qualifier, what can we offer as security?"

"I'll give the bastards a million up front and five hundred thousand in two years secured by a mortgage on my assets which are worth at least three million. Tell 'em that and if they don't want that deal, I will be beside you at counsel table in the morning and you can take some more of my money trying the damn case." Having delivered this ultimatum, he stiffly walked to the bar to fix another drink. Before he got there Brad was on the phone.

"You've got a deal, sort of," he said.

"What sort of a kind of deal?" Michael inquired.

"One million in cash and five hundred thousand in two years, secured by a mortgage on the company's assets."

"And of course interest at the rate of six percent per anum on the five hundred thousand?"

"Hold On." The attorney covered the receiver and said to Barnes: "He wants six percent interest on the balance." Cy Barnes looked like a man who could go no further. He just wanted out. He made an affirmative hand gesture to his attorney who then resumed the conversation with Michael. "Yes, interest in the bargain."

While he listened Michael jotted down the terms in a quick scrawl on a legal pad in front of him, tore off a piece of the paper with his note and a question mark and pushed it across the table to Dick. The client looked down, read it quickly and gave Michael a thumbs up sign. "All right Brad I have the authority to accept, you've got a deal. I'll have one of my people call your office in the morning for details on the assets to be mortgaged and a settlement agreement. Will you inform the court of the decision and tell Barnes it has been nice doing business with him and it's always a pleasure to work with you."

"You've got it Michael, I'm sure I would have gotten that jury to see it my way." He laughed at his own joke.

"We'll never know will we? See you in court next time,"

Brad hung up, told Barnes it was done and went down to the bar and fixed himself a double scotch. "Cheers," he said to his half asleep client, then took a long swallow from his drink, put the empty glass on the table, slipped on his hat and coat and helped the old man struggle out to the elevator and into a cab. It started to rain as the cab drove off into the night.

CHAPTER 26

While Michael worked building the law firm, Mary labored in the suburbs raising the Sullivan Children. Jack, the oldest, received the most attention recovering from his near fatal injury. Michael took a half year off to be with his son and as he regained his health and use of his limbs, his care fell to Mary more and more. Jack became close to her, and in his father's absence, tried to act as the man of the house. Mary told Michael his eldest had leadership qualities; the children listened to him and followed his lead in all things, which proved a great help to her. Jack knew his father was busy earning for his family and didn't resent the fact; he took it on himself to fill in for his dad to help Mary in every way he could. Mary loved Michael without qualification and realized his interest lay in her welfare and that of the children. Knowing her husband, as she did, she appreciated the fact he was not in it for the glory or fame he might achieve as a successful trial lawyer. He valued her and his family above all. Religious, in an unpretentious manner, they let actions speak for themselves and trained the children by action and example. In the same manner the children had total faith in their parents, comfortable in the knowledge they were loved and they would be protected, an advantage many children do not enjoy.

In her senior year at Trinity Mary managed a part time job at the White House library located in the Old Executive Office building adjacent to the West Wing. After graduation she went on a tour of Europe and on her return secured a job as a legislative aide to a U.S. Senator. Her job on the Hill put her in a front row seat to watch the Reagan administration in its first year of operation. She met Michael through a friend of his and he found her dazzling, intelligent, and at twenty two, the wisest girl he had ever met. Nine months after their first meeting they married, Michael got a plumb job as clerk to a state Supreme Court Justice, and after a year found a job with the oldest firm in the city. Their first child came and they were happy, ambitious and full of hope.

In the early years of practice Michael stuck pretty much to learning the law and working hard in the community to attract clients. At first the going was slow but as years passed he acquired the reputation of being a first rate trial lawyer and clients sought him out. By the time Sullivan & Connolly reached its fifth year Michael's reputation in the community had grown apace with his law practice. The more successful he became, the more the community called on him for his leadership qualities, thus, in addition to a burgeoning law practice, he served on four charitable boards, two as president, and became involved in Republican politics. At first his duties were confined to serving as counsel to the central committee; as his reputation grew he became legal counsel to the State Republican Party. Notwithstanding all his outside activities, his law practice took precedence yet, he found the time to act as advisor to elected candidates and those who aspired to run for office on the Republican ticket. In addition, he and a like-minded coterie of Republican lawyers had been instrumental in raising funds to support incumbents and those seeking office.

It came as no surprise then when he received a call from Betty O'Donnell, a state legislator, who he'd met and had a passing acquaintance with. She asked if they could meet and he arranged to meet with her over lunch at the University Club. After the call he did some research on Mrs. O'Donnell and his search turned up the facts: 47 years old, served four terms in the legislature, first elected at 39. Prior to a political career she taught at a parochial school and been active in Catholic charities. From her picture in the legislative pictorial she appeared attractive. Her biography noted her husband was a doctor and they had three children. He assumed she wanted some political, or perhaps legal advice which he always gave freely. He arrived at the club early and instructed the maître de he would be having lunch with Mrs. O'Donnell and would he direct her to his table.

When she entered the dining room he recognized her immediately from her picture which did not do her justice. With just a tinge of gray in her hair and flashing green eyes she made an impression on him as elegant, at the same time feisty. As she approached the table he stood and extended his hand. She shook it and he waved the maître de off as he moved to hold her chair for her. Once seated he took his own chair and asked if he could order her something to drink.

"I'll have a Pellegrino soda if they have it."

He turned to the waiter standing at his elbow and said: "Please make that two."

When the waiter passed out of earshot she said: "Mr. Sullivan, I'm so pleased you agreed to meet with me,"

"Please call me Michael, and it is a pleasure to make your acquaintance and I must confess that after we made the date I conducted a little research on you and I must say your record is impressive, so just let me say I am at your service."

She smiled in a pleasing manner, exposing beautiful white teeth which enhanced her smile even more. "I'm not so sure you'll want to be when I tell you the purpose of my asking you to meet with me."

"Try me," he responded, thinking to himself, what could she possibly want from me, this is obviously not a meeting to seek legal advice. Anyway let's wait and see what she has in mind. I'm sure, in dealing with most men, she gets what she wants.

"I'll be very forward if you don't mind." Before she could complete her sentence the waiter interrupted to ask if they were prepared to order. She stopped midsentence and gave her order in compliance with his request. "A cobb salad."

"And you sir?"

"I will have a roast beef sandwich and may I have potato salad in place of French fries?"

"Very good sir," He jotted it down and gracefully pivoted and headed for the kitchen with their orders.

"You were saying," he prompted.

She smiled that enchanting smile again and said: "I was saying I didn't want to be too forward, so let me come to the point. The smile disappeared replaced with a look of earnestness. Her smile was not the flirtatious smile of a temptress, rather a disarming smile, one that made you like the owner, even go so far as willingly trust the owner without question. "I know you've been interested in politics and I'm wondering if you would be willing to help me? I've decided to run for Mayor against the incumbent, Tom Dominelli."

He didn't bat an eye and quickly decided she was not only attractive but ambitious. The sitting Mayor, someone less than competent, had held the seat for eight years and sought a third term. The city had not yet reached the stage of machine politics, but the mayor, Tom Dominelli had lots of friends in the unions and in the business community. He also knew they would not cotton to a woman as Mayor. "I'll be happy to help you anyway I can," he paused, "within reason."

"I'd like you to be chairman of my campaign!"

For the first time since he sat down Michael became flustered. "Well, I don't know what to say. Why me?" The server appeared suddenly with their lunch, placed it before them and withdrew.

"Eat your sandwich and allow me to explain and I don't mean to flatter. I plan to win this race but I can't do it alone. You're somebody in this town and highly respected, although you may not realize how respected. I've sounded out twenty people in this city who I think make up what might be called the Republican establishment.

Your name has come up in every conversation. At least ten of those individuals suggested I ask you to back me and run my campaign. The office is non-partisan and Tom Dominelli is a Democrat, as you know, and he's loaded city hall with Democrats which has made it difficult for Republicans to get much attention from the Mayor's office. I believe that should change; the city should be run as it was meant to be—nonpartisan. The campaign will be nine months, you'll be the boss and I'll be on the street. Now I'm not a fool, I know you have one of the busiest law practices in the city and now your firm has become a major player. Be that is it may, I want to win, I'm qualified and I'll campaign like you've never seen. But I can't win without the best and that's why I've come to you, hat in hand, to ask."

She flashed that smile again and he looked at her and it was like looking at a small child asking if she could go riding on the merry-go-round.

"Betty," he paused, and then said: "if I may call you that, I'm deeply flattered. You are right, you are qualified and you'd be a great improvement over old Tom Dominelli. I'd have to think about it before giving an answer."

A look of angst came into her eyes but not defeat. At that moment he realized she was going to be nice about it but she wouldn't take "no" easily, gracefully yes, but not easily.

"Michael I don't take that as an ultimate no. I realize for you to take it on will require a lot of time on your part and sacrifice by your law firm; I can guarantee it will be an experience neither of us will forget, especially if I'm elected the first woman Mayor of the city."

"Ok, let me do this: I'll be talking with my wife Mary, my partners and everybody else I can think of and give you an answer in one week. Will you promise me something if I say no?"

"Certainly, and I pray you won't."

"Promise me that you will understand that I gave it my most careful consideration and truly believe I could not give you all that it would take to accomplish your goal. I clearly understand that it will take everything either of us has to unseat Dominelli. If I decide I can't give it my all, the answer will be 'no' and you will understand."

"That is more than fair and I tell you I will understand and will go forward but it won't be the same without you." She reached across the table and they shook on it.

After lunch he returned to his office, sat at his desk, and looked out the window. What have I got myself into he pondered? I don't have time to run a law firm, run a major political campaign, serve on three boards, and the board of bar governors, not to mention family responsibilities. I can't see Mary going along with it or even thinking it makes any sense.

That night over cocktails they discussed it, and contrary to what he had been thinking about her reaction, she treated the idea with enthusiasm. "It would be a real challenge, and it might be a lot of fun for the whole family. Jack's going to be a senior in high school, Sharon a sophomore at St. Anselm's, Peter a freshman at Blanchet and Kathryn a seventh grader at St. Elizabeth's; they could all participate. A real experience for all of us." He caught her excitement and by the time dinner had been dispensed with they both decided he should do it. Michael didn't think the partners a problem and many of them might get a kick out of helping, even giving money to the campaign. They had been in Washington the first two years of Reagan's presidency, he at law school she finishing her last year at college and working on the Hill for a congressional committee. The Carter years had brought high inflation, the Iran hostage taking, a country drowning in malaise, according to the President. He claimed the country had grown too big for one person (the President) to handle. That attitude resulted in a sweeping win for Ronald Reagan and a new optimism he brought with him from California. The country prospered in those years and the Soviet Union brought to its knees after President Reagan stood in front of the

Berlin wall and said over the loudspeakers: "Mister Gorbachev Tear down this wall!" After he left office, his Vice President, George H.W. Bush followed him into the presidency and the country continued its prosperity until late in his term when the economy took a downturn. When that occurs, the American voter votes his or her pocketbook.

A young governor from Arkansas with little experience beat Bush in 1992. Under Clinton the country rebounded economically and re-elected him in 1996 by a margin under fifty percent.

The country didn't know at the time of the election Clinton had been engaged in a sexual relationship with a young intern in the White House. After the election the scandal came to light. He became the first President since Andrew Johnson to be impeached. His trial in the Senate ended in acquittal with all Democrats voting to acquit there being two thirds necessary to convict. His acts besmirched the Office of the President of the United States and he suffered suspension as a lawyer. He finished his term in disgrace.

All this political history had been followed closely by the Sullivans and after the Clinton debacle the country ached for a President who would restore respectability to the highest office in the land. That man was George W. Bush the second son to follow in his father's footsteps in the office of the Presidency, the first being John Quincy Adams elected February 9, 1825. Early in his administration George Bush and the American people suffered a devastating blow when two aircraft, loaded with hundreds of passengers slammed into the one hundred storied twin towers of the World Trade Center in lower Manhattan killing three thousand people and reducing the buildings to piles of rubble. Before this tragedy could be grasped a third plane crashed into the Pentagon in Arlington, Virginia. A fourth plane, loaded with passengers, crashed to the ground when those on board became heroes attacking the Islamic savages who had captured the plane. In all, nineteen radical Muslims tried to break the spirit of the American people.

Against this background Michael decided to get into the political arena running Betty O'Donnell's campaign. Mary was right, it would be a new challenge, one that would not always be framed as an adversarial contest, as in a trial, rather one that required moving voters in the direction of a political leader through a contest at the ballot box. Like litigation, it involved persuasion but unlike litigation it demanded discussion of ideas instead of facts presented to a jury for determination. Again, Mary's instincts were keen predicting Paul Connolly and the other partners would have no objection to his running Betty O'Donnell's campaign for Mayor. Indeed several offered to help in every way possible.

As promised, he met Betty at the University Club for lunch and he saw by her look she was apprehensive and not her smiling self he'd witnessed at their first meeting. Once settled he broke the news. Her face lit up and she gave him the smile that dazzled and gripped his hand like he'd tossed her a life preserver.

"Oh I'm so pleased Michael, I know we will win." Her mood became buoyant for a few seconds and then quickly changed to one of seriousness. "Really? You've thought about it. Can we win?" Delighted with her reaction he began to lay out his thoughts on whether they could win and what they had to do to bring it about.

"The answer is 'yes' I think we can, or I would have told you 'no,' there is little or no chance. To the question: will we win? At this point I can't say; the election is nine months from now, you have a tough opponent and one who will do whatever it takes to win. As far as managing the campaign—that I will do with one caveat: you have the final say on major policy and strategy. If I don't agree with you I will so advise."

"Agreed," she interrupted.

"Have you talked with anyone or appointed anyone to raise money?"

"Yes, Barkley Johnson, a banker, you may know him."

"I do but I think we will need someone with more clout; he's an awfully nice fellow, probably too nice to be able to put the arm on the diehards. I'll meet with him, and in a gentle way I'm going to suggest he co-chair your finance committee."

"Anything else boss?" she said with a delighted gleam in her eye.

"Yes, you're going to have to be on the road for the next nine months, recruiting, speaking, making phone calls and personal appearances for money. The Mayor, I've found out has a million dollars in his war chest and will certainly raise two or three million more from the downtown businessmen he so diligently works for. How much have you raised?"

"Fifty thousand in my re-election for senate account which can easily be transferred to a mayoralty campaign."

During the remainder of the lunch they discussed various individuals she had asked to be in her campaign, when she might announce, and a tentative short term schedule for speaking engagements. Michael said he planned to hire a day to day manager, a scheduler and an advance person as soon as possible, followed by a press aide and a treasurer. They all had to be paid which meant fund raising had to start immediately.

"For all we know Betty, there may be several who will run for Mayor, if they are well financed they could take votes from you or the Mayor. I think important to announce as soon as possible to intimidate others who are thinking about running. I want you to start speaking at neighborhood coffees with the idea of recruiting volunteers and sharpening your ability to field questions under fire."

Already February 2002 when he agreed to run Betty O'Donnell's campaign, Michael, like every project he undertook, from law school, to passing the bar, to preparing for trial, through himself into the campaign. Within a week from his second meeting with the candidate he'd prepared an analysis of the city's voting precincts, Republican and Democrat, ordered a study of where the Mayor's strength lay in each of the city's four quadrants, ordered a poll to test Betty's name familiarity against the Mayor's and hired a fund raiser to fill campaign coffers with two million dollars—a million more than the Mayor had on hand when he realized O'Donnell would not be a pushover like two prior opponents.

In Michael's keen mind it was a matter of sitting down with strategists, and determining where to go for votes within the confines of the city's six hundred thousand population. The race would be city wide rather than state wide which offered an entirely different set of logistics. Following up on what he told the candidate he sought a day to day manager, and that's when he met Ron Fitzgerald, a young man aged twenty seven, single, crew haircut, friendly face and unbridled enthusiasm. The latter trait convinced Michael he hired the right man. Fitzgerald had been Betty's recommendation having known him as legislative assistant to the Speaker of the House in the state legislature. From the first days of the campaign Michael knew he had someone he could depend on to follow orders and complete assignments. After a week, campaign headquarters had been acquired, and Ron rounded up seven full time volunteers and ten part timers. Showing genius at begging and borrowing equipment he had computers installed at ten desks, all on an interconnected network, a scheduler hired to start arranging appearances for the candidate and an advance man to accompany her everywhere and in some cases precede her to the next stop.

From the start Michael enjoyed working with Ron Fitzgerald and found him very innovative with ideas. One of his first acts was to secure a hotel ballroom for the candidate's announcement and mail a thousand invitations to people they hoped would attend. He followed that up with a bank of thirty volunteers calling ten hours a day encouraging people to attend. He personally contacted twenty press, television people inviting them to the opening and furnished each a twenty page press kit giving a complete background on the candidate. Michael could not have been more pleased.

February twenty fifth Betty O'Donnell came into the ballroom of the Hilton Hotel. Seven hundred people packed the room. Behind the stage a large banner had been strung reading: "Betty O'Donnell for Mayor," Each person entering the room received a pamphlet containing biographical information about the candidate and a white sticker lettered in red and blue with the caption: "Betty O'Donnell for Mayor." Others were given placards with the same message. Michael marveled at the scene Ron created, people would think the announcement was for someone the stature of the President of the United States. Ron had provided for a raised platform in the rear of the room for T.V. and still cameras. Even the press seemed to sense the excitement in the air. When all were seated, Betty, followed by her husband and two children came into the room and the crowd broke into applause. In a brown tailored suit she looked every inch the executive; watching the scene from the back of the room, Michael thought she made a startling contrast to the stereotyped politician Tom Dominelli. With the family seated on stage Michael came forward, mounted the stage, took the microphone and introduced himself and gave a four minute introduction of who Betty was, her qualifications for Mayor, why the incumbent needed to be replaced and introduced her with the send off, "Your next Mayor."

Acknowledging the introduction, Betty flashed the same smile she exhibited on their first meeting at the University club. The smile disarmed the gathering, they relaxed the press noticed, and she launched into a twenty five minute explanation of what she wanted to accomplish for the city, why the city needed new leadership and how she intended to be elected. At the conclusion the crowd came to its feet. When they settled down she took questions from the press. Afterward with the press in tow she exited the hotel and began a walking tour, clasping hands, handing out literature. Television cameras followed her for two blocks as she shook hands on the street and entered shops along the route chatting with customers and workers alike, all of it making perfect footage for future television commercials.

They were underway with eight months and six days to go. The following day the *Daily Ledger* carried a news story of the announcement but more importantly wrote an editorial about the race: "A new political star has emerge on the horizon in the person of Betty O'Donnell, running against Tom Dominelli who is counting on a third term and will be almost impossible defeat with his political organization solidly in place and the backing of the city's business elite. She's no novice and has eight years of experience in the state legislature. Like they say: 'anything is possible' and that holds true in this case. We take away from her opening at the Hilton, Mr. Dominelli, will face the biggest challenge he's faced so far in the likeable Betty O'Donnell."

The afternoon paper, *The Herald* carried a favorable review of the announcement saying: "Betty O'Donnell, appears as a refreshing new face on the local scene and the election for Mayor suddenly becomes more interesting. O'Donnell will not be a walkover and, if elected, will be the first woman in history to occupy city hall."

Michael decided to find out what kind of a fund raiser he might turn out to be and in his first effort invited thirty five men and women he knew who could afford to underwrite the campaign if they felt the candidate worthwhile. (Can she win?) At least half were lawyers from the major law firms and the rest business people. Through extensive research he found out most of those invited had not given in prior mayoralty campaigns and none had given to the sitting Mayor. He also realized for some, being on the wrong side of the incumbent, could adversely affect their economic outlook, at the same time, he knew they were all risk takers and if Betty won they also would win. Some might give to both campaigns just to cover their bets. He arranged a late afternoon meeting for the thirty five to chat briefly with Betty in a small setting, coffee, tea and light sandwiches for refreshments after which she would give a short talk, telling of her aspirations, the office she sought, answer questions and then exit the room with Ron Fitzgerald, leaving Michael to ask each of those present to raise over a million dollars initially, with more later. For twenty five minutes Betty held sway over the room; between burst of statistics, ideas, criticism of the sitting Mayor, and her vision of what the city would like under her leadership. She gave that winning smile, they listened; to questions, she gave short, concise answers, which, in every case seemed to satisfy the questioner and everyone else in the room.

When she left, Michael took his stance in the center of the room and told them they Had seen the candidate, now the question facing them was: would she be a benefit to the city, as opposed to the current corrupt administration? He passed out cards and asked each to sign signifying willingness to raise the needed funds, giving the option to those who weren't convinced from what they heard and seen to turn the card back in blank. He gave them time to fill out the cards and thanked each one for taking the time to come and hear his candidate. When the room finally emptied, he picked up the house phone and called Ron and Betty who were waiting in a nearby room.

"Come on down we'll go through the cards together, I'm not even going to guess how we did until you get here and we count our winnings—or losses." On their arrival they asked Ron to sift through the cards. On the first one he laid on the table he said: "Bingo! George Wilson is in for $45,000! Giving a thumbs up sign he turned over the next card and saw a repeat from Peter Jenkins. Another thumbs up. Unable to contain his excitement he spread them out on the table and the three checked them. Each person present had checked "yes."

"If they all come through we'll start with $2,500,000 in the bank, Betty said with Unrestrained enthusiasm. "Michael you're a genius. Where did you get these People? Will they keep giving?"

"First, they're friends and acquaintances, and second they will

Michael J. Walsh

continue to give depending on how we perform. Each of them were carefully picked and each is a competitor not afraid of risk. And if we have to go back to the well they'll do it again when they see name identification established and the first poll shows we're in the ball game.

In the next two months Michael beat a path daily between his law firm and campaign headquarters. He got to his office at seven in the morning, went through his mail, answered e-mails, dictated at least twenty five letters and memos, interrupted only by telephone calls from clients and members of the firm. At lunch he grabbed a sandwich which had been specially prepared for him, and ate it on the way to the headquarters, three miles away in a suburb rather than downtown. He decided the suburb was a preferred site allowing volunteers to come and go at their convenience and have a place to park when they got there.

March turned to April and Michael began a routine he followed until the last month of the campaign, coming to Headquarters every day for an update with Ron Fitzgerald. He usually found him in the back room covered with maps of the city, with precincts overlaid on them, brochures stacked in the corner and a large picture of the candidate smiling beneficently on Ron and all the workers. The place always looked like a newspaper office and by April first Ron had managed to acquire another fifteen computers for a total of twenty five from unknown sources and he had twenty five volunteers manning each one, updating data, turning out "thank you" notes, contacting volunteers and designing routes for door to door walkers. Every afternoon they huddled in the back room reviewing the day's events and planning a theme for the next day.

They discussed what issues Betty should address in her speaking engagements in accord with the theme. Ron designed a program in which Betty made a fifteen minute tape with the topic of the day distributed to ten radio stations and all the talk show hosts. With luck, the taped speech ran free on five or six stations a day. Once

284

they made a policy decision, Michael called fifteen or twenty of his fund raisers to keep them abreast of what the donors should know when being asked to give. Five college students spent their free hours writing speeches and memoranda sent out to the volunteers, and for use by Betty in her daily appearances. In the early going they had to build name familiarity and, as time wore on, they did so, so that by summer Betty O'Donnell had become a household name across the city.

At first, Dominielli paid no attention to the O'Donnell campaign, choosing to ignore her presence. That worked well through the end of April when her name familiarity ran at twenty five percent. Early polling showed her trailing 66% to 32%. Michael assumed the Mayor's polling showed the same or better. That didn't bother him a bit. His idea was to lay in the weeds as long as possible and then throw everything they had at him, hoping it would be too late to fathom the dynamism of O'Donnell's well oiled machine.

CHAPTER 27

After he and Paul Connolly founded Sullivan & Connolly Michael made it a point to visit every attorney at least once a month to talk shop, review cases, and mentor the lawyer, if an associate. Even though it put a terrific price on his time he continued this practice until the firm reached thirty lawyers. He wanted to avoid losing a protégé, as happened in the case of Ben Armstead. It paid dividends to make every lawyer in the firm feel an integral part of the team, like a football coach calling each player into his office for a personal chat giving the player a sense of being part of something bigger then himself. After Armstead withdrew there were no further defections from the firm. When the firm reached sixty five lawyers Michael began addressing practice groups within the firm, rather than individual lawyers, early every Tuesday morning in the conference room with a catered breakfast. By 2000 Sullivan & Connolly had expanded its initial practice from litigation to corporate, estates, probate, securities and tax with the primary practice remaining trial work with thirty lawyers devoting themselves to defending and prosecuting clients business concerns. In time they discovered the clients they had been serving solely as trial lawyers, needed other services and thus the expansion. Michael, and to some extent, Paul remained head of the trial lawyers.

Strangely, Clients came seeking Sullivan & Connolly representation because of Michael's reputation as a trial lawyer, even though the advice they sought did not require litigation. He and Paul often discussed this phenomena and finally concluded people wanted a successful trial lawyer in charge of their case no matter the problem, because if things got worse they would have a fighter in their corner.

No longer tasked with day to day trials, Michael's and Paul's attention turned to trying the most important cases with the most at risk. When he agreed to run Betty O'Donnell's campaign for Mayor it placed a great strain on time available for his many activities including bar committees, charitable organizations, of which he was chairman of two, and deep involvement with his family. To an outsider it would appear no one could have enough energy to do all the things he did and do it successfully. But Michael had a philosophy: he understood he had an abundance of energy, was blessed with good health, worried like everyone else but the one thing that carried him through every crisis and helped maintain his equilibrium was his faith.

Often his day started with seven o'clock mass at St. Patrick's three blocks from his office, then to the firm for breakfast at his desk or with a client, Tuesday morning breakfasts with his attorneys, lunch with clients, or in trial, meetings with other attorneys in settlement discussions and outside board and committee meetings and finally home at seven in the evening. With the campaign in full swing he tried to get most his legal duties taken care of by three, and to be at O'Donnell headquarters by three thirty to lend a semblance of order and be on hand for people who needed decisions beyond Ron Fitzgerald's authority.

Ron turned out to be a Godsend to the campaign and to Michael. Twenty years his senior Michael thought there might be some difficulty between the two due to the difference in age. He found, instead, they got along like father and son. Not a lawyer, Ron had no knowledge of the law, other than would a normal citizen. He knew Michael Sullivan had the reputation of an important personage in the city and famous as a skilled trial lawyer. Parallel to Michael's fame Ron considered himself a nuts and bolts professional political operative and felt extremely comfortable with the lawyer as his boss. In some ways Ron made Michael feel like he was in his twenties again. They never talked law or cases, they talked politics. In that sense they were equals.

"Ron," Michael asked, "when do you think we should start running television ads? We're building a pretty good reservoir of money."

"Michael, with no disrespect, and as one professional to another, I think it's too early."

The first time Ron addressed him by his first name he felt a little taken aback but it was done in such an innocent way, he didn't resent it. And after a few initial sallies it became "Ron" and "Michael" and they both felt comfortable with it.

"Here's my thinking: we've got to get her as much free press as we can, that means having three or four events a day that will draw press and a barrage of direct mail. Summer will be a little slow with people on vacation and their minds on other things. I think we should wait until the first of September when the kids are back in school and then let the Mayor have it with all the money we can raise and spend."

"I'll have to think on that," Michael responded, "one ad can reach a hundred and fifty Thousand people and I'm concerned about falling too far behind in name identification. I know you and Mary are working on building a field force but I wouldn't be adverse to running a week's ads just before school is out to plant seeds and let voters see her on the screen. That smile is going to win a lot of votes." After thinking about it for twenty four hours Michael decided to go with a sixty second television commercial designed to introduce Betty O'Donnell to a huge swath of voters; he believed it would raise her name identification and her standing in the polls against Dominielli. It turned out to be the right move at the right time. Her name ID rose to ninety percent and poll numbers to forty percent with six months to go.

The Firm

Early on Mary suggested to Michael she get involved in the
O'Donnell campaign; he had no objections, so in the first month
she managed to get the four children busy after school doing tasks
around the headquarters as a means of making the campaign a family project. She and Ron put together a plan to send a thousand volunteers into the precincts beginning October first, through election
day. The plan she developed called for a door to door route for each
volunteer consisting of fifty households. At each house the volunteer knocked on the door, handed a piece of literature to the inhab-
itant, asked if they would allow a lawn sign on their property, or a
bumper sticker on their car. If they said yes, the headquarters would
be notified; instantly another volunteer would be dispatched within
the hour to plant the sign or affix the sticker. She arranged for five
thousand lawn signs to blanket the city and four thousand bumper
stickers with "O'Donnell" emblazoned in large letters. Dominielli
could never match her foot soldiers and countered her efforts with
expensive television. As envisioned, the plan Ron and Mary were
working on, resembled an army going into battle, with captains,
coordinators, constant cell phone communications and an elaborate
computer tracking system that recorded every visit and how many
times a voter had been contacted.

Whenever Michael happened to be in the headquarters he saw
and talked with Mary and the children but they were always too
busy to spend much time with him. Watching Mary work, giving
orders, answering questions, talking on the phone to her cohorts
made him happy. In his mind the family was doing something
together and being productive at the same time. Sometimes late
at night when everyone had gone home and just he and Ron were
alone they sat and talked about how the campaign was going, what
had to be done the next day and the next week. On these occasions
Michael listen to what Ron had to say. His knowledge of politics
seemed encyclopedic; in the four years he'd been a legislative aide
in the legislature he managed to know the names of every legisla-

tor, lobbyist, state employees high and low and most of the Judges. He had a disarming, non threatening personality that allowed him to make friends easily. People trusted him, and told him things, better left unsaid. They did so because they knew if they asked him to keep it to himself, he would. Having worked with him for five months Michael trusted him implicitly. Ron remained cool under fire, as Michael witnessed on several occasions; he didn't panic. With five months of politics under his belt Michael understood it is easy to panic, get discouraged and want to give up in a political campaign. The time is short, mistakes are made and events have a way of shaping a campaign having unintended consequences. It happened, when the Mayor's forces put out a direct mail piece raisingthe specter Betty O'Donnell favored abortion and voted for it in the legislature. Within an hour of it hitting the streets Ron suggested Betty call a press conference denouncing the piece setting the record straight. She hesitated but Ron and Michael convinced her it had to done quickly. She followed their advice, called the conference and to her surprise all the television stations sent cameras and reporters. The print fraternity sent reporters and still photographers. She gave an amazing performance, calling the mail piece a slanderous attack laying it at the Mayor's doorstep and touting her record against abortion which she referred to as licensed killing. Moreover she said the issue had no relevance in a campaign for Mayor.

For ten minutes that night every station ran her press conference in the six o'clock news slot and again at eleven o'clock. The newspapers carried stories on it and overall members of the fourth estate talked among themselves and collectively decided they had a donnybrook in the making which made for readers and advertising dollars. O'Donnell's forces had had their first clash with below the belt politics and they met the test. There would be more between May and November; they got their feet wet and were satisfied with their response.

The Firm

From June on Michael talked or met daily with Ron or Betty or both making sure everyone knew what each part of the campaign was doing insuring they put out a unified message. Ron made it a point to talk with news reporters and television producers every day, first to promote his own candidate and second to ferret out any adverse information floating around concerning the Mayor. Through talking with a number of reporters covering the Mayor's campaign he found the Mayor and his aides were not taking Betty O'Donnell's challenge seriously except to poll her traction with the voters. Michael and Ron felt if O'Donnell's numbers were moving up after Labor Day, they had the troops to mount a strong pre-election push, and most importantly, a "get out the vote," army. The Mayor's only recourse: flood the airways the last week and hope to overcome O'Donnell's Army.

Besides working out all the logistics and organization necessary to conduct a lawn sign and door to door campaign, Mary came up with the idea of a chain letter to women voters. She put together a meeting of ten of her Junior League colleagues who agreed to write ten letters to friends endorsing Betty O'Donnell and asking the recipient to send out ten letters to friends. By late July thousands of such letters had been mailed and the campaign began to see an upward tick in women favoring O'Donnell fifty to forty five—a very good sign.

. . .

Michael took time off in August to catch up on cases he'd been juggling until the campaign ended in November. During that time he received a call from John Kennedy who said he and Edward Malloy, also a client, wanted to meet to discuss a project they had undertaken and needed the firm's help. Malloy had been a client of Michael's at the old firm and had started with a small grocery store that grew to a chain of fifteen stores in a few years.

"What are you two up?" he asked, greeting them in the reception area.

"No good," Kennedy laughed and they followed Michael down the long hallway with offices on either side with secretaries in front of each office. After they'd gone some distance Malloy said: "I've counted twenty offices in this hallway Michael, how many more before we get to yours?"

"Seventeen Ed, mine's the last one. We've grown some since we last met."

As they made their way down the hall they glanced in each office and saw lawyers, men and women, in their mid thirties and early forties studying law books, on the phone, working at computers, talking to clients— all very busy. A visitor could easily grasp the firm was all business, men dressed in suits, the women in conservative suits or dresses. Some firms in the city had grown lax in what they allowed their lawyers to wear in the office when they weren't meeting clients or going to court. Not at Sullivan & Connolly. Michael and Paul had too much respect for the clients to allow their attorneys to be seen in the offices and the corridors dressed like college seniors on spring break. Admittedly this attitude was not in keeping with current law office vogue, but then Michael and Paul Connolly had never catered to conventional wisdom and Sullivan & Connolly lawyers knew that when they joined the firm. They were different and proud of it.

The two were ushered into the office which had been expanded to accommodate a conference table that sat ten. One wall contained law books and rest of room had a couch, coffee table and some chairs. Simple and organized.

They sat at the conference table and Michael ordered coffee and Danish. Still impressed with the offices he had seen, Malloy, a big six foot, five inch husky with black Irish eye brows and steely gray hair commented: "Sully, it's certainly been awhile, I checked all those offices and secretaries and it looks like you've tripled in size since we last did business."

"That we have," Michael acknowledged with a wide grin, "we've been lucky Ed and we've also worked hard to get where we are."

"That's obvious. Me and John have been busy ourselves the last six months and that's why we're here"

"Tell me about it." A knock came at the door, and two paralegals brought in a big carafe of coffee and a tray containing an assortment of pastries. They ate while John Kennedy detailed how he and Malloy had pieced together sixty acres of land and hoped to turn it into one of the biggest shopping centers in the state. The first hurdle required acquiring all the parcels needed for the project. The toughest part had to do with getting it zoned commercial, going through planning commission hearings and later the city council on which the Mayor sits.

"We'd like Sullivan & Connolly to handle it for us."

Michael didn't hesitate, "Yes we can do that but you should be aware I'm involved in the O'Donnell for Mayor campaign and Tom Dominelli, if he wins, could be adverse to your position."

Kennedy scoffed, "Young Ron Fitzgerald put the bite on us for a substantial contribution to O'Donnell's campaign so we have the same problem you have. Dominelli doesn't bother us and besides I think your candidate is going to win."

John Kennedy, when he first became a client of Michael's, had already amassed a large fortune in the vicinity of eight hundred million dollars, building shopping centers and land investments. He went by the motto: "buy land they're not making it anymore." Whenever asked: "how do you make money?" He'd reel off his motto, they'd laugh, but when they thought about it later on, they marveled at the truth and simplicity of it. The interesting thing about Kennedy, he understood the money didn't belong to him, he simply had the use of it while on earth. His religion (Catholic) and his understanding of life taught him: better to give than receive. That principle guided his life, so as a good steward, he multiplied his wealth while giving it away to charity and other pursuits he deemed beneficial to people. Since working with Michael Sullivan in the early days at the homeless shelter he had financed not only the education of his own four children but those of another seventy five. He and wife Sally built a home for the elderly, built two eight story dormitories at his alma mater, Notre Dame. They felt blessed and they shared those blessings with those in the community. At the time Michael Sullivan was making a reputation for himself in the law, John Kennedy built a reputation as one of the smartest men in the country in the world of finance. When he met with Michael and Ed Malloy to discuss plans for the shopping center he had already been investing in building sites in Maui, Hawaii, and the Dalmatian coast in Croatia. Over the previous five years much of his time had been spent flying to foreign soil, viewing and evaluating properties. His co-partnership with Malloy was an effort to help a friend make some money.

For Michael, zoning presented an area of law he had not engaged in, but the firm had an excellent real estate practice. For two days he availed himself of the group bringing himself up to speed in zoning and shopping centers. No novice, Kennedy commissioned a mockup of the center featuring all the stores, parking areas complete with landscaping. On seeing it Michael expressed admiration for its ingenuity. He anticipated one of the objections to the development with its one hundred retail outlets would be the amount of traffic generated which guaranteed resistance from nearby residents. A further hurdle would consist of ample water and sewage facilities as well as adequate ingress and egress points. With this in mind Michael chartered a helicopter and a professional photographer to fly over the area taking pictures of the distance between the nearest homes and businesses and the development site. They took a whole day flying back and forth over the area, Michael pointing what he considered the most advantageous views to the photographer. He wanted to be able to show in court how "out in the country" his client's new shopping center had been located purposely to avoid traffic problems for nearby residential areas. For him this became a key piece of evidence convincing a zoning board, planning commission, and if necessary, a judge or jury, that the shopping center made the best and highest use of the property. He put an economist to work developing a reasoned prediction of the numbers of jobs the project would generate, taxes paid to the city and the ease of shopping at a close by retail outlet.

All these measures were taken anticipating opposition to the project. Only when sure he had every base covered did he approach the planning commission with the development plan. Normally the developer worked with the planning staff to clear all preliminary problems and Kennedy and Malloy did that with Michael attending every meeting. He wanted to craft a record of documents and witnesses to be used in court if the administrative process failed. He sought to first get approval from the planning commission staff. After some weeks the planning staff furnished its analysis and agreed to recommend the plan to the commission.

At the hearing before the commission Michael represented the developers in a carefully planned one hour presentation included all facets of the shopping center: job growth, parking, tax revenue and overall benefit to the immediate community. Opposition appeared from the neighborhood in the person of one hundred agitated home owners. For three hours they harangued the five commissioners, ten speakers in favor and forty against, the rest interested in the outcome. At eleven in the evening the chairman called a halt and announced the vote, three to two in favor. Threatening voices were heard muffling a small cheer by those in favor of the center.

Afterword John Kennedy and Ed Malloy thanked him for the close win. Michael knew better and warned they'd just been through round one of a longer fight. "That mob will be back with a lawyer or a brace of lawyers. It will cost them a pretty penny and from the looks of the ring leaders they'll come up with the money."

Kennedy laughed, "The bigger the fight, the larger your fees Michael. My money is on Sullivan & Connolly no matter who they hire."

. . .

Most of the summer they spent on the O'Donnell campaign with Betty making daily appearances, weekly press conferences and Michael making the fund raising circuit trying to build a cash surplus over operating expenses which would be used strictly on television the last three weeks. By the first week of September internal polls were showing Tom Dominelli at fifty percent and O'Donnell at forty five. Michael was satisfied. They had raised her numbers from forty two to forty five and her name identification to just short of one hundred percent. So far so good he thought to himself. Sensing a problem, when public polling showed the challenger making headway, Dominelli quit sitting on his laurels, and decided to hire the top advertising agency in the city. Michael knew, from press rumors, they were already preparing negative ads to run against Betty.

In mid September he called for a meeting at his home to plan the remainder of the campaign. Present were the top fund raisers, two political consultants, the candidate, the pollster, Brad Darby, Mary, Ron Fitzgerald and John Kennedy.

"We're mid September Brad, what are your new numbers?"

"She's still doing fine with the females, losing the males but not too badly. She losing the above sixty vote which is sticking with the Mayor and she's doing better than average with thirty five to fifty five crowd. As of last night he's got 45, she has 40 and the rest are undecided. If that trend continues we could lose unless we get the undecided to break for us. Something has to happen or we make it happen."

"Ok, let's leave it there for a minute and see what we've got on hand." Kennedy said, a serious look on his face, and then his mouth widen to a gigantic smile and he said: "If it's money we need to win, were gonna win. My horses and I have great faith in our candidate," he glanced at Betty,

"We've got a seven hundred thousand dollars to spend on television and by October first we'll raise another five hundred thousand. We are not going to be outspent." They broke into applause and you could feel their anxiety leave the room.

"We needed that John and we'll take you at your word. He turned to Jeffrey Wilson, the twenty six year old "whiz kid" ad consultant they hired to produce the commercials.

"What's our inventory look like Jeff?"

"Michael we've got ten spots ready to go on all the major issues, comparing the Mayor's record to Betty's positions on the same issue. If he gets rough, we've got two ready to drop on him for his promise to raise property tax versus ours to cap the rates. That should grab the above sixty voter Brad spoke to. The other, his vote to turn down charter schools. We are ready to act to blunt any funny stuff he puts within twenty four hours or less."

"That sounds good." He turned to Mary and asked if her volunteers were ready to roll October first.

Mary laid out her program, just as the other hired consultants had done. Michael treated her like a consultant, differentiating between his wife and mother of his children and another hired gun. They both appreciated their respective positions, she a campaign worker and he the chairman. Everyone in the room treated her same way, except Betty, who realized how much she had done for the campaign and loved her for it. They had grown close over the last year, often when Michael and Ron were not around, commiserating with each other over the ups and downs of the campaign. Betty's husband stayed clear of interfering in the campaign while Michael led a dual life, running the campaign and his one hundred person law firm. Mary understood Betty's situation as a woman far better than Michael. He treated her as the Mayor to be and as a professional; Mary saw the soft side of her and communicated with that side far better than the men in the campaign. She found herself pointing out things to Michael he would have never perceived in Betty's makeup. He saw a woman politician with an engaging smile, which, in his judgment made her a winner. It went much deeper than that and Mary understood this and had become a real listening post for Betty when she had concerns.

"As I've said we have a thousand volunteers ready to go door to door every day from now to election, besides lawn signs, and bumper stickers they will do two literature drops, ten days out and five days out. We have a hundred volunteers to drive people to the polls election day. We have a mole or two in the Dominelli campaign and as of now they have no ground game ready to go and doubt they will mount one. I'm told they are relying entirely on radio and television to drown out our message." Everyone nodded in admiration at what sounded like a prodigious effort to take place in the dwindling days of the campaign.

"Ron where are we on the arrangements made for the debate before the Cosmos Club on October 25?"

"It's going to be televised, one hour duration, each standing at a lectern facing each other. A three person media group will ask questions giving each man a thirty second rebuttal. Each has one minute to open and close. Our advance people will get plenty of tickets to counter any loud clapping for the Mayor. We may even pack the place if we can outhustle them for tickets. Three stations will be covering it and we'll be filming it to use in our television ads."

After another hour Michael wrapped it up and admonished the group eighteen hour days would be the order of the day until the election.

CHAPTER 28

Four days after Mary Sullivan put her troops in the precincts, O'Donnell lawn signs began to sprout like daffodils in spring. Michael continued to hold back on television, husbanding his resources until the last seven days. Ron grew more and more agitated as the Mayor continued to up his television exposure and warned Michael if they let the Mayor continue unopposed on television, independents would start moving to the opposition and even some of Betty's hard won gains might start to erode. By October fifteenth Ron's fear came home to roost. A poll done by the afternoon newspaper showed the Mayor had upped his number to forty nine and Betty had dropped to forty three leaving eight undecided. Still Michael held back on the television campaign, to the point where even Betty began to question his judgement.

"Michael, Tom is killing us with negative ads, if we don't shore up our position quickly, this campaign is going down the drain," she complained with undisguised apprehension. She was not the only one exhibiting concern, but as principal, she had the most to lose.

Mary didn't join the corps of skeptics, nor did the fund raisers. All these men and women knew Michael, trusted his judgement and had undiluted faith he knew what he was doing. He'd said at the outset they would hold their fire until the last minute, the gamble being Tom Dominelli would use up most of his television money by October twenty fifth pushing up his poll numbers and then lay back on his oars and run out the clock, thinking he had built up enough of a lead to win even if Betty O'Donnell surged at the end.

"Michael have you seen this morning's paper?" The call came seven o'clock in the morning and Ron had him out of bed and on his feet.

"No, but it must be pretty important for you to call this early."

"Well I'll just read you the headline and you can judge for yourself. 'Prominent Lawyer Heads O'Donnell campaign.' It goes on to say: 'John Kennedy and Edward Malloy, clients of Michael Sullivan of Sullivan & Connolly who heads the O'Donnell campaign for Mayor plan to build a gigantic shopping center on the outskirts of the city and need Betty O'Donnell's vote, if elected, to close the deal. Incumbent Mayor, Tom Dominelli says he is the swing vote on the five person council, plus two other members who share his views and the council has the final say.' The Mayor goes on to tell the writer he deplores this tactic to get the shopping center at the expense of all those voters living in the district. He claims a vote for O'Donnell will insure the building of the shopping center, a vote for him will stop it cold. This could kill us Michael. There's eleven days left to the election and we're already slipping in the polls."

"Ok Ron, call Betty and the consultants. I'll be at headquarters at eight thirty. By that time I'll have a plan." He hung up the phone.

"What's that all about?" Mary anxiously asked as he sat on the edge of the bed now fully awake. So this is politics flashed through his mind. No Marquis of Queensbury rules? Just plain hardball!

He turned to Mary who had slipped into her robe: "That was Ron Fitzgerald. The morning paper is running a story, obviously given to them by Dominelli's campaign, that I'm running Betty's campaign for the sole purpose of gaining her vote for John's shopping center."

"That's preposterous," she shouted, and he heard the pain in her voice. "The fact you're running Betty's campaign and you have two clients trying to develop a shopping center that can help the city is totally irrelevant."

"I know that and you know that but the public often reads the headline and concludes something diabolical is afoot."

"You can't let that skunk get away with that Michael. What can you do?"

"Mary, you're angry," he said laughing. "You're beautiful all the time but when you get angry you really look beautiful."

"This is no time for admiring beauty Irish, you get dressed and I'll get some coffee made and you take care of that rascal."

He came down stairs dressed in a gray pin stripped suit, white shirt, a blazing red tie, freshly showered and shaved. He looked ready and Mary said so.

"Now Michael Sullivan you go down there and go on the offensive and I'll be in around ten. My troops are going to redouble their efforts and we're going to clip that buzzard's wings."

He rarely saw her that worked up. She was always calm when upset, no reactionary. Somehow she had the ability, God given or acquired, to stand back, look at an event or situation and realize what was happening when others didn't see the consequences of the act. As a perfect example, he thought of how the week end before the presidential election in 1992, Lawrence Walsh, a special counsel appointed to look into the Iran-Contra affair, brought indictments against Casper Weinberger, Secretary of Defense and George Schultz, Ronald Reagan's Secretary of State. At that point, four days before the election, George H.W. Bush, the incumbent, behind in the polls but catching up rapidly would have won. Mary said the indictments would finish Bush. Michael, who considered himself a student of history and politics, told her the indictments had come too late to stop Bush's momentum. He didn't realize the impact they had on the public's consciousness. She did and, of course, she was right. This happened many times in their life and she seemed to have an uncanny ability of seeing things before others did. As a result he learned early to value her judgment in everything he did.

When he reached headquarters he found they were all awaiting his arrival. Betty, Ron, the consultants, and the pollster looked to him for an answer.

Betty opened up the minute he sat down: "Michael, this is so unfair to you, you've never represented me as a client, I have no knowledge of Mr. Kennedy's project and if I'm elected and have to vote on the issue I will recuse myself. I'll tell that to the press!"

"You don't have to make such a concession to thwart this attack, they're trying to knock you out using me as the bait. I'm confident we can turn this dirty trick back on them. On the way over I've been trying to work out in my mind how we should proceed. Does anyone have any doubts about whether we should respond to this article immediately?" Silence. "All right here's my thinking. We call a press conference for eleven o'clock that's two hours from now. I will open the conference with a complete version of how and when you asked me to run your campaign Betty and how and when John and Ed Malloy asked me to represent them. I'll then turn the mike over to you and you confirm what I have said and explain you met these gentlemen for the first time after you asked me to be your chairman, that you are not now or ever have been a client of mine and that I have every right to represent whoever I choose. That if elected, you will look at the issues that come before you, or, if you prefer, you will recuse yourself from considering any vote on the Kennedy project these two gentlemen have pending before the Mayor and council, even though you see no conflict whatsoever. You end by saying this is a last minute ploy by a desperate candidate to stave off imminent defeat and that you don't intend to let him get away with trying to destroy you by slandering those who have volunteered to help you. Finally you think his vague allegations are an attempt to confuse the voters and steal the election."

"Whew, that's tough Michael," Ron volunteered.

"It's perfect Michael, I don't need a script for that I'm so mad I'm ready to call the press in right now."

"Not now Mary, eleven o'clock. We want coverage on the twelve o'clock news, night news and the eleven o'clock wrap up—all day coverage."

An hour and a half later the headquarters was packed with cameras, still photographers, reporters from four news outlets including The *Herald* and two hundred O'Donnell supporters holding aloft "O'Donnell for Mayor" signs. Some yelled, "Call the Fire Marshall there's too many people in here." Someone else shouted: "Throw the bum out, he's a Dominelli supporter."

Thinking they needed a backdrop for the conference Ron put out an urgent call for volunteers to man "battle stations" requesting they come to headquarters for the press conference. At eleven o'clock Michael stepped before the microphones, klieg lights went on and the room grew dark. He purposely kept his remarks short but clear so no listener could miss the point, the Mayor's allegations were a smoke screen designed to make the voters believe there was a fire when in fact his representation of Betty O'Donnell and his representation of two clients pursuing a business objective were completely separate matters, totally unrelated, and any attempt to link them to some vague conspiracy amounted to fraud.

Betty, fired up by the attempted besmirchment of Michael's reputation and consequent reflection on her honesty, gave a brilliant summary of her relationship to Michael Sullivan, her acquaintance with John Kennedy and Ed Malloy, her total unfamiliarity with the project they were engaged in, and most damaging to Dominelli's allegations, her promise to recuse herself from any vote on the project "when I become Mayor." For twenty five minutes she answered every question posed to her providing an uninterrupted platform to accuse the Dominelli campaign of fraud and hinting at The *Herald's* complicity for not fact checking the story before running it in the paper.

The T.V. stations and the opposition newspaper lapped it up as a chance to hit the Mayor and a competitor at the same time for sloppy journalism. When the room cleared they sat around and watched a monitor replay the conference. Ron insisted it be taped on the chance the networks might want some of it and they could use it in their television spots, if necessary.

"If they even do half a job Betty, you knocked it out of the box, you too Michael, one of the consultants offered. Mary winked at him and they both knew a blow had been struck for the truth. The consultants were ecstatic and couldn't say enough about Michael's decision to retaliate quickly before the Mayor's red herring could take root. The next day they saw an uptick in the polls, and the *Ledger* reported: "we're tracking every day now until the day before the election. We pay no attention to public polling, we'll trust our own findings. Today O'Donnell is at 42, Dominelli at 45 and 13 undecided."

Despite O'Donnell's dramatic rebuttal, Tom Dominelli kept hammering on the alleged "conspiracy." What had been an effective press conference, had not slowed the opposition. They just kept repeating the lie. The consultants came up with the idea of taking the most dramatic parts of Betty's press conference, combining the rebuttal with her charge of fraud and duplicity on the part of the Mayor, and producing a 60 second spot. Ron objected, reasoning it would only highlight the issue and add to the controversy Dominelli was trying to keep stirred up.

"What do you think Michael?" Betty asked.

"I think we should do it, but can we get it on the air tonight? We've only got Friday, Saturday, Sunday and Monday before the election."

Jeffrey Sloan, a gangling twenty seven years old and a six year veteran of the political wars as a T.V. spot producer said: "I can do it. I'll edit the film and be back in four hours with a product. I watched the screening yesterday and thought some of the press conference could be dynamite if edited into thirty or sixty second spots. I've already got great ideas but Betty did such a great job the only tough part will be picking out the best scenes.

In the last week of campaign Michael, Mary and the children were practically sleeping at the headquarters. Like a Field Marshall, Mary maintained contact with her captains from eight a.m. in the morning until eight at night, constantly moving her door to door workers around the city. Jack, Sharon and Peter dropped out of school to stay on the sidewalks knocking on doors. Sharon bragged to her mother she and her high school mates had put up four hundred lawn signs in the last week. The Sullivans were engrossed in a challenge together and no one was more enthusiastic than the children, partly because they admired the candidate but more they loved being part of something bigger than themselves, and working with their parents.

True to his word Jeff Sloan put together a pretty piece showing Betty doing all the talking, the one subtitle consisting of: "O'Donnell for Mayor." When he screened it for their approval, they saw his genius and Ron more than anyone praised the commercial.

"It's a gamble," Michael admitted, "but we have to cut this guy down. Get it out to the stations, we'll know by Sunday if it hurts or helps."

On Sunday morning the Sullivans returned from seven thirty mass at St. Agatha's and were sitting around the sun room they added on to the house which became the most used as a family room and featured floor to ceiling paned windows, creamed colored walls, colorful print sofas and a wood stove which heated the entire room. In the kitchen Mary cooked breakfast while Michael and the boys sat on their favorite sofa watching an early morning preview on television of the day's professional football programing. Somewhere in the house a telephone rang. "Dad, it's for you. Take it in the kitchen."

Exhausted he heaved himself to his feet and by the time he reached the kitchen, the smell of sizzling bacon and sight of the counter loaded with breakfast rolls, scrambled eggs, toast, doughnuts, potatoes O'Brian and two steaming pots of coffee brought life back into his weary bones. Sharon handed him the phone and he said warily: "hello," thinking, who would call this time on a Sunday morning, it couldn't be good news.

"Michael, it's Ron. Are you awake?"

"Sure we've been to church already. Where are you?"

"I'm on the street and I have in my hand the Sunday edition of the "*Insider.*"

"Is that that underground city paper put out by what we used to call the counter culture?"

"Very good," Ron laughed at his knowledge of those opposed to the current society.

"You're not as old as you act. But let me get to the point. On page sixteen they are reporting the District Attorney is investigating the Mayor and an aide, 'close aide' is the phrase used, getting kickbacks on fees collected from parking meters. The investigation has been underway for a month."

"Do they cite any sources?" Now all tiredness dropped from his body and he became fully alert, as though prepared to cross examine a witness.

"Unnamed, but if they don't have it, you're talking a defamation law suit from the Mayor. I'm on my way now to try and run down the author and see what can be verified. I also have calls into the *Ledger* and the *Herald* to see what they know."

Michael could hear the excitement in his voice, and it began to well up in him as well. "We've got to alert the radio stations, this has to be on the street this afternoon to do us any good, and even then it may be too late. I don't know Ron, we may have a case of the old 'Lawrence Walsh' syndrome, stopping the Mayor in his tracks. You keep at the detective work; I'll alert Betty and the rest of our people for a noon meeting; if you can make it fine, if not, keep in touch by phone. We will be putting something out this afternoon quoting the 'Insider.'"

He hung up and looked around to see five faces staring at him waiting to hear what had been said. Briefly he repeated Ron's information and said: "Look it's going to be a long day so let's eat this beautiful breakfast Mother's made, we're going to need it. Then everybody to 'battle stations.' "

At noon, the front office hummed with staff and volunteers coming in to get handouts and going out to plant lawn signs, phones ringing off the hook, fax machines sending out excerpts from the "*Insider*" article to every news outlet in the city and state. Michael, Mary, the pollster, consultants, and the candidate huddled around the small conference table in the back room. The candidate poured a fresh cup of coffee as Michael spoke the first words: "Where are we in our tracking poll?"

"We've stopped the bleeding from the *Herald* article, that's the good news, still we're stalled at forty four, the Mayor at forty seven and nine still undecided. Betty's commercial is working; we came up from forty two to forty four. From here on out it's all about door to door and getting our voters out Tuesday. Plus the underground newspaper has done us a real service publishing the story of the Mayor's parking meter activities. Assuming that hits the T.V. screens tonight and the two dailies tomorrow we have a fighting chance. All we need is seven of the nine percent undecided and anything we can take from the Mayor. I won't know where we are until we poll tonight and tomorrow night. By Tuesday morning I should have an inkling of whether we're going to have a new Mayor.

Betty excused herself to attend seven church suppers and bazaars with her volunteers to spread literature and talk to the voters. Michael counted heavily on the Catholic vote and made sure the community was aware Betty O'Donnell was a staunch Catholic and pro-life. Church goers were her core support no matter what domination.

At three thirty Ron called to say: "The *Herald* is going to cover the investigation despite their endorsement of the Mayor. They've already put two investigative reporters on the case. My guess is, if the guy's guilty, they don't want to be tarnished by association. These people at the *Herald* are really something. They've boosted the Mayor all along, but give them a chance to sell newspapers and they'll opt for it every time. What hypocrites. The question now is: will the investigation raise enough doubts in people's minds between now and Tuesday or will the cynics say it's just dirty politics, or worse, the O'Donnell campaign is behind it."

"I don't think so Ron, after the Dominelli fiasco blaming Betty for having me as her campaign chairman and her rebuttal, they're going to give the story credence and who knows, the D.A. may leak the details which could really put us in business. We'll just have to watch the news shows tonight to see how they're going to play it."

At six p.m. everyone in the headquarters stopped what they were doing, the room grew quiet, all eyes focused on the television set sitting up on a raised stand near the back of the room. Michael, Mary and Ron sat in three folding chairs near the front door.

"Good evening ladies and gentlemen our lead story this evening deals with the political contest for Mayor set for Tuesday when the city's two hundred and fifty thousand voters go to the polls. A story appeared this morning in the *Insider*, a so called underground newspaper, to the affect, District Attorney, Dennis Johnson has been investigating the Mayor and one or more associates over the last month allegedly for taking kickbacks from parking meter collections for some period of time. That's the essence of the story. We have queried the Mayor's office which is denying the story and the district attorney's office has not acknowledged the story. However, reliable sources in that office have confirmed to us that indeed there is an ongoing investigation, but no indictments are ready to come down. When we have more on this story we will report it to you..... In other news...."

Someone turned off the set and an immediate buzz set in. People started yelling, some cheered, Michael turned to Ron and said: "It's a strong statement and creates doubt but the denial gives hardliners an excuse to stand by the Mayor since the allegation lacks proof."

"I think it's the shot we need," What do you think Mary?"

"I agree Ron, the 'thick or thin' voter will stick with the Mayor to see if it's true or not. But I think the 'faint of heart' will move to us. Too much smoke, it just doesn't pass the smell test. People want a 'clean' candidate, and Betty is our 'clean candidate. Tom Dominelli has a cloud over him."

"You're probably both right, this thing is not going away. Let's hope there's time for it to sink in with the electorate. Just thirty six hours before the first vote is cast."

"I think we should have a drink on it," Ron said, "if we can retire to the back room, I'll do the honors. Scotch everyone?" They nodded in unison and for the next several hours discussed the day's extraordinary events.

At the Monday morning meeting they all sat around in the back room: Mary, Ron, Michael, and the consultants, coffee mugs in hand, curiously awaiting returns from Sunday night polling. Brad Darby, the pollster arrived at nine sharp with charts in hand.

"The first chart shows the overall situation. We've come up one to forty five, but more important, the Mayor has dropped two to forty five with ten undecided. We're tied Ladies and Gentlemen!"

They cheered like high schoolers when the winning basket drops through at the buzzer. "Hold it down," he shouted over the excited chatter, the *Herald* is coming out with its own poll showing the race at 46-44 in the Mayor's favor. Groans all around. "Don't worry," he continued excitedly, his eyes twinkling, we have the momentum, we'll poll tonight, and if all goes well, I'll release our results to the *Herald* at four tomorrow afternoon. My guess is we're going to go to 46 overnight with the Mayor remaining at 45. The undecideds will decide the race in the voting booth. If we get four or more of the late deciders, we win narrowly. One caution: if the *Herald* is right and I'm wrong, fire me!" They all laughed and Michael said: "We'd fire you if we knew where to find you." (more laughter) For the first time in weeks a feeling of hope crept back into their beings and they all began to believe they might pull it off, but no one voiced what they were all thinking.

"Mary, this is your biggest day yet, today and tomorrow. We're all exhausted but everyone is giving one last push. The lawn signers have joined the door to door group so you'll have a thousand volunteers in the field all day including your sons and daughters, Kathryn has raised such a ruckus about not being included, Sharon is going to let her tag along with her."

"I can't do anything around here today, you and Ron are in full charge," Michael said, "I'm going door to door with the kids and with that Michael grabbed his coat and baseball cap and headed out of the headquarters whistling as he wended his way through controlled chaos in the main room as a hundred people in white sweatshirts with "O'Donnell for Mayor" emblazoned on the front attended to tasks they were assigned. He had no idea what they were doing but he was confident Ron and Mary knew and that gave him a warm feeling as he hit the street on the last day of the campaign. It had been a long ten months with the people's verdict due on the morrow.

Some twenty houses into his route he knocked on a door, as he had at the previous houses and a man in his sixty's, bearded, somewhat unkempt with a sneer on his lips opened the screened door and barked: "What do you want?"

Not wanting to antagonize the man any more than he presently appeared, Michael explained he was campaigning for Betty O'Donnell for Mayor and had a brochure he would like him to have. The man closed the screen door and in an angry voice said: "I wouldn't vote for her if you paid me. She and that Sullivan fellow are up to no good. Some kind of conspiracy!"

"How do you know that?" Michael asked innocently.

"I read it in the *Herald* and they don't lie. I've been taking it for twenty years."

Michael made a split second decision to ignore the fellow and move on to more friendly territory or try to win his vote. He opted for the latter on the theory in a close election every vote counts. Remembering Ron's exhortation about Paul Laxalt running for the Senate in Nevada (he lost by a narrow margin) he stuck his right hand out and said: "I'm Michael Sullivan, the fellow you read about. The man, completely taken by surprise, stuck out his and squawked" Tom Bradly."

Before Bradley could shut the door, Michael quickly explained the unfairness of the *Herald*' s story and that whether he (Bradley) was for against the development, the question was before the Mayor and the council and the planning commission voted for it. "Did you hear Mrs. O'Donnell's on television?" Michael asked.

"No I didn't but the whole thing sounded ominous to me."

"Do you still feel that way?"

"Well no, Mr. Sullivan, now you've explained it, in fact I don't think that shopping center might not be such a bad idea. It'll create some jobs for people, and Lord how we need those. I've heard of you. I hear you're a pretty good lawyer, do you do wills?"

"Yes I do Mr. Bradley, I'd be happy to do one for you."

"Corse I'd pay you."

"Naturally," Michael agreed.

"Tell you what Mr. Sullivan, you seem like a nice young fella. Me and the wife may just give you a call to do our wills, and I'll tell you what else I'm going to do for you. Everybody in the neighborhood is for the Mayor. I'm goin to tell my forty or so neighbors about our little conversation and I'm goin to persuade em to vote for Mrs. O'Donnell. If you're her manager she can't be too bad, besides I'm kinda known as the Mayor in these parts and if I tell um O'Donnell is ok chances are she'll get a few more votes."

"I salute you Mr. Bradley, and when you call, ask for me and say I said 'I would be taking care of your estate needs personally.' "

"Much obliged Mr. Sullivan, a good day to you sir."

Michael Sullivan bounced off the porch with a new found friend, convinced, if Bradley came through, he would have won the election all by himself in this one block. A short while later he ran into Peter and Jack campaigning in a nearby precinct and related his recent experience. They laughed and slapped him on the back saying Bradley appeared to be another juror overwhelmed by a Sullivan closing argument.

"We've been getting a good reception all day," Jack said, "I don't know if this is an O'Donnell neighborhood but the people we've been running into are really enthusiastic for her."

"I tell you son I've had nothing but fun today talking to the voters. It's amazing what you see when they open the door and you get a glimpse of their living rooms, it's a real eye opener. I've been running this thing but you, walking the streets knocking on doors, probably have a better handle on what's going on than I have."

"Dad you've been so busy between the firm and the campaign we haven't been able to tell you what we've seen and heard, but we've told Ron and mom and they pay attention. We've been out here every day for the last forty five days and there's a certain rhythm you get into that tells you whether things are going good or bad….."

"What sort of vibes are you getting today?"

"Positive, the natives are restless and ready to vote. They've chosen their side."

At six a.m. election day they gathered, for perhaps the last time, in the backroom of the headquarters, Betty, Michael, Mary, Ron, the consultants and the pollster, Darby. A large plate of Danish and doughnuts sat in the middle of the table with two pots of hot black coffee. Collectively, they looked bone weary, yet exhilarated, because win or lose the end was in sight. Michael called the meeting to order and gave the floor to Darby for his educated guess on the day's outcome.

"I give you good news and bad news. First the bad. In our overnight based on five hundred calls, we have them dead even, forty five-forty five, the same as a day ago. The undecideds are going to make us or break us. We also find the 'kick back' story is making headway and based on that we detected sleight momentum in our favor and that is good news.

Betty reacted to the news; she put her head on the table and started to laugh: "Oh my God, we've spent twelve months, three million dollars, two hundred and seventy appearances, TV ads, radio spots and we're tied. They all started laughing at her analysis, except the pollster.

"What's so funny, you started at about sixteen and nobody had ever heard of you, now you're even with the corrupt Mayor with momentum. I think we've done a great job."

"Oh Brad, you miss my point," Betty said and laughed again. "All that time, energy and money only to be tied. Of course we've done well, and I'll tell you something else, due to all our work we're going to take the fellow out."

"By the forty votes old Tom Bradly's going to scare up for us in precinct 45," Michael said. They all laughed and the tension drained out of the room. They speculated about turnout and came up with the figure two hundred and fifty thousand and thought if they could get one hundred and fifty two thousand they'd have a landslide. At eight a.m. the meeting broke up, Mary left to get her callers and drivers activated to get shut-ins to the polls; everyone else started making calls.

CHAPTER 29

They were to spend election night at the Wilson Hotel, where Betty arranged for a suite on the fifteenth floor and set the ballroom aside for a hopeful victory celebration. Betty and Tom O'Donnell, her husband, invited sixty of their close friends to a buffet supper in the suite, along with key campaign workers.

Michael, Mary and Ron stayed at headquarters on the phones getting out the vote until the polls closed at eight o'clock. Worn out, they slumped in their chairs, tired but happy. They were the last three left, everyone else had adjourned to the ballroom or the suite at the Wilson to await returns and hopefully see a new Mayor elected. They just looked at each other and Mary said: "That's that. I haven't eaten all day can we get something before we go over to the hotel?"

"I think I can take care of that," Ron answered and removed everything on his desk, reached into a lower drawer, pulled out a white table cloth, spread it on the desk, took out silverware and set the table, went into the back room and returned with two candles in sticks. They watched with awe as he went over to a cabinet stacked with campaign literature, got up on a chair, and extracted a bottle of Johnny Walker, black label and three glasses. Without uttering a word he poured the scotch into three glasses as the Sullivans dared not say a word to break the spell.

"After we down these, I've prepared a scrumptious feast of cold chicken, potato salad, rolls and corn on the cobb I will heat." They raised their glasses and toasted each other.

"Amazing," Mary said. "To genius," and raised her glass a second time. "You are not only a good fellow and a masterful campaign manager you are a master chef par excellence."

"To genius," Michael repeated and drank to his own toast.

They ate ravenously and by eight thirty were on their way to the hotel in a cab. On arrival they strode through the lobby and down an escalator, two levels, to the ballroom. They stepped off into a crowd of a thousand trying to get into the packed room. The first thing they saw were large signs on all the walls reading: "Mayor Elect-O'Donnell." Facing the entrance, a huge board divided into eight frames representing districts in the city, each flashing the tallies coming in from Registrar of Elections headquarters.

"It's like a tote board at the race track," Michael marveled. People milled about, laughing, talking, excited for the victory they hoped to celebrate. They tried to reach one of two cash bars stationed at either end of the room but the one they chose had a long queue so they abandoned the thought of getting a drink. Some of the crowd recognized Michael and Mary and came over to chat. Ron Quickly got lost in the crowd and made his way back to the bar. The first time they looked up at the tote board the totals ran: Dominelli: 22,000, O'Donnell: 19,500. Close but not as close as they would have liked to see it early in the count.

At the first opportunity they broke away from the crowd and made it back up to the lobby and to the O'Donnell's suite on the fifteenth floor. Entering the suite they realized they were seeing a replica of the scene they witnessed in the ballroom. They were mobbed by well-wishers, Betty and Tom being among the first to greet them.

"We're going to do it Michael," she yelled above the din. He could tell Betty and Tom were already celebrating, drinks in hand. At the first opportunity he pulled her off to the side and said: "If we're going to win we won't know for hours and you are going to have to greet your supporters down in the ballroom. Have you got something worked out to tell them?"

"I have some remarks, but they're based on a winning scenario."

"I think you better have something in case it goes the other way or it's still highly in doubt. Mary will help you change it to: 'it looks promising. It could be a long night.' Don't have anything more to drink and concentrate on what you want to say besides thanking everyone for their support."

At first she was taken aback, but quickly realized her euphoria was premature, saw his point and became very business like. "You're absolutely right Michael, we've come too far and worked too hard to get up before a thousand people and sound boozy. When do you think I should appear in the ballroom?" People were crowding in on them and trying to speak to her but they paid no attention. For all intents and purposes they were in the backroom of the head-quarters at one of those early morning meetings plotting strategy.

Michael cast a glance at his watch, saw the time: nine thirty. Ron suddenly appeared at his elbow and seeing the two of them in deep conversation, asked if they were aware of the status of the race. Before they could respond he gave the answer. "The Mayor still leads, thirty nine thousand to thirty six thousand with forty five precincts reporting."

"That's hopeful, but no way conclusive. I think you should go downstairs Betty at 10:30 and hope we are close if not, tell it like it is."

"Ok, Boss," Betty gave that magnificent smile and said: "I have to mingle with the some of the donors, you understand." He nod-ded and asked Ron to get Mary to help Betty with her speech and see if he could find a quiet room with a television set where he could quietly figure out the probability of winning

Ron had requisitioned a room across from Betty's suite with phones linked to four outposts in the city, and the Registrar of Elections office, receiving vote updates from individual precincts.

From this information he could tell whether they were doing better or worse than expected in a given precinct. In a room off this "war room" stood a bed, two chairs, a desk and a television set. Ron gathered up slips of paper from the phone callers and he and Michael slipped into the little room far from the maddening crowd. Michael turned on the set and saw an announcer interviewing a guest; running across the bottom of the screen the vote total appeared: "Dominelli-45,320; O'Donnell-43,270, twenty nine percent of precincts reporting. Michael again glanced at his watch: 9:45 p.m.

Mary joined them and said: "Do you two mind if I turn on the light," and laughed, "you're getting far too serious." Ron turned on a stand up lamp that cast a soft glow around the room, erasing the depressing bleakness caused by the television in a darkened room. He left to check with his precinct callers next door and two minutes later returned and handed Michael more slips of paper.

"Michael you can see we're doing a lot better on the south side than we figured."

"I see that. How's my Tom Bradley precinct doing?"

"I don't have those figures but I'll get them before the night's over," Ron answered. With that he brought out a bottle of Johnny Walker he brought from headquarters and from the outer room where his callers remained huddled over their phones he produced a platter of crackers, cheeses, raspberries, strawberries, black berries and pineapple rings. He poured out three glasses of scotch and they raised their glasses: "salude."

"You are a marvel Ron, in the midst of a typhoon you think of a snack. Your talents are wasted in politics, you should have your own restaurant."

"Ron's what they call in the service, a 'scrounger,' Michael said, "you tell him you need something and he gets it, no questions asked." He looked at his watch nervously and saw the time: 10 p.m. The polls had been closed two hours. The television screen flashed

"Breaking News" and new figures appeared: Dominelli-50,210; O'Donnell-49,652. (50.5% to 49.5%)

"Ok Ron it's ten fifteen, get Betty and Tom and head down to the ballroom. You can see they're revved up the deficit is shrinking. We know from the boys next door we're actually ahead by five hundred votes at least, tell her that. She will know what to say based on that information. Mary and I will wait here and watch. After she makes her speech bring her back up here for an analysis." Ron left and Michael gave Mary a hug and squeezed her hand: "We're going to do it, but it's going to be razor thin."

Betty graciously came on stage with her husband Tom and their two children followed by a fifty person entourage. Television cameras zoomed in on the family and a close up of Betty's face captured her endearing smile. Michael clocked her speech; eight minutes long. Just right. As she came to the end the tote board flashed: Dominelli-60,100; O'Donnell-60,951, her first lead. A roar went up from the crowd: "O'Donnell, O'Donnell."

Betty waved and put her hands over her head like a boxer and shook them. The crowd roared all the more. She followed Michael's directions, thanking everyone, telling her supporters it looked promising but way too early to claim victory and then at the end, with perfect timing, the board showed her forging into the lead. Up in the room Mary and Michael watched with fascination; they were glad for Betty and proud of her performance. They knew they had accomplished something good for themselves, for Betty O'Donnell and for the city.

Around midnight it became clear Betty O'Donnell would be the first woman Mayor in the city's history. The analysts, vote counters and exit polls had it: 125,907 to 120,206 for O'Donnell. They went back to the O'Donnell suite to offer congratulations and when they left Betty said: "Michael and Mary it couldn't have been done without you, we'll never be able to thank you enough, but I will try to justify your faith and confidence in me. God bless you both." They embraced as people do when they've been through something hectic together and survived. When they left Betty and Tom turned to their other guests and celebrated into the wee hours of the morning the first woman Mayor of the city.

. . .

On his first day back in the office full time, Michael cradled a cup of coffee in his hands and looked out the window of his fifteenth floor office, thinking: "I have to admit I'm going to miss the excitement of the campaign, Ron Fitzgerald, the consultants, the loyal volunteers." It gave him real pleasure to be a part, if not the cause of Betty's victory. Plus the firm now had a friend at city hall.

A knock at the door interrupted his reverie and Paul Connolly came in and plunked his lanky form in a chair opposite Michael's desk.

"Welcome back boss, we missed you around here."

"I've been thinking Paul, I've been at this campaign almost a year and it would be unfair, in my view to take out a full partnership share. Do you have any idea how much that share would amount to?"

"That's nonsense," Paul answered, your name on the door brings in more business then you could possibly take out of the firm."

"That's all well and good but do you have a rough idea what that take would be this year?"

"I guess half a million dollars, and besides you were here at least half the time and business with the city should bring in three times that much next year."

"Ok Paul here's what I want to do, and don't try to persuade me otherwise; you fellows have had to carry a heavier load with me gone no matter how you look at it. I'll draw a hundred thousand and my share above that will be divided into two pools, one for the partners and one for the associates. That won't amount to a great deal but it will be a token of my appreciation."

"Very generous pal, yet I don't think the partners will hear of it."

"I'm still the head guy around here."

"Yes Michael you are."

"Then it's a done deal, now let's talk business."

"Do you mind if I get another cup of coffee if were going into executive session?"

"Sure, will you get one for me?"

Michael and Paul had established a rule in the firm, you get your own coffee. You don't ask a secretary to bring it into you. They found it a way to keep the lawyers level headed and the staff appreciative of not having to be waitresses as well as secretaries. The one exception to the rule occurred when a lawyer had a client or was in conference with other lawyers, or a deposition being taken. Under these circumstances lawyers and staff worked as a team to service guests and clients making them feel comfortable. A simple rule that contributed to the feeling at Sullivan & Connolly, everyone in the house played an important part in making the wheels go round.

In a few minutes Paul returned with two cups of coffee on a tray and with a sly grin laid a plate of Danish on Michael's desk.

"Paul, I couldn't have chosen a better partner, you're always thinking.......of your stomach."

"Actually I was thinking of your stomach, and now that I see you reaching for one I'm convinced I did the right thing."

"Enough jesting, bring me up to speed on what's happening around here."

"We've hired three new associates, two of them young women which brings us to fifty five associates and thirty five partners."

"I'd like to meet them."

"You will. They'll be joining us next week. Business has been excellent and the best thing that's happened to us is losing Boniface Insurance. Six companies wanted to take their place and we accepted four as clients and had conflicts with the other two. The interesting thing about the firm is you and I are the oldest guys on the staff except for a couple of secretaries."

"And how old am I?"

"47, I looked it up in Martindale-Hubble."

"Well, Paul we're going against the grain; most of the big firms in this town are raiding each other as a means of growing. I still believe building one brick at a time, what you sacrifice in slow growth you gain in loyalty. Our only loss has been Ben Armstead and the three he took with him and that was years ago. What ever happened to him do you know?"

"A brilliant guy Michael, just like we figured when we hired him, but he's searching for something and hasn't found it. He's got two partners and he's had eight lawyers leave him including two of the four who left here. He can't seem to get along with people. I think he's going to wind up as a solo practitioner."

"Too bad," Michael said regretfully, "we had such high hopes for him here." Changing the subject abruptly he reverted back to his previous request. "I meant what I said about those two pools, will you take care of it?"

"Reluctantly, I will, and thank you, you unselfish scoundrel." He drained his cup, collected Michael's and his tray and left. An hour had passed without either of them realizing it. They liked each other's company yet neither had taken the time, since the early days of the firm to just meet and converse on a social basis, each had been too busy trying cases, getting clients, hiring lawyers and building Sullivan & Connolly into the most sought after firm in the city.

When Michael became campaign chairman for Betty O'Donnell, Paul understood he would have to step in and fill the role Michael had always played—head of the firm. He had no intention of usurping that role, but only to fill the vacuum in his absence and keep the firm growing and acquiring new clients. As Michael got deeper and deeper into the campaign Paul found himself moving into a management, something he was not accustomed to. Trial work he thrived on and while Michael remained top gun in the firm for litigation, Paul Connolly had carved out a name for himself within the state trial bar. Law firms in the city and around the state had now come to acknowledge the top trial lawyers in the state, man for man were to be found at Sullivan & Connolly. When faced with a lawyer from the firm, the opposition warned their clients: "Be ready to go to trial, those fellows don't settle cases, they try them." As much as he enjoyed trial work, when he took over Michael's role as manager, he found himself fascinated by the complexities of managing the firm. Psychology seem to be the most useful quality to have. Dealing with over a hundred people, all with their own well developed persona, required a combination of tact and compromise. He found himself quite good at it and the lawyers and staff responded well. Where Michael was the leader, and slowly becoming an icon, the lawyers felt comfortable with Paul's ready smile and easy going personality. On the other hand Michael Sullivan was a very focused and serious man. He quipped and kidded with the best of them and he had an understated dry humor but beneath that exterior lay a calm, steel like approach to work and play. He was a competitor, he liked to compete and he liked to win, but not at any cost. Competition in sports, all sports, had been thrilling to him. In high School he played basketball, baseball and tennis. Tennis became his favorite and he considered it the highest form of competition, one against one. In college he starred on the tennis team and later in the air force participated in world wide tournaments. That's one of the reasons he and Paul meshed so well. Like Michael, Paul had been an athlete during his student days and excelled as a baseball pitcher. On the mound his 6' 4" frame threaten the hitter never more than when he threw fastballs, striking out batter after batter. As good as he was, and scouts had approached him, he knew he would never make the majors and decided to get on with a professional career in the law. He graduated after Michael at Georgetown University Law School.

Now Michael had returned and Paul receded back into his pre-campaign roll. However after a month and a lengthy discussion they decided Paul should take over management of the firm, if willing. Surprisingly Paul agreed, confessing to Michael he found it more interesting than he thought it would be. They agreed Michael would take the high profile cases and devote himself, as much as possible to expand the client base.

A month into Betty O'Donnell's first year as Mayor, the zoning case came before the city council. Because of the ruckus raised by Tom Dominelli, during the campaign, Betty, at first, considered recusing herself but later determined that would be cowardly. At the last minute she decided the issue too important to the city's growth to let the four council members decide it without her weighing in. She studied the issue carefully and decided to vote in favor.

Michael appeared before the Mayor and council members, sitting as a legislative body. He presented a brilliant argument pointing out the benefits and countering the arguments of the opposition point by point. The head of the planning commission, represented by its counsel laid out all the preliminary studies completed by his staff and the conclusion they reached. He noted a full hearing had been held before the commission which adopted the plan unanimously. In summary he urged passage of the plan to build the Kennedy Development. Two hundred residents of the affected area, had chosen ten spokespersons to represent their interests plus a lawyer. For two hours, first the lawyer, and then the residents hammered the panel, first making legitimate arguments until it got to the spokespersons at which point it degenerated into threats of reprisal and name calling against the Mayor and city council. Finally the junior member of the council called for the vote.

"Will the clerk call the roll," Betty intoned

"Brown," the clerk requested:

"No!"

"Persky?"

"No."

"O'Donnell?"

"Yes!"

"Markowitz?"

"Yes."

The room grew silent. No sound. Perhaps two hundred and fifty people leaned forward in their chairs to listen for the deciding vote.

"Shipstan?"

"No!"

Pandemonium broke out, the residents were on their feet, yelling, laughing, clapping. The lawyer for the homeowners accepted congratulations from his adoring constituents.

"Order, Betty shouted into the microphone. Order, or I will clear the room. We still have two matters to cover."

They were already leaving the room in droves. They got what they came for—defeat of the project. Michael turned to his clients and said; "Round two is over, we won the first, they won the second. If you're game, we will move to the third round beyond the bureaucrats and into the courts. The law is on our side. The council made an arbitrary decision, one the court will not look favorably on." They got up to leave and Michael winked at the Mayor as they turned and made their way up the isle to the exit and he saw Betty with a slight twinkle in her eye signaling she did the best she could.

A few months after the hearing, Michael was on his way to the courthouse for a settlement conference with Judge Gregory Appleby when he ran into Ron Fitzgerald bounding down the courthouse steps shouting at him: "Hello boss." Breaking into a wide grin Michael greeted him extending his hand and grabbing him by the shoulder in an embrace. Anyone watching their greeting would have drawn the impression the older man found genuine pleasure in meeting the younger. Michael put his arm around his shoulder and asked: "What's happened to you my friend, you disappeared the day after the campaign?"

"I got on down to the state capital to see if I could get my old job back at the legislature. No dice."

"What are you going to do now?"

"I'm working part time for a title and trust company checking plat maps in the court house, and looking for a full time job on the side."

A thought flashed across Michael's mind; he admired the work Ron had done in the campaign, especially the long hours he had to put in sometimes sixteen to eighteen hours a day. He never asked for any increase in pay or time off. On every assignment undertaken, he performed with a minimum of instructions, often devising his own modus operandi. Moreover, Michael loved his puckish sense of humor and the fact, at his young age, unlike so many others, he didn't take himself too seriously. Despite a twenty year age difference, they had chemistry.

"Ron, why don't you come to work for Sullivan & Connolly?"

"That's awfully nice of you Michael, but what could I do? I know nothing about law."

"Look Ron, this is no gesture to help a fellow out; I think you can be a huge help to us. I had the chance to watch you for nine months, you can do things some of my lawyers can't do. We have an office manager who's swamped with work. We have a hundred and twenty five employees, and that's a crowd for one person to manage. He could use an assistant and I'll guarantee you'll make more than you made in the campaign or legislature. How about a start at thirty thousand dollars? Ron looked stunned, grateful, doubtful and completely taken aback. For a moment he remained silent.

Michael broke the silence saying: "All right, how about thirty five thousand?"

His aplomb returned and he said: "Michael, I'm overwhelmed, I wasn't being quiet to up the salary, I thought thirty thousand too much. Sir, if you think I'm worth it, I am honored to work for you.

"Ok, then it's done, thirty five thousand, and Ron I think you're going to like working at Sullivan & Connolly. I'll tell Paul Connolly, our managing partner, about our court house conference and ask him to give you a call so we can get underway. Now I've got to run, I'm already late for a conference with a Judge. They shook hands and Michael hurried to the fifth floor.

He got off the elevator and practically ran down the long corridor to court room 22. As he did so he passed court room after court room and became generally aware of witnesses hovering outside each, waiting to be called, people in clusters listening to their lawyer's instructions, people sitting quietly on wood benches between court rooms, others wandering up and down the hall sporting juror badges. As he approached 22, a group of perhaps forty individuals listened to final instructions from a bailiff before entering the court room to begin a new trial. He pushed open the double doors, and saw Timothy Brian, the court clerk, sitting in the empty court room.

"His honor is awaiting your presence Mr. Sullivan, other counsel arrived five minutes ago."

"Plead my case Tim, after I leave, if I leave," and gave the clerk an engaging smile.

"I'll be doin' that Mr. Sullivan and a good day to you sir."

Not knowing what kind of a reception to expect, being five minutes late for a meeting with the most punctual Judge in the Courthouse, Michael knocked on the door, stepped in and bowed to the Judge.

"All right Sullivan cut the act, you're late but counsel and I are grateful you showed up."

"I don't know how to take that Judge, I would never deliberately fail to appear at your summons, late yes, but never abstention."

"You Irishmen are all the same Michael, you have an excuse for everything. Sit down, Bart here has no time to waste on your shenanigans. The "Bart" referred to by the Judge was Bartlett

Jacobson, a renowned land use and zoning lawyer with the reputation of winning difficult cases representing land owners and residents in zoning appeals. Michael didn't know him personally but, like all adversaries, he had to go up against in trial or on appeal, he had done in depth research on Jacobson, down to his wife and family and cases he had been involved in. Michael found his reputation well earned.

"All right Gentlemen, shake hands," the Judge ordered "and come out settling; save the court's time and your own." He did not say this in jest or with a smile. The lawyers knew he meant every word of it and would try to force settlement to avoid what he deemed a two week trial.

"Bart, is it your position there should be no shopping center at all?"

"Pretty much your honor."

"Michael, is it your position you want the center with all the bells and whistles?"

"Not necessarily. My clients have suggested several modifications to cut down noise, traffic and frustration on the part of the homeowners. Nothing seems to appease the opposition."

"Is that true?" the Judge asked.

"Generally, yes. I represent hundreds of homeowners and it's hard to get them to agree to anything, accept keeping the shopping center out of the neighborhood. Once we won at the council level they're implacable."

"I can understand that, but you can lose this thing at trial, I'm sure you realize that."

"I do, still my clients are committed to total victory."

Judge Appleby intimidated many lawyers who appeared in his court, especially the young ones. He respected Michael as a top flight trial lawyer, having been a trial lawyer before appointment to the bench. Unlike many of his fellow Judges, with little or no trial experience, he appreciated lawyers who knew their way around the court room. In many ways it made his job easier. Any time a lawyer from Sullivan & Connolly appeared in his court, he knew they were prepared to try, and came to court with well thought out briefs on the law of the case.

Michael said nothing, letting the Judge do all the talking. He knew Bart's hands were somewhat tied, but he also understood homeowners are reluctant to pay attorney's fees. If he won at trial the homeowners would be reluctant to appeal after paying Bart Jacobson twenty five thousand dollars to try the case, plus another twenty five thousand to finance the appeal. Realistically Michael believed settlement not to be an option; to win he had to win at trial. So he sat silent, content to let the Judge conduct settlement discussions. Jacobson and Judge Appleby argued back and forth the risks of trial versus the certainty of settlement.

When the hour reached five, the Judge clasped his hands behind his head, leaned back in his chair and said: "Gentlemen, trial will commence Monday morning at ten o'clock. Briefs in my office by then." Both lawyers agreed to have the Judge try the case, rather than a jury, believing the complexity might confuse a jury and Michael was doubly willing to go along with a court ruling, fearing an emotional jury could be swayed by the homeowners against the large land developer.

CHAPTER 30

Prior to trial Michael submitted a fifty page brief citing applicable cases from the state's highest court and the courts of other jurisdictions on zoning law to be applied in the case before the Judge. The central issue in these cases was whether the administrative tribunal (in this case the city council) had made an arbitrary and capricious decision based upon insufficient or lack of evidence. Michael took the position the city council bowed to the wishes of a room full of angry homeowners without taking into account the evidence presented by his clients. His opponent argued ample evidence had been introduced to support the council's decision.

The trial received full coverage in the local news media, so that, on opening day when the Judge took to the bench the room was filled to capacity with homeowners, press and the usual court watchers. The economic stakes were high, with the city bursting at its boundaries, the test came down to whether expansion could be legally undertaken, given the need and precautions taken, or would there be fighting and litigation every time a developer sought to bring a commercial development into or near an existing city. Both lawyers and the Judge, hearing the case without a jury, knew the consequences would be a turning point for the city—expansion or retraction, progress or status quo, depending on one's point of view.

In a one hour opening statement Michael outlined the quantity and quality of the evidence to be presented. Jacobson, in half the time, gave the drawbacks of allowing the project to be built. Preparing for trial, Michael spared no expense enlisting, as expert witnesses, city planning authorities, architects, and economists from the city and comparable cities in the tri state area. A detailed mockup of the east end of the city, showed the distance between the eastern outskirts and the proposed development. Photographs taken from the helicopter were introduced into evidence showing an aerial view of the development.

During a week of testimony, Michael called as witnesses, members of the planning staff who initially recommended approval of the plan submitted by John Kennedy and Ed Malloy. In direct testimony they told the court they deemed the project of benefit to the community, and in furtherance of long range plans they had prepared for gradual development east of the city. Next he called members of the planning commission who, after a hearing, voted in favor of the project. At the end of the second week of trial, Kennedy and Malloy told of initial discussions and the decision to build the shopping center, hiring architects, Cost estimates, traffic studies, financing, costs of delay and expected revenue. Beginning the third week he called to the stand members of the city council who voted against the project. They were called as hostile witnesses, which gave Michael the opportunity to cross examine before they could be used by Bart Jacobson to present his case. Michael, not unaware of the danger in calling such witnesses, because they would have been well prepared to testify during Jacobson's case both on direct and cross examination, decided to call them out of order on the chance they would be taken by surprise and forget what they were supposed to say.

It proved to be the right tactic. He led them through a series of questions, that established their prejudice against the project, by showing they decided to adopt the Mayor's position, believing he would re-elected, and they ultimately based their decision on the homeowner's opposition. He got them to admit it would mean thousands of jobs for the community, additional tax revenue for the city, and provide convenient shopping for those living east of the city. Their rationale came down to: homeowners vote in elections, developers didn't.

Being able to cross examine them as hostile witnesses before Jacobson could put them on the stand as his witnesses served to gut the testimony they were prepared to give as to: traffic, congestion, pollution and homeowner objections. When he completed his examination he informed the court: "The plaintiff rests, your Honor." In two and a half weeks time Michael produced twenty five witnesses, multiple exhibits, and created a record, he felt, would assure victory on appeal no matter what decision Judge Appleby rendered.

Bart Jacobson spent the rest of the third week of trial calling homeowner after homeowner voicing their individual objections, two traffic experts, who swore traffic would be unbearable without further development of the highway extending eastward, an economist who stated jobs created would be low paying and harm done would outweigh benefits. At the end of the trial both attorneys agreed the Judge should "view" the property. Judge Appleby acceded to the request and he, both lawyers, the court reporter and other interested parties went out to the site. The attorneys described for the record what they were seeing, the Judge, likewise, dictated his statement for the record detailing what he saw, asked several questions of the lawyers and then they all returned to the courtroom. From the bench Judge Appleby advised a written opinion would be issued within two weeks, after studying the transcript, (2,500 pages) and reviewing exhibits. He thanked everyone involved and retired to his chambers.

Back at Sullivan & Connolly, John Kennedy and Ed Malloy talked about the trial and speculated on the outcome. "I'll say this for the Judge," Malloy theorized, "I don't know how smart he is but I watched him throughout the trial and he took notes every time a witness testified or an exhibit introduced. He appeared interested in what the experts had to say."

"I don't think he paid much attention to those whining landowners," Kennedy quipped. What are your thoughts Michael?"

"John I tend to agree. What impressed him, I think, was the 'mock up' we prepared and his view of the site. He's going to make up his own mind; he listened to the experts, but it's his city too and he'll do what he thinks best for the city. I think it important he's going to write his opinion. If it's favorable, you fellows are going to have a much easier time with future projects and so will other developers. It's really a case of: 'do we grow or stay small?' It's a question every city in America faces."

"I'm betting on you Michael, you tried a hell of a case. What do you say Ed?"

"Absolutely," and gave a thumbs up sign.

Michael blushed because he knew these two had no need to and did not flatter. He smiled and said: "We wouldn't have stood a chance without your financial backing."

Laughing, Kennedy said with a smile, "We can't wait for the bill."

Two weeks later Michael reviewed one of fifty current files he kept in a credenza behind his desk. He prided himself on the fact when a client called and wanted to know, "What progress is being made on my case," he could swivel his chair around, reach for the alphabetically labeled file, flick through it quickly and give the client a precise update, as to whether a complaint had been filed, an answer filed, discovery requests, depositions scheduled, trial dates and often answering a legal question the client may have become aware of in the case. These calls he generally kept to minimum to save the client money and allow him to quickly get back to the business of the moment, without having to refresh his recollection. Michael Sullivan was neither a "clean desk," lawyer, or a "disorganized desk" lawyer. His desk always had ten to fifteen files neatly stacked in the order he intended to work on them. He scrupulously tried to work on one file at a time until he had dictated a memo, letter, note to file or whatever else had to be addressed before returning the file to the credenza.

His concentration was broken one afternoon two weeks after the zoning case had concluded when Maggie Johnson, his secretary, came into the office with a bundle of mail cradled in her left arm and a large envelope in her right hand. She'd been with him a year and he considered her the best he had worked with. At thirty six, she was very attractive. No flamboyance, always beautifully dressed, and most important, highly intelligent. For Michael it was a perfect match. She anticipated his needs, remained calm in a crisis and gave advice only when asked. Extremely pleasant to look at, as many in the office did, she was happily married to a doctor and had two children, ages four and six. Her marriage wouldn't have stopped some men; Michael was different. For him, the only women in his life were Mary, his mother and his two daughters. Sometimes single women associates, having the opportunity to work with him on a case, tried to flirt, but he remained totally unaware of their attention, which caused some to think him naïve or a "straight arrow," in the vernacular of the day. However, once they spent time working with him, observed his courtly manners and dedication to the task at hand, their thinking underwent a radical change to admiration and respect. They considered him a gentleman, loyal to his family and members of the firm. When that realization set in the women associates looked upon him as the type of man they would choose for a husband, a man they looked up to and respected. Though older than most of the associates in the firm, Maggie Johnson had the same feeling about Michael Sullivan.

Holding the envelope out, she cheerfully said: "Mr. Sullivan, I think you may be expecting this." He looked up and replied mischievously, "Maggie, have you been going through my mail?"

"Well, yes I couldn't help but notice the return address: "The Honorable Gregory Appleby," and we all know, you and everyone at Sullivan & Connolly have been waiting for a decision on the zoning case."

"Thank you Ms. Johnson," he took the envelope and said: "I hope you are the bearer of good news."

As soon as she left the office, he carefully opened the envelope, and removed what he assumed to be the Judge's decision. He thumbed through it quickly, noting the number of pages, forty, and bracing himself, turned to the last page. A smile slowly crept across his face as he read the conclusion:

"In view of the above findings of fact, I make the following conclusions of law: The decision of the City Council was arbitrary and capricious based on a paucity of evidence and therefore must be overturned and plaintiff's petition granted. Counsel for the plaintiff is hereby instructed to prepare an order of judgment containing findings of fact and conclusions of law consistent with this opinion and submit them to the undersigned for signature."

He started to call Paul Connolly but checked himself and went to the opening paragraph of the Judge's opinion and continued to read until he reached the conclusion. In his judgment the Judge had carefully laid out the progression of the case through the initial planning staff findings to the planning commission hearing and decision and proceeded to the hearing before the city council. In doing so, Michael felt the Judge laid out a careful prelude to his decision which began on page fifteen with a recital of testimony from the transcript accompanied by page citations, exhibits considered and references to case law much of which had been adopted from Michael's brief. All in all, Michael believed it would be difficult to overturn on appeal with the appeal court giving great deference to the judge's finding of facts. He took into consideration the homeowners would have to pay upwards of twenty five to thirty five thousand dollars to appeal with a twenty percent chance of success.

Instead of calling Paul as he had originally intended, he called Mary, who had sat up with him many nights prior to trial discussing the issues. She knew it was a great win, important to him as well as the firm, but neither of them at the time realized the publicity it would generate for Michael and the firm.

The next call to John Kennedy elicited a confident, "I never doubted the outcome, congratulations Michael." Last he called Paul Connolly, told him he'd received the opinion and invited him to come and read it and notify members of the firm.

When he arrived at his office the next day a copy of the *Daily Ledger* lay on top of his desk with a note stapled to the front page: "Congratulations Boss, you're finally getting some deserved recognition—Maggie."

The story began on page one with the headline: "Court rules in Favor of Developers." And a subhead: "Michael Sullivan Wins Again." The story, written by Jason Barbur, lauded Michael's role as lawyer for the developers: "In a three week trial before Judge Gregory Appleby, Michael Sullivan, of Sullivan & Connolly, put on a dashing show of examining witnesses, cross examination, brilliant oral argument and a scholarly legal brief, plus a view of the property his clients intend to build a shopping center on all of which proved convincing to the Judge who, in a written opinion, labeled evidence produced by the opposition and accepted by the city council in its decision, as arbitrary and capricious, which in legalese translates into the council acted emotionally, without creditable evidence." The *Herald* followed suit with a day by day review of the trial for its readers sparing no compliments on Michael's presentation of his client's position.

In the ensuing week a writer from the *Herald's Sunday Magazine* requested an interview with Michael explaining she wanted to do a profile for the Sunday edition of the news magazine to include his early career in the law, the firm and how it came to be a power house legal establishment. He acquiesced and two days later Valerie Schwartz came to his office for the interview. Although leery of what the story might contain, he felt it wouldn't hurt the firm's reputation in the long run. He sized up Ms. Schwartz as a tough no nonsense reporter. Short in stature, bespectacled, her hair drawn back in bun, and except for her age, reminded him of Justice Elizabeth Goldstein of the Supreme Court. Her questions were sharp, she wasn't interested in fluff.

Michael seated her on the couch in his office, while he sat at the end facing her. She urged him to tell her everything and she would make a judgment what to use. Over the course of three hours she elicited he had gone to high school locally and then to Georgetown University in Washington D.C, served in the U.S. Air Force for two years, then enrolled at Georgetown University law school, passed two bar examinations, the District's and his own state bar, clerked for a state Supreme Court justice, joined the law firm of Barron, Walker, Youngman & Hamilton, left that firm after fifteen years, and founded Sullivan & Connolly with four lawyers and grew to over a hundred in seven years. The first hour melded into the second and Valerie Schwartz began to see the prospects of a Horatio Alger story. She jotted in her notebook, Sullivan was an achiever. Her area of inquiry moved to his marriage and the children. Jack, the oldest, a junior at Georgetown University, Sharon, the second a senior in high school, Peter a sophomore and Kathryn a freshman. They reviewed his recent activities as Chairman of the Betty O'Donnell campaign for Mayor, his love for sports and his choice of tennis as his favorite sport in which he excelled in high school and college. By the third hour, tough reporter Schwartz was totally immersed in the life and times of Michael Sullivan and sure she was on to the making of the presidency in some future year. She queried him on his trial victories and losses and he assured her he had many losses to go along with the wins. She finished the interview asking if he minded if she talked to people in the firm, and possibly lawyers he'd done battle with. He had no objections and warned: "It won't be all bouquets."

A captivated Valarie Schwartz followed up on her request, interviewing members of the firm, other lawyers, the Mayor and people Michael served with on various charitable boards. Her article appeared in the *Sunday Magazine* two weeks later covering three pages and a picture of the two of them sitting on a couch, he being interviewed. The picture brought out a youthful look despite his age, forty eight, with not a hint of gray in his hair, a dark suit, white shirt and tie, in sum, a look of confidence and maturity, with a smile at the corner of his mouth. Anyone viewing the picture and reading the story might sum it up with the word: "formidable."

Sharon Sullivan, up early Sunday morning, still in her pajamas put on a rain coat and went to the mailbox to get the Sunday paper. She scanned the front page with the headline: "U.S. Threatens War With Iraq." Meandering to the kitchen she tossed the paper on the table, went to the cupboard and pulled down a package of breakfast food. When she finally got seated and started to scoop her first spoonful she started to read the *Sunday Magazine*. On the first inside page she saw the story about her father. Her first impulse: scan the article to see if her name was mentioned. "Oh Joy," she shouted, "yes and the whole family is mentioned." Excited she returned to the first paragraph and was surprised to learn so much about her father. She never knew, for example, he served as law clerk to a Supreme Court Justice. Actually, she thought: "My dad is a pretty famous person."

Finishing her serial in four gulps, she couldn't contain her excitement any longer and rushed from the kitchen, up the stairs announcing to everyone she had news. When she burst into her parents room they were just sitting up in bed startled at all the noise coming from the stairwell.

"Dad, Mom, our family is in the *Sunday Magazine*. I read the whole article and the writer really says some nice things about dad. She jumped on the bed and laid the paper in front of them. Michael and Mary sat up propped with pillows and she read the story aloud. Mary laughed, "Are you going to be able to keep your head to its present size, Michael?"

He paused for a moment and then answered, knowing Mary was having some fun with him. "She probably got a little carried away but I'll try to handle it."

"But dad, you're a famous guy, Sharon exclaimed. Mary spoke up and said: "Sharon that article will be lining the garbage cans all over this city tomorrow. You'll find as you grow older fame is fleeting and your darling famous father knows that better than any of us. They all made fun of Michael and laughed at his modesty. Secretly they were proud of their dad, Mary most of all.

. . .

As the firm grew, Michael's energy took him in many directions, besides the day to day practice of law. Even before the breakup of Barron, Walker, Youngman & Hamilton he donated hours to the bar association serving as chairman of two committees and eventually president of the state bar association. Paul Connolly had encouraged him to run for the office, even though it would require time away from the firm. Paul saw things in Michael he was probably unaware of. The stuff that leaders are made of, indefatigable energy, love of competition, an astute mind and the ability to attract others to a cause, in their case, the firm. No one in the firm resented his outside activities; in fact they reflected well on the firm. Most of the lawyers followed his lead doing pro bono work, serving on bar committees and boards of nonprofit charities—giving back to the community. Michael operated on the theory: throw bread upon the waters, use your talent helping others and it will come back a hundred fold.

By every measure, Michael Sullivan's growing fame, as a lawyer and leading citizen brought notoriety to the firm and as he gained stature the firm reaped the benefits. From a financial standpoint, Paul Connolly and all the lawyers in the firm had prospered. He realized, without Michael Sullivan, they could still be at fifteen lawyers, rather than the one hundred they were. Success breeds success.

Paul Connolly did not seek fame, only a reputation as a top lawyer in his profession. The firm's rapid growth had forced him to become more of an administrator than he had wished, and at the same time revealed his genius for organization, planning and recruiting legal talent which had great effect on the firm, like Michael's court room victories. They were a perfect team working in tandem, neither jealous or envious of the other. The model they settled on, growing out of Michael's experience at Barron, Walker, Youngman & Hamilton, worked beautifully for the firm, equity for all and an appreciation of each lawyer's talent and contribution to the firm. They were achieving an almost unbelievable result; a hundred person firm with the feeling of a small, close fifteen person law firm. A truly remarkable result when other firms were raiding each other, competing for super stars, and merging to survive.

Paul and Teresa Connolly remained close to Michael and Mary from the days they opened the doors at Sullivan & Connolly. Teresa, short and perky, Paul, tall, lanky and easy going. The four worked hard, raising their children, three girls and a boy for the Connollys; two boys and two girls for the Sullivans. They attended different schools, the Sullivans at St. Agatha and the Connollys at St. Mary's yet the children were like cousins because of time spent together. Both women were the core of their families, religious, smart, generous and terrific wives and mothers. They brought that same spirit to the sixty wives of the firm. Family was paramount. This spirit permeated the firm and contributed to the closeness of all its members.

Like Michael, Paul had been a standout student at Georgetown

University and the Law School, he'd clerked for a federal court Judge before hiring on with the white shoe firm, Tallyrand & Morris. He assumed he would make partner there and spend the rest of his career with the firm. That is, until he met Michael Sullivan. Somehow he didn't hesitate a minute when asked to partner with Michael. It seemed so natural. From the day their plaque went over the door, he never looked back, he knew he would be with the firm until he could no longer practice.

As it grew and Michael brought in more and more business, Paul naturally filled the roll of making it all the mesh. The lawyers looked up to the two senior partners, Michael as the leader and Paul as the one they brought their problems to. It wasn't that Michael was above it all, he just didn't have time to try the big cases, get clients, be immersed in civic affairs and run the firm too. Paul felt secure in the knowledge that if anything happened to either of them, the foundation laid was so well grounded it would continue to thrive no matter happened. He and Michael had discussed such an eventuality and both agreed the firm could withstand the loss of either or both.

Serving as president of the state bar demanded more than Michael had foreseen, yet he determined to visit every one of the thirty six county bar associations during his term. He accomplished the feat in his first three months in office. In his inaugural address, the night of his election, he told two thousand lawyers and their wives of his goal to visit all the local associations to find out their needs and how the association could help them better serve the citizens of the area.

On that evening he told the assemblage, it was his hope lawyers could set an ethical example for others to emulate, pointing out when he entered practice firms were still relatively small and congenial, where all the lawyers knew each other and cases could be settled on the street corner. A lawyer's word to a fellow lawyer was gold. All that rapidly changed over a twenty five year period.

Lawyers were now urged to operate like a business, fight each other through the discovery process, go back on their word, raid each other for talent, merge to survive, become multi-state, bill an impossible number of hours, in short conduct their practice as a business not a profession. With what result? More money—yes. But loss of community esteem. He pointed out lawyers had a higher calling than just making money. "Society is built and dependent upon the framework of the law. Without law there can be no civil society," Lawyers, he argued, are stewards of the law, society has granted them that high status, because they are the bulwark against tyranny. To abuse that stewardship, to lose that trust, to be less than professional is to abandon those who have placed their trust in the law. He urged members of the bar to treat each other with respect as their predecessors had done. To treat the law as a sacred trust, and in so doing, set the example for their fellow citizens to follow. For a few seconds—silence. Then they stood and they cheered. Every lawyer present longed for the same kind of professionalism he described. Each had studied the law, and assumed they were entering a profession of high honor only to find out greed permeated the ranks of some but not the majority of lawyers. He pointed to a higher standard. One, he reminded them, they were imbued with when they graduated from law school.

Traveling around the state with Mary, he thought, would bring much more to the meetings with his fellow lawyers and their wives, and she would be able to get a sense of what the wives felt about their husband's profession. As they traveled from town to town, he speaking in grange halls, theaters, hotels and in one case a court room, and Mary mixing with the wives afterwards, they found a wonderful group of men and women, most of them in small law firms or solo practitioners, practicing law exactly the way Michael had described it in his inaugural speech, untouched by the greed he had referred to. They found it refreshing to meet such people.

In talking to and visiting with lawyers in some of the rural areas he found many were not taking advantage of or not even aware of the technology being employed in the larger urban practices. Spurred on by this realization, he put together a three day seminar with technical specialists, lawyers using state of the art equipment in trial practice, law firm organizers and experts knowledgeable in internet and electronic research teaching their expertise to small and middle town lawyers allowing them to compete on a case by case basis with their better equipped electronically sophisticated brethren in the larger firms. He and Paul Connolly had spent hours on the phone getting the experts to donate their time and five of the larger firms, including their own, to shoulder the costs. Six hundred lawyers from around the state showed up. Michael gave the welcoming address telling the participants what he had learned in his travels around the state and that the seminar they were attending would enhance their practice and improve the services they were currently furnishing to their clients. During the three days he was all over the pavilion conferring with fellow attorneys encouraging them to learn the new ways. He had top lawyers demonstrating trial techniques, using visuals and power point presentations, designed to simplify the job of Judges, juries and witnesses. At the end he asked: "Should we do this next year?" and they answered with a thundering "yes" followed by loud applause for all who had contributed to its success. He had no idea then the conference would be held in succeeding years and become known as the "Sullivan" seminar drawing up to fifteen hundred lawyers annually.

CHAPTER 31

While Michael Sullivan and Paul Connelly were busy practicing law, the outside world continued to spin and not for the better. William Jefferson Clinton, forty second President of the United States, had brought himself and the presidency into disgrace. In complete disregard for the position he held, he recklessly became involved sexually in pursuit of a young woman intern working on his staff at the White House. He would have gotten away with it perhaps but for the fact, a reporter for Newsweek magazine, Michael Isikoff, had completed an investigation into the affair and written a story for Newsweek. Newsweek's editors tried to quash the story to protect Clinton, but news blogger, Matt Drudge, got wind of it and published the story on his web site. The country gasped in embarrassment and dismay. Surely Clinton would have the grace to resign opined the pundits but they didn't fully understand the Clintons. He was willing to and did plunge the country into the depths of despair while he tried to deny what was obvious to all. Ms. Clinton blamed others.

Ken Starr, a federal appeals court Judge, was appointed to investigate Clinton, and in the process uncovered ample evidence of Clinton's lies warranting impeachment. Only the second President to be impeached since Andrew Johnson in 1868, Clinton, like Johnson, was acquitted in a trial before the Senate by a partisan Democratic vote. During the investigation, impeachment proceedings and trial the country ran on automatic pilot, while Clinton spent all his time defending himself.

Representative Henry Hyde, Chairman of the House Judiciary Committee, presented a brilliant case demonstrating, without contradiction, the President's guilt. The rationale for the Democrats to acquit: Clinton did not commit high crimes or misdemeanors. He only took advantage of his position with a young inexperienced intern. The American people were not fooled by the Democrat charade. At the time, Michael, like others, thought Clinton had the sense to resign and spare the people going through another Nixon-like drama and impeachment. They misjudged the man. His interest lay in saving his own hide, not of the people who elected him. Michael watched Clinton stumble through the remainder of his term, a stain on the soul of the country.

As a Republican, active in politics, he took heart in the election of George W. Bush in 2000, a two term Governor of Texas, and forty third President of the United States. Bush promised to restore honor and decency to the White House and the presidency after the black mark left by the Clintons. His presidency plunged into a new era on September eleventh 2001 when Islamic terrorists crashed two planes into the World Trade Center in New York, another into the Pentagon in Washington D.C. and a fourth crash in Pennsylvania. Transfixed by the greatest foreign attack on American soil in history, George Bush became a war President, placing national security at the top of the nation's agenda. Within months of the attack President Bush launched the country into war against the terrorist Taliban regime in Afghanistan which continued to give sanctuary to Osama bin Laden the architect of the attacks. Four months passed before the Taliban were driven from power and bin Laden chased into hiding.

For Michael, and all Americans, after a long cold war which saw the crumbling of communist Soviet Russia, a new enemy arose, far more elusive, to stalk the world. A fanatical brotherhood of Muslim terrorists sworn to destroy the United States. In 2003 America invaded Iraq with a twofold purpose: overthrow of the dictator Saddam Hussein and destruction of Hussein's weapons of mass destruction. Three weeks after the invasion U.S. armed forces surged into Bagdad and ousted the Hussein regime. American had now established a presence in the Middle East where it would remain for the foreseeable future. In keeping with his promise after destruction of the twin towers in New York, President Bush set out to destroy Islamic terrorists wherever found.

. . .

Mary and Michael sat in the third row of bleachers beside the tennis courts at Georgetown University watching Jack Sullivan playing a singles match against a player from Johns Hopkins. As a freshman Jack had made the team at number five singles. Now, as junior he held the number three singles position on a Georgetown team hoping for a shot at the national championship. At six foot two topped with a head of black hair, heavy eye brows like his father and a tan body Jack looked every inch an athlete.

When the children were young Michael saw to it they all had tennis lessons from a seasoned professional, something not affordable by his family when he was growing up. He learned the game by watching others and imitating their ground strokes, serve, overhead and volley. Being a natural mimic he incorporated several styles into his own, and as a junior in high school he played well enough to earn an athletic scholarship to Georgetown. In four years he set a record for wins and along with it a lifelong love of the game. It was only natural that he sought to instill that same love for the game in his children. Each, in his or her turn, took to it like a duck to water so that by the time Jack enrolled at Georgetown they had all played in tennis tournaments and proved to be fierce competitors against their opponents as well as between themselves. Peter, the second son, was doing so well in high school and on the verge of winning the state high school championship, as his father had done thirty two years earlier, caused Michael to hope he'd go to Georgetown and follow in Jack's footsteps. As a freshman at Georgetown, Sharon Sullivan made number two on the varsity squad.

Although they had seen Jack play many times they delighted in watching him. The way he gracefully moved around the court. He moved to the ball with cat like swiftness, always set and waiting when the ball arrived, hitting it to the opponent's opposite side until he maneuvered him out of position, finishing with a kill shot. What beauty. They clapped in appreciation. In Washington for parents weekend at Georgetown University after their two eldest enrolled in the Jesuit school on the Potomac, they stayed at a little hotel on Wisconsin avenue and attended festivities on campus, and lectures in Gaston Hall. Over a hundred years old, completed in 1901 the two story hall, seating seven hundred and forty, in dark wood, bedecked with coats of arms of the twenty eight Jesuit Universities and colleges in the United States enjoyed the reputation of campus jewel much like the Bodleian at Oxford University. Kennedy, Nixon, and Clinton had spoken from its stage, Secretaries of State had proclaimed policies, Gorbachev, Thatcher and other world figures had delivered historical speeches to students, faculty and friends. They thrilled walking around the green campus, mingling with students and their parents. They attended Sunday mass at Dahlgren Chapel in the quad bordered by a building named "Old North" where George Washington addressed listeners from its steps and where the constitution of the United States rested in safety during the civil war.

These were heady days for the Sullivans with the children growing into adulthood, Michael heading up one of the largest and fastest growing firms in the city and Mary more and more involved in charitable activities. The future unknown they found the present an exciting place to be.

"Hey Dad how'd I do?" Jack said, coming off the court after a 6-2; 6-2 win over his Johns Hopkins opponent.

"Great Jack, I thought you looked pretty mobile out there. Sit down with us for a minute before you shower."

"Mom, it's so great you're here. Where are we going to eat tonight?"

"Your father likes the Tombs, how do you feel about that?"

"That'd be great, probably run into some of the buddies there but that's ok."

"Bring the team with you Jack, if you want, I'll buy the beer."

"Very generous. Let's leave it at this. I'll see you at the Tombs at seven thirty with or without the squad. I'm off to take a shower."

At seven fifteen that evening the Sullivans descended ten steps down from thirty six street N.W. into a narrow alley leading to the entry of the Tombs restaurant, a Georgetown University hangout founded by Richard McCooey. Michael spent many happy hours at the Tombs during college and law school years and as did Mary during her years at Trinity. For them it always brought back fond memories. The first thing a visitor sees coming in from a narrow passage way is the round bar with old World War I pictures on the walls. A mid twenty year old bartender or two is always serving twenty or thirty people. To the right is the restaurant with glass stained windows and booths along the walls. Long tables with benches sit in front of the booths where students, faculty, visitors and the regulars sit on either side eating and drinking out of large pitchers of beer. Half the room has tables of four with white table cloths for more formal dining. A second room two steps down from the first sports leather booths, walls decorated with college flags, and boating scenes from the 1800's. A fireplace with crossed oars from the rowing teams anchors one wall. Noise greets the visitor: loud voices, arguing, laughter, deep conversations, all perforating the air; college boys, girls and their parents experiencing the college scene together for one night.

"We're expecting five or six for dinner," Michael told the young waitress in the tombs uniform: oxford blue button down shirt, black bow tie and kaki skirt. That's what he liked about the tombs, besides the college décor, all the waiters were between twenty and twenty five, dressed alike, the boys sharp, the girls pretty, a college scene out of the fifties. Before long Jack and his friends arrived dressed in t-shirts and shorts. Michael frowned, and Mary kicked him under the table code for: "Keep your mouth shut about the dress code."

Introductions made Michael ordered pitchers of beer and they all started to talk at once and soon they were calling Michael and Mary, Mike and Mare, so the senior Sullivans kept pace with the times and started calling them by the names Jack assigned them in his introductions: Harry, Dudley, "fast Eddie", Floyd and "pretty boy" Wilson. The food arrived along with more pitchers of beer and soon the Sullivans found themselves transported back to their early days in Washington. Someone in the room started singing and soon song welled up in the entire restaurant. Around midnight Michael and Mary looked at each other and she gave the sign, "time to go." As they got up to leave Jack and his friends, stood and sang: "Good night Lady," accompanied by the entire complement of the Tombs. When they got back on the street he gave her a hug, and hailed a cab. Back at their hotel they laughed at the evening's shenanigans and fell asleep in each other's arms.

. . .

On his way into the building Michael picked up the morning edition of the *Herald* and since he'd skipped breakfast at home he decided to go over to a small arcade just off the lobby and get a large coffee and blueberry Danish. Breakfast in hand he crossed back over to the bank of elevators and proceeded to the fifteenth floor. The time: seven o'clock. Usually at that early hour ten or twelve lawyers were already at work along with several secretaries and paralegals. As he entered his office rain began to pelt against the windows and he congratulated himself for narrowly missing the deluge. He looked at a stack of depositions sitting on his desk awaiting review, and made a decision to first eat the Danish and drink his coffee before attacking the pile. He sat down on a couch in a corner of the office, sipped the coffee, and opened the newspaper. The first thing that caught his eye was a headline: "Congressman Tom Bennings Seriously Injured." Michael put his coffee down and leaned over to read the story more closely. It continued: "On his way home last night from a meeting with officials of the Tri County Irrigation Commission Bennings's car was hit head on by an intoxicated driver, William Stacy. The Congressman remains in critical condition at Providence Hospital. Stacy miraculously survived the crash, and is being held in custody by the police, pending a hearing. The driver of Bennings's car died on impact."

Michael knew Tom Bennings well, having worked with him on a number of occasions. A feeling of sadness came over him and he put the paper down no longer interested in its content. He reflected on the suddenness of death. Bennings had just turned fifty six and had a great future ahead of him in Congress. A lawyer, he had served in the state legislature for two terms and the Senate for one. A total of ten years before his election to Congress. The district had prospered from his representation with many facilities funded by federal grants. He will be missed Michael thought to himself. There will surely be a scramble for his seat.

"Mr. Sullivan, Mr. Kennedy is on the line for you. Will you speak to him?"

"By all means Maggie, put him through." He looked at his watch, 7:30 a.m. Pretty early for a call from a client. Must be urgent.

"Michael lad, have you seen this a.m.'s newspaper?"

"That I have John, quite a shock wouldn't you say?"

"Yes I would, and a serious setback for the district if he is lost. That's what I'm calling about, can we meet for lunch?"

"Sure, where do you want to meet?"

"I know a little out of the way Italian restaurant on Ballard Avenue. Can you meet me at noon?"

"Ok, but do we have to meet halfway out of town?"

"I'd prefer it that way if it's all right with you."

Michael hung up, sat back on the couch and looked out his fifteenth floor window. Rain continued to beat against the glass running down in rivulets. He didn't particularly like rain, yet sitting up fifteen floors in a warm office surrounded by books and briefs gave one a sense of security. He left his office and walked down the hall four offices, nodding to the occupants, turned left, crossed the width of the suite and headed for the firm's lunch, coffee room. He poured himself a cup of coffee and made his way back. When he reached the hallway leading to his office Paul Connolly came ambling down the hall.

"Hi, I was just on my way to your office."

"Get a cup of coffee and come on down."

Four minutes later He and Michael were discussing the "Bennings tragedy." In his position as a state legislator, and later as Congressman, Bennings had been a great source of business for the firm. Always on the lookout for new enterprises wishing to come to the state, as often as not, he referred clients and inquiries to Sullivan & Connolly. Referrals became clients when the firm performed satisfactory work. Paul speculated whether Bennings would make it out of the hospital, and if not, its impact on the firm.

"The news is sketchy at best; there should be a hospital bulletin later this morning," Michael informed. My thought is to pray that he pulls through. I'm not a close friend but l know he has a wife and five children, and from the dealings I've had with him, he is first class fellow."

"I suppose the party is already thinking about a replacement."

"I feel a little awkward answering that question when the man is fighting for his life, but if I were to bet I'd say state Senator Jack Johnson or Watson Smith the Attorney General. Johnson has represented the district for eight years and Watson is from the city, giving him a slight edge I think. Who do you think the Democrats would put up?"

Michael J. Walsh

"I don't know Michael, except if Hillary Johnson ran, she'd be tough to beat."

"Let's see, she's been District Attorney for eight years now, has name familiarity and I think she's done a pretty good job. That might be a good guess Paul."

"Well, I've got to get back to work but Bennings is a real shocker, it just goes to show you never know when or how." With a shrug and a wave Paul left.

After his conversation with Paul, Michael's thoughts turned to Kennedy's phone call. The more he turned it over in his mind, the more curious he got. Kennedy would never call that early in the day unless he really had something serious on his mind. Moreover he usually gave a succinct briefing of what he wanted to discuss. And why meet essentially out of town? I'll just have to wait for the answers and he turned to the depositions he intended to read at 7:30 that morning. Already nine o'clock the office buzzed with the sound of telephones, voices, computers, arguments and lawyers scurrying off to court. Another bustling day at Sullivan & Connolly.

At ten thirty Maggie came into Michael's office, saw he was alone totally absorbed in studying the document in front of him, so she rapped gently on the door to get his attention. He looked up.

"Sorry to interrupt," she said apologetically; "We just heard Congressman Bennings died fifteen minutes a go and I thought you should know."

He hesitated on hearing this news and thought back to his conversation earlier with Paul Connolly, "I'm truly sorry Maggie. Thanks for the information and will you make sure Paul knows. He and I were just talking about Tom a few hours ago, what a waste of life and the guy who killed him walks away unscathed. It doesn't seem just does it?" She nodded in agreement.

By the time he arrived at the appointed place, John Kennedy was already seated and had a scotch highball in front of him. "Drink Michael?"

"No, John, too much to do this afternoon, but I'll enjoy watching you down yours."

Kennedy motioned to a waiter who came to the table immediately and appeared extremely solicitous; from this Michael gathered Kennedy had been at the restaurant before, maybe many times, realizing you don't get that kind of attention on the first visit.

"Are you ready to order Mr. Kennedy?" the waiter asked, pencil poised over his notepad.

"Yes, Phillips, we are. Michael, your choice?"

"A hamburger, no cheese please."

"A steak and home fries for me, Phillips."

"Very good sir."

While Kennedy ordered Michael glanced around the room and noticed it populated with well dressed businessmen, no one he recognized. So this is Kennedy's club, away from the University club. Interesting! The restaurant appeared busy and the Maître de seemed to know everyone by name as they entered the room. He made a mental note to come again.

Kennedy interrupted his thought, asking: "I suppose you've heard about Tom Bennings tragic death?"

"Yes, about ten thirty my secretary advised me of it. Early this morning Paul and I were discussing it and hoping he would make it. Obviously he didn't. He was very good to our firm and we'll miss him.

"Who do you think will run?"

"Paul and I were batting that around this morning and I ventured Jack Johnson or Watson Smith."

"Who will the Democrats run?"

"Hard to say, Paul thought Hillary Johnson would be tough to beat if she ran."

"Interesting," Kennedy said as he motioned to Phillips and pointed to his drink. "I've been doing a little thinking on the subject after I heard about the accident, in fact I've been on the phone for an hour and a half before I got here talking to about ten people I know pretty well. Funny, at my suggestion we all came to the same conclusion who should run for the Republicans."

"Let me guess," Michael smiled, Betty O'Donnell."

"That's a good guess but no cigar. She's only been Mayor a year and doing a good job. She should stay where she is for now."

"I didn't know you were that interested in politics John, other than fund raising."

"Tom did well for the district but I'd like to see a better candidate take his place, one who could go all the way—to the top."

"And that would be who?" Michael asked now genuinely fascinated by the conversation and curious to know who Kennedy and his friends were obviously backing for the seat. He knew enough about Kennedy from their years of association that he put his money where his mouth is and he could persuade others to do the same. He also knew when he put his mind to a project he was relentless in pursuit of success. Michael became aware of that trait watching Kennedy raise money for Betty O'Donnell's campaign. Kennedy had given money and raised lots of it at crucial stages in Betty's campaign; when he became aware finances were stretched; he quickly replenished the coffers. Michael thought, if a candidate had John Kennedy as a financial backer, he would have a real fighter in his corner.

"None other than Michael Sullivan, Esq." Michael started to speak, but Kennedy stopped him.

"Before you say no, listen to me."

The waiter appeared at the table with their fare and Kennedy's scotch. They said nothing while he placed the food at their places. The minute he left, Kennedy resumed the conversation. "You should see the look on your face," he laughed, "I've always thought you were a pretty calm fellow."

"Are you crazy? What in the world are you thinking?"

"I'm not crazy. I'm thinking you should run for the United States Congress to fill the vacancy left by our friend Tom Bennings. Here's why." He proceeded to outline his thinking as Michael tore into his hamburger. When upset during meals he invariably ate faster. As Kennedy talked he ate furiously, one eye on Kennedy and both ears attuned to what he was saying. The points John made were simple and straight forward: Michael had practiced law for twenty two years, a tremendous success in his chosen profession, built Sullivan & Connolly into one of the most successful law firms in the city and become President of the State Bar Association. Kennedy guessed his worth over twenty million dollars from practicing law. He argued the country needed leaders, and while Michael had made great contributions to the city and to the bar, he could triple that as a member of Congress. He acknowledged it would be a financial sacrifice, especially with two children in college and two more close on their heels.

"In short Michael, you are a born leader, you've got a lot to give and as far as financing a campaign is concerned, my friends and I will underwrite a hundred thousand up front and whatever it takes beyond that. In all likelihood the Governor will call for a special election, preceded by a nominating convention and the winner will serve out Tom's unexpired term until 2004."

Half in jest, Michael asked: "Has this idea sprung into your head since Tom's death less than four hours ago?"

"As a matter of fact I have thought about it for a year or more. I watched you and Ron run that campaign for Betty O'Donnell, and I don't know whether you realized it or not, but you and Mary looked like you were having the time of your lives. I watched you at events with voters, you're a natural. They talk to you. I watched it with my own eyes. There's something else to consider if you enter the race and lose, which I don't foresee, you can always go back to the law firm as the 'Sullivan' in Sullivan & Connolly."

At that, Michael laughed again in a kind way and said: "You've got it all figured out, you and your anonymous friends. Do you realize if I were to be elected, I wouldn't turn into a crook, I couldn't be managed, I'd be independent, have you advised your friends of that."

"Listen, Michael, you know me better than that, "John snapped, red creeping into his cheeks.

"The guys I'm talking to are people you know and respect. They share my thinking about you, their motives are the same as mine, they want a candidate who will help the district, and the state, a demonstrated leader, not some hack who's in it for all he can get, like so many."

"I know that John, did you feel I pulled your leg a little bit?"

"No. I'm very serious about this Michael, we feel you are a born leader and you can do more good for people in Congress than you can serving clients like me. You have all the money you need, the country needs men like you. Do this for me, before you say no. Talk it over with Mary and see what she thinks."

"That I will do John, and I must say I'm flattered...no that's the wrong word. 'Gratified' is the word and humbled you and your friends would think of me in the way you've spoken. I owe it to you think about it and I will discuss it with Mary and get back to you in four or five days."

"Fair enough, because if you should decide to do it, we'll have to move quickly. If you and Mary, especially Mary are opposed, we'll call it a day and figure it's the Republic's loss."

Michael picked up the check, they shook hands and both departed. He took a quick check of the time: 3:00 p.m. Three hours had passed, without realizing what a momentous discussion had just taken place. On his return to the office he did not mention his conversation with Kennedy to anyone, not even Paul Connolly. By six o'clock he was so preoccupied with his lunch conversation, he decided he could do no more in the office and left for home. Mary had talked to him about five o'clock, but he made no mention of the conversation with Kennedy. That would come later when they sat down for a cocktail before dinner.

She greeted him with a smile and a kiss as he came through the door. That's what he loved about her, no matter what kind of a day she had had, for him there was always that great smile and affectionate kiss. It made coming home a joy and he looked forward to it; when he was up she calmed him down, when down she bucked him up. Mary had a fire lit, the flames cackled as he eased himself on the couch opposite the fireplace. He loved the couch where he could watch the fire and gaze at the bookshelves on either side of the fireplace.

Books were his pride and joy, all or most of them used. Over the years, whenever he had time at lunch, he loved to get away for an hour or so in used book stores. He'd go to book sales on Saturday sponsored by schools and libraries. His library numbered two thousand books, almost all of which he bought used. It contained books on politics, law, economics, religion, history, biographies, theater and of particular interest, biographies, of Nixon, Kennedy, Johnson, Clinton, Reagan, Dewey, Truman. All the historical figures, Churchhill, Washington, Jefferson, Jackson, Disraeli, Ghandi, Mao Zedong, the dictators, Hitler, Stalin, Togo, Mussolini, the Popes, John twenty three, John Paul II, Pius XII, the stars, Hepburn, Bergman, Tracy, Grant and Cagney.

He and Mary were voracious readers in their early years as a married couple. They maintained stacks of books beside their bed, sometimes reading two or three at a time. Reading became the family hobby. In the early years the children accompanied Michael to book sales and they would come away with a stack of their own. Enjoying the sight of the books, his thoughts were interrupted when Mary returned with a glass of scotch whiskey for him and one for herself.

"Here's to us my Darling," He said

"What's on your mind Michael? I know you."

"What makes you think there's something on my mind?"

"We've been married twenty one years Mister, I know that look on your face, that's why I fixed that drink. Notice anything unusual about it?"

"So that's it—I thought it was pretty strong. Yes, I have something on my mind I want to share with you."

Knowing Michael, she intuitively sat back on the couch ready to take it all in, good or bad.

"I had lunch with John Kennedy today........"

Interested in John Kennedy's wellbeing Mary interrupted him to ask: "How is he and his family?"

"Oh, he seems fine. Stupid of me I didn't ask about Sally and the children. Anyway we didn't get into family talk, his purpose at lunch was to ask me to run for Tom Bennings seat."

Silence! Mary didn't move, said nothing and looked at him in the most benevolent way. Then she spoke: "What did you tell him?"

"I told him I would have to think about it and discuss it with you. He was quite adamant that if you were against I should forget about it."

"That John is a prince; that is so like him. What do you think about it?"

Slowly, deliberately, he answered, measuring his words. "At first I was stunned; the idea never crossed my mind when I heard of Tom's death. After I got back to the office from lunch I tried to put the pieces together, think it through, measure the idea against what we've got, what we've built together, our life here, how it would affect the children. The challenge it presents professionally—actually a switch in professions, the effect on my partners, Paul and the others."

"And what answers did you come up with?" she asked giving him a loving look, a look that said, I'm with you whatever you decide to do.

"I think it would be a challenge. Lord knows we've had our share, but the words: 'representative of the people' had a certain, warm ring to it. I was flattered, of course, that anyone might think of me as congressional timber, but Kennedy and his cohorts are tough business men and realistic with a dash of idealism. Maybe they know me better than I know myself."

"They do Michael, but you're more than 'congressional timber' as you put it. In fact Congress would be a step down from what you've accomplished. John may be right though, maybe it's time to move on, you've practiced law for twenty one years, built one law firm into something, got forced out only to build the best firm in the city. We've got a son and a daughter at Georgetown and a third headed that way. We've made great friends, raised our children here, maybe it's time to accept a new challenge, a new city."

"Whoa, not so fast. I might not be chosen by the party, and if chosen, may not beat the Democrat."

"Oh, you'll win all right, I know that and Kennedy knows it, otherwise you wouldn't have had that conversation."

"I gather then you're not opposed?"

"If you're ready to have a go at it, I'm with you Michael you know that, but if we are going to go through a major life change, I believe it has to be a family decision."

"All right sweetheart, you call Jack and Sharon and have them grab a morning flight out of National and they can catch a 'red eye' back to Washington Sunday morning. We'll have a family conclave all day Saturday and give it a full outing. If it's a go I'll tell John Sunday night and talk with Paul and the partners Monday morning. Now that I have that off my chest, what's for dinner?"

"By the strangest coincidence, steak, potatoes and salad and a bottle of California pinot noir, from Napa. She raised her glass: 'To the House of Representatives.' "

"To the House of Representatives," he answered and they laughed together. They felt a sense of adventure and wonderment at what the future might hold.

CHAPTER 32

As planned, the family met early Saturday morning after Michael had cooked his specialty, scrambled eggs, sausage, bacon, potatoes O'Brian, toast, coffee and orange juice. The menu never changed and they loved it. They all agreed he had a certain way with scrambled eggs. After breakfast they trooped into the library and he repeated his conversation with John Kennedy, the fact he and Mary had talked about it that night when he got home, and had come to a tentative decision pending the family having a chance to discuss it. Jack and Sharon were all for it, the younger two, Peter and Kathryn were reluctant because of friends they had made since grade school. Jack argued they'd soon be in college and Peter could go to Gonzaga and Kathryn to Georgetown Visitation in Washington.

"You'll love it," Jack said, it's different but you'll meet kids from all over the world at Georgetown Visi."

After listening to Jack regale them with stories of Washington, aided and abetted by Sharon the freshman at Georgetown, the two younger ones began to see a different picture and finally volunteered it might not be such a bad thing.

"But dad, can you get the nomination and win?" Jack raised the most important question of the day; to that point, the children had been talking like Michael had already won, now it became a question of could he win.

"That I can't say Jack, but I know we, and I mean all of us can give it a whale of a try." After four more hours the family decided it was the right thing to do. Their rationale: if a door opens walk through it. "I think the first step will be a nominating convention called by the party. There will be at least two or more competitors besides myself. If we win, we go to a special election between the Republican and Democrat. The winner will hold the seat until the general election in 2004."

"I've got another question dad. If you're elected, do you have to give up your place in the firm?"

"I'm not sure, Jack but I think the answer is yes. If I'm not mistaken, the firm would have to change its name."

"You mean no Sullivan & Connolly," Jack asked incredulously with a look of alarm.

"I think that's right, no Sullivan & Connolly. Does that change your mind about me running?"

"No dad. But in my opinion you'd be giving up a lot for a lot less, but what the hell, if you and mom want to do it, I'm with you all the way and I think I speak for my brother and sisters." They said nothing and nodded in assent.

That night he called Kennedy and they talked at length; then decided Michael should talk with the partners the next day, and assuming that worked out, the finance people could be notified the candidate had committed to the race. Ron Fitzgerald would be asked to act as operations manager based on his experience in the O'Donnell mayoralty race. Both the Republican National Committee, and Republican Congressional committee to be notified Michael Sullivan intended to run for Congress on the Republican ticket in the special election to take place on a date specified by the Governor. Kennedy took the first step to hire a political consultant, and had two in mind for Michael to interview. The next morning the *Daily Ledger* carried a headline: "Governor Sets Date for Special Election," followed by a story both parties were likely to hold nominating conventions to choose their candidates.

By the time Michael got to his office the next day rumors were circulating around the firm there could be an important announcement sometime later in the day. The first call came from Paul

Connolly. Not wanting to beat around the bush Michael advised Paul he had decided to run for Congress and before he could say more, Paul told him he'd come right down to his office. When he got there, Michael picked up where he had left off. Paul listened to the tale beginning with the Kennedy luncheon through to the family conference. He did not interrupt until Michael finished and then reacted to the news.

"I think you can win it Michael, no doubt in my mind. But you'll be giving up a lot. We've built this firm together into a power house and we're both making more than we ever dreamed possible when we started out. Plus we are practicing great law with the cases and clients we have. I know you've had as much fun as I have building the firm. I can understand though, you're the kind of a guy, who relishes new challenges, new worlds to conquer and I know you'll do us all proud and do great things for the state at a great loss to us." Michael started to interrupt him but he raised his hand indicating he wasn't finished. "I don't mean to sway you in any way, we all do what we have to do, I can tell you it will be a blow to the partners; I think we should advise them right away; before doing so let me say on my own behalf, I couldn't agree more with John Kennedy, you have the ability to lead Michael, it may well be that Kennedy is right you should turn your talents to a larger arena. We'll miss you but the country needs you more."

"I appreciate that Paul, now let's get everyone in the conference room at noon and I'll make the announcement. And Paul, if I'm elected, you'll have to change the firm name."

"As you were telling me your decision the thought crossed my mind we'll have to change the name of the venerable firm of Sullivan & Connolly to Connolly and X. That will take some time getting used to. They laughed and embraced each other. Michael thought he saw a tear in Paul's eye and said: "I could lose and then we can keep the name."

"I know you Michael, you're not going to lose, and the firm will just have to get used to it."

They gathered at noon, not sure of what the meeting was about, called on such short notice without announcement of an agenda, the partners knew something serious was about to be discussed. Of the partners only one guessed what the topic might be yet it seemed so farfetched he didn't bother to run it by the other partners, not wanting to be an alarmist. When the room grew quiet, Michael stood up in front of the partners and calmly told them what he had decided to do and his reasons for it. At first those in the room, except Paul and the partner who speculated about the purpose of the meeting, appeared stunned. Their first thought: what will happen to the firm? As Michael went further into his explanation, they relaxed, realizing the firm would survive. He told them they had all built the firm together, as such, its growth and success didn't depend on any one partner, it was too strong for that. When he ended, they were on their feet, offering congratulations, slapping him on the back and each offering to do everything in their power to see him elected the next Congressman from the district. He had changed the atmosphere from one of sadness to enthusiasm for what he had decided to undertake, and based on his optimism for the firm's future and his confidence in them, they were no longer concerned whether the firm could survive without him, they knew it would.

In time to make the afternoon *Herald* Ron Fitzgerald circulated pictures of Michael in the Sullivan & Connolly library with a press release announcing his candidacy for the Republican nomination for the vacant seat. Every outlet had the news and it attracted wide spread coverage in the evening news broadcasts.

Valerie Swartz of the *Herald* wrote: "In a move that totally caught the district Republican Party off guard, super lawyer, Michael Sullivan, announced his candidacy for the seat left vacant by the untimely death of five term Republican Thomas Bennings. Two other candidates vying for the nomination are Jack Johnson,

State Senator and Watson Smith, Attorney General, both highly regarded in Republican circles. Francis Tobin, local party chair, has been quoted as saying: 'This is a totally new ball game with Michael Sullivan in the ring. He brings a new dimension to the race and demonstrated competence.' He hastened to add 'I'm not taking sides but with the addition of Sullivan in the race the party has three strong candidates.' Delegates to the convention will consist of district party leaders, elected officials and precinct committee men and women from the district Tobin said. Asked whether any one of the three Republicans could defeat the Democratic nominee, he pointed out the seat had been held by a Republican for ten years and anticipated that trend to continue for the foreseeable future.

Questioned about Sullivan's sudden interest in the race Tobin responded, he didn't think it such a surprise, in view of the fact he had recently run a successful campaign to elect the new Mayor, been active as a fund raiser for the party and counsel to the state party chairman. 'At the same time,' he said, 'some have wondered why the senior partner of one of the most prominent firms in the city would seek a seat in Congress holding far less prestige than his present high profile position.' In the coming days, that question and others will be put to Mr. Sullivan, who must now enunciate his position on issues of concern to the voters. He will be matched against seasoned politicians whose positions are well known. It will be interesting to learn where Mr. Sullivan stands on the issues."

Mary looked up after reading the Swartz article and said: "It's a new game Michael, have you thought about issues and your public positions?"

He smiled and said: "I have my dear, and my 'public position' will not differ from my private feelings."

"You won't cut your sails to please your new audience I take it?"

"You know I won't and don't be tempting me with that Oh you're going to be Mr. perfect look. I'm going to see if I can get nominated by the convention. I'm sure some of my views will differ from my opponents. This will be the first test—if my views are out of kilter with my fellow Republicans we'll know it soon enough."

"I'm just kidding you, my friend, once you've taken a position, it's in concrete unless you can be persuaded by a rational argument. I've seen that myself after twenty one years of marriage. I think you'll do all right on the issues Michael."

. . .

Even as they made plans for the convention, world events were taking place that were sure to shape the policies and politics every Congressman and Senator would face for years to come. The United States had just launched an attack on Saddam Hussein in Iraq. The same dictator who put down the Shite population in the southern portion of his country after the United States had withdrawn from Iraq in 1991, following its successful war to thwart Hussein's invasion of Kuwait. Three weeks after the second U.S. invasion of Iraq, American troops had driven straight to Bagdad causing Saddam and his Baathist party to dissolve, and he to disappear from sight. Congress had been fully briefed on the danger he posed and had given President Bush the authority to drive the dictator from power and dismantle any weapons of mass destruction found. All this after the U.S. had mounted a war against the Islamist, terrorist Taliban in Afghanistan and driven Osama bin Laden into hiding.

After bombing of the world trade center in 2001, America faced a new deadly and dedicated enemy, perverters of the Islamic religion, a small group of terrorists seeking to threaten not only America but the nations of the world. By terror, stealth and barbarism these radical Islamists hoped to destroy the will of the west and promote their backward ideas throughout the world. It was a new type of war, one America had not had to face before. Iraq had been won by the overwhelming strength of American forces, but now it must cope with the problem of setting up a governing body to insure a peaceful Iraq, one we hoped could be an ally in the Middle East.

Michael knew the war and its consequences would be important issues in the shortened campaign to fill the vacant seat. He
expected it to come up in the first press conference he gave after the
announcement. It did. The first question asked was: "What should
we do about Iraq? Afghanistan?"

"I believe we must help the Afghans rebuild their country and
that means furnishing security while they do it. It will mean a new
constitution, new laws, a legislature or parliament if you will, a
democratically elected President. All this will take time. The country was ravaged by the Russians from 1979 to 1989. It will not be
healed in a day. As for Iraq, the same blueprint is going to have to be
employed. Our forces have cleaned out the dictator, now a vacuum
exists. It must be filled quickly. Again, security is the key while a
political solution is reached."

"How long will that take?" came a follow up question from
another reporter.

Without hesitating, Michael averred he did not know and in any
case felt it was too soon to speculate, but the salient fact remained:
two terrorist had been dethroned. "Now we have the responsibility of forging a stable Afghanistan and Iraq." From years in the
courtroom and engaging the press in the process, Michael Sullivan
understood reporters wanted short easy to understand answers to
their questions. He felt it would be the same with the voters. They
may not like the answer but they would get a straight one from him.

The day after the press conference, Valerie Swartz wrote a fol-
low-up column for her paper:

"Michael Sullivan is no different as a candidate than he was as a
trial lawyer. He answers questions directly and understandably. I've
seen him in the courtroom and now I've watched him in a political
setting. What you see is what you get. He's recognized in this city
as a great lawyer and now shows every promise of being a major
leaguer in this new game of politics. He has come to play.

As to why a prominent lawyer, the head of one of the state's largest and most successful law firms chose to run for one of seven house seats allotted to the state, listen to his answer: 'I've been doing a job representing individual clients for over twenty years and I've loved every minute of it, however, I believe it's time for me to expand the clientele and apply whatever talents I have to represent the people of this state in Washington. In Tom Billings, we had a wonderful leader and a friend. I hope I can continue to do the job he was doing so well.' There you have it, noblesse oblige."

Minutes after Michael gave his answer to John Kennedy he'd decided to run, Kennedy made calls to ten cohorts who had offered to back Michael for the seat; they were not only Republican fund raisers but active in party affairs. On a word from Kennedy they began to put together lists of delegates voting in the convention. Party leaders decided and advised the Governor, the convention should be held April 15 with three hundred delegates in attendance. Kennedy's men got the names, addresses, e-mails, phone numbers and biographies of each delegate. Following the announcement Mary, Michael and John Kennedy had a conversation as to who could run the campaign for the convention and through November when a full two year term would be at stake. The same name came up—Ron Fitzgerald.

"Well and good, Michael but he's doing a beautiful job at the firm and I know from talking to the wives, the lawyers love hm. You may get some resistance from him, not to mention Paul Connolly."

"I agree Mary, all I can do is ask and see what he says."

On receiving Michael's call, and hearing his request, Ron said: "I hoped you'd call, I can't wait to get started, but you'll have to talk with Paul. He's been so great, I hate to leave him and the firm in a tough spot finding a replacement."

"I'll speak to Paul, I'm sure he'll give you the go ahead. In the meantime the most important task now is to put together a two week campaign to win delegates to a nominating convention. John

Kennedy has put together a dossier on every delegate and Mary has some ideas how we get to them. Will you meet with her?"

The Democrats, instead of having a nominating convention, opted at the last minute, for their nominee to be chosen by various interest groups within the party, including unions, pro-choice leaders, feminists, leftists, gays, traditional Democrats and party leaders. At the end of a two day conclave they finally picked a compromise candidate, Hillary Johnson, the District Attorney, serving her eighth year in office, just as Paul Connolly had predicted; adding she would be tough to beat.

Michael followed up on his call to Paul on behalf of Ron Fitzgerald, and found Paul not too happy with Ron's leaving the firm to join Michael's quest for Congress. After they chatted a while Paul said: "It's really Ron's decision Michael and I think he's made it. I'm sorry I jumped the gun. I've been thinking a lot about what you are about and I'm excited. To show you how excited I am, I'm going to detail four associates for the delegate gathering process."

"Overly generous of you Paul, I can't thank you enough. Before this political thing gets too far along, I'm betting you'll become a part of it, not as a candidate, but as a wise counselor and backer.

"I'm already a backer; I don't know how wise a counselor I will be but I'm willing to try partner. Good luck Michael."

Kennedy, Ron, Michael and Mary had dinner at the restaurant where the idea of running had first been raised. Over drinks and a steak dinner, they made decisions how the campaign should function until the nominating convention. As usual Kennedy had booked a table in a far corner of the room, out of the limelight, and instructed his friend, the maître de,' to have the meal served and refrain from coming to the table unless he signaled for refreshments, which he did over the course of the four hour dinner meeting. Michael and Mary confined their thirst to one scotch before dinner while Kennedy and Ron had several over the course of the evening excusing themselves each time claiming Johnny Walker sharpened their wits.

After the meeting Michael and Mary joked the scotch seemed to animate the two of them beyond their normal lucidity.

Sketched out on a legal pad Ron brought to the meeting, a six month plan of battle taking into account the convention process and the special election took up most of the discussion. Michael, Mary and Kennedy were to work with the associates Paul selected to assist them gathering delegate commitments. Ron assigned himself the task of finding four regional leaders in the district and twenty volunteers for each, the leaders to be paid staff. Betty O'Donnell offered the use of her volunteers, which she had built into a formidable political machine, to assist Michael's organization in every way possible. The quartet agreed the stakes were high enough that it necessitated enlisting the help of consultants located in Washington D.C. with experience running congressional campaigns.

To aid the local effort, they agreed polling essential and Ron contacted two national firms, notwithstanding local pollsters had good reputations for thoroughness. He reasoned, better someone from the outside to give honest, objective results, than local concerns that might have conflicts. Near the end of the evening Mary broached the subject of costs. By her reckoning, the plan being discussed would cost at least a half million in administrative expenses for six months, none of which included promoting the candidate. Kennedy assured her he and his partners would be able to raise as much money as needed and match the Democrats dollar for dollar. The evening ended on an optimistic note; the participants felt, at least, they had a blueprint, something for all to work with. The key, they agreed, was for each one to carry out their assignment, independent of anything else going on in the day to day campaign. Michael had a good feeling, even though they had no idea whether they could secure the nomination, if they did, they were ready to go full throttle the day after preparing for the special election in November.

On leave from the firm until the convention, Michael moved from his fifteenth floor office at Sullivan & Connolly to a one story leased space with a small room in the back for a private office empty except for a few tables and chairs. In a couple of days it became the headquarters of "Sullivan for Congress" fully equipped with computers, work tables for volunteers, shelves loaded with campaign literature, lawn signs, bumper stickers all on the assumption he would be the party nominee for the special election.

Good to his word, Ron Fitzgerald came up with a five page, multicolored press packet that included a biography, picture of the family, positions on issues and all kind of facts about the district. All this accomplished in forty eight hours of the dinner meeting at Kennedy's favorite restaurant. Every delegate received a packet hand delivered by volunteers. All these steps were taken in preparation for Michael to start calling as many delegates as he could, the rest to be contacted by associates and volunteers who knew the delegates personally.

His first calls were a little inhibited, the responses tentative; not used to calling people asking for their vote he sounded diffident but by the fifth call, he began to hit his stride and his confidence grew, and as it grew the responses from the delegates became more encouraging. Most listened courteously to his explanation, some made no commitment and thanked him for the call, two said they were voting for someone else. Three committed and three said they were leaning and knew of his reputation. After ten calls he viewed the loose leaf notebook Ron had prepared containing all the information on each delegate. He counted three positives, three leaners, two opposed and two non-committals. Not bad for a couple hours work. At the end of the day that ended at eight o'clock he totaled up the results: 40 calls; 20 yes, 10 for the opposition, 4 leaning and 6 undecided. Exhausting work yet beneficial because the calls disclosed issues of interest to the delegates which could then be used to garner convention votes. As day four came to a close, Kennedy, Michael and Paul's four associates had contacted over two hundred delegates, getting about a hundred and twenty five potential votes.

Two more days of calls and contacts netted another thirty votes ranging from: "yes," "possible," to "lean."

The other two candidates, decided to forego a delegate contact operation, instead they toured the television stations and radio host shows, hoping to exploit their name familiarity and political experience in an effort to dampen enthusiasm for the newcomer—Michael Sullivan. Michael remained isolated in his frugal office making calls until seven days before the convention and then making the rounds of television and radio stations, giving interviews and holding press conferences. Whereas his uniform in the little office had consisted of a white button down shirt, gray slacks, old crew sweater and loafers, now as he made the rounds, he transformed himself into a high powered trial lawyer dressed in a gray pinstriped suit, bright blue tie, and white shirt. Two stops at the *Herald* and *The Daily Ledger* were taken up with questioning by respective editorial boards.

At the *Herald* they grilled him on his stands contrasting them with those of his opponents. He articulated each position clearly and succinctly so there could be no misinterpretation of where he stood knowing full well the paper would probably endorse the Democrat. The most he dared hope for from the *Ledger* was a truthful exposition of his views on the issues without too much distortion. The *Ledger* turned out to be the friendliest of the two, more in tune with his positions. Ron accompanied him to the interviews and afterward ventured his opinion both papers would endorse him for the Republican nomination but only the *Ledger* for the special election.

At the end of the day Michael asked Ron: "How did we do with those editorial boards?"

"I think you did great, of course I may be a bit prejudiced. I didn't detect any underlying hostility and that's a good sign. I'll tell you where we've made significant headway and that's your phoning delegates. We're getting good feedback, the delegates are impressed with the fact you called them and asked for their vote." Ron's cell phone rang, he listened, said "thanks," and hung up.

"Interesting news, Michael. There's a rumor going around Wilford George might throw his hat in the ring at the nominating convention and make a big splash, promising to spend his own money in the special election if the delegates select him."

Michael took the news with typical calmness, knowing full well George might prove to be a distraction but no real threat. A handsome man of thirty, tremendously wealthy because of his father's business acumen, a socialite and patron of the arts. His fame, if any, came through society columns not trade journals, although he occasionally put in a day at the office. Michael speculated he might draw some votes but could only help their cause. He reasoned, four in the race improved his chance of winning.

"You know who this fellow is, don't you?"

"Yes Ron, I've run into him on a few occasions and he's a nice enough man, but I would guess even if he spent a bundle of money on the convention, he won't be able to stampede it. You have our campaign too well organized to let the likes of him beat us. Those other two are a different story. They're professional politicians, and from my phone calls, generally well liked. Even those who promised me their vote said I didn't have the political experience they had but......they think I have more talent." Michael gave him a gentle nudge in the chest and laughed at his own joke.

. . .

Three days before the convention, Ron summarized their position in a conference call with all the principals. "It looks like the toughest opponent is going to be Senator Jack Johnson, the other two I don't think are going to make it to a third ballot. I've arranged to have forty of our people on the floor to make sure the delegates, we think we have in tow, vote and stick for three ballots. The way this thing works is after the first ballot the bottom vote getter drops out and the three remaining go on the second ballot. I'm assuming we'll be on the second ballot and go on to the third which will decide the nominee.

Again assuming our vote counters are accurate, it will be us versus gentleman Jack Johnson. Each candidate will have the opportunity to address the delegates for no longer than fifteen minutes with the festivities getting underway at 10:30 a.m. Saturday. The public and press will be invited, of course, and will be restricted to balcony seats. Mary has secured tickets for hundreds of our supporters and they will be shouting their heads off when Michael speaks. If other candidates don't fill there allotment of tickets I have another two hundred volunteers who will be standing by to use those tickets. Now to the vote. I estimate we should get a little over a hundred for sure on the first ballot, guaranteeing a place on the second. Finally, Michael will continue to make calls through Friday night."

"Speaking of phone calls I've learned a great deal about human nature; these delegates want answers, there not giving up their vote unless they're satisfied you believe in the things they believe in. It's been a very telling learning experience."

"How many have you talked with?" someone asked.

"By my count, two hundred and fifty and I hope to get another fifty by Friday night. As far as I can tell the only other candidate who's contacted them besides myself is Senator Johnson and that's been spasmodic."

"If we win this thing Michael," someone said, "you will have damned near earned it by yourself."

"Correction: If we win, it will be due to hundreds of volunteers helping us out. The phone calls will have helped."

Mary held dinner until the last call had been made by Michael at eight p.m. Friday night. Her tired but exhilarated husband joined the family at the dinner table and as usual Michael offered the grace:

"Bless us O Lord and these thy gifts which we are about to receive through Your bounty, through Christ, our Lord. It our hope we are successful tomorrow and that Your will be done. Amen"

"Amen" echoed around the table and the chatter began. "Are we going to Washington dad? What do you and mom think?"

The Firm

"Of course, we are Kathryn, Mary responded in a strong, clear voice, voicing an opinion she didn't feel certain of yet, leaving no doubt in the minds of her children. "Wait till I take you on the subway in Washington," she told Kathryn; "you're going to get all around the town for a dollar. What do you think of that? "

"I'd be scared to go alone but if you'll go with me I think it will be fun." The chatter was light, but they all felt anxious, even Kathryn, the youngest. Each understood, if their father won, their lives would change and the uncertainty of what form that change might take caused apprehension, yet the thought of their father winning and going to the nation's capital outweighed their fear of change.

CHAPTER 33

They drew straws to determine the order of speakers. Senator Johnson drew the short straw and walked to the rostrum to make his presentation to a packed arena. Convention workers had strung bunting and banners around the balcony overlooking the floor. Posters, and placards were affixed to the walls at ground level sporting red, white and blue colors and carried pictures of the candidates. Four large pictures of the candidates were mounted behind the rostrum and two large screens sat on either side of the hall so that everyone, on the floor or in the gallery, could view the speakers at close range and gauge their facial expressions as they spoke. For all intents and purposes it looked, to the casual eye, like a miniature national convention. While the Democrats chose the back room method to select their candidate, the Republicans, with their one day convention, were creating all the excitement and reaping free publicity and press, so important in any election. Anyone slightly interest in politics would have been caught up in the excitement of the moment. Americans, no matter what their party, love a political fight. The convention drew national press attention, the *New York Tribune* and the *Washington Star* sending political reporters instead of relying on wire services or stringers to cover the event, which meant the special election in the fall would draw a measure of national attention in the eastern press.

State Senator Johnson used his fifteen minutes to relate his life story, beginning with his birth in 1949, marriage, law school, his two terms as State Representative, followed by six years in the State Senate and concluded in a thunderous roar that he was indeed the most experienced candidate in the field of four, and for that reason alone his candidacy represented the best chance to keep the seat in Republican hands. From the sound of applause he had his share of support from the delegates and those in the balcony gave him a good hand which he hoped would influence the delegates.

Wilfred George took the stage as the second speaker and it turned out he had a gift for speaking and a humorous bent. The first seven minutes of his time he spent explaining how he was a late comer in seeking the seat, how he became interested and his assurance to the delegates his candidacy gave the party the best chance of winning the special election; in pronouncing this assurance he had the crowd laughing at deprecating humor. On the eighth minute he turned serious and started to discuss the Democratic opposition, how difficult it would to win in a run-off. In closing he came to the chief claim for his candidacy—he could personally raise the money needed and spend his own which he intended to do unstintingly.

Ron and Michael, sitting side by side, waiting to go on stage judged the applause for George loud but not as enthusiastic as Johnson's reception. Polite clapping from the balcony evidenced he didn't have much of an organization behind him, although his supporters had more signs in the hall than the other candidates, except for the Sullivan campaign. The chairman called out Michael's name and after a brief introduction beckoned him to the microphone.

Michael Sullivan had spoken publicly hundreds of times and to audiences as large as four thousand people, and he knew from experience a crowd is always apprehensive for themselves and for the speaker. After a minute and a half has gone by they instinctively know whether the speaker is in control or not, and if he or she is, they sit back and give their attention. He compared it to addressing a jury, if they liked you they would listen, if not, a faraway look crept into their eyes. Juries instinctively liked Michael Sullivan whether he won or lost. What they saw and what the delegates were seeing was a man elegantly dressed, but not in a way to offend or patronize his listeners, a man very serious and sincere about the message he meant to convey, a man prepared and not there to waste his or their valuable time and a man with an understated sense of humor that made you laugh with him as he laughed at himself. He had a gift and he never abused or misused it. When sincere, his audience became deeply aware of it and they too became serious to match his sincerity. They found him believable because he believed in what he said.

As he looked out over the delegates on the floor and two thousand in the balcony he hesitated until you could hear a pin drop. He believed he would get the nomination but it had to be earned by convincing these delegates he and only he could defeat the Democrat in the fall. He not only wanted to win, he also wanted their enthusiastic support—after he'd secured the nomination. The speech he delivered was patterned after a closing argument to a jury, commencing with a statement of where he stood on the issues, something the previous two speakers had failed to do, he talked about the district itself and how people in the district would benefit if he were to be their representative in Washington, that he'd return to the district to report on legislation before the Congress, and hear their concerns, that his profession had taught him how to negotiate and work with others, traits a successful legislator must possess. He told of two or three humorous incidents in his work before the courts. In all he presented the figure of someone you'd want to be your representative in Congress. Young, fifty one, an attractive wife, a fine family and no scandal. Yes, he looked like a winner, six feet, one inch, not a gray hair and at ease with himself. He stepped down to loud and long applause; Mary and Ron had turned out their troops, and they applauded long and hard.

He took his seat and listened to the sustained applause; he did not deceive himself by their demonstration, there were those who applauded a capable performance yet withhold their vote, no matter what he said or stood for. The question for him turned on whether there were more who felt the opposite. Mary slowly let her hand slip into his unnoticed and that was her code to convey her opinion: "A great speech Michael," though they never looked at each other.

A murmur went through the crowd as the last speaker, Watson Smith, approached the rostrum. He proved eloquent, describing how he had grown up in the district and presently lived there, and even though he'd won state wide office as Attorney General and served in the state capital, he continued to make his home in the city. He praised the other candidates for entering in the November election. Michael listened carefully as he spoke and found himself impressed by his manner, relative youth at thirty nine, and his sincerity. Like Michael, he had been in private practice attained partner, and then appointed Attorney General, when his predecessor resigned. He stood for election, won and was serving the last year of his term. They knew each other casually through bar activities and Michael thought him a good fellow. In the course of his speech he briefly touched on the issues but not as completely as Michael had. When it ended he sat down to lusty applause and Michael sensed, for the first time, this young man might be his chief rival.

Abruptly, one hour and a half into the session, the Chairman announced the first ballot would be taken. Cameras, focused on the counting sheets, transferring the image on to the two large screens so those in the hall could see the actual vote as it progressed. Not twenty minutes elapsed before the chair announced the results:

Michael Sullivan	105
Jack Johnson	93
Watson Smith	62
Wilfred George	40

At the conclusion of the vote the chairman declared a one hour break for lunch, all delegates to be back in the hall by one p.m. ready to vote on the second ballot. Mary, Ron, Kennedy and Michael and a number of their floor leaders retired to a corner of the hall and ate sandwiches and cola delivered at intermission.

"This thing is going to be close Michael," Kennedy said, Johnson is within range and Watson is showing surprising strength. I think he took votes from Jack Johnson."

"You're right John, with Wilfred George out, all three of us are going to get some of his votes."

Ron Fitzgerald returned from a brief meeting with his floor leaders and told Michael one hundred and five votes were firm, they only needed 46 votes to win less to get into the third round. Also they picked up talk Johnson's vote might be moving away from him. Outwardly Michael and Mary maintained a calm composure, inwardly they both knew his career in politics could be over before it began, if they didn't win on the third ballot. Fifteen minutes passed before all the delegates were back in their seats and the second ballot called for. An agonizing twenty minutes passed before an announcement on the results of the second ballot:

Michael Sullivan	115
Watson Smith	100
Jack Johnson	85

The crowd sent up a roar and Smith delegates began crossing into other sections to try to sway Johnson's votes sensing they had the momentum. The Chairman, rapped the gavel for order and advised the delegates a fifteen minute recess would be in place before the final vote.

Ron conferred with his vote counters who informed him there was talk of a deal by the Johnson delegates to throw their vote to Watson. He quickly informed Michael and Kennedy; the two had a hurried conversation and when it ended, Kennedy told Ron to go to the leader of Johnson's campaign and tell him any such deal would result in campaign funds being denied to Johnson in his campaign for re-election to the state Senate. "Tell them a rigged vote would tarnish the party's reputation and make difficult, if not impossible, to defeat the Democrats in the fall." At the end of the recess Ron called Michael on his cell phone and reported the leaders believed they had quelled whatever deal had been in the making. Johnson got the message and passed word to his delegates to vote their conscience.

The call to order came and the third and final vote got underway. Quiet came over the crowd, no one left the hall as they awaited the outcome. Vote counting took place under the watchful eyes of campaign workers for both candidates, and tallies appeared simultaneously on the large screens. An agonizing, thirty minutes went by before the Chairman stepped up to the microphone holding up his hand for silence. "Ladies and Gentlemen we have a nominee and the next Congressman from the district. The official vote is: Sullivan-165; Smith-135."

At a signal from Ron all the Sullivan delegates on the floor and Mary's door to door and lawn sign volunteers in the balcony let loose with shouts filling the hall with deafening noise. Even non Sullivan voters clapped, though their candidates had lost, they knew Michael Sullivan would be a worthy contender for the seat. All four candidates gathered on the stage and raised their hands in a show of unity. Michael Sullivan had made the finals and awaited, a yet unknown opponent, for the honor of representing the second district in Congress!

After delivering a short five minute speech to the delegates and hearing their cheers, he stepped off the podium down into the crowd, the first to greet him, Mayor Betty O'Donnell, whispered in his ear: "Welcome to the world of politics Irish, how does it feel?"

"Embracing," he answered, and gave her a hug. Before they had a chance to speak, the crowd surrounded him asking for autographs and photos. Fifteen minutes passed and they still waited in line to shake his hand and whisper a word of encouragement; then Mary came to stand beside him and she shook every hand he had shaken. A half hour passed and the end of the line could not be seen and they stood there until four o'clock when the last admirer thanked them and said he had go home for dinner. They laughed and speculated how many people they had met in three hours. Kennedy and Ron had been standing off to the side watching the whole time, and when the Sullivans went to join them, Ron asked if they realized how many hands they had shaken, and they said they had no idea. He had been counting and floored them with the number: "one thousand two hundred and fifty good souls, many from the Johnson and Smith camps."

"It's amazing Ron, many said they had not voted for me today but they intended to volunteer for the election in November."

"Well, Michael, you're finally on your way, where it stops, nobody knows," Kennedy said, delighted and relieved Michael had come through beautifully in his first test in political waters.

"We can't waste time sitting on our laurels. Michael, tomorrow at nine you'll have to return to that little room we gave you to make your finance calls and you will find a hundred and fifty other people there sitting at desks and computers at work on your behalf, all volunteers, ready to finish what we started today."

The family did not assemble for dinner until nine that night and all they could talk about was the day they had just been through. The crowds, the cheering, the candidates, the balloting—all new and exciting. They talked about his speech, the thrill watching the vote, impressions of the crowd and its size. For Mary and Michael, the feeling they got from shaking all the hands afterward and getting little snippets of conversation from each person as they passed down the line, left the greatest impression of the day.

"It was a new experience for me, and I'm sure for your mother. I've got to tell you I got a tremendous kick out of it. The people seemed so enthusiastic but more than that, they weren't just well wishers, they were saying in effect 'ok, you won now go out there and beat the Democrat.' Did you get that impression Mary?"

"I did Michael, it's as though they passed on a sacred trust and you're the trustee."

As they lay in bed with the lights out Michael gazed thoughtfully at her and said: "You know, I realized something today I didn't understand before...."

"And that would be what Congressman?"

"We're not there yet, but I saw today what you can do with a crowd—you can convert them into fans—just like movie stars do. They want your autograph, they want to touch you, in their eyes you're something bigger than they are. You can make them feel good just talking to them. I can see where you'd get carried away with your own importance, by becoming the subject of such idolatry. I find that a little unnerving."

"I want you to go to sleep Michael it's been a long day. I think I know what you mean but at least you have the brains to figure it out. Most politicians think they really have risen above the crowd and don't realize if they slip, the crowd will trample them. As long as you use that power you've just discovered, to help people and make them feel good about themselves, we'll be all right. I don't think you're going to be susceptible because you're smart enough to realize there are people smarter than you, and no matter what you are doing in law or politics you have to work harder than the next fellow, and keep your head down to regulation size."

"You are smart Mrs. Sullivan, I'll give you that."

"Thank you, now if you will go to sleep, the household will be much appreciative."

"Good night Mrs. Sullivan, I'll think about what you said."

CHAPTER 34

"Three weeks away," the nominee said, sitting on a couch in their makeshift headquarters, addressing what had become known as "the team," Mary Sullivan, Ron Fitzgerald, John Kennedy, Dan Streetmeier, advertising consultant, Ab Tweet, political consultant and Norm Towsen, pollster.

"The first thing I saw in the *Herald* this morning was a negative ad for Hillary Johnson, her first."

"Any ideas how we counter Dan?"

"I think we should put out two ads immediately and Ron agrees with me. First, we have one ready to roll which is biographical, pictures of you, Mary and the children, you as a young lawyer, president of the bar, etc...."

"Have you got it here?"

"Yeah. Bill plug it into the television." The ad ran sixty seconds, and Michael thought to himself as he watched: "How amazing it is what they can do in sixty seconds."

"All it needs is your ok, we've already bought time."

"I think you've done a good job, let it roll. What's the second ad you have in mind?"

"The following day we come back with a sixty second spot, showing your position on taxes, spending, health care, abortion and social security; we juxtapose your position with hers which is soft on crime, pro-abortion, higher taxes, an advocate for socialized medicine, and her intent to support higher taxes to pay for social security instead of allowing the taxpayers to take a credit in a heath account much like they do now with their 401K accounts. In other words, letting the voter know there is a stark contrast on basic issues between you and her. What do you think?"

"I say go with it, we'll be attacked by the media as going negative but she beat us to it with her ad this morning." Turning to the political consultant Michael asked what he planned for the next twenty one days.

"Saturation television for the entire run-up, match her negative advertising ad for ad, but only with provable facts. Unfortunately we can expect the opposite from her ad team based on what we've seen and her prior campaign for District Attorney. The last two days we change tactics, emphasizing your strengths, proven leadership and values. I think the abortion issue could the clincher—she's for partial birth abortion. She should be hammered on that. Finally, everything depends on turn out and I think we're well positioned on that with Mary's volunteers."

Mary interrupted to add, "Our troops will be in the field tonight and every night going door to door; she has union volunteers doing the same but we have four times as many."

"The Republican National committee is committing a hundred thousand dollars to this race," Kennedy spoke up, adding a note of cheer to the meeting."

"When did you get that news?"

"They called last night and said their people had been analyzing the race for a week and decided to make the buy, taking the position it's a Republican seat and has to be held. The money is welcome but be assured we'll have all we need, I promised you that Michael and my people are as good as their word."

Ron changed the subject to appearances: "We've got you booked into six events a day for the next two weeks and I have a team put together that will advance every event. Also I've been contacted by Jack Swanson, President of the City Club last night; they want to sponsor a debate between you and Hillary Johnson. I assume you have no problem with that?"

"None whatsoever, it will be our opportunity to make the case, and hopefully clinch the deal, but on one condition: that it's covered by all the television stations."

"That will not be a problem," Ab Tweet shot back. "A one hour debate with a newscaster from each of the local stations posing the questions. They'll love it." The agenda concluded they went back to their assignments.

Paul Connolly loaned two of the firm's top associates to travel with Michael daily as he made his way through the scheduled round of events: Tim "Buddy" Simpson and Taylor Williams. Simpson an up and coming litigator and Williams about to make partner in the firm, both bachelors, took up their posts the next day. Together, with Michael, they made an impressive trio, all over six feet and all business. As they made their rounds on the first day, Tim became the "wheel man," Michael sat alongside in the front seat and Taylor in the back of their five year old Chevrolet. (Don't drive up in a limousine, Ab Tweet warned.)

"How did Paul feel about letting you fellows get involved?"

"No problem Mr. Sullivan, the day after you got the nomination Tim and I decided we'd like to help you, and Mr. Connolly encouraged us to do it. We said it would only be a few weeks and he said that would be fine and for us to give it everything we've got."

"Call me Michael, will you fellows? It works better for me, if it works for you."

"Yes Sir," they responded in unison and by mid-afternoon, after the fourth stop, it became Michael, Tim and Taylor.

At each event Michael strode into the room, followed closely by Tim and Taylor, and although there were just three of them, anyone seated in the room could easily think of the term, "juggernaut," for that's the impression they gave. As the candidate, Michael electrified the room as he made his way to the platform. He gave his set piece and then came off the stage and shook every hand in the room, with a word for each. To the person addressed he gave full attention so that person felt there were just the two of them in the room. One said: "I'm a Democrat, but damn it that guy gets to you. I asked him a question and he took his time answering it and damn I agreed with him. I don't know, it's going to be tough to vote for 'ol Hillary."

When he finally got home at ten p.m., after his last event, Mary prepared a hot dinner for him. He felt exhilarated, still on a high from the day's campaigning. She judged his mood and asked:

"Would you like a scotch before I feed you?"

"Why not sweetheart, I'm all fired up, must have shaken two thousand hands today. I couldn't have done it without those two associates Paul let us have. They are really competent, move thru the crowds forcefully, but graciously, relieve me from those who have great ideas how I should run the campaign, take every name and sign up every one who offers to volunteer."

"I'm thrilled that Paul's men are working out for you. I can report I also had a good day at headquarters, everyone and everything has meshed and tomorrow we will be at top production. I just got home a little while ago myself; our people will hit three thousand doors tonight."

"Great. What else is happening in the world?"

"In our world, Hillary Johnson gave a press conference today lambasting your stand on abortion. President Bush is going full tilt in his campaign for re-election, the Democrats may be sending some heavyweights out here to pump up Hillary, two women Senators are rumored to be coming, probably Boxer and Feinstein."

"I think that will help us more than hurt us. Boxer will go over here like stale fish to male voters, Feinstein might help her but not by much. I suppose if they bring in people like that, we can hope the Republicans counter with some hitters of our own. Tomorrow will you have Ron contact them and tell them what's afoot with the Democrat surrogates?"

"That I will do."

They finished their drinks, ate the dinner she had prepared and dragged themselves upstairs, completely beat, after a day on the trail. He fell asleep immediately, Mary could not. She thought how their lives were changing daily. She knew it would be hectic, but it was turning into a daily crisis with the whole family caught up in it.

With Michael at the head of the firm immersed in practicing law, and she raising the children and participating in the community as much as he, life had been exhilarating yet manageable. Jumping into politics brought a whole new dimension into their lives, exciting, confusing and far different from what they were used to. She told herself she wasn't complaining, simply mystified by the rapidity of change in their lives. How would they adjust? If she had a nagging worry, it was how to adopt to a new life in politics. No thinking beyond tomorrow she thought wistfully—tomorrow will take care of itself.

After a week of campaigning Norm Towsen, the pollster, passed on news Hillary Johnson had jumped to an early lead with forty percent to Michael's thirty five, the rest undecided.

"It's not good news Michael," he said, telling the candidate where the race stood with two weeks to go.

"Ok, we know what we have to do and it has to be done in the next two weeks, so let's start working harder."

"A lot harder," Ron Fitzgerald added. "we just found out there's a circular being dropped off on the porches stating you've got a record of womanizing, you're just a high flying personal injury lawyer, and an ambulance chaser. That calls for an immediate response and as hard as we can hit."

"All right Ron," Michael directed, showing no sign of concern, "get a press release out to all media saying we have become aware a scurrilous piece of literature is being distributed to the voters by unknown individuals. Issue a firm denial of everything alleged in the document and that we have filed a criminal complaint with the

U.S. attorney. Second, arrange a press conference for this afternoon where I will address the contents in the document and its use in the campaign."

Standing before a battery of press and television cameras that afternoon with Mary standing at his side, Michael made an opening statement, charging the circular was an example of the worst kind of politics, packed with untruths. He rebutted each point made in the tract and then took questions.

"Mr. Sullivan, one charge made is that you are a womanizer. Care to comment?"

"The only women I have ever 'womanized,' your word, is the lady standing next to me, the mother of our four children. My treatment of her cannot be labeled, in your word, womanizing.'

I defy anyone to prove otherwise." He turned to Mary and asked: "Have I stated the truth?"

"You have stated the unvarnished truth, and I must add, I abhor the anonymous slander against our family."

"Mr. Sullivan, you don't deny that you are a personal injury lawyer do you?"

"Your question implies there is something wrong with being a personal injury lawyer. There are many lawyers that specialize in bringing law suits for injured clients. They are good lawyers contrary to your question's implication. I've been a trial lawyer, and yes, I have taken personal injury cases and malpractice cases, however, they are a small part of my practice, so in a sense it is incorrect to call me a personal injury lawyer. I have not specialized in that field."

"Mr. Sullivan, do you attribute this tract you've denounced to your opponent, Hillary Johnson?"

"There is no doubt it will poison the minds of some voters who read it. I think most will think it the trash it is. The allegations are so outlandish and unsubstantiated. On the other hand it can't be denied it helps Ms. Johnson. We have no evidence her campaign is behind it. My purpose in holding this press conference is to expose this piece of garbage I'm holding in my hand for what it is, and to call attention to it so the record is clear as to my personal and professional life. We all know politics is a rough, mean business but this pamphlet is a libel and that is why my campaign has brought it to the attention of the U.S. Attorney, the Attorney General and the voting public."

The six o'clock news, carried Michael's press conference on all local stations as well as the eleven o'clock wrap up. Each station also carried a small clip of Hillary Johnson denying her campaign had any connection with the circular, and complaining Michael Sullivan had left an implication it had.

Overnight polling disclosed Michael's forthright exposure and denial of the tract's contents brought an uptick in a daily tracking poll conducted by the *Herald*; Johnson-39; Sullivan-36, with 25 undecided.

Surprisingly, Johnson had heavy money coming in from an unknown source, enabling her to make television buys at a two to one pace over Michael. One of her main themes emphasized his pro-life, antiabortion position. In the second district, "choice" had been a big issue in the 2002 congressional race and Tom Bennings, the Republican, had endorsed the pro-choice position. Johnson hoped to draw off Republican women using it as a wedge issue against Sullivan.

He took a solid position on the Iraq invasion backed by a majority of the voters in the district, Republican and Democrat. Johnson, a liberal Democrat, had voiced opposition to the war but so far it had not become a major issue. In his stump speech, and in answer to questions from the press, on the issue of abortion, Michael made it perfectly clear he believed life began at conception and therefore the fetus was entitled to protection under the constitution. As a lawyer, he believed, along with many constitutional lawyers and scholars, that the Supreme Court, in carving out a so-called "right of privacy" created a right out of thin air, without a legal premise to support it. The decision, *Roe vs Wade*, he believed to be a political decision not a legal one. Johnson, thinking she had the winning hand, continued to pummel Michael on television and radio and he countered arguing abortion was a legislative prerogative not a judicial one and in deciding *Roe vs. Wade* the Supreme Court had usurped the authority of fifty state legislatures.

Both camps agreed, after tense negotiations, to one debate before the City Club with a week to go before the election. As he'd done so many times preparing for oral arguments before the state's Supreme Court, and the Federal Circuit Court of Appeals, Michael put together a team acting as press interrogators in a mock debate, with a woman standing in for Hillary Johnson. Ron had gone so far as to duplicate the set that had been approved by both campaigns for the City Club debate. During the Day, Michael made his routine six appearances; in the evening he went through rigorous questioning from the three mock reporters, and responses from the synthetic Hillary Johnson. Meantime, Ms. Johnson gave minimal attention to debate rehearsal, instead concentrating all her efforts getting free and paid television.

Five days before the debate the team met at the headquarters to plot the attack line.

"We've made sure at least fifty percent of the crowd will be our people, a hundred standees are permitted and I'm assured we will get fifty tickets for that, so nobody is going to shout us down," Ron explained. This will be the one chance we have to nail her. You've got to be aggressive, Michael, the fact she's a woman should have no bearing on your treatment of her. She's plenty tough and if she senses any courtliness she'll light into you like a wounded banshee." Laughter.

Kennedy spoke up: "You're too rough on her Ron, if he beats on her too much, the ladies won't like it."

"How about treating her as a man?" Mary volunteered. (laughter)

"I'm a professional, so is she," Michael said, "I'll be treating her as I would a court room opponent, courtesy, without mercy." They all laughed. Seriously, I think she's going to home in on the abortion issue, and I'm well prepared and the question is: will the legal argument prevail over an emotional one. If presented calmly and logically I think it will. I'm sure you people have put every possible question to me, so being stumped will not be a problem." With days to go the race tightened; Johnson stubbornly holding her lead 46-41-13, the undecideds moving evenly to both candidates.

Sitting around the conference table at headquarters the team met, with the exception of Michael, who continued his six event a day routine, sometimes adding an event or two if presented the opportunity. They traded ideas on how to handle the final days.

"What's the latest tracking?" Kennedy asked Norm Towsen.

"We're stalled at forty one, she's dropped to forty four and the undecideds have gone up a little bit which means they've moved from her to the undecided column. A good sign; still too early to show a trend. We need something to happen in the next four days and to my mind it has to be the debate."

"Well the fact she's dropped two in the last couple of days is not a discouraging sign."

"True, but they haven't come to us, they've just left her," Ron answered.

Everyone at the table had a solution or a theory but it all came down to the City Club at noon and they all knew it. They decided to tape the debate in the hope they could use parts in a commercial to be run for three days before the election. On the day of the debate Ron went to the hotel, where it was to be held, anxious to get a picture of what it would look like and where to place the camera taping Michael. The room had been set up the night before and he had it all to himself except for a couple of City Club officials making sure it had been set up to specifications. The room held one hundred tables and they were in place with white table cloths, crystal, silverware, each with a centerpiece of daisies in a small pot with an American flag stuck in it. Perfect for television he thought. They had set up a special section for television cameras, still photographers and the print press. After an hour the media people began to come in and set up their equipment. Some waved at Ron and he acknowledged with a wave back. He knew most of them from his work on Betty O'Donnell's campaign for Mayor, and renewed acquaintances with all of them when he signed on for Michael's congressional campaign. Most of the press were neutral, but some, openly favored Johnson because of her gender. Not that they didn't like Michael, it was just that she happened to be a woman and they wanted a women to win.

Ron deliberately put in place a system whereby his people were to come into the room in groups of three or four at a time and strategically take positions in all parts of the room so that Michael's applause would come from every quarter. He made sure all his people were in place by 11:30. When that time arrived he could see his five hundred plus Sullivan backers blanketing the room sitting in the most advantages places. Two days prior, he had obtained from the hotel a seating chart for the debate, and using that he carefully plotted, on a ten by five mockup of the room, exactly where he wanted his forces seated. Each Sullivan guest had been apprised of the table they were assigned. By 11:45 the room quickly filled with people not committed to either candidate, the curious, and Johnson backers identified with campaign buttons bearing one word: "JOHNSON." Not wanting his people to be identified, Ron instructed Sullivan attendees to wear no insignia so when they let loose with their applause it would appear to be coming from a non-partisan audience and hopefully the media would think it spontaneous applause for a well turned argument or a telling quip by Michael Sullivan. Nothing was left to chance, because Ron and the political consultant felt they had to win in that room or not at all.

The program called for lunch to be served, dishes cleared, and the moderator to introduce the candidates, which he did, and then stepped down off the stage and joined his fellow interrogators. At Michael's introduction his supporters gave a lusty cheer, Ms. Johnson received scattered applause from which Ron concluded the modified response demonstrated Michael's supporters outnumbered hers' giving him control of the floor. This came as a welcome surprise because he had given a lot more credit to Johnson's team, thinking they would want to pack the hall or get at least fifty percent of those present. Obviously it had not occurred to them.

Counting members, guests of members, standees, press and kitchen help, who deserted their posts to watch the proceedings, Ron estimated fifteen hundred in the room. Wall to wall people. A hush came over the crowd as the moderator put the first question to Michael: his position on crime nationwide and what to do about the increase. For Michael it was like answering a bar review question. He had sixty seconds to answer and he made ten important points within that time frame clearly setting out his position—tough on crime. Johnson had thirty seconds to respond. She did, and tore into Michael for his tough position, punishing those convicted of three felonies to serve longer penalties. After six questions had been asked it became obvious the candidates were far apart on the issues; Johnson began attacking Michael personally, implying his positions were not taken in good faith. As she used this tactic more frequently, Michael's claque began cheering after his rebuttal to her answers and a low hum of boos when she kept up the attack.

Early in the debate Michael realized she had decided to attack him, acting the part of the aggressor, hoping to portray him as weak. Rather than play into her ploy he decided to answer the questions with all the facts and statistics at his command and to address her as Ms. Johnson in a courteous and firm manner. What the crowd would have seen and heard from their vantage point was a suave six foot, one inch gentleman dressed in a dark blue suit, white shirt, striped tie, not overly handsome but strikingly masculine delivering measured answers to questions, often dropping a quip at Ms. Johnson expense which brought instantaneous laughter, not only from his supporters, but from crowd as a whole. He came over as likable, not mean, not rattled by her attacks.

Johnson, a short five foot five woman of stocky build with glasses, was relentless in downplaying issues, more intent on going after Michael on his stands. Near the end of the debate, one of the panel asked Michael when he thought life began, a typical question he had received during the course of the short campaign.

"I believe life begins at conception. Reason tells me this, but more importantly, medical science has reached the advanced stage where life is unmistakably in the womb. Abortion has taken too many lives in this country. Statistics tell us thirty million have died and counting. We cannot afford to snuff out the lives of the unborn. The constitution protects life. As an elected official I come down on the side of life."

"Ms. Johnson, your response?"

"Mr. Sullivan's response is irresponsible. He knows full well the Supreme Court has declared it a women's right in case after case. I have had an abortion. My husband and I could not afford a child when we were very young and it was my choice to have an abortion. I do not believe, as Mr. Sullivan does, that a fetus has life. He's obviously against women who choose to have an abortion." She stopped and glanced at Michael with a triumphant look on her face, confident she had quashed his argument and gained support for her position.

"Mr. Sullivan you have thirty seconds to answer."

He paused before answering, waiting for the buzz from her remarks to grow silent. Every eye watched him, waiting for his response.

"I'm very sorry Ms. Johnson you thought it necessary, and that you had the right to take the life of a child. A defenseless unborn.

It is that kind of attitude that has stifled morality in this country in pursuit of self. We fail as a country when we fail to protect the unborn. I repeat, if I'm elected to Congress I will work every day I serve to protect life in every form and at every stage."

For a fleeting moment, there was silence then a roar and then three quarters of the room were on their feet cheering. Ron, standing in the back of the room knew it, John Kennedy, sitting at a table near the front of the stage with Mary knew it, the press knew it. Michael Sullivan had just laid his candidacy on the line and made no apology for it. He had spoken calmly with sincerity and conviction, no one in the room doubted that. He was willing to lose the "choice" vote for a principle. His people cheered for a full thirty seconds before the moderator brought order to the room.

For those assembled it was over even though the debate went on for another ten minutes. They knew who won. When they left the room you could hear a loud buzz. They expected fireworks and they weren't disappointed. The irony of it all was the question on abortion and her answer were completely unplanned for. By revealing she'd had an abortion and proud of it, Johnson showed an unflattering side to her otherwise commendable resume. When it ended, her supporters raised signs, they had brought with them and kept hidden throughout the debate, and now pushed them in front of the cameras screaming: "Johnson for Congress," "choice" "choice." Had the abortion question not been brought up the demonstration might have proved effective, but after the candidate proudly claimed she had an abortion, the celebration seemed hollow and artificial, and enthusiasm died. The question now: what would the public's reaction be to her revelation she'd had an abortion—would she get credit for a brave act or condemnation for a selfish act.

. . .

Saturday morning Mary read over Michael's shoulder while he read the lead story in the *Herald*.

Johnson Reveals Abortion. The writer details what happened at the City Club debate and the positions taken by the candidates. "Johnson's startling announcement she had an abortion, and was proud of it, caused a stir and Michael Sullivan's denunciation of the practice took center stage crowding everything out as far as other issues were concerned." He looked up and said: "What do you think Mary?"

"Like I told you right after the debate, it broke the camel's back. That question Brady Sorenson asked was loaded with dynamite. Up to that point I don't think the crowd was overly impressed with her ad hominem attacks on you. It looked like a mad dog trying to bite a giant's ankle. Whether the voters got the same impression we had in the hall is another question."

"You know, I think Ms. Johnson thought she was going to bag a lion when she literally bragged about having an abortion. I don't think she had the vaguest idea the impact it had on the crowd. It's funny how people think."

Later that day, Dan Streetmeier, the ad consultant, came to Michael with idea for a commercial to be used at the last minute. "It starts with Brady's question to you on abortion, your answer, and her blurting out she'd had an abortion and took pride in it. It will be in black and white, with a fade out with the words: "You make the choice life or death." Paid for ...... What do you say Michael? Can we run it?"

He didn't hesitate, "Make the spot, we'll review it and make a decision."

"Actually Ron is down at station KZDT where it's being prepared. He's waiting for your decision and now that you've given the ok, I'm going to call him and tell him it's a go." He made the call and was told to have Michael and Mary come down to the station to preview it.

"Ok, Mary and I will be down there in fifteen minutes."

"I'm skeptical, Michael the ad sounds pretty tough. It tells women who've had an abortion, they've killed their unborn, and to those thinking about it, they are potential murderers."

"Your analysis is correct Mary but facts are facts. If abortion kills a person, and we believe it does, then we should fight for what's right. Johnson hit first, obviously thinking I would back off. So I say ask and ye shall receive. She asked for it."

Arriving at the television station, they went directly to the screening room where Ron and Streetmeier were standing by. They took their seats in a small theater set up for screening commercials, programs and movies. Ron raised his arm signaling the projectionist to run the commercial. It ran exactly sixty seconds and was dramatic to say the least. The cameraman had caught it all, the facial expressions of the candidates, Michael's devastating reply.

"You're right Mary it may be a little too tough but it does show her in a bad light. Most women who have had an abortion don't brag about it. Some even have remorse. This woman was flouting it. I don't think even the pro-choice advocates are going to be too excited about that so I say let it roll we'll know soon enough whether it makes a difference." Ron left the room with Streetmeier to start the ad running on all stations.

"I don't know Michael, I hope you're right."

"Don't worry, Mary, it's a tough ad but it has to be said win or lose. If Johnson is elected there is one more abortion advocate in the Congress. If I'm elected there's one less. I willing to take the gamble.

The night before the election, after a full day of campaigning, they all sat around the headquarters. "This is our last night of polling and I hope to have the numbers about two a.m. this morning. Anyone care to stay up for it?" Norman Towsen looked to see if he had any takers.

"Are you kidding Norm? We'll all be up except Michael, he'll be sound asleep." Kennedy spoke up and said: "We've spent thousands on polling, I don't think I'll be asleep when you analyze the results."

"Ron is right, I'm going home and sleep like a baby. I think the die is cast and we'll just have to wait for the ultimate poll—the voters."

"You're going by yourself, my husband, I'm staying with John and Ron for Norm's numbers."

"The information will come in here to headquarters," Norm volunteered, "why don't I come down to the house afterwards and you can go home now with the candidate. Take everyone with you and get some sleep."

"That's a better idea Norm, I'll cook something up for everybody when you arrive."

Just as the pollster had forecast, calls were made, data weighed and analyzed, and for brevity's sake, put on a single sheet and Xeroxed for each of the six gathered around a table in Mary Sullivan's kitchen at two a.m. Election Day.

Kennedy read aloud from the sheet: "The third night of three night tracking: Johnson-45; Sullivan-44; 11 undecided." "Brother, eleven undecided on the eve of an election. I've never heard of such a thing. Four or Five, yes, But eleven. Unheard of. I think that television ad is going to make or break us." What does it mean, Norm, you're the pollster?"

"We've come up three, she's down one. I've been conservative in my analysis—undecided usually break for the underdog which we happen to be. She needs five of those undecideds we need six. All I can say is it's a tossup. I realize that's not a definitive answer but with that many undecideds, your guess may be better than mine."

When he finished Mary drew the line pointing out her watch read three thirty and they had to get some sleep before voting started in four hours.

CHAPTER 35

Mary, with four hours sleep, and the candidate made their way at 7:30 a.m. to the precinct in the parish hall at St Agatha to cast their vote. T.V. cameras and three reporters waited to take the usual "candidate voting" shot. Unlike his wife, he enjoyed a full night's rest and felt energized and expectant, shaking hands with the poll workers and people waiting to vote. As they exited the hall, a reporter with a camera man in tow cornered Michael and asked for a statement on the outcome of the election.

"Close, very close, but we win by a nose." He laughed and they laughed with him."

"That's what we'll use on the twelve o'clock news, Mr. Sullivan, if that's your call. Thanks."

The campaign leased out a suite of rooms in the old Ambassador Hotel, a place Michael had made deliveries to in his high school days and one that held a lot of memories for him. As a young lawyer he enjoyed meeting with other lawyers every Friday morning at seven a.m. in the old hotel. As a board member of several charities he'd attended meetings in its old fashioned private rooms. It seemed natural to culminate the campaign in the sedate old hotel, with the ornate ballroom, now festooned with red, white and blue bunting, a large tote board set up to show vote tallies, two cash bars attended by uniformed bar tenders and food tables laden with salads, meats, shrimp, cheeses and strawberries. At Michael insistence, a Dixieland band joyously played the Muskrat Ramble. Upstairs on the tenth floor Michael's entourage gathered, comprised of lawyers from the firm, their wives who had worked in the campaign, Paul and Teresa Connolly, John and Sally Kennedy, several senior partners and their wives, Ron Fitzgerald, the four children and the "team" who worked so closely with him. Concern for the outcome permeated the room; talk at a low hum, no one had an idea of the outcome and another hour would pass before the polls closed.

Weary, but excited, Mary hosted the reception, and although the meal was catered she moved around the suite, passing hor d'oeuvres, getting people drinks, while Michael, calm and looking happy, chatted amiably with his guests, every once and a while laughing uproariously at one of Kennedy's Irish jokes. If Michael was the calmest in the room, Ron had to be the busiest, working off the main suite in a bedroom with four direct phone lines in front of him, awaiting calls at eight p.m. from twenty key precincts where, when the first votes were announced, he would have some idea of where the race was headed. Jack Sullivan sat beside him, legal pad and pencil in hand, ready to jot down numbers as Ron called them out, then take them to his father.

The main suite grew uncommonly quiet when John Kennedy turned on two television sets at opposite ends of the room at exactly eight p.m. Guests gathered in two groups, one clustered around the set on the east side of the room the other on the west. A voice from the television announced : "The polls have just closed and we have our first returns from the Special Election for Congress and you see them on the right side of your screen, Johnson 1,090 to Sullivan's 850, Johnson leading fifty six percent to forty four percent. Remember this vote is just a fraction, and a small one at that, of the total votes cast. Turnout is predicted at about two hundred forty thousand votes."

Concern flashed across every face in the room, but they told each other first returns were indicative of nothing except a close race. To be sure, they expected Michael to break out on top, when he didn't, the pessimists began to worry but kept their concerns to themselves. Off the main suite Ron Fitzgerald began to harvest phone calls from his correspondents placed in key precincts.

"Take this down Jack, precinct 153; Sullivan 206, Johnson 203. We were supposed to lose that precinct by thirty votes. I like it. Don't tell anyone yet, let's get some more reports over the next twenty minutes." For another twenty minutes they both bent over the phone, Jack writing down the precinct numbers and votes counted when Ron shouted them out.

"We've got a good sample Jack, I can't say we're going to win but we're keeping right up with her and doing better in five key precincts I thought we'd lose. Xerox that sheet and slip into your mom and tell her to get it to your dad." In his mini office Ron had set up phones, a copy machine and a small television set that allowed him to monitor the commentators while taking calls from his men in the field. Jack left, as instructed, motioned to his mother in the main suite, gave her the sheet with Ron's figures, which she quickly digested and then made her way over to Michael talking with members of his firm and shoved it in his pocket. He excused himself and made for Ron's bedroom office.

"What's your read Ron?"

"Doing good Michael so far. Way too early for a call, still we're even."

At nine thirty with the count standing at seventy five thousand votes for Johnson and Seventy three thousand five hundred for Michael, he announced he and Mary were going down to the ballroom to speak to their supporters who had been gathering since five p.m. and were on edge watching the television sets and the large tote board. Everyone in the suite trooped down with them to the ballroom. Ron and Jack remained on station in the bunker. When they came into the ballroom a huge roar went up from fifteen hundred people now packed in until the fire marshal said, "no more."

"Sully-van," they shouted. Just the sight of him and his look of confidence boosted Their spirits. The sound reverberated around the room. He waved and finally a hush came over the crowd; they listened for any news he could bring them and they expected good news otherwise why would he have come to the ballroom so early when no one knew the outcome. On television sets around the huge room, Michael appeared at the microphones with a large crowd standing behind him and Mary to his right looking out into the sea of faces.

"I've got good news, we're close." They reacted with loud cheers. "It will be a long night, don't go home because you're going to be rewarded for your hard work. In the end all your labor, pounding signs, making calls, getting our voters to the polls will pay off. I'm not declaring victory. Too early for that, but I'm predicting it." They erupted again with the chant "Sully-van," "Sully-van." He waved his arms for their attention and the cheers subsided.

"No matter how the returns come in, and they will go up and down, keep the faith, do not waver, we will win. God bless you all and now Mary and I will wait and watch with you until the last ballot is counted." He kissed Mary and told her to go back up to the suite and wait.

"What for?" she asked, "I'm sticking with you Sullivan, you stuck your neck out predicting victory, you better be right."

"We'll be ok Mary, I can feel it. Let's meet some of the people down here, we have a lot of people to thank." For the next half hour they moved through the crowd, shaking hands, chatted with workers, and gave a television interview. They were surrounded everywhere they moved. At ten o'clock they broke away and went back up to the suite. The first thing they saw were new numbers posted on the television: Johnson 95,000; Sullivan 94,520. An hour passed and the room grew quiet, everyone clustered around the two sets as the returns came in slower than earlier in the evening. "BULLETIN," flashed across the screen and new numbers appeared: 100,200 to 99,906, the announcer repeated the numbers and commented, "Johnson still leading by 294 out of two hundred thousand and six votes cast. That's about as thin as it gets" he added.

Michael slipped out of the suite over to the bedroom office where Ron informed him he couldn't predict the outcome despite the fact eighty five percent of the votes had been counted. He reported the Registrar of Elections office had difficulty getting results from certain precincts and no one could articulate why. The candidate returned to the main suite and found it packed, not only with the guests but well- wishers who arrived from the ballroom. The eighth of April turned into the ninth and the clock in the suite turned to twelve ten a.m.

A political pundit on the television explained to his host: "This is a horse race, the closest political contest I've seen in ten years. Tom Billings won the seat in 2002 with fifty six percent of the vote, so it's pretty clear, Johnson, the Democrat is waging a tremendous battle for what has been a safe Republican seat. Neither party, it seems, has a great advantage in the second district with the independents making the difference between winning and losing. Sure there has been polling but the polls have been ineffective in predicting the winner....... Wait a minute, I'm going to have to break off here and switch to Johnson's headquarters, she's about to make a statement....."

In Michael's suite and the ballroom a thousand people were standing and sitting, tired but keeping eyes on the screens to listen to Hillary Johnson. Michael glanced at his watch and saw the time: twelve fifteen. Most people had already gone to bed content to find out the result in the morning. Now her crowd had thinned to three hundred people. Nevertheless, they gave her a hearty cheer and she told them they were leading in the latest count 106,401 to 106, 250 and assured them she would put the race to bed in the next hour and when they awoke Wednesday morning she would be the Congresswoman to lead the second district. Pandemonium broke out among her workers, believing she had inside information so late in the count.

A perceptible groan sounded emitted from the Sullivan suite. Someone spoke up: "She's bluffing, keep the faith like Michael told us......." The room broke into laughter, easing the tension. Another turned the sound down on the televisions, while Johnson continued to address her faithful.

"Congresswoman, my foot," "Ex congresswomen," another shouted, "step up to the bar, Sullivan's buying, we're going to win this one. Keep the faith." That's all it took, the mood changed from somber to giddy, and to reward their faith new numbers appeared on the screen showing Michael with his first lead of the night, small, still the lead, 108,551 to 107,950. No landside but a lead of 601 votes.

In the bunker Ron had the phone to his ear, and Jack had four pages of figures on his legal pad. He reported there were only thirty precincts left to report, and Michael's lead had grown to seven hundred. The clock now read one forty five and only one station remained on the air and many in the suite had melted away to the point only a hundred remained, those closest to the Sullivans. Jack kept shuttling from the bunker to the suite with new numbers, always two minutes ahead of the television.

At 2:15 a.m. Ron told Jack to tell his dad: "Four precincts still to report and we've got an 820 vote lead out of two hundred and twenty thousand plus cast. Another fifteen minutes passed before the television anchor announced the final vote: Sullivan 110,525; Johnson 109,212.

They were too worn out to celebrate. Instead everyone, embraced, congratulated Michael and Mary and slowly found their way out of the suite into the night satisfied a great victory had been won. Only the team remained amidst empty glasses on the tables, empty plates everywhere, banners coming loose from the ceiling, the television sets still blaring out results of the election; what had been a beautiful hotel suite now looked like the scene of a wild two day party. Mary told Michael it would require a battery of maids to bring it back to life. Ignoring the clutter, they all sat around, the Sullivans, Kennedys, Connollys, Ron, the pollster, the consultants and Jack the oldest who told them he'd been saving a bottle of Johnny Walker Blue Label scotch for just such an occasion. Michael did the honors pouring a full measure for each and they lifted their glasses and he toasted: "to faith."

"To faith," they answered in unison.

. . .

Hearing a muffled sound at his bedroom door, Michael sat up drowsily, looked at Mary, saw she had not been disturbed by the sound and said softly: "Come in."

"Dad, sorry to barge in on you but I thought you should know, Hillary Johnson has asked the Secretary of State for a recount."

"What time is it Jack?"

"Seven o'clock, here's the *Daily Ledger*, read it for yourself."

"Mary stirred: "Can you two go somewhere else, we didn't get to bed until four o'clock?"

"You heard her Jack let's go down to the kitchen; I'll make us some coffee." Down they trudged, Michael made the coffee poured two cups and sat down across from his son. The story in the *Ledger* informed the reader Johnson had signaled her intent to file the necessary papers that day to request a partial recount. The recount, the story continued, would be held ten days from the date of the election and consist of a partial recount in the county in which the city was located and required a recounting of upwards of seventy five thousand paper ballots...

He looked up from the paper as Jack sat down with a bowl of cereal and said: "Nothing is easy Jack, I'm sure you've discovered that in your twenty one years."

"So true dad, however it's my understanding a recount seldom results in reversing the outcome of an election."

They sat there in their pajamas silent, thinking their own thoughts when the phone rang. Jack got up from the table, went over to the wall where the kitchen phone hung and picked it up.

"Hello, yes, are you kidding? Dad it's the White House calling, they say the President wants to speak with you."

Michael took the phone from his son, suddenly fully awake. "Yes, yes Mr. President....well thank you....your very kind....yes sir, I'll see you in Washington....yes and you have a good day too sir." He hung up and said nonchalantly: "That was George Bush, President of the United States."

"I can't believe it dad, what did he say?"

"What a nice man, he said he just wanted to congratulate your mother and I on our victory, that he had been following the race along with a number of key races and to have no concern about the recount. He said he had a lot of experience in recounts and we both laughed."

"Did he say anything else I should know?" Jack said, laughing and proud the President of the United States took time to call his father.

"You heard part of it, he said he looked forward to seeing your mother and I at the White House."

"Is all I can say is: whata guy!"

"What's all noise down here you two, I couldn't sleep with all the racket. Mary went over to the stove and poured herself a cup of coffee: "Can I get anything for you gentlemen now that the house is awakened?"

Neither said a word, just sat there innocently with semi hurt looks at being accused of waking up the household.

"Who was that on the phone? I heard it ring upstairs."

"George Bush," Jack said matter-of-factly.

"Jack, I didn't get to bed until three thirty this morning, don't joke with me."

"I'm not kidding mother, it was the President. I answered the phone and the caller said the White House was calling and the President wanted to speak to dad."

Mary's face broke into a beautiful smile and she felt a tingle go up her spine. "Michael, was it really the President?" Then she realized Jack would never joke with her about something so important.

"It was he Mary," Michael confirmed and proceeded to tell her, as best he could recall, the President's exact words.

"What a darling man to take time when he's running the most important office in the world to call my husband, your father. I hope we do get to meet them."

"There is other news Mary, we haven't mentioned not wanting to detract from the President's call and that is, Hillary Johnson is filing for a recount today, the story is in the *Ledger*."

For perhaps ten seconds she said nothing a frown coming to her face. Then as suddenly as it had appeared a smile replaced it and she said: "So be it. It's not going to detract one bit from celebrating a call from the President of the United States."

"She's steel Jack, you can't intimidate her. Get the gang down here. In honor of the President's call, I'm going to cook everybody a breakfast fit for a king including bacon, eggs, potatoes O'Brian, sausages and pancakes to be served in the next half hour. We'll worry about the recount tomorrow. Today we celebrate.

CHAPTER 36

On the eve of the partial recount Hillary Johnson announced, with great confidence, she would receive enough votes to overturn Sullivan's win. She claimed, her sources told her the votes were there, and when queried by the media, who her sources were she declined to elaborate, merely repeating she had confidence in the outcome.

Paul Connolly took personal charge of the Sullivan recount team. He recruited thirty lawyers, from firms across the city to volunteer for the three days needed to complete the recount. For half a day they gathered in the offices of Sullivan & Connolly reviewing rules of the recount and were told to be aware of expected aggressiveness on the part Hillary Johnson's recount team. The opposition, composed of union members and Democrat lawyers, were sure to challenge every ballot Paul told them. If they tried to do this on an indiscriminate basis, and it appeared they had every intent to overturn the result of the election at any cost, retaliation would be the order of the day until Johnson's team understood they might wind up losing votes.

A huge empty warehouse had been chosen as the site for the recount. Ominously a storm raged outside and the patter of rain drummed against the windows as the two teams gathered to start the count. Thirty picnic like tables in rows of six manned by ninety volunteers ready to count ballots stacked on each table. At the sound of a whistle they began; one volunteer to pull a ballot from the stack, call out the vote, one Democrat and one Republican monitor to review it quickly for flaws, one to record the tally and one to put it on the "counted vote" pile. At other tables officials collected the votes as recorded, and a special table was set aside for the press to cover any aspects of the count they deemed necessary to write about in their stories. More tables were set up at one end of the warehouse with coffee urns and doughnuts to be replaced at noon with box lunches for all the workers and observers. The scene struck one as stark and a certain dreariness hung over the room. As Connolly predicted, the Democratic challengers began to challenge any ballot with a tear or smear or minor error that could be seen visually. After a half hour of this aggressive challenging, and complaints from his people, Paul called his team into a huddle during a break and authorized his lawyers to go after every Johnson ballot. They went back to the tables and began to challenge a Johnson ballot every time a Sullivan ballot was challenged. This went on until noon when the total votes picked up by Johnson came to twenty five. During the lunch hour the Registrar of Elections called Paul and Johnson's attorneys and suggested a truce on challenging what appeared to be perfectly valid ballots in his view. After a prolonged discussion they returned to their respective counters, told them what had been worked out with the Registrar and instructed them to only challenge "if there is a genuine doubt about what the voter intended with the ballot." By days end everyone involved was exhausted and the Democrats discouraged at only picking up fifty votes.

Paul met with Michael, Mary and Ron late the first evening and recited the day's events from early morning until six at night. "The exercise is arduous but has to be done; if you don't watch those rascals they'll have a hundred votes stolen in an hour; I think by late afternoon they realized any shenanigans would be dealt with in like kind.

Ron interrupted to ask: "What's your feeling on whether they're going to improve their numbers?"

"Not possible to predict but at the rate they're going they're not even going come close to turning this election around. We'll know tomorrow night for sure. I spent my day answering questions, arguing with their attorneys and the rest of the time at each table observing the counting. Almost uniformly the ballots are clear as to the voter's intent and in remarkably good shape. The bad ones are rather obvious and it's impossible to tell who they voted for and those are tossed. We'll see a much different batch tomorrow from what we've seen today. Right now Michael you're still 740 votes ahead."

On the second day the atmosphere at the warehouse became less tense not as adversarial as the first day, with everyone, county officials and monitors getting to know each other; humor and wise cracks began to creep into the conversations. Johnson picked up another fifty two votes which brought her two day gain to one hundred and two votes. Day three started with less enthusiasm on the part of the Democrats knowing they might not gain enough votes for a full recount. By noon their hopes dimmed as Michael lost only twenty more votes. Six o'clock came and the total for the one hundred thousand votes counted turn into a net gain for Johnson of a hundred and forty votes. Extrapolating that gain to a two hundred and twenty five thousand recount would result in roughly a two hundred and eighty vote gain, five hundred short of Michael Sullivan's vote.

An announcement to the press assembled to hear the final total read as follows: "Sullivan, Republican, 112,502; Johnson 112,002. Both Ron and Paul Connolly were in the hall when the Registrar made the announcement and Ron called Michael: "You won, it's over you're the officially elected Congressman from the second district. Not by much, but a win is a win—congratulations."

"Thanks Ron, I couldn't have done it without you and Paul and all that gang at the warehouse. Will you convey to them how thankful I am for their hard work the last three days. In fact we've got "thank you," letters to get out to everyone who played any part, no matter how small. Can you start that process as soon as tomorrow?"

"It'll be a pleasure, the most fun I've had in weeks."

"And Ron, I want you with me in Washington, will you come?"

"I'm a disciple Michael, we won the Mayoralty, now a Congressional seat, who knows where it will lead? I'm ready to ride the bronco if you are."

"I'll tell you, I'd be handicapped without you, Mary's going to have her hands full setting up our household and only the Lord knows what I'll be doing the next three weeks. We can talk salary and position next week."

He settled back in his chair at Sullivan & Connolly and gazed out his office windows; the sun slowly descending and shadows creeping up the facades of surrounding buildings. I'm now a public man, he mused, does that make me a politician? Michael reflected on the change in his life over the last six weeks, no take that back, since the campaign for Mayor that he ran with Ron as his assistant. That's when he went public. To him, going public meant exposing yourself, your family and your friends to public scrutiny, sometimes even worse, calumny, slander, libel. Moreover, the public man or woman must go out and literally get up on a soap box and proclaim to the electorate, "Here I am folks, I want to represent you and lead you." For some it's the fame, or power or in many cases money, that thrusts them into the spotlight. For most it is a profession. He didn't put himself in that category. For Michael Sullivan, the law was his profession, in particular, a specialty that required great skill—trial lawyer. He asked himself: "Am I reluctant to leave the law to become a "politician?" No. he looked upon it as a duty after talking with Kennedy, Paul Connolly, his partner, and others. A duty to serve. In practicing law, he served his clients. Now, he reasoned, it's time to serve others; by winning a seat in Congress he could serve his country again as he did when he wore the uniform of the U.S. Air Force after graduation from college. Yes, a different arena to be sure, a larger stage, and perhaps that's what made him listen to John Kennedy's entreaties to run.

Life is not static, it's about change. He had to learn new skills, deal with new and different problems than he had dealt with in the law, at the same time he knew he would bring to this new calling the experience he had logged to date, building a firm, experiencing betrayal, founding a new firm, great triumphs in the profession and the courtroom. All this he would bring to the U.S. Congress, and from what he knew of that body, that was as much, and in most cases more, than most of those serving.

An hour passed in reverie, and now he knew his motive: not fame, power or fortune, he'd already achieved those goals, no, his motive boiled down to service. To whom much is given, much will be required. That's why he was going to Congress and he knew all the Sullivans felt the same, because he and Mary, from the time they were married, felt the same way and each day they tried to pass on to their children those same values.

Before they were to embark on their journey to the nation's capital, John and Sally Kennedy threw a party in honor of the new Congressman, his wife and two hundred and fifty key workers on their ten acre estate. A perfect evening awaited the guests. Cocktails served on the terraced back lawn. The grounds surrounded by ten foot Thuja Occidentalis hedges. At one end of the lawn a large swimming pool framed in a semi-circle of white Roman columns topped with connecting white beams and bath house, all in the same classic style of the main house, a white colonial with seven bedrooms to accommodate Kennedy's growing family of six children. In the front of the house a circular drive way, with an offshoot to a three car garage.

Twin bars sat under white tents doing a land office business and the crowd hummed with excitement as a jazz sextet played background music in soft mellow tones. Kennedy decided the party afforded a perfect opportunity for Mary and Michael to meet, on a more intimate basis, those who had worked the hardest for his victory. At eight o'clock the dinner bell sounded and the guests slowly moved toward the buffet tables laden with ham, turkey, shrimp, salads, roast beef, and six kinds of dessert. All the while the Sullivans worked their way through the crowd, exchanges remembrances, asking about children, grandchildren, showing a genuine interest in each person they talked to. They laughed at someone calling Michael "landslide Sullivan."

Michael, with Mary at his side, made a touching speech, how, but for the assembled and their back breaking performance, he would not have been elected. Yes, he and Mary would be headed for the nation's capital but they would be back time and again to work in the district, to justify the faith the voters had placed in him. He noted his partner, Paul Connolly would be heading the firm they had built together and he wished all the partners and associates great success in the years ahead.

Paul Connolly took the floor following Michael's remarks and reminded his listeners how after Michael had left Hamilton, Sullivan, Collins & Phelps, the two of them, with two associates, formed Sullivan & Connolly and over the years built the firm to its present size, one hundred and twenty five lawyers and a place in the city's top law firms. Attributing the firm's growth and prestige, in good measure, to Michael's skill as a trial lawyer and his business getting ability he went on to say he would be missed yet the firm's loss was the country's gain. In a final toast he said: "Michael you will always have a place at the firm you built, and you always be a great lawyer and I predict you will not be back but will go to the top of your new profession—1600 Pennsylvania Avenue."

They raised their glasses and gave a mighty cheer; at Paul's signal the band played "Hail to the Chief." Michael and Mary embraced Paul and Teresa Connolly and suddenly it was over. The next day they emplaned for Washington D.C. and a new challenge—the United States Congress.

Made in the USA
Middletown, DE
13 May 2022

65713642R00248